Artaud and His Doubles

THEATER: THEORY/TEXT/PERFORMANCE

Series Editors: David Krasner and Rebecca Schneider

Founding Editor: Enoch Brater

Recent Titles:

Artaud and His Doubles

Kimberly Jannarone

THE UNIVERSITY OF MICHIGAN PRESS : *Ann Arbor*

First paperback edition 2012
Copyright © by the University of Michigan 2010

Published in the United States of America by
The University of Michigan Press
Printed and bound by CPI Group (UK) Ltd, Croydon, CR0 4YY

2015   2014   2013   2012   5   4   3   2

A CIP catalog record for this book is available from the British Library.

Library of Congress Cataloging-in-Publication Data

Jannarone, Kimberly.
     Artaud and his doubles / Kimberly Jannarone.
         p.   cm. — (Theater: theory/text/performance)
     Includes bibliographical references and index.
     ISBN 978-0-472-11736-9 (cloth : alk. paper)
         1. Artaud, Antonin, 1896–1948—Criticism and interpretation.
     2. Artaud, Antonin, 1896–1948—Knowledge—Performing arts.
     3. Experimental theater—France—History—20th century.   4. Drama—
     History and criticism—Theory, etc.   5. Cruelty in literature.
     I. Title.
     PQ2601.R677Z685   2010
     848'.91209—dc22   2010024619

978-0-472-02794-1 (e-book)

ISBN: 978-0-472-03515-1 (paper : alk. paper)

For Olive Raeder and in memory of Richard Raeder,
for making so much possible.

A madman, helpless, outcast and despised, who drags out
a twilight existence in some asylum, may, through the insights
he procures us, prove more important than Hitler or Napoleon,
illuminating for mankind its curse and its masters.
　—ELIAS CANETTI, *Crowds and Power*

PREFACE

This is an unlooked-for project. Like many others, I first saw Artaud through the filters of American experimental theater and post-structuralism. My earliest work on Artaud began from accepted familiar premises, largely established in the 1960s: Artaud as prophet, madman, genius, was the thing to study; his significance lay in his status as an inspirational figure manifesting a largely ahistorical impulse; his denunciation of civilization's discontents implied a progressive critique. My research led me in different directions, however. Fueled by a desire to really *read* Artaud's works closely—especially his early writing and his productions—I dug into the archives to research Artaud's theatrical practice. There I found, much to my surprise, that he had a gift for directing that had been recognized by his contemporaries but completely ignored by his successors. I began to wonder what was at stake in keeping Artaud's theory separate from his practice, in deciding that Artaud *meant* only insofar as we abstracted him. In 2005, I published some of this research in an essay on Artaud's directing in the Alfred Jarry Theater. To highlight the very real practical talents of a figure known almost only for his theories, I avoided discussion of his later, most famous work, *The Theater and Its Double,* and its key term, "cruelty." I initially had expected the archival research to feed into a book on Artaud's theater practice. While that material does inform the study at hand, the significance it has assumed has changed significantly.

Reading his work in the context of the 1920s and '30s confirmed that the young Artaud had plenty in common with other young Parisian artists of the early twentieth century. At first, he seemed to fit in with these idealists, ready to starve for their ambitions, working with the feeling that they were about to create a revolution. But I noticed that the path Artaud took had a radically different fundamental orientation than that of his Parisian peers. In order to both get my own bearings and understand what set Artaud apart from his contemporaries, I soon felt I needed to examine his most well-known work, *The Theater and Its Double,* on its own terms, historically situated, outside of received associations with avant-garde ideas and especially outside of the concerns of his latter-day followers. The process was a de-familiarizing experience.

Artaud's writings reflect an implacable belief that every material thing, every differentiated object and every force compelling them, is cruel, corrupt, sick, evil. The only true peace his works envision lies in undifferentiated- or nonbeing. The force animating Artaud's oeuvre—what gives it its inexhaustible power—is the desire to expose the underlying foundation of *le mal* and, more still, to call for the material annihilation, liquidation, or erasure of all those debased concrete and discrete objects that constitute our world.

The dark view underlying Artaud's oeuvre is not unique to him, especially in a French literary culture full of *poètes maudits,* but its extremity and form are striking. Artaud wrote that "the face within is evil," a worldview repeated throughout his oeuvre with relentless ferocity. Further, he yearned to enact his vision on the bodies of others: he conceived of spectators at his Theater of Cruelty as unindividuated *organismes,* and he voiced the most autocratic ideas on directing yet articulated. Yet a particular use and interpretation of his writings have become so established among people pursuing radical ideas for life and the theater, who have wished to make artistic innovation and social progress synonymous, that the singularly disturbing event called for by *The Theater and Its Double* has been obscured.

A number of intangible things let us know when encountering a work of art that an artist may be taking us on a journey that is unpleasant, disturbing, but we are confident of the motivation; we feel a kind of human sympathy or questioning guiding the work that establishes the common ground of the journey. Whatever those intangible things may be, they are missing in Artaud's work, especially when read in its historical context.

As I researched Artaud's work in the context of the interwar era, I found numerous and undeniable connections to contemporaneous ideas and theaters no one had discussed—the flourishing, reactionary line of what Isaiah Berlin called counter-Enlightenment thinking; the historically concurrent theatrical developments of the rise of the director and the taming of the audience; the (under-studied) people's theaters in fascist Italy and Germany; and the history of the rise of mass politics. My readings on crowd theory—initially intended for another work—proved to be a kind of decoder ring that enabled me to recognize a reactionary, fascistic tendency that is undeniably present and provocatively under-examined in Artaud's writings.

As a consequence, this book is a long way from the one I had expected to write. I thought I would be reading Artaud in connection with the leftist camp of the avant-garde; I now believe that was dangerous wishful thinking. The danger comes not from believing that students or practitioners of theater who use Artaud as an inspiration will suddenly find themselves fascists, but from the implications of the inability to *read* Artaud's work in light of what's patently there. If we've embraced his works, incorporated his ideas into our own, we need to examine more closely what desires and impulses we nourish when we do so.

Many of us have assumed even before reading Artaud that he was aiming for any number of things—greater understanding, freedom, individual creativity, a "better world," perhaps—because of how we were introduced to him. We have read our own hopes into the confusion of his revolutionary-sounding rhetoric, adding on to sentences that were already complete our own conclusions ("so that we will, in the future, x, or y . . .").

Alternately, we have read him backward, our perception colored by the last photos of him after he emerged from the asylums, toothless, haggard, scribbling his fury into worn notebooks that immediately were snatched up by his new, young acolytes, fetishized, and published. Like those who only knew him in those last two years and treated him as an inspirational but harmless, destroyed, holy fool, we strip him of any will or intent to participate in the "real" world, in any world of action.

To help avoid repeating some of these reading patterns in my own study, I have, in addition to reading Artaud's works in their historical context, confined most biographical information to footnotes. In this, I may be slightly overcompensating for the preponderance of biography in other studies of his works (and, indeed, decisions about what to put in the footnotes when discussing his work as a director became particularly challenging). But I have attempted to respect a boundary between an analysis of ideas and structures and an analysis of a man—although Artaud himself did not respect these boundaries—for the sake of interpreting his work in a context other than his personal life. Who "Artaud" might have been, I could not presume to know.

ACKNOWLEDGMENTS

Many colleagues and friends have been generous with their support on this project. I warmly thank, in particular, James Bierman, Michael Evenden, Patricia Gaborik, James Harding, Olivier Penot-Lacassagne, Kara Reilly, Cindy Rosenthal, and Mike Sell, all of whom took the time to read sections or drafts of the book and provide me with thoughtful feedback. I thank Brandin Baròn, Kathy Foley, and David Marriott for timely contributions of references and perspectives from their areas of expertise. All these contributions were valuable, but I alone am responsible for the conclusions presented here, as well as any residual errors.

This work is happily indebted to the University of California, Santa Cruz, in many ways. Multiple grants from the Senate Committee on Research and the Arts Research Institute supported this project at crucial stages of its development. Many thanks to my research assistants, Nathaniel Bogie, Megan Fox, Emily Gift, and Sarah Kelly. Three chairs of the Theater Arts Department—David Cuthbert, Mark Franko, and Danny Scheie—each encouraged me to teach a seminar on Artaud, for which I thank them, as well as the students in those seminars, whose questions, ideas, reservations, and enthusiasms all pushed me forward. Thanks to Catherine Soussloff and the UCSC Visual and Performance Studies Colloquium and to Chris Connery and Gail Hershatter at the UCSC Cultural Studies Colloquium for inviting me to present portions of my research.

The staff of the Bibliothèque Nationale and the Cinémathèque Nationale (Paris) assisted me tremendously in accessing archival material and images.

A version of portions of section II first appeared in *Theatre Journal* 61 (2009): 191–211, for which I thank Jean Graham-Jones and David Saltz. Also thanks to Jody Enders and James Harding for publishing research that found its way, in different form, into chapter 6, in *Theatre Survey* 46, no. 2 (2005): 247–73.

The Comparative Drama Conference, the Twentieth/Twenty-First

Century French and Francophone Studies International Conference, the International Federation for Theatre Research, and the American Society for Theater Research (ASTR) all provided invigorating environments in which to present portions of my research. I am especially grateful for discussions at ASTR with the participants in our many avant-garde seminars, as well as colleagues and friends, including Sarah Bay-Cheng, Michael Chemers, Shawn-Marie Garrett, Odai Johnson, Carol Martin, Cary Mazer, Joseph Roach, and several others already thanked here, with whom sharing research and ideas has been lively and gratifying. Also thanks to Elinor Fuchs, Marc Robinson, Gordon Rogoff, Catherine Sheehy, and especially James Leverett for encouraging my earliest investigations into Artaud's work.

I am indebted to everyone at the University of Michigan Press, especially LeAnn Fields and David Krasner for their support, and LeAnn for her unflagging generosity and perspicacity.

Three people were conspicuously valuable in this process. Blake Morris was a brilliantly talented research assistant (whose passion for Canetti was critically infectious), and I am glad he has yet to stop thinking with me about these ideas. Kathy Chetkovich's clear-sighted feedback on my writing was but part of her profoundly multifaceted support, for which I am inexpressibly thankful. Finally, Erik Butler has read more drafts, suggested more sources, listened to more ideas, and given me more encouragement and help during this process than could possibly be accounted for by any motivation other than love. For this, I can only thank him in kind.

CONTENTS

A NOTE ON THE TEXTS AND
TRANSLATIONS USED

A small fraction of Artaud's writing is available to the English-language reader. Only four volumes of the twenty-six-volume *Oeuvres complètes* have been translated into the English *Collected Works*. Although it would have had the advantage of citational elegance, I did not quote and translate entirely from the *OC*—that is, Antonin Artaud, *Oeuvres complètes d'Antonin Artaud, nouvelle édition revue et augmentée*, vols. 1–26 (Paris: Gallimard, 1976). Instead, I opted, when possible, to cite from texts the reader might be able to readily locate. The primary sources for this are:

CW   *Collected Works of Antonin Artaud.* 4 vols. Trans. Victor Corti.
         London: Calder and Boyars, 1968–73.
SW   *Selected Writings.* Trans. Helen Weaver. Ed. and intro. Susan Sontag.
         Berkeley: University of California Press, 1988.
TD   *The Theater and Its Double.* Trans. Mary Caroline Richards. New
         York: Grove Weidenfeld, 1958.

I use Richards's translation for *The Theater and Its Double* because hers is the book most people are likely to have on their shelves; it has also been the most influential translation. For works by Artaud not contained in these sources, I translate myself, unless otherwise noted, and provide the original in the footnotes. For other French material, I cite from existing translations in the body of the text whenever possible, but translations from all French sources are mine unless otherwise noted.

A NOTE ON THE TEXTS AND TRANSLATIONS USED

INTRODUCTION : The Uses and Abuses of Antonin Artaud

Je n'ai jamais rien trouvé d'éclairant dans
ce que les gens disaient sur Artaud.
—PAULE THÉVENIN

An apocalyptic sensibility drives the writing of Antonin Artaud, infuriated and propelled by a sense of the world's utter and unimaginable wrongness. Artaud's works, expressing exhilaration in brutality and seeking peace in annihilation, describe a universe in which evil rules without its dialectical term of good, and in which the best existence would be one without body, shape, or consciousness. The fight for impossible absolutes—the staging of a hopeless and devastating struggle—is what Artaud called the Theater of Cruelty, and it is for imagining this that he has become one of the most renowned theatrical figures of the twentieth century.

Artaud envisioned the Theater of Cruelty as this: an epidemic event that would destroy the individual and overturn every human creation, including language and civilization; liberate itself from all logic, matter, and history; "assault and benumb" the individual; operate in the realm of myth and image; and impose the vision of an omnipotent director on a "hypnotized" and surrounded assembly. His vision was rooted in a strong belief in the dark nature of man, the omnipresence of evil, the foulness of the body, and the need to systematically employ "cruelty and terror."[1] Artaud sounded this call in *The Theater and Its Double*, which was written between 1931 and 1935, a period when Europe was still shattered from the devastation of World War I; people were being politically conceptualized as masses; and charismatic leaders denouncing the world's corruption were orchestrating their way into World War II through spectacular manifestations of sensorial, rhetorical, and emotional manipulation.

Seen in this light, the traditional reception and interpretation of Artaud's work appear inadequate, if not indeed inappropriate, in several ways. For almost half a century, *The Theater and Its Double* has been shadowed by a peculiarly persistent set of doubles of its own: those of 1960s radicals in the United States, England, and France. The era's experimental theater artists, cultural revolutionaries, and progressive thinkers established the dominant tenor of subsequent interpretations. Most of us encountered Artaud by way of the '60s; that is to say, through the concerns of critics, editors, and interpreters such as Susan Sontag, Jacques Derrida, the *Tel Quel* group, and Paule Thévenin, and artists such as Peter Brook, Jerzy Grotowski, and the Living Theatre. In the '60s, Artaud's works were embedded in a context that we can broadly call leftist: one characterized by a striving, through the advancement of human awareness and creativity, to create a new social and political world in which a greater number of people could enjoy a greater amount of individual liberty and happiness.

While *The Theater and Its Double* had an undeniable impact on the 1960s and seemed to anticipate many of that generation's preoccupations, our interpretations of the work have been curtailed by reading it as if it had sprung from that period itself, ignoring its actual—and disconcerting—historical context: the interwar era in Western Europe. The task of *Artaud and His Doubles* is to firmly situate Artaud's theatrical writings and practice (almost entirely produced in the 1920s and '30s) in the political, intellectual, and theatrical climate of its time. Such a contextualization dramatically alters our associations with his works and his thought. Through historical examinations and close readings of his works, we uncover a set of previously undiscussed doubles in France, Italy, and Germany who were voicing a very different set of values and concerns from those of the 1960s interpreters with which we are so familiar. These new doubles are the reactionary post- and pre-war Europeans who eventually channeled their frustrated, cataclysmic sensibility into tirades against reason, glorifications of unthinking homogenized masses, and calls for wide-scale destruction in the name of a higher truth. Artaud posited that the double of theater was life; that the theater came first, and it had the ability to create a new reality. It is worth, then, closely examining his ideas for the theater in light of the life around him and what soon followed.

Artaud entered the public eye in 1923 with a series of letters denouncing the inadequacy of language, and he exited the world in 1948 doing the same, leaving, in addition to a substantial body of performance and visual art, approximately ten thousand pages of this inadequacy behind. Reading Artaud, one is struck by his vehemence and single-mindedness and by how force, rather than sustained argument, holds the often contradictory and illogical pieces together. The works push and strive, yet never articulate their end; they turn back on themselves; they denounce the very form (writing) of their articulation. They give the impression of fragments and traces—what Artaud called an early collection of his writings—"Fragments of a Diary from Hell."[2] Indeed, much of what is collected in the enormous twenty-six-volume Gallimard *Oeuvres complètes* is unedited and unfinished material—correspondence, notes, journals, and drafts. In a body of work such as this, containing, as it does, a wide variety of contradictory ideas, it can be relatively easy to extract provocative or memorable phrases, isolated terms, and opportune passages that serve the immediate needs of a critic or artist. Instead of extrapolating from decontextualized quotations, we must read Artaud's work with a broad, structural view in order to accurately discern the world picture it reveals. Certain obsessions, desires, images, and strategies repeat themselves incessantly and unreflexively in Artaud's rhetoric,[3] and these repeated terms ground the analyses of the study at hand: Rupture. Catastrophe. Abjection. Paroxysm. Self-annihilation. Bodies dissolving their limits among other bodies. Power. The chapters of *Artaud and His Doubles* examine these terms in detail; for now, in order to set the stage for the readings that follow, I will briefly point out the landmarks of Artaud's brief but legendary career.

The 1923 series of letters referred to earlier is *Correspondance avec Jacques Rivière*, which announced Artaud's appearance on the French literary scene shortly after he moved to Paris from Marseille (having spent most of the war in sanatoriums).[4] This epistolary work, initiated by Rivière's desire to know the author of several poems submitted—and rejected—for publication in the prestigious literary journal *La nouvelle revue française* (of which Rivière was the editor), establishes themes that run through every part of Artaud's subsequent oeuvre. In the letters, Artaud argues for the validity of his refused poems on the basis not of their "literary merit," but of their value as fragments salvaged from a besieged consciousness. He argues he is a "genuine psychic anomaly" whose torment gives him "the right to speak," however imperfectly:

> And here, monsieur, is the whole problem: to have within oneself the inseparable reality and the physical clarity of a feeling, to have it to such a degree that it is impossible for it not to be expressed, to have

a wealth of words, of acquired turns of phrase capable of joining the dance, coming into play; and the moment the soul is preparing to organize its wealth, its discoveries, this revelation, at that unconscious moment when the thing is on the point of coming forth, a superior and evil will attacks the soul like a poison, attacks the mass consisting of word and image, attacks the mass of feeling, and leaves me panting as if at the very door of life.[5]

Rivière was struck by how Artaud's description of his sickness, anger, alienation, and paranoia opened into a wider discussion of perceived boundaries between impulse and expression, formlessness and structure, experience and language that other artists were also challenging. The publication of the correspondence immediately attracted the attention of the Surrealists, who were likewise attempting at that time to redefine literary and artistic principles and forms by prioritizing impulse—rather than intellect or practiced craft—as a creative force. Subsequently, the letters also served as a launching pad for influential theoretical analyses of Artaud's work in the 1950s and '60s in terms of post-structuralism and psychoanalysis (discussed later). Artaud described the flaws in his poems as signs of the collapse of an entire mental universe:

This scattered quality of my poems, these defects of form, this constant sagging of my thought, must be attributed . . . to a central collapse of the soul, to a kind of erosion, both essential and fleeting, of the thought. . . .

There is something which destroys my thought; something which does not prevent me from being what I might be, but which leaves me, so to speak, in suspension. Something furtive which robs me of the words *that I have found*. (SW [emphasis in all quotations is per the original, unless otherwise noted], 34–35)

Artaud insists that he was struggling not with lack of skill or inspiration, but with the possibility of coming into full possession of his self and creative potential because something was interfering with the actual functioning of his mind. Rivière's publication of Artaud's letters validated Artaud's impulse to describe his tortured mental universe, something that, from that point on, Artaud continued to do throughout the rest of his career. The correspondence established Artaud as a singularly defiant figure in the face of widely experienced creative and intellectual dilemmas brought on by the compromises, restrictions, and limitations of established forms. Artaud's descriptions of why his poems would never be "perfect" on the "formal level" (*SW*, 32) thereby took on a heroic aspect, emphasizing the torment a maliciously flawed world could provoke in a creative individual.

In the 1920s and '30s, Artaud immersed himself in the work of the theater. He acted and worked with Aurélien-Marie Lugné-Poe at the Théâtre de l'Oeuvre, Charles Dullin at the Atelier, and Georges and Ludmilla Pitoëff at the Comédie des Champs-Élysées, among others.[6] He wrote reviews, scenarios, and production plans for the stage. He saw much international theater, including productions by Reinhardt in Berlin, which influenced his own work. From 1926 to 1928, he directed, designed, wrote for, acted in, and produced works in his own Théâtre Alfred Jarry.

His film career, also from this period, provides us with much of our Artaud iconography. He played over twenty roles in French, German, and Italian avant-garde and commercial films, for major directors including Abel Gance, Carl Dreyer, Fritz Lang, and G. W. Pabst. Notable roles included the monk Massieu in Dreyer's *La passion de Jeanne d'Arc*, Marat in Gance's *Napoléon*, and Savonarola in Gance's *Lucrèce Borgia*. He was cast as a bishop, a monk, and a fanatical priest; as a mad revolutionary and a crazed lynch mob leader; as an ethereal spirit, visionary, and outsider. In each role, he projected a radiant, raging, otherworldly persona that has enormously influenced our reception of his works.[7]

From about 1931 through 1935, Artaud wrote the essays that eventually comprised *The Theater and Its Double*, his most well-known theatrical work, in which he developed his idea for a "Théâtre de la Cruauté" (Theater of Cruelty). His one attempt to bring this theater to life occurred in 1935, when he adapted, co-produced, acted the lead in, and directed his own version of *Les Cenci* (*The Cenci*). The essays and the work on this production developed to their fullest articulation Artaud's ideas about the ideal theater event, the role of the director, and the desired effect of the event on the audience. The Theater of Cruelty is what he is most known for in the theater, and for this reason it is the primary focus of this study.

The final significant part of Artaud's career are the last twelve years of his life, including two major travels, confinement in asylums, and his final two years in Paris. In 1936, Artaud journeyed to Mexico. After half a year in Mexico City, he visited the Tarahumara Indians for a month and participated in their peyote ritual. In the context of this trip, Artaud wrote profusely about an idealized primitive culture and spirituality, which he saw standing in violent opposition to Western society; in the process, he took special aim at the rationalism and materialism of Marxism. In late

1937, he visited Ireland for a month. An obscure altercation outside a church and a subsequent fight on the boat back to France landed him in an asylum shortly before the eruption of World War II. Artaud stayed in different asylums for the next nine years, in mostly horrific conditions during the war and the Occupation. After art therapy and controversial electroshock therapy at an asylum in Rodez, Artaud began to write and draw again. His writings from 1943 to 1948—obsessed with self-creation, scatology, god and overturning god's dominion, evil, and the invocation of primal energies through incantatory sounds—are hardly classifiable, and they form the basis of much Artaud scholarship in France. Upon his re-emergence into the literary and cultural scene in 1946, Artaud was hailed as a hero. Back in Paris (in a hospital in the suburb Ivry), "crowned with the image of a mad poet or *poète maudit*, he became for many a symbol of combat for liberty."[8] This symbology has not left him. We will now see what specific forms it has taken on since his death.

Uses and Abuses

What Nietzsche argued with regard to history, we might argue with regard to Artaud: he serves the ends of various critical and artistic schools so exceptionally well that we may easily forget he ever existed outside of their interpretations. Artaud's life and works have been used to support an array of critical, cultural, social, theoretical, and artistic positions in the last half century, being drawn into service for arguments about capitalism, collectivism, individualism, psychiatry, civilization, madness, and much more. Some of the most complex discourses of late-twentieth-century criticism and theory and an enormous number of influential modern theatrical works draw from readings of Artaud. Throughout these interpretations and receptions, two tendencies recur: to see in his work the foundation of a revolutionary protest that is primarily leftist, and to view his writings ahistorically, as existing almost outside of time. These are the tendencies this book confronts.

A constellation of terms anchors both English-language and French Artaud reception: suffering, revolution, resistance, liberation, and freedom. Both schools of interpretation approach Artaud's work as seen through his biography—or, rather, they discuss not so much a body of works but a life itself. They refer not to "Artaud's writings" or "Artaud's work," but to, simply, "Artaud." Both schools, also, use "Artaud" to advance broad theoretical positions on culture, politics, and identity. The idea of suffering underpins both. The English-language school exemplifies the ideas of revolution associated with the fantasmatic "Artaud," while the French concentrates on the ways Artaud and his oeuvre can represent resistance. By giving readings of these three terms—suffering, revolution, and resistance—through his interpreters, I provide a sketch of the doubles of Artaud that have been handed down to us. This clears the way for the historical analysis and close readings that are the task of this book. We will return to these inherited doubles through the lens of the other key terms—liberation and freedom—in the conclusion.

The Suffering of Antonin Artaud

The English-language Artaud came into being with the 1958 Grove Press publication of Mary Caroline Richards's translation of *The Theater and Its Double.* The book opened—and subsequent editions maintain this tradition—with nine photographs of the author: one hauntingly beautiful portrait by Man Ray, in which Artaud's face emerges from darkness, looking into a narrow strip of light accessible only to him; the other eight a series of photographs taken near the end of his life, a showcase of his deterioration, as he appears in turn menacing, harmless, crazed, anguished, and ridiculously French (cigarette, scarf, stacks of papers, art, etc.). This series of photos (taken at Ivry) presents the Artaud who emerged from the asylums sick, with no teeth (due to malnourishment and electroshock therapy), haggard beyond his years at age fifty, raging more violently than ever before. They also constitute the bulk of visual information most readers have of Artaud.

A tenth photograph further shapes Artaud's image. It is taken from his performance as a monk in Carl Dreyer's *La passion de Jeanne d'Arc* and is featured on the cover of the second-most well-known edition of Artaud's works in English, the 1976 *Antonin Artaud: Selected Writings,* which contains Helen Weaver's intensely readable translations of almost six hundred pages of Artaud's work. In this film still, Artaud is looking up into a bathing and mysterious light. He appears simultaneously anguished and beatific, at the height of his beauty (the upward angle of his face conceals the tonsure he had for the role). Behind him, the shadow of a corner of a rooftop frames his head. The roof is decorated with protruding knobbed spikes, and the corner is angled so that the apex appears just at the crown of his head. He plays only a minor role in the film, but from this still you would think he was the martyr himself. His slightly aslant crown of thorns and his intense inwardness and charisma situate him as the noblest sufferer in history.

The commentaries of both editions reinforce the implications of these images. The only commentary provided in the Grove Press edition of *The Theater and Its Double* comes in the curious form of an essay by Maurice Saillet, written on the occasion of Artaud's death and translated into English ten years later as a post-scriptum for the book. The only striking part (aside from the choice of this mediocre essay by one of the less prominent observers of Artaud) is the first paragraph, which describes Artaud's death as a resurrection:

> Antonin Artaud died March 4, 1948, at the age of fifty-two. The date should be remembered as that of a new and terrible birth: the moment this body and this mind, riveted together by long agony, parted company, Artaud's *real life* began. The hailstorm of his thought now batters our own; the harp of his nerves vibrates in the world's void; and the knell has rung for several transitory forms of literature and art. (*TD*, 147)

Artaud has transcended this earth to begin a new life in us; his nerves and thought, having swept away imperfect forms, now fill our lives. We are not speaking of an author or an artist when we speak of Artaud; we are speaking of a messiah.

Susan Sontag pushed this vocabulary even further in her influential introductory essay to the *Selected Works* (the essay was originally printed in *The New Yorker* in 1973), which crystallized the tone of American Artaud scholarship:

> Both in his work and in his life, Artaud failed. . . . What he bequeathed was not achieved works of art but a singular presence, a poetics, an aesthetics of thought, a theology of culture, and a phenomenology of suffering. (*SW*, xix–xx)[9]

Presence, theology, suffering: Sontag's essay fixed the messianic terms that have become Artaud's unshakeable doubles.[10] According to Sontag, "Artaud offers the greatest *quantity* of suffering in the history of literature" (*SW*, liii). His suffering is "heroic" (a word repeated frequently throughout her essay); he has a "purity" of "moral purpose" (*SW*, xxiv); "Artaud is someone who has made a spiritual trip for us—a shaman" (*SW*, lviii). He is all this and more: his suffering is, explicitly, Christlike:

"Some of Artaud's accounts of his Passion of thought are almost too painful to read" (*SW*, xxi). For Artaud, "thinking and using language became a perpetual calvary" (*SW*, xx). His effect on the world of theater is analogous to that of Christ's on earth:

> Upon that art, theater, he has had an impact so profound that the course of all recent serious theater in Western Europe and the Americas can be said to divide into two periods—before Artaud and after Artaud. (*SW*, xxxviii)

Artaud is not a precursor, but a presence; his works represent not a landmark, but an era. Our new A.D. is *Artaud domino*.

English-language reception focuses on *The Theater and Its Double* and the image of Artaud as one who suffered for a new theater that he prophesied but was unable to bring into being. Artaud also serves as a Christ figure in France, but with the focus not on his theatrical vision, but on his life in the asylums.

Artaud scholarship in France generally assumes the shape of a barely secularized Christian narrative. Coming from humble origins in the South of France, Artaud established himself in Paris, accumulating followers and some notoriety. His confinement in the asylums from 1937 through '46 represents a dormant period when he was shunned, abandoned even by his friends—he himself said he was "dead" during these years. In 1946 he emerged miraculously, with the characteristics of a martyr of society, a man who had been rejected because of his unassimilable but inspired visions. He moved from a position of abject outsider, a pariah, to an outsider who is now sublime—from disease to sanctity. His trips to Mexico and Ireland were his Gethsemane, his incarceration his crucifixion and burial, his emergence at Ivry his resurrection. As with Christ, we read his story backward, using the knowledge of his divinity/incarceration as the necessary key to interpreting his earlier life and works.

Artaud's image has been shaped through the imagery of holy suffering, and people often write about him from the position of apostles. Many publications on Artaud exhibit a rapturous religious style with a vocabulary of fervent idolatry. After his death, especially, as Alain Virmaux and Odette Virmaux illustrate in their survey of his reception, "the general tendency was to lyricism and fanatical veneration."[11] People wrote of his superhuman status, his inability to be understood by mere humans. Paule

Thévenin, his editor and, during the last two years of his life, his friend, wrote in 1948:

> Je ne puis parler d'Antonin Artaud dans cette langue-ci, car elle n'est pas la sienne. Il parle la langue des siècles des siècles dans les espaces des espaces et peut-être est-ce seulement à l'infini des siècles des siècles qu'il me sera permis d'approcher avec des mots ce que j'appelle maintenant la mort et pour quoi Antonin Artaud ne m'a pas laissé de nom.[12]

> [I can't speak of Artaud in this language, for it isn't his. He speaks the language of the time of times in the space of spaces and maybe it's only in the infinity of the time of times that I will be allowed to approach with words what I now call death and for which Antonin Artaud has not left me the name.]

As a final example of the extravagant heights all this can reach, Sylvère Lotringer begins a recent collection of essays, *Fous d'Artaud,* with the argument that Artaud's early onset of insanity and his later frighteningly zealous conversion to Christianity in the asylums were due to the (alleged) discovery that he was Jewish. The essay concludes: "Artaud wasn't mad, he was Jewish. Like Jesus Christ."[13] Artaud is so spectacularly exceptional he's not even mentally ill: his erratic behavior is attributable to the fact that he is as unclassifiable as Christ.

As Shakespeare is the unquestioned father of all drama—even, according to Harold Bloom, the inventor of the human—Artaud is the master sufferer in the world of art and culture. He incarnates the greatest conflation of life and art, anguish and creation, ever experienced. Maurice Blanchot wrote in 1956 that Artaud's experience makes us ask, "Is to suffer, ultimately, to live?"[14] Jacques Derrida pursued a similar thought throughout a series of essays on Artaud spanning decades, culminating in 2002 with, "Artaud is suffering itself."[15] Artaud is the abstract embodiment of pain, a nonpareil artist-as-sufferer in a cultural tradition not lacking candidates.[16]

The status of heroic sufferer, martyr, messiah, has conferred on the figure of Artaud a kind of immunity, it seems, from comparisons of the sort this book undertakes.[17] To suffer makes one sympathetic, and Artaud's terrible anguish has earned him a noble and frankly holy status.[18] But does suffering necessarily ennoble every facet of a person's thought? Did it do so with other great modern sufferers, from Schopenhauer to

Nietzsche or Strindberg? Does pathology, in short, invalidate, erase, excuse, or elide politics?

Elias Canetti comes right out and says no at the end of *Crowds and Power*, his monumental book on the dynamics, imagery, history, psychology, and politics of power and community. Discussing Daniel Paul Schreber—who, like Artaud, lived a life of mental and physical anguish, apocalyptic visions, compulsive writing, and years of confinement—Canetti compares the ideas of the madman to those of totalitarian leaders in the interwar era. Schreber's 1903 *Memoirs of My Nervous Illness*, written in an asylum and presented (successfully) as justification for his release, describes his vision of himself as a figure of unparalleled torment, connected by his nerves to a persecutory god and his angels, only finding peace in the fantasy of controlling the rest of the world. Canetti dedicates his book's final two chapters to the patterns of thought underlying the inmate's tortured universe and to the products of that thought, such as Schreber's fragmented texts, transcriptions of visions, detailed cosmological systems, and hallucinations. Canetti dares to assert that the madman's structure of thought, his megalomaniacal fantasies of persecution, power, and retribution, anticipate the fascistic dynamic of crowds and power in the interwar era. *Artaud and His Doubles* suggests, as shown in the choice of epigraph, that the madman in his cell who sheds light on the most troubling systems of thought in the twentieth century might also—and more directly than Schreber, given when he was writing—be Artaud.

Translation and Revolution

More than half a century after his death, Antonin Artaud's name conjures for Americans the dreams of our 1960s radical theater artists. In the United States and in England, Artaud's works have been received primarily as inspiration for experimental performance practices in the service of liberationary social and political ideals. Any research into Artaud's work quickly leads one into a crowd of largely leftist doubles working at the vanguard of experimental theater. In fact, the list of theater artists and companies that *The Theater and Its Double* has influenced or been said to have influenced is almost as long as the list of our experimental theaters itself: Judith Malina and Julian Beck of the Living Theatre, Peter Brook, Sam Shepard, Richard Schechner and the Performance Group, John Cage, Karen Finley, Joseph Chaikin and the Open Theater, Charles Marowitz, Richard Foreman, Spalding Gray, Liz LeCompte, and the Wooster Group just begin the list. *The Theater and Its Double* remains the bible for those at-

tempting to find a non-Brechtian way to use theater to provoke the revolution, a seminal inspiration in the decades-long quest for the non-didac-
tic revolutionary project envisioned by the counterculture. Artaud's call
for an end to masterpieces, his rejection of tradition and the constraints of
civilization, and his unrelenting cries for freedom have been interpreted
as a radical critique, a foundation for a revolutionary praxis that forms an
essential part of experimental theater.[19]

However, this appropriation of Artaud's work is surprising given
that Artaud explicitly opposed a materialist political use for his works
and demanded they be interpreted in the realm of the spirit and not
among the contingencies of daily life. Artaud's desire to remake human
existence from an artistic and ontological level drew him to the Surrealists
in 1924, but the abhorrence of a politically engaged move—such as the
Surrealists joining the Communist Party in 1927—pulled him away. For
Artaud, communism was "a lazy man's revolution" (SW, 162); the real
revolution would be "beyond" material politics and economics. "À la
grande nuit" ("In Total Darkness"), Artaud's 1927 retaliatory letter of rupture with the Surrealists, articulates his absolute objections to political action: "As if from the viewpoint of the absolute there could be the slightest
interest in seeing the social armature of the world change or in seeing
power pass from the hands of the bourgeoisie into those of the prole-
tariat" (SW, 140).[20]

Scholars who want to read Artaud's theater in a leftist political framework have thus had to radicalize his apolitical stance. For example, his
works have been read in light of an "engaged" art—not explicitly political, but aiming to alter the ontology of its society—an idea some have
rooted in Sartre, Camus, or even Adorno. The Theater of Cruelty, in this
vein, "contributes to a transformative tragic politics that seeks to overcome unpalatable social regimes by interrogating the epistemological formations and structures of representation from which they spring."[21] This
kind of argument takes as its cue Artaud's call for fundamental human
change, which Artaud situates in the metaphysical realm. Writers searching for potential political or social uses of Artaud's works, then, investigate the possibility of reading Artaud's ideal theater as effecting a metaphysical revolution, aiming at the foundations of life and thought, not the
details, "engaged" according to Adorno's definition, or revolutionary according to Camus's notion of "revolt." Artaud's project, according to this
logic, works toward a radical revisioning of life that aligns itself with
philosophically liberationist ideals.

Such critical approaches point to a prevalent wish among theater practitioners to enlist Artaud's work in the service of a liberal revolution against restrictive and oppressive systems of thought, politics, and society. To take one recent example, Peter Sellars staged Artaud's 1947 radio play *To Have Done with the Judgment of God* in 2002 as an indictment of America's war fever and its human consequences in Afghanistan. This piece, performed again in 2004 in San Francisco as part of Yerba Buena's Art and Politics series, emblematizes a recurrent desire on the part of English and American theater scholars and practitioners to find in Artaud's howls of defiance support for political and social change.

This desire is extremely common, especially among progressive theater practitioners: we want Artaud on "our side." We want Artaud's revolutionary theater to be revolutionary politics, and, since his reception has come to us almost exclusively through works born in the 1960s, it has become a matter of habit, rather than thought, to welcome him into our projects, as a countercultural and a liberatory political force.[22] In general, we have taken Artaud's project, his "revolution," in terms of experimentation and exploration, his "cruelty" in terms of ruthless honesty and self-exploration.[23] Artaud's project has been interpreted as a call for a revolution that has as its goal a fundamentally constructive restructuring of human thought and existence.

The Living Theatre provides some exemplary instances of how Artaud's ideas for a Theater of Cruelty have been used in the service of a liberal "revolution." The Living Theatre has worked for decades to encourage radical changes in material politics, social openness, and individual freedom: as Julian Beck said, "We are a revolution disguised as a theatre."[24] Though the group began its work in 1947, before reading Artaud, once founders Judith Malina and Julian Beck read the translation of *The Theater and Its Double* in 1958, "the ghost of Artaud became our mentor."[25] They began referring to the Theater of Cruelty in writings and interviews, quickly becoming a dominant force in Artaud's reception. They interpreted Artaud's cosmic rage as a call to revolution against the coercive effects of government, repressive society, and personal inhibitions. They used *The Theater and Its Double*'s language of rebellion, revolution, and resistance in the service of utopian political goals and personal spiritual fulfillment. Artaud's "cruelty" served as a necessary precursor to their end goal, which was realization of a free community here on earth, or "Paradise Now."

The Living Theatre was the first American company to base production work on Artaud's ideas. Its 1959 piece *The Connection* and its 1963 production *The Brig* enlisted the Theater of Cruelty to make the suffering of those living the brutal underworld life of the junkie or prisoners in a U.S. Marine Corps camp palpable to their audiences. Beck and Malina hoped, by showing the suffering, to explode it, to make it disappear. Malina, who directed, wrote of *The Brig:* "When the audience can know violence in the clear light of the kinship of our physical empathy, it will go out of the theatre and turn such evil into such good as transformed the Furies into the Kindly Ones."[26] Beck's description of their interpretation of Artaud's desires crystallized the tendency for artists to attach their own hopes and ideals to what would happen in the aftermath of Artaud's onslaught of "cruelty":

> Artaud believed that if we could only be made to feel, really feel anything, then we might find all this suffering intolerable, the pain too great to bear, we might put an end to it, and then . . . we might truly feel the joy, the joy of everything else, of loving, of creating, of being at peace, and of being ourselves. (Beck, "Storming the Barricades," 25)

This hopeful outcome, however, is superimposed on Artaud's work, added after an imaginary ellipsis where *The Theater and Its Double* ends.

A later project, *Paradise Now* (1968), made clear the fundamental difference between the Living Theatre's goals and those embedded in the Theater of Cruelty. Initially, in productions such as *The Connection* and *The Brig*, Beck and Malina used Artaud's ideas in combination with the ideas of Meyerhold and Piscator in a way they hoped would clearly agitate against oppression. They sought to immerse their audiences in the horror of the situation (using Artaud), framing it theatrically (with Meyerhold) and intellectually (with Piscator) in such a way as to provoke the will to fight against that horror. When, in *Paradise Now*, they discarded the intellectual agitation and theatrical distancing techniques of Meyerhold and Piscator, leaving only the Artaudian, the political views they still held got clouded. The Artaudian immersive experience, left on its own, came across to some as deeply reactionary and itself authoritarian, revealing a troubling relationship between radical liberation and collective conformity that we will return to in the conclusion. The Theater of Cruelty, on its own, clearly did not effectively advance "The Beautiful Non-Violent Anarchist Revolution" that the Living sought.[27]

Artaud wrote in 1927 of his rupture with the Surrealists, "the whole

root, all the exacerbations of our quarrel, turn on the word 'Revolution'"
(*SW*, 139). One of the questions *Artaud and His Doubles* asks is this: what
kind of revolution does Artaud demand? Examining his writings in
depth, we find that, unlike the language of the Living Theatre, which is
accepting, relativist, and focused on beauty, Artaud's rhetoric is intoler-
ant, absolutist, and focused on abjection. The idea of sexual freedom and
celebrating naked bodies, so crucial to the Living Theatre, is anathema to
Artaud's vision, which expresses a loathing of the body and of sex. Even
Artaud's use of drugs—mostly a laudanum addiction begun while in a
sanatorium—doesn't stem from a pursuit of self-revelation, but a need to
ease his physical pain, and he writes almost not at all of using psyche-
delic drugs before his 1936 trip to the Tarahumaras. Artaud's accounts of
his personal hallucinations sound less like liberating experiences than
nightmares, lacking the pleasure, absurdity, or playfulness of an ideal
1960s acid trip. What would be the revolution brought about by "cruelty" if we viewed it not as a metaphor for a kind of metaphysical
strength-building and a necessary precursor to joy, but in Artaud's own
terms?

"Revolution," after all, does not always represent a progressive
move—many right-wing movements, and indeed fascism, have called
themselves "revolutions."[28] We must ask what is targeted for destruction
and what is envisioned in its aftermath. The Surrealists, with whom Artaud collaborated briefly on the journal *La révolution surréaliste*, worked to
destroy hindrances to self-expression and cultural exploration so that a
greater number of people would be happy and so that the individual
might come into his or her own unique voice. This liberal attitude, as we
will see, is the opposite of Artaud's, and he loathed it. In 1927, Artaud
wrote, "What divides me from the Surrealists is that they love life as much
as I despise it" (*SW*, 141). He never writes of people being happy, and his
dream for the individual is its dissolution, not its fuller articulation.

French Resistance

If Artaud is a pillar for U.S. radical theater, in France he is a pillar of radical theory. Artaud serves as a key figure in French intellectual movements
that sought to challenge the boundaries between studies of literature, art,
psychiatry, and politics in the 1960s. French reception centers not primarily on Artaud's theatrical innovations, but on his poetry, person, and confinement.[29] The French Artaud is accompanied by a theoretical discourse
on the poetics of madness and resistance perhaps unparalleled by that on

any other single modern figure. His oeuvre signifies a refusal that many disparate projects have theorized and wielded as a radical critique: "The writing of Artaud, the sensation of excess that it gives," observes Olivier Penot-Lacassagne, "more than anything else serves as an impulse to a subversive position, to the negation of the existing social order."[30] Derrida used Artaud's writings as key texts in developing his concept of deconstruction, reading them as concrete resistances to interpretation, wholeness, and completion. Julia Kristeva used Artaud's oeuvre to theoretically tie political and poetic resistance together in terms of the "subject in process," arguing that Artaud's very being, manifested in his "déchirements" of language and his "éructations," defied and ruptured the order of logic and law.[31] Other writers of the *Tel Quel* group, at the height of their excitement over the possibilities of the cultural revolution in the late 1960s, read Artaud's texts as radically subversive in Maoist terms. Gilles Deleuze and Félix Guattari used Artaud's image of a "body without organs" as a model of desire in their critique of the functioning of the capitalist system in *Anti-Oedipus: Capitalism and Schizophrenia*. "Artaud," by resisting any final interpretation, by confusing the line between the "critical" and the "clinical" with his insanity and poetry, mirrors the twisted structures of inherently dynamic and unstable systems, representing an eternal, defiant struggle against that which has seemed stable, natural, or eternal.[32]

U.S. radicals adopted "Artaud" for body politics, the French for language politics. The problems of writing and representation find fertile ground in the ten thousand pages of Artaud's struggle. The endless paradoxes of Artaud—his irresolvable conflicts, his stream of eternal tensions—serve as ideal foundations for theories of resistance. The Rivière correspondence established how Artaud's suffering both blocked his creativity and fed it; how his psychological torment both constituted his work and prevented it; how his life was his art, which was an attempt to live his life. Blanchot, reading Artaud, asks if to suffer is to live. Derrida asks, while examining the idea of the Theater of Cruelty, if to represent is to betray. Foucault proposes that Artaud's writing marks its own absence. The paradoxes signify eternal movement and undecidability, resistance to fixity and definition.

To hear Artaud's voice in the radio play *Pour en finir avec le jugement de dieu* (*To Have Done with the Judgment of God*) (1947) is to hear dramatized a central paradox of what the French refer to as Artaud's "case." In this performance, Artaud reads the last section of his play himself, taking on the characters of both hostile interviewer and defensive respondent, his barely modulated voice switching from accusatory contempt to near-hysterical defiance:

—Vous délirez, monsieur Artaud.
Vous êtes fou.

—Je ne délire pas.
Je ne suis pas fou. (*OC*, 13: 103)

[—You are raving, Mr. Artaud.
You are mad.

—I am not raving.
I am not mad.] (*SW*, 569)

Artaud's inability to reconcile himself with himself has made him an ideal starting point for post-structuralist analyses of the modern individual. Further, his anger at this inability, his defiant stance in the face of tormentors both real and imagined, tangible and intangible (ranging from friends to psychiatrists to evil spirits), seems to represent a kind of principled, righteous resistance—somehow both voluntary and involuntary— to the flaws and inadequacies of the world.

Michel Foucault gravitates toward Artaud at the end of his book on the institutionalization of insanity, *Madness and Civilization*, as Artaud's ruinous position in an asylum during wartime warrants. Foucault's discussion of cultural conceptions of madness culminates in an evocation of the poetry of Artaud's struggle:

Artaud's *oeuvre* experiences its own absence in madness, but that experience . . . all those words hurled against a fundamental absence of language, all that space of physical suffering and terror which surrounds or rather coincides with void—that is the work of art itself: the sheer cliff over the abyss of the work's absence.[33]

Foucault's brief discussion of Artaud does not focus primarily on him as a historically representative asylum patient, but as another instance (together with Nietzsche and Nerval) of a poet fighting against the impossibility of expression, someone whose struggle imposes on us "a task of recognition, of reparation" (*Madness and Civilization*, 288). Like many thinkers of the French school, Foucault, even within a book that otherwise concerns itself with the historical and political contexts of the cultural and psychological situation at hand, presents a strikingly ahistorical reading of Artaud's work. Artaud's poetic singularity seems to have removed him from history.

Derrida, when pressed to explain, in 2002, why he said that he had been "haunted" by Artaud all these years, pointed to the "intensity" of Artaud's experience rather than its actual content (which, he admitted, was not that unusual). He referred to Artaud as a kind of "enemy" who had pursued him for decades.[34] This brings us back to the person-centered discourse around Artaud and the specific character it takes on in France.

In 2006–7, the Bibliothèque Nationale held a huge retrospective of Artaud's works, including poems, notebooks, drawings, film clips, reviews, photographs, correspondence, source material, and more. Everything was set at oblique angles, including the big yellow letters that greeted you at the threshold, spelling, "Moi, Antonin Artaud, je suis mon fils, mon père, ma mère, et moi" (I, Antonin Artaud, I am my son, my father, my mother, and myself).[35] The first room, dedicated to his face—photographs and self-portraits—invited an identificatory approach. On the sides of the panels holding the pictures, one found mirrors at viewer height. Noise music from his production of *The Cenci* played from multiple hidden speakers, creating an atmosphere in which, as you turned from images of Artaud to images of yourself, shrieks, crashes, bangs, howling winds, church bells, and the eerie sounds of a Martenot surprised you from different sides. This room opened into the exhibit's central corridor, from which all others branched off: a stark rectangle of all-white walls, floors, and ceiling, with little barred windows, lit by fluorescents, filled with works relating to Artaud's asylum years. As you looked at his most outrageous creations—murderous spells cast on former friends, encouraging postcards to Hitler—you heard the sound of Artaud's voice saying "electro-shock" over and over. The yellow text cutting diagonals across the walls, floors, and ceiling spelled out: "Mort au monde"; "Je suis l'infini"; "Je suis votre irréconciliable ennemi" (Death to the world; I am infinity; I am your irreconcilable enemy). Being forced to traverse this corridor in order to even begin to consider Artaud's theatrical career, film work, drawing, or art criticism parallels the act of moving through Artaud reception in France. It begins with the asylum and uses his suffering at the hands of society as an emblematic critique in which you, the viewer, are implicated.

The French version of Artaud's martyrdom centers on his internment and his rage; it is an intellectual "Artaud," rather than the American visceral "Artaud." It creates sides, and there are enemies everywhere, as the decades-long battles over the editing of his complete works, his treatment at Rodez, and his legacy demonstrate.[36] He suffered not from weakness but from principle; he existed in order to demonstrate the inadequacy of the world and its systems. His anger is always highlighted, his most menacing, blasphemous, scatological, violent texts quoted the most often, as if to keep up a steady stream of furious opposition to the "system" (translations here in the footnotes): "Chiote à l'esprit," "Toute l'écriture est de la cochonnerie," "rien qui m'apparaisse maintenant plus funèbre et mortellement néfaste que le signe stratifacteur et borné de la croix, rien de plus érotiquement pornographique que le christ, ignoble concrétisan sexuelle de toutes les fausses énigmes psychiques"; "Cogner à mort et foutre la gueule, foutre sur la gueule est la dernière langue, la dernière musique que je connais."[37] His oeuvre—battering rationality, desecrating religion, condemning society, shattering social taboos into as many pieces as possible—serves as one long howl of resistance to civilization.

Artaud had achieved some recognition for his writing and theater work in Paris before he was incarcerated, but it pales in significance to his acclaim there afterward. A study of the publication of works both by and on Artaud in French journals from the 1920s until today reveals what Guillaume Bridet describes as "the overwhelming privilege given to the last ten, and especially last two, years of Artaud's life," evidenced in an extraordinary jump in publication numbers of critical and, after 1948, posthumous works by Artaud.[38] Although he had been published in leading journals in the 1920s and '30s, after his move to the asylum at Rodez in 1943, editors fought with one another for the privilege of first publication of one of his works. Then, in the 1940s, "after the death of Artaud, the myth of the *poète maudit* grew. To publish Artaud became an editorial imperative."[39] In the 1960s, as Penot-Lacassagne writes, "Not to publish Artaud was to remain in the margins of lucrative polemics; to publish him was nothing but to respond to the demands of the moment."[40] Today, debates over Artaud's treatment by the psychiatric establishment and legal issues with the publication of his works keep the irons hot (in fact, one of the last letters Derrida ever wrote was a heated letter to Gallimard accusing it of not giving Artaud's editor, Paule Thévenin, enough credit in its recent edition of Artaud's works).[41]

The mythical, person-centered discourse has limited the scope and breadth of Artaud scholarship by focusing attention away from the works themselves.[42] All these "fragments hurled against the void" rarely receive close, contextualized readings. Provocative phrases and quotations get picked out and used in an extraordinarily uncontextualized manner. Bridet describes how journals and newspapers have used the Christlike figure of Artaud, "a man . . . who was sacrificed on the altar of super-human revelations," in the service of their own political, critical, or social agendas and neglect actually reading the works.[43] In its usage in the French press, "Artaud's oeuvre," observes Bridet, "leaves the domain of art and creativity" and is "caught up in the rivalries caused by the economy of symbolic commodities."[44]

But while his works themselves have been largely neglected in the literary sense, they have been collected with an extraordinary fetishistic fervor. The clinical focus on Artaud's insanity and unresolvability has led to a bizarre sacralization engendering a belief that every fragment rescued from his consciousness represents crucial testimony to his condition and to his genius, evidence of his special clinical and artistic status. This is evident in the editing practices employed in collecting his works: each scrap of paper—whether a call for heroin, an unfinished letter detailing the minutiae of renting a new room, or a barely legible scrawl on a napkin— has been collected for the *Oeuvres complètes.* More than with any other literary figure, the banal and the exalted are not separated from each other, which sometimes takes Artaud's career from the sublime to the ridiculous, from tragedy to farce.

Paule Thévenin, to whom Artaud entrusted the editing and publication of his works and who spent decades collecting documents for the Gallimard *Oeuvres complètes,* encountered the severe drawbacks of this attitude.[45] She remarked on the extraordinary difficulty of getting materials such as Artaud's letters, artworks, and manuscripts from the people who owned them: "All the people who come into contact with [*toucher à*] Artaud are paranoiacs. . . . That posed problems for everyone, everyone. It's this attitude that people take in relation to Artaud. That even struck the editor. He had never seen that."[46] Everyone who enters into imaginary communion with post-Rodez Artaud threatens to be drawn into this circle of insanity, a fact driven home to me in 2002 when I requested some Artaud documents at the Bibliothèque Nationale. A librarian told me the original documents didn't circulate anymore, not because they were fragile, but because everyone who studied Artaud was "complètement fou" (completely mad).

Lotringer's *Fous d'Artaud,* then, is aptly named: it mimics the madness not only of its subject but also of some of his critics.[47] Lotringer—to bring this point to a close with a return to a particularly striking recent example—goes to incredible lengths to establish Artaud as a visionary/outsider/prophet in the opening essay of the book. Framing his discussion in terms of Artaud's (alleged, according to Lotringer) Jewishness, Lotringer turns to Louis-Ferdinand Céline for support, quoting from Céline's most outrageous anti-Semitic diatribes to establish parallel persecution complexes of Artaud and Jews. Lotringer ends by linking Artaud to Jesus—both Jews and both misunderstood and uncategorizable by their fellow men. When we get to this point—enlisting Nazi sympathizers to buttress the argument for Artaud as not only the Eternal Jew but also Jesus—I think we have to take a big step back and ask what on earth is going on here.

What is missing from the majority of the French school is distance: from Artaud as a person (whose presence was obviously more than commanding); from "l'affaire Artaud" (i.e., all of the legal and editorial wrangles with his works that occupied a significant place in the French press for decades); from Artaud as a case study; from the Romantic legacy of poet as sufferer, of artist as spiritual visionary. Artaud's oeuvre has inspired an extraordinary number of works in late twentieth-century French theory and criticism, but when it comes to Artaud, the criticism is identificatory and, in general, conspicuously ahistorical.

Artaud in Context

Artaud lived in a world constituted only by his own self, oblivious to the political conflicts around him. Ought we, also, to live there? Or shouldn't we rather examine his works themselves to see how he absorbed and reworked ideas, imagery, and impulses of his time, whether consciously or unconsciously? *Artaud and His Doubles* does not take sides with any existing school of thought. Instead, it attempts to move beyond current paradigms by examining elements missing from these readings. By focusing on Artaud's interwar writings, his productions, and the worldview they reveal, I illuminate connections to contemporary modes of thought outside as well as inside theater, while establishing fundamental ideas that thread their way through Artaud's entire oeuvre that may be of use to subsequent scholars. Although I make reference to certain biographical details, this book is emphatically not a biography and does not employ a biographical approach. I do not pretend to know "Artaud"; I am reading his works themselves and not his person, and I read them in the context of the history of ideas, politics, and theater.

This study focuses on *The Theater and Its Double,* primarily for the reason that it is by far the most widely read work of Artaud's and thus provides a critical focus for the question, which I address in the conclusion, of *why* such a reading of Artaud has been avoided. Artaud's theatrical writings were composed in the 1920s and '30s, and all of his work in the theater also occurred during these two decades;[48] in fact, the period of 1920–35 encompasses the entirety of his acting, directing, playwriting, and design work, between his first performance with Lugné-Poe and his last theatrical role in *The Cenci* in 1935, including the 1924 publication of his first theatrical essay "The Evolution of Décor" and the final edits in 1935 of *The Theater and Its Double.* Thus to speak of Artaud's theatrical work and ideas is necessarily to speak of theater of the interwar era, which is what *Artaud and His Doubles* does. I reference other works Artaud wrote during this period, such as novels and poetry, insofar as they shed light on his vision for a theater, and I dedicate one section to analyzing his directing work. I do not venture into the period when he was incarcerated, nor do I debate questions of his sanity; I focus instead on his theatrical works, their immediate contexts, and their implications.

Artaud and His Doubles reveals another dimension to the Theater of Cruelty by pursuing correspondences across sociological, psychological, artistic, and political formations. Sets of concerns grounded in comparative research shape each section: intellectual history and the cultural climate of Western Europe in the interwar era, the historical development of modern theater audiences and the director, and crowd theory. The preceding pages have exposed one set of Artaud's doubles: his interpreters themselves and their focus on suffering, revolution, and resistance. Now, we leave them behind to move on to examine the historical doubles of his writings, ideas, imagery, and impulses: his contemporaries in interwar Europe, largely outside of the French avant-garde and far removed from his traditional associations. These historical doubles are, in section I, the European counter-Enlightenment, irrationalist, vitalist, and mystical thinkers; in section II, the theorists of people's theaters in Italy and Germany; and, in section III, the figure of the crowd leader and its associated discourse in interwar Europe. The sections designate these three sets of doubles. The individual chapters make the demonstrations through historical contextualization and close readings of Artaud's work.

Section I, "The Fight against Civilization; or, The Rebirth of Tragedy," reads "The Theater and the Plague," Artaud's famous opening essay of *The Theater and Its Double,* in light of the moment of its composition: the aftermath of World War I in Western Europe. Artaud's images have been read as metaphorical, taking their power from ahistorical poetic license. Yet the specificity of Artaud's catalogs of catastrophe is not entirely metaphorical or out of history. His rhetoric and imagery mirror the ravages of World War I and the thinking of those who called for more, who, within a few years, coalesced their irrationalism and mysticism into a body of ideas that fed directly into fascism. This section examines the imagery and polemic of "The Theater and the Plague" alongside contemporaneous resurgences of irrationalism and mysticism, interwar interpretations of Nietzsche and Wagner, and troublingly resonant images of trench warfare. Artaud's essay reveals a desire to keep war alive during peacetime, demonstrating affinities with interwar counter-Enlightenment and reactionary thinkers who reacted against the nineteenth century's embrace of science, liberal individualism, belief in progress, and human achievement with a belief in a vague vitalism; a distrust of science and civilization; and apocalyptic images of disease, evil, abjection, and a new, heroic era. The first set of Artaud's undiscussed doubles is comprised of this grim congregation.

Just as Artaud was not alone in feeling a *mal du siècle,* he was also very much a product of his times in thinking in terms of crowds and wanting to channel their energies. Section II, "Audience, Mass, Crowd," interprets the Theater of Cruelty's ideal spectator in light of early twentieth-century theater audiences and the field of crowd theory. Artaud was writing at a moment when the role and identity of the audience were being radically redefined. The late nineteenth century transformed the audience from an active assembly to a refined, domesticated, and physically restrained group of people who obeyed the command to contemplate in stillness what transpired behind the proscenium. While much of the avant-garde rebelled against this new bourgeois audience and developed strategies to attempt to re-invigorate the spectator, many other performance theorists built on the new means of control. In the 1920s and '30s, some sought to intensify the audience's emotional experience while keeping it physically restrained, orchestrating an ecstatic loss of self. The doubles revealed in this context are again outside the avant-garde altogether: they are the creators of peoples' theaters in fascist Italy and Germany. While the avant-garde was still thinking in terms of "audience," these theorists were thinking of "crowds."

The crowd between the wars in Western Europe provides an illuminating context for Artaud's ideal theater event and another way of interpreting his call for resistance, revolution, and liberation. Crowd theory provides us with a critical vocabulary that helps us orient our notions of "freedom" in the context not of the 1960s but of Artaud's interwar Theater of Cruelty. Crowd theory analyzes how people behave differently when in crowds than when alone, and it establishes critical terms for the relationship of crowds to leader figures. It reveals the strategies by which masses could be given a feeling of exaltation and communion while being directed, a subject of particular interest in the interwar era. Artaud intuitively taps into this with his Theater of Cruelty. Freedom, here, is found through loss and immersion rather than individual liberty and self-realization. This dynamic combines with Artaud's dark, mystical worldview to create a very distinct kind of freedom. Freedom for the Theater of Cruelty takes the form not, as we will see, of empowerment or peace, but of an ongoing experience of convulsive, ecstatic misery.

Section III, "Visions of Power," contextualizes Artaud's ideal director in terms of the phenomenon of the rapid rise of the theater director, from approximately the 1850s to its entrenchment by the interwar era. The rise of the director served as the final, decisive move in the historical restraint of the theater audience. It also accompanied the rise of the modern mass individual and the emergence of charismatic leaders. Nowhere is this historical contemporaneity and the connections across cultural spheres better illustrated than in Artaud's oeuvre, which mirrors the historical shift in power in the theater away from the audience and toward the director. This section uncovers the history of Artaud's first and most sustained theatrical venture, the Théâtre Alfred Jarry (1926–28), and his 1935 production of *The Cenci* to examine his directorial strategies in theory and in practice. Through these productions and his theorizations about directorial control in *The Theater and Its Double*, we consider Artaud's exaltation of violent figures of power (such as Count Cenci and the mad Roman emperor Heliogabalus) and their doubles in charismatic, authoritarian leaders on the rise during this period.

The language of political power in the interwar era expressed itself in terms of suffering and overcoming, mysticism and higher laws, catastrophe and revelation, fear and menace, myth and destiny. Emotion, not reason, ruled the discourse of Italian Fascists and German National Socialists. Their commanding rhetoric focused on style and emphasis more than argument or dialectical exchange, and it presumed that the needs of the flesh, psyche, and soul were identical. This language bears unsettling similarity to the most radical voice of theater directing as it found its articulation with Artaud. Thus, Section III explores the language Artaud uses to describe the director of the Theater of Cruelty and compares that with other visions of directorial control. Some of the earliest directors, such as Firmin Gémier, Jacques Copeau, and Edward Gordon Craig, often viewed themselves as not only leaders but also visionaries, speaking in terms of reshaping not just an art form, but existence itself—society, community, the world. To an extreme degree, Artaud's works abound in metaphors of sorcery, hypnotism, the occult, and dreams of power. Artaud envisages this kind of alchemical energy as wielded by the director, an energy that is, in the Theater of Cruelty, aggressively one-directional. These may be dismissed as imagistic fantasies of a madman, outsider, or artist, but people who, in this same period, actually managed to impose their will on the world show us what these ideas could possibly mean in more concrete terms. Artaud's metaphysical language, centering on visions of power, control, and leadership, places him in the company of parties with whom he's not normally compared: those who share not only his historical moment but also his fascination with leadership in a totalizing, vengeful, and mystical context.

Establishing Artaud in these frameworks—the postwar mentality in Europe and the development of political and artistic strategies for seizing control in the wake of the era of the masses and a newly submissive audience—forces us to consider his Theater of Cruelty in a new, if disturbing, light. The conclusion, "Longing for Nothingness," asks why a historical approach to Artaud has been avoided up to this point and investigates the key term of freedom in the context of the complex intersections of formal experiment and political affinities. It focuses on the element of desire in the work of Artaud and that of all his doubles: the desire for de-individuation, for losing oneself, the desire for super-human goals, for a broad notion of freedom at any cost. By resituating Artaud in the context of non-progressive thinkers and artists between the wars, I ask what desire led post-structuralists and American experimental theater practitioners to idealize this power-hungry, reactionary, deeply pessimistic artist. Perhaps the most significant association with Artaud's oeuvre is that of freedom, which *Artaud and His Doubles* follows in multiple forms, including chaos, liberation, lack of inhibition, and loss of self. Liberation sounds empowering, and freedom carries with it a promise of happiness, but to be free does not necessarily mean to be empowered; to be liberated does not equal self-fulfillment. The hidden double of the kind of freedom Artaud promotes—dismantling systems without establishing a vision for what would take their place—is chaos, which leads not necessarily to liberation, but just as often to its opposite.

Beyond Poète Maudit

The historian George L. Mosse has written, "It is the task of the historian to destroy old myths in order to encourage new confrontations with reality."[49] It is my hope that this book's examination of an unexplored side of Artaud's oeuvre will provide new confrontations with not only his works and time but also the reality of our own embrace of him and the complex relationships among experimental theater, liberationary ideals, and the dynamics of power between groups of people and charismatic leaders.

The structure of thought that flowed through the age of crowds and culminated in fascism is to be found in Artaud's work in a distinctive and disturbing manner. It is not exclusive, but it is undeniably present, and it is drastically unstudied. This blind spot calls for an examination. As totalitarianism and fascism may rear their heads again in new—perhaps unrecognizable at first—ways in this century, I believe we must consider why an author, thinker, artist, and icon so valued by experimental theater practitioners and progressive scholars has escaped this analysis; indeed, the embrace of him itself is due for a serious evaluation.[50]

I don't have many fellow travelers on this road. Roger Shattuck wrote in a brief 1984 essay of Artaud's "significant quantity of nostalgia for violence along with a tendency to capitulate to undefined collective forces that speak in an unknown voice."[51] He concludes: "Over the long haul and in his most crucial writings, Artaud is prepared to surrender individual consciousness and even individual life to a higher collectivity. Some might call it a prophetic mind. I call it a totalitarian mind—or at least one deeply pulled in that direction" ("Artaud Possessed," 186). Rainer Friedrich and Naomi Greene have explicitly tied Artaud to, respectively, totalitarian thinking and fascism in similarly brief essays, and Stephen Koch provided a persuasive polemic against the seductions of the violence in Artaud's work in 1966.[52] Although few scholars and practitioners have investigated the claims these writers make, *Artaud and His Doubles* takes these propositions seriously and explores them at length.[53]

Similar work has been done on Nietzsche and Wagner, two figures whose works and ideas, as we will see, connect with Artaud's on multiple levels. It is not terribly popular; "defenders" of these artists may reject investigations into this aspect of their work as "the tyranny of suspicion."[54] Stephen Aschheim, in a study of the diverse and contentious field of Nietzsche reception in the worlds of culture, politics, and philosophy, points out that some critics have been accused of "Nazi pedigree hunting in the realm of ideas" (*Nietzsche Legacy*, 319) in their discussion of Nietzsche and the Third Reich, while others, such as Walter Kaufmann, surely went too far in the other direction, attempting to rescue Nietzsche from the "radical inversion of everything that the prophet of creativity, cultured and critical individualist, and good European had actually stood for" (315–16). As the field of reception runs from pole to pole in both the political and the aesthetic realm, studying Nietzsche—and, I believe, Artaud—must take into account the studying itself.

Aschheim cites a commentary on the Nietzsche debate that usefully serves as a framework for my investigation. Commenting on "the explosive and experimental Nietzsche corpus" (317–18), he cites Eric Vögelin's argument that we can find a "structure of thought" whose interpretation will prove more meaningful than the emphases on the most outrageous passages taken singly:

> What deserves some attention . . . is the fact that Nietzsche's work lends itself easily to . . . misinterpretations. This fact should not be denied. There is no sense in pretending that the horror passages which are quoted with equal delight by the critics and the National Socialist admirers are not to be found in the work. Their existence should not be an incentive either to whitewash or to condemn Nietzsche, but rather to explore the structure of thought which produced them. (317n)

It is the task of *Artaud and His Doubles* to explore undiscussed parallel "structure[s] of thought" to Artaud's most famous work. Artaud's "explosive and experimental" oeuvre also contains myriad possibilities with repercussions throughout the world of theater history. It is also reflective and anticipatory of social, political, and philosophical currents throughout Western Europe. It contains passages that avant-garde and experimental theater artists found inspiring, that influenced the development of innumerable progressive thinkers and artists, but it also contains "horror passages," and these demand further investigation.

Georg Lukács argued in his controversial *The Destruction of Reason* that thinkers have to be examined in light of their social, political, and historical significance, whether or not the authors deliberately positioned themselves in these categories. Their ideas have "historically necessary influence. In this sense, every thinker is responsible to history for the objective substance of his philosophizing."[55] This resulted in his famous examination of Nietzsche, which attempted to uncover "how philosophical formulations, as an intellectual mirroring of Germany's concrete development towards Hitler, helped to speed up the process" of Germany's path to Hitler (Lukács, *Destruction of Reason*, 4). Lukács argued that the accusation of pedigree hunting pales in significance to the importance of tracing a web of thought subtler than superficial alliances. Explicit declarations, dedications, temporary allegiances—all these are visible to the most casual observer. What is more difficult is to see how fascistic structures of thought manifest themselves among the intellectuals, artists, leftists, and "ordinary people" who, throughout the twentieth century, have found themselves part of a totalitarian world and have no idea how they arrived there.[56]

The field of examination of political affiliations on the level of culture rather than allegiance is continuing to grow, perhaps not surprisingly as the unpredictability of our political future continually manifests itself, often to our dismay, in spite of our efforts to learn from the past and foresee our progress. Hannah Arendt wrote repeatedly of the difficulty we have seeing the totalitarianism in ordinary events. Her "banality of evil" formulation in *Eichmann in Jerusalem* helps us understand how political extremism does not necessarily—or perhaps at all—stem from one fantastic manifestation of power, but from undramatic yet decisive attitudes of a people. Alice Yaeger Kaplan has studied fascism in France not because it manifested itself there in any lasting political sphere, but because "France is a pedagogical place with respect to theories of fascism" (*Reproductions of Banality*, 52). Zeev Sternhell's controversial book on fascism in France, *Ni droite ni gauche* (*Neither Right nor Left*), applies this approach to the literati, assuming that the works of minor authors and journals can penetrate culture more deeply than an overtly fascist newspaper such as the Parisian *Je suis partout*. The subtler embodiment of ideas and the professedly apolitical stance of such writers may hold even more power because of the near invisibility of their politics.

Artaud was writing in a country that never developed fascist government but that developed "powerful intellectual and cultural preparation for it."[57] The following examinations situate Artaud in his historical moment, one in which aesthetic fantasies translated far too easily into calamitous politics.

SECTION I : The Fight against Civilization; or, The Rebirth of Tragedy

*The Great War was the psychological turning point. . . . The urge
to create and the urge to destroy changed places. The urge to destroy
was intensified; the urge to create became increasingly abstract. In the
end the abstractions turned to insanity and all that remained
was destruction, Götterdämmerung.*
  —MODRIS EKSTEINS, *Rites of Spring*

SECTION 1 · The Fight against Civilization, or, The Rebirth of Tragedy

CHAPTER 1 : Invocation of the Plague

The penultimate stage direction of Artaud's only original play, *Jet of Blood* (1925), presents an image of perverse fecundity characteristic of his writings:

> *An enormous number of scorpions emerge from under the Wet Nurse's skirts and begin to swarm in her vagina, which swells and splits, becomes vitreous, and flashes like the sun. (SW, 76)*[1]

Horrific new life spreads rapidly over its progenitor in the form of a million poisonous creatures. A ruptured sexual organ lights up the world, "flash[ing] like the sun," after which a brothel keeper flees and a virgin rises from the dead. A wet nurse midwives destruction, purity arises from decay, death takes the form of life, and the agent of these inversions is disease. Infestation and birth bear no difference in this universe: the passage of life occurs through biological organisms that sicken and kill.

Artaud's writings teem with such malignant offspring arising from the disastrous proximity of conception and destruction. In *Heliogabalus* (1934), the depraved new Emperor inaugurates his reign by walking into Rome backward, imagistically inverting the course of natural birth and insemination, "wearing over the pubis a kind of iron spider whose legs flay his skin and draw blood with each . . . movement of his thighs" (SW, 321).[2] Heliogabalus's inaugural procession includes ritual musical objects "made from male members that have been stretched, tanned, blackened . . . affixed to the ends of staffs like candles impaled on nails, like the barbs of a mace" (SW, 321). In his 1925 description of André Masson's painting *L'homme*, Artaud highlights the images of "a slender belly" (SW, 65) and a burst *grenade*—*grenade* meaning both artillery and the obscenely fecund fruit, the pomegranate. Out of the exploded *grenade* spiral cells, eggs, germs.

Invocations of menacing new life come to a head in "The Theater and the Plague," the first essay in *The Theater and Its Double*. The scorpion swarm of *Jet of Blood* resembles nothing so much as the plague raging through Europe in Artaud's imagination, spawning a dangerous new universe as it annihilates the old. Artaud's images of comprehensive devastation, of new life equated with torment, come hard on the heels of World War I, whose aftermath left much of Western Europe feeling that the new world just arrived had originated in horror and was very clearly heading back into it. This context—a grotesque new life emerging historically as well as in Artaud's frequently considered ahistorical writings—is where we must begin in order to interpret the worldview made manifest in *The Theater and Its Double*.

In the early 1930s, when Western Europe was still reeling from the damage of World War I, Artaud chose the plague as the central metaphor for his ideal theater. *The Theater and Its Double* (written between 1931 and 1935, published in 1938) stands out in Artaud's twenty-six-volume oeuvre as the most concrete and most sustained articulation of his vision for the theater we have in writing, and "The Theater and the Plague" (written in 1933) encapsulates the book's violent concerns and unresolved tensions. All the examinations of this study, in fact—including that of the crowd, of the audience/performer relationship, of fascism, and of Artaud's leadership role in a politics of ecstasy—find root in this essay. Therefore, my interpretation of Artaud's work begins with a sustained close (re-) reading of "The Theater and the Plague" in its historical context in order to bring to the fore pervasive themes that previous readings have neglected or taken ahistorically, specifically highlighting the worldview defined by disease, cataclysm, and aggressive dynamics of power and submission. After a detailed look at *The Theater and Its Double*'s first chapter, we can situate the book in its true context in cultural and intellectual history. Read against the backdrop of World War I and alongside contemporary strains of milleniarism, ecstatic images of degeneration and purification, and fantasies of orchestrated broad-scale devastation, this, Artaud's most famous work, clearly establishes a far more troubling vision—of the world and for the theater—than has generally been assumed.

Nouveau mal du siècle

The Theater and Its Double begins as any avant-garde manifesto might: with a call to sweep away existing systems, artistic as well as social. Strikingly, *The Theater and Its Double* does not present utopic visions of the sort that normally followed avant-garde manifestos' opening moves, no pictures of health, transcendence, or progress. Instead, written in the aftermath of a nearly worldwide self-destruction, *The Theater and Its Double* dwells, with intense concentration, on cataclysms, on moments of suffering, on abjection and terror, on annihilation and gratuitous violence, on the dark nature of mankind and life and the forces that regulate them. The book does not reveal a salutary project or even a death wish;[3] it demonstrates an absolute fascination with the painful moment before death and the energetic manifestations of that pain, with what Artaud's Viennese contemporary Egon Friedell described as the intoxication of sickness.[4]

In the eternal tug-of-war for primacy in human values between civilization and nature, between the rational and the intuitive, Artaud comes down unhesitatingly on the side of the natural and intuitive. *The Theater and Its Double* pits all manmade systems against a chaotic, pre-rational organic condition. The book rests on the premise that theater can be used to return us to a primal experience of the "fragile, fluctuating center" of life (*TD*, 13). To turn to a cultural form—the theater—to get past civilization is not paradoxical in Artaud's world, because he considers "true culture" a state that operates regardless of and beyond manmade systems and objects. "True culture" represents not a progression of systems, ideas, or aesthetics but instead "savage, i.e., entirely spontaneous" impulses; "bestial essences"; and the movement of "the secret forces of the universe" (*TD*, 10). Ripping the concept from its moorings in human activity and production, Artaud uses "culture" to indicate an organic totality, a natural condition. "True" culture is found not in products or activities but in living itself; it is "action," "protest," "exaltation," "force" (*TD*, 8–10).

To restore us to the condition of "true" culture would require a radical conflagration of what has always passed itself off as culture. In this destructive desire, Artaud echoes other avant-garde artists, such as the Italian Futurists in their call to raze stagnant institutions and the dadaists in their rage against existing systems. However, Artaud's ideas unfold in a distinctly sinister and atavistic atmosphere. While primitivism forms a crucial foundation for much of the avant-garde, Artaud's writing reveals a desire not for a utopia but for a re-encounter with primal forces and energies closely akin to those of the brutal Dionysos of Euripides's *Bacchae*.[5] This lineage of extra-civilized energies that enrapture as well as devastate moves through theater history from Dionysos to *The Birth of Tragedy* to *The Theater and Its Double*. In the 1920s and '30s, this will for an ecstatic yet menacing loss of self, vividly articulated by many artists and theorists clamoring for its physical realization, found its political home in fascism.

Believing that traditions, art, and received ideas represent only the stagnation of true culture, Artaud envisions countless ways of demolishing them: "The library at Alexandria can be burnt down. There are forces above and beyond papyrus: we may temporarily be deprived of our ability to discover these forces, but their energy will not be suppressed" (*TD*, 10). In his yearning for "true" culture, Artaud champions what historians mourn: "It is right that from time to time cataclysms occur which compel us to return to nature, i.e., to rediscover life" (*TD*, 10). This is one characteristic thread of Artaud's thought: he inverts the aspirations of Western civilization and glorifies their negations. Everywhere in *The Theater and Its Double* Artaud exalts anything—the burning of the library at Alexandria, the Black Plague, the story of Bluebeard, the work of the Marquis de Sade, the fall of Jerusalem—that contributes to the collapse of civilization. In his reading of *'Tis Pity She's a Whore*, Artaud celebrates the pair of lovers who "overthrow . . . law, morality, and all those who dare set themselves up as administrators of justice" (*TD*, 29). Annabella weeps "not with remorse but for fear I shall not be able to satisfy my passion" (*TD*, 28). As Artaud describes it, Giovanni rips his lover's heart out in an act of "heroic" defiance: "Vengeance for vengeance, and crime for crime" (*TD*, 28). The triumph of the lovers' brutal excesses of passion reverses the *Oresteia*; we move backward from Athena's court and erase the progression of civilization by revoking the Eumenides and restoring the Furies as champions.

Cataclysm rules Artaud's rhetoric, and the plague serves as his emblematic image. "The Theater and the Plague" calls for the theatrical event to have the force of a plague ravaging a city. The essay asks that the theater mimic the inversions of the epidemic and its attendant generation of destructive forces. The plague appeals because of its comprehensive nature: "The theater, like the plague, is in the image of this carnage and this essential separation" (*TD*, 31); at the onset of the plague, "the regular forms collapse" (*TD*, 23). Carnage and collapse: Artaud's writings repeatedly turn to conflagration, disease, war, rape, and murder as images of the desired event. Cataclysms are necessarily cruel; they represent devastation on the broadest possible level. They also represent the power to overturn the order of the world, to unleash a host of energies free from manmade—and therefore, according to Artaud, imperfect—systems. In Artaud's vision, cataclysms are movement, cruelty, power, life.

Artaud was far from alone in this kind of cataclysmic thinking after

World War I.[6] The 1920s and '30s found large swaths of Western Europe entertaining apocalyptic fantasies fueled by violent metaphysical pessimism. This thinking found articulation in a wide range of works, including Spengler's *The Decline of the West* (1918); Ortega y Gasset's *The Revolt of the Masses* (1920); Freud's bleakest work, *Civilization and Its Discontents* (1929–30), in which he allows that civilization may be quite possibly "not worth the trouble"; and Malraux's *The Temptation of the West* (1926), in which an observer on Western civilization notes that *"Man is dead,* following God."[7] In many circles, despair and anger led to what Modris Eksteins, in his history of the cultural ramifications of World War I, calls an "increasingly abstract" urge to create, dominated by an intensified urge to destroy.[8]

The postwar period gave rise to a peculiar frustrated mindset resulting from the realization that the Great War hadn't produced the "apocalyptic resolution" (Eksteins, *Rites of Spring,* 292) it had seemed to promise. In Germany in particular, "the burden of having been in the eye of the storm and yet, in the end, of having resolved nothing, was excruciating" (Eksteins, *Rites of Spring,* 293). An acute sense of a thwarted climax led, in some circles, to an intensification of the yearning for destruction. This prolonged yearning, a desire to keep the violence of the war alive until resolution or death, manifested itself in France with authors such as Louis-Ferdinand Céline, especially in his rabid interwar pamphlets, such as *Bagatelles pour un massacre* (1937):

> I've got a hunger! . . . an enormous hunger! . . . a world-wide hunger!
> a hunger for Revolution . . . a hunger for planetary conflagration . . .
> for the mobilization of all the charnel-houses in the world! An appetite which is surely divine, divine! Biblical![9]

Works like Céline's—which are very much in tune with Artaud's—manifested end-time thinking with no clear end in sight, a furious desire for a continual build of the most violent and forceful energies, a distinctive, if localized, feature of the *entre deux guerres* period.[10]

This kind of apocalyptic thinking led Artaud to the plague. He had company. Egon Friedell, writing at the same time in Vienna, also turned to the medieval catastrophe as a way to connect the interwar moment to a kind of higher inevitability. Friedell's work articulates a Spenglerian view of history as a series of cycles: *A Cultural History of the Modern Age* (1927) locates modernity as beginning in 1348 with the Black Plague and ending with the catastrophe of World War I: "The hour in which the new age was born is marked by a heavy sickness of European humanity—the Black Death" (81). The plague, for Friedell, manifests the painful birth of a new era, a twinning of sickness and power.

The plague provides a way to conceptualize an otherwise incomprehensibly comprehensive catastrophe: it is a dynamic totality of immeasurable power. The Great War, like the plague, heralded a completely new world in material, psychological, and spiritual terms, proving the link between the destruction of human bodies and that of civilization. The plague reveals the body politic in its carnage: it demonstrates the identity of matter and consciousness by deranging them simultaneously. "At these points," Friedell writes of periods of prolonged psychological upheaval after great catastrophes, "it is a matter of *real* disease" (*Cultural History*, 70).[11]

In Friedell's vision, such periods of destruction and mass psychosis lead to temporarily increased creativity and insight, and the world perpetually moves through eras of psychosis, sickness, and inspiration.[12] Artaud's thinking is less cyclical. In his vision of the plague, the epidemic engenders its own dangerous offspring to populate the new era. Both Friedell's and Artaud's works reflect the belief that the plague is no accident, but indeed a manifestation of a "new spirit" (Friedell, *Cultural History*, 82) or "Will" (Artaud). Artaud goes even further than Friedell in this intentionality: "a social disaster so far-reaching, an organic disorder so mysterious," he writes, indicates "extreme strength" at the moment "when something essential is going to be accomplished" (*TD*, 27).

The worldview we're sketching reveals a Romantic strain in its exaltation of suffering, in its belief that civilization occludes the forces that really matter, that laws and society stifle the organic individual will. In fact, the interwar era nourished what Nicholas Hewitt has called a *nouveau mal du siècle*—a sickness or evil of the century that resembled the *mal du siècle* of the earlier Romantic period, but which took on new and darker forms after the Great War and with the next war looming.[13] The exaltation of sickness, malaise, and melancholy prevalent in earlier nineteenth-century writers such as Novalis, Nerval, Baudelaire, and Hoffmann, to name just a few, grew more pessimistic after World War I, more violent, and much larger in scope. The identification of objects and systems to reject multiplied, while the ideals fueling creative production became increasingly obscure. In the *nouveau mal du siècle*, there was no place for a cult of youth, a rhapsodic description of an age, or a secret harmony between the indi-

vidual writer and the cosmos. The Romantic idea of limitless personal creativity and individual transcendence lost its hold on the imagination for
writers such as Céline, Malraux, Léon Daudet, and Drieu la Rochelle. After the Great War, sickness seemed, to many, to no longer serve as a privileged state through which an individual might gain access to unique visions, but to form the very fabric of society.[14] *The Theater and Its Double*
was born in this moment of the *nouveau mal du siècle*, exuding a fervor to
resist succumbing to any enervating morbidity. "The Theater and the
Plague," instead, enthrones sickness as the arcanum of power.

The Residues of War

"The Theater and the Plague" runs on currents of fear, *le mal* (sickness or
evil), and what Artaud calls "cruelty." It invokes a role for the theater that
consists of bringing forth a monstrous swarm to overturn the old world
order and establish a reign of terrifying energies in its place: "Like the
plague the theater is the time of evil [*le mal*], the triumph of dark powers"
(*TD*, 30). To read the essay is a matter not so much of following an argument (there are many internal contradictions and breaks in logic), but
rather of tracking a set of images the essay continually evokes and circles.
"The Theater and the Plague" is less an explanation of a program than an
initiation into the worldview upon which the Theater of Cruelty rests.[15]
The essay demands to be read as we read avant-garde manifestos such as
those of the dadaists or the Italian Futurists: as an articulation of an artistic vision that reaches beyond theater, a vision embedded in its cultural
moment, inextricably linked to a complete world picture.

In this section, as we pursue Artaud's imagined course of the plague
through body and society, we find recurrent images of abjection and inversion; a system of cosmic equivalencies; a deep interest in decay, violence, and corruption that never transforms into an equally specific vision
of health; and the darkest possible depiction of mankind. These form the
basis for Artaud's ideal theatrical experience. Throughout, *The Theater and
Its Double* invokes these images in a distinct historical context: they echo
specific horrific events that were resonating in the minds of Western Europeans between the wars.[16] After a war that killed or wounded 11 per-
cent of France's entire population, direct knowledge of the carnage was
inescapable, and the images flooded the nation's consciousness for
decades afterward. Highlighting the historical context of this imagery

and examining what Artaud does (and does not do) with it moves us beyond seeing his connections as primarily with artists such as those discussed in the introduction who yearned for new social or cultural systems brought about by artistic innovation that emphasized liberality and progress. "The Theater and the Plague," reveling in images of broad-scale human destruction after World War I and betraying the darkest possible worldview, suggests affinities, as we will see, with an unsettling politics.[17]

"The Theater and the Plague" uses imagery from historical, legendary, anatomical, and mystical accounts of the bubonic plague in Europe to establish an ideal theatrical event.[18] Artaud describes in clinical yet fervent detail the physical demolition of society and the plague victim's body. His prose reaches its most precise and vivid heights in the course of these descriptions. From the appearance of red spots to the dizziness, fever, and rising blisters that lead to the individual's death, from the initial panic to the universal apotheosis of perversion, Artaud's language focuses intently on the most graphic, painful, and intimate effects of the disease.

Artaud's vivid descriptions of decay evince an infatuation with dark powers that reign equally in micro- and macrocosmic realms, illustrating a "passionate equation between Man, Society, Nature, and Objects" (TD, 90). His world picture is one of equivalencies, one in which matter, energy, and spirit all spring from and are driven by an indefinable but profound and exalted foundation of le mal. Drawing from disparate sources such as the Paracelsan paradigm of grounding theories of equivalencies in natural sciences, the Gnostic worldview that the world is inherently bound in error (both modes of thought being re-explored in the early century), and a kind of medieval body politic (also emerging as an interwar trope), Artaud uses the plague to construct a cosmology of universal suffering with a distinctly sinister and ecstatic character.[19] We will begin with the physical body and move to the body politic in following the course of the plague.

As the plague moves through one victim in "The Theater and the Plague," Artaud's imagery connects corporeal, terrestrial, and cosmic realms. As the plague attacks the body, the "crazed body fluids" of the victim flood through his flesh, "his gorge rises, the inside of his stomach seems as if it were trying to gush out between his teeth" (TD, 19). This corporeal attack corresponds to earthly forces: "The body fluids, furrowed like the earth struck by lightning, like lava kneaded by subterranean forces, search for an outlet" (TD, 19). And they reach toward the cosmic:

"the skin rises in blisters like air bubbles under the surface of lava, and these blisters are surrounded by circles, of which the outermost, like Saturn's ring around the incandescent planet, indicates the extreme limit of a bubo" (*TD*, 19). All the while, the victim is "seized by [the] terrible fatigue . . . of a centralized magnetic suction, of his molecules divided and drawn toward their annihilation" (*TD*, 19). Contained in one body but imagistically reaching across all spheres, the plague represents for Artaud a focused destructive energy revealing correspondences across body, earth, and universe.

Consciousness occupies an equally crucial place in the essay's picture of corresponding corruptions. Artaud argues (through a selective anatomical analysis of the interior of a plague victim's body) that the afflictions described here occur, in the interior of the body, on only two organs: the brain and the lungs. These are the organs in which Artaud locates awareness and will, because we can command the brain and lungs to arrest their functions (thinking and breathing), but we cannot stop our hearts from beating or our other organs from functioning. In the plague victim, the brain and lungs alone "blacken and grow gangrenous," falling into chips and granules of an unknowable "coal-black dust" (*TD*, 20). The disease physically and deliberately crumbles away our sense of self and power; it seems to "have a preference for the very organs of the body, the particular physical sites, where human will, consciousness, and thought are imminent and apt to occur" (*TD*, 21). The plague hastens the collapse of individual thought and will in its victim because it naturally is drawn to similar forces—and the plague itself has thought and will. Artaud insists the plague is not a bacillus but "a psychic entity" (*TD*, 18). Thus, it achieves its ruthless assault on the body guided by a symmetry of consciousness. It demonstrates its superiority to individual consciousness, which is similar to it in kind but not nearly equal in scope.

In addition to the corporeal, the terrestrial, the cosmic, and the conscious, the plague operates on the societal level: "We can comprehend the troubled body fluids of the victim as the solidified and material aspect of a disorder that, on other planes, is equivalent to the conflicts, struggles, cataclysms and debacles brought about by life's events" (*TD*, 25; translation modified). The liquefaction of the body, the self-destruction of the universe, and the annihilation of individual consciousness match the collapse of civilization. Artaud notes that the sixteenth-century plague in Provence "coincided with the most profound political upheavals, downfalls or deaths of kings, disappearance and destruction of provinces, earthquakes, magnetic phenomena of all kinds, exoduses of Jews" (*TD*, 18). The force of the plague more than equals that of the social order; it can overturn it as easily as it can waste the body: "Beneath such a scourge, all social forms disintegrate" (*TD*, 15). The attack on civilization completes the essay's picture of a world whose unity is best perceived in its destruction.

"Once the plague is established in a city, the regular forms collapse" (*TD*, 23): this yearning for the disintegration of forms connects to other avant-garde yearnings, but the way it plays out reveals the characteristic nature of Artaud's project. The regular forms collapse in the most wretched ways:

> There is no maintenance of roads and sewers, no army, no police, no municipal administration. Pyres are lit at random to burn the dead, with whatever means are available. . . . The dead already clog the streets in ragged pyramids gnawed at by animals around the edges. The stench rises in the air like a flame. Entire streets are blocked by the piles of dead. (*TD*, 23)

Piles of dead recur throughout Artaud's cataclysmic rhetoric, bodies stacked on bodies with no means to inter them. The specificity of these images should bring the historically minded back to the trenches of World War I. No one, including Artaud himself, has ever acknowledged how close his imagery is to that of the recent war, but taking it into consideration, we see that his metaphor is not in fact much of a metaphor, but more of a recycling of a horrific—and nearly contemporaneous—reality.[20]

Artaud's descriptions of the effects of the plague on the city bear a disquieting similarity to that of reports and diaries from the front lines. Compare the earlier quotation to one of Eksteins's descriptions of conditions in the trenches:

> The odor of decomposition—masked only by the almost equally intolerable reek of chloride and lime—and clouds of flies attracted by the carrion were [inescapable]. Limbs and torsos were churned up again and again by the shelling. Working parties digging or repairing trenches repeatedly uncovered corpses in all stages of decay and mutilation. . . . Fragments of bodies [found] their way . . . into sandbags. (*Rites of Spring*, 151)

Artaud's "appeal to cruelty and terror" (*TD*, 86) sits strangely after a war that left nine million dead and twenty-one million wounded, with almost no one in France, Germany, or England escaping some personal bereavement. His vision of an upside-down world stalls in its emancipatory feeling when looked at next to real descriptions found—for one example among thousands—in accounts of the new horrors of artillery:

> When the huge shells burst, they ravage the earth with their violence, hurling trees, rock, mud, torsos, and other debris hundreds of feet into the air. Craters the size of swimming pools remain. When a lull comes and the rains return, men bathe in these cavernous holes. (Eksteins, *Rites of Spring*, 140)

This is truly an upside-down world. Ernst Jünger, the German soldier whose *Storm of Steel* recounts his experiences in the trenches, frequently refers to how the war caused reversals so total they became absurd, how it broke all alignment with normality, how each town affected by the war experienced "the ties of bourgeois existence . . . loosened by frequent bombardment" (192). "The Theater and the Plague" invokes, then, a repeat: life had indeed already turned itself inside out, and civilization had been demolished, along with millions of men. And it was, as many people sensed by then, about to do it again.

But Artaud's imagery unfolds without acknowledging its proximity to reality, fervently summoning the collapse of an already collapsed civilization. His rhetoric is animated not by sympathy or outrage but by exhilaration—it is vibrant, lavishly detailed, and completely intent on the abjected objects: "poisonous, thick, bloody streams (color of agony and opium) . . . gush out of the corpses" (*TD*, 23); "the gall bladder, from which the hardened pus must be virtually torn . . . is hypertrophied and cracking in places" (*TD*, 20); victims "spread howling through the streets. The disease that ferments in their viscera and circulates throughout their entire organism discharges itself in tremendous cerebral explosions" (*TD*, 23). Artaud protests in *The Theater and Its Double* that "cruelty" does not refer to bodily violence (although he admits it may be necessary on occasion), but his prose tells another story.[21] He at times articulates a desire for health, but he has no vision and no enthusiasm for it. Devastation is what fascinates him.

As Naomi Greene accurately observed, Artaud's "prose is at its most impassioned, its most overheated, when he is describing scenes of violence and bloodshed" ("'All the Great Myths,'" 110). His meticulous and extensive descriptions of the plague's effects emphasize and laud its brutality, amorality, and the "gratuitously absurd" acts it inspires (*TD*, 24). Artaud's prose relishes the carnage, pointing us away from any wishful interpretation of this as an imagined restorative event. The plague instigates a world of sustained trauma akin to that of World War I, but far from lamenting or acknowledging this, Artaud imagines a theater precisely in its image.

Abjection supplants transcendence in Artaud's vision: while his manifestos have been seen to employ the revolutionary approach of a healer, his rhetoric focuses on the disease. Artaud's work foregrounds life's humiliating and painful physical condition—the tortures of the body, its private functions, its hidden parts, its illnesses. His images of the plague crystallize his fascination and disgust: blisters appear on the anus and armpits of the victims, the dead and dying are raped by the newly insane. There is no protest against this suffering driving the language, but a celebration of its ferocity.

Ferocity manifests itself not only in bodily suffering but also in behavioral inversions. The essay exalts actions so extreme that they are themselves a cruelty. In a representative paragraph, Artaud depicts how, with the onset of the epidemic, the rules of civilization as we know it crumble:

> The last of the living are in a frenzy: the obedient and virtuous son kills his father; the chaste man sodomizes his neighbors. The lecher becomes pure. The miser throws his gold in handfuls out the window. The warrior hero sets fire to the city he once risked his life to save. The dandy decks himself out in his finest clothes and promenades before the charnel houses. . . . And how explain the surge of erotic fever among the recovered victims who, instead of fleeing the city, remain where they are, trying to wrench a criminal pleasure from the dying or even the dead, half crushed under the pile of corpses where chance has lodged them. (*TD*, 24; translation modified)

The lascivious turn virtuous; the survivors rape the dead. The plague creates reversals; the direction of change is more or less irrelevant. Pillaging or repudiation, purgation or defilement—the essential thing is that the accumulated reversals tap into violence as a cosmic process.

"The theater," Artaud writes, is "an immediate gratuitousness provoking acts without use or profit" (*TD*, 24). In this, it resembles the Great War itself: frenzied, gratuitous, and unconcerned with individual life or progress. As Eksteins demonstrates in his history of the war, "gratuitous-ness" reached a historical height in 1916 with the invention of trench war-fare and the terrible new principle of attrition: "For over two years the belligerents on the Western Front hammered at each other in battles . . . that cost millions of men their lives but moved the front line at most a mile or so in either direction" (*Rites of Spring*, 144). As the German poet Ivan Goll phrased it, "Whole regiments gambled away eternity for ten yards of wasteland."[22] Years of slaughter produced nothing beneficial to either side. The war climaxed not in victory but in a perversion of victory. Ernst Jünger describes the land that the French "won" in 1917: "As far back as the Siegfried Line, every village was reduced to rubble, every tree chopped down, . . . every well poisoned, every basement blown up or booby-trapped . . . everything burnable burned."[23] For both the winners and the losers, the war represented the triumph of ruin.

The plague, as a model for the theater, does not cure in any recogniz-able sense: it only unleashes. Each of its ideas is submerged in an impas-sioned and rhetorically exclusive invocation of "gratuitous" violent ac-tion. Crucially, however, the force that drives the violence is neither accidental nor unthinking. The plague, for Artaud, represents a great "Will" manifesting itself. It is an omnipotent "psychic entity," a focused force of destruction, "the direct instrument or materialization of an intel-ligent force in close contact with what we call fatality" (*TD*, 18). Although its purposes are hidden to most observers, the plague is decidedly not ar-bitrary in its course. In Artaud's interpretation, it purposefully attacks the most private, the most vital, and the most sensitive areas of the human body. It prefers to cause the most pain, the most humiliation possible dur-ing its course through the victim: "Around the anus, in the armpits, in the precious places where the active glands faithfully perform their functions, the bubos appear, wherever the organism discharges either its internal rottenness or, according to the case, its life" (*TD*, 20). Its "preferred ap-pearances" (*TD*, 20) make the sufferer as abject as possible; the plague de-constitutes him or her physically and metaphysically. Artaud emphasizes the plague's deliberate nature because he is calling for the theater, an or-chestrated event, to perform the same function: the theater must learn to wield such powers itself.

A sense of betrayal pervades Artaud's writing: what life we have, and what we have given life to, corrupts rather than ennobles. Our bodies, our social structures, our ways of thinking are diseased, cruel, dissolute, bru-tal. Humans suffer and must continue to suffer, the essay insists, because it is the nature of our existence. "The theater, like the plague, . . . releases conflicts, disengages powers, liberates possibilities, and if these possibilities and these powers are dark, it is the fault not of the plague nor of the theater, but of life" (*TD*, 31). The plague is not evil; life is.

"The Theater and the Plague" repeatedly hammers home the idea that the plague comes from within. It makes manifest what is latent, magnifying existing evil (*mal*) and bringing it to a point of paroxysm—it represents humanity's true nature being unleashed: "If the essential theater is like the plague, it is not because it is contagious, but because like the plague it is the revelation, the bringing forth, the exteriorization of a depth of latent cruelty" (*TD*, 30). It reveals what is already there: the corruption and foulness of man-made systems, "the lie, the slackness, baseness, and hypocrisy of our world" (*TD*, 31). The rottenness of the human body and civilization needs to be revealed by an equally dark power that works both internally and externally: the lies and evils of society will be stimulated to grow, to take over, to spill into the streets.[24] The plague punctures the "gigantic abscess" of mankind, "releasing"—not eliminating—our foulness, torturing us with our own worst impulses. Our own bodies dictate the plague's course: the buboes follow our natural concentrations of "rottenness" and "life." Thus, we not only deserve the plague; we *are* the plague: this is the vision of humanity "The Theater and the Plague" articulates.

"The Future of the World"

"The Theater and the Plague" is Artaud's expression of an aggressive, bloody, and apocalyptic worldview far removed from the private spiritual worlds of mystics, Symbolists, and Surrealists; from the political engagement of outraged anarchic dadaists or the leftist Brecht and Piscator; from any of the poetic, philosophical, or artistic schools between the wars defined by nuance, absurdity, irony, laughter, beauty, or tranquility. It has an affinity with the dark, conflict-oriented, pessimistic, totalizing worldview of the counter-Enlightenment and, particularly, of its manifestation in fascism. Artaud was not alone in embracing destruction as a response to World War I, of thinking that civilization needed a violent overhaul that art was called to provide. But his approach to it betrays fundamental differences from contemporaneous avant-gardists. Artaud lacks the playfulness, humor, and collective energy of the Surrealists, dadaists, and even the Italian Futurists and instead speaks in an aggressive, univocal, dictatorial voice. He does not share with the Surrealists (whom he joined for a while) an appreciation of the beauty of life or the possibilities of human creativity. The dadaists provide an interesting point of comparison in this context: their short-lived Cabaret Voltaire (1916) thrived on fragmentation, absurdity, black humor, and a kind of grinding anarchy in response to the horrors of war, manifesting the unique combination of intense engagement and ironic distance that was the gift of much of the avant-garde. Their Zurich cabaret served as a dark carnivalesque mirror of the language, art, and culture that made World War I possible.[25] But after the war, the dadaists backed away from that angry fragmentation and attempted, in several different ways, to envision a next step.[26] Their frenzy was brief, self-destructive, unsustainable. Unlike the disunited dadaists who followed individual creative paths after an initial embrace of destruction, Artaud remains focused on the moment of denunciation, lingering on the turmoil, seeking a way to create what he calls "organized anarchy" (*TD*, 51), to forge a method of directing and controlling the unleashed chaos.

The Italian Futurists present an even more revealing comparison to Artaud's work in the context of the avant-garde. They, too, manifested a desire for a comprehensive attack on what they considered a sick society and developed fragmentary and aggressive artistic strategies in this pursuit. But their project exhibits two crucial differences from Artaud's. For one, the Italian Futurists, although led by a strong-willed impresario, Filippo Tommaso Marinetti, operated as a diverse collection of artists. Marinetti encouraged contributions from a wide range of individuals, styles, and genres. Dozens of members over the years presented a multilayered artistic front, in stark contrast to Artaud's Theater of Cruelty, which is rigorously monologic. Just as importantly, the Futurists channeled their destructive urges in pursuit of a new culture on the ruins of the old. However deluded their vision of a healthy Italian state may have been, the Futurists certainly had a vivid ideal of sanguinity: they maintained a steady faith in the eventual institution of a strong Italian people and state.[27] Artaud agreed that society was sick, but, as the plague metaphor announces, his answer to its disease is the marshalling of an even greater force of destruction.

What might we gain from this destruction, this sustained paroxysm? "The Theater and the Plague" climaxes with a long passage in which Artaud articulates what possible "benefit" could arise from the violent unleashing outlined earlier. It coalesces the essay's apocalyptic, totalizing rhetoric of frenzy, eruption, dark forces, and suffering and puts it in the service of an orchestrated ecstasy. The essay builds to this remarkable call to arms:

> The theater like the plague is a crisis which is resolved by death or cure. And the plague is a superior disease because it is a total crisis after which nothing remains except death or an extreme purification. Similarly the theater is a disease because it is the supreme equilibrium which cannot be achieved without destruction. It invites the mind to share a delirium which exalts its energies; and we can see, to conclude, that from the human point of view, the action of theater, like that of plague, is beneficial, for, impelling men to see themselves as they are, it causes the mask to fall, reveals the lie, the slackness, baseness, and hypocrisy of our world; it shakes off the asphyxiating inertia of matter which invades even the clearest testimony of the senses; and in revealing to collectivities of men their dark power, their hidden force, it invites them to take, in the face of destiny, a superior and heroic attitude they would never have assumed without it. (TD, 31–32)

Critics have been too inclined to view this passage as an out-of-time poetic metaphor. But while Artaud is ostensibly writing about ancient history and aesthetics, what he asks for directly evokes the past war and invokes the next. *The Theater and Its Double* hymns the absolute, annihilating catastrophe of the plague in terms of intoxication with cosmic reversals, heroic attitudes, and death just as many extolled the apocalyptic nature of total war. Returning to the frontline diaries of Ernst Jünger—whose descriptions of his experience exude equal doses of horror and ecstasy and who unhesitatingly signed up to fight again for Germany in the next war—we find similar desires articulated in uncannily kindred language. In the barren landscapes, the smell of corpses and gunpowder invoked in him "an almost visionary excitement, that otherwise only the extreme nearness of death is able to produce" (*Storm of Steel*, 93). During the "Great Battle" (the Somme Offensive in 1918), when walls of flame overwhelmed the landscape, when the ground convulsed, when artillery generated an "absolute noise," man achieved the ultimate reversal: "Even the laws of nature appeared to have been suspended" (Jünger, *Storm of Steel*, 229). "What was at stake was the future of the world," Jünger writes. "I think everyone felt the individual in them dissolve" (231).

Artaud writes of theater in these terms: as if the individual must dissolve under the power of catastrophic higher forces, as if the future of the world depended on it. But what will follow the dissolution of the individual, the cosmic inversion, the divinely overwhelming experience to which the Theater of Cruelty aspires? "The Theater and the Plague" advocates throwing oneself into a "total crisis" in order to experience a "heroic" feeling and unleash one's darkest powers. Its purpose: "death or cure"; "death or an extreme purification." As we have noted, *The Theater and Its Double* does not articulate a positive vision to follow the total crisis the event brings about. But if we are tempted to spend time with the (nearly isolated) use of the word "purification" here and read it in a theatrical, Aristotelian sense, we need, even more, to note the word's more immediate resonances in the contemporaneous world.[28] The plague's withering corruption, its devastating course through society represents, for Artaud, a vital and violent "purification" that the theater must duplicate: "In the theater as in the plague there is something both victorious and vengeful: we are aware that the spontaneous conflagration which the plague lights wherever it passes is nothing else than an immense liquidation" (*TD*, 27). "Victorious and vengeful": Artaud wields the language of purity and assault in the same manner as frustrated-apocalypse authors such as Céline, whose ideas soon found a warm welcome among the fascists.[29] In line with Céline's sweepingly exalted aggressivity, Artaud's essay even allows for the possibility of total annihilation if the unspecified "cure" fails: "Perhaps the theater's poison, injected into the social body, disintegrates it . . . but at least it does so as a plague, as an avenging scourge, a redeeming epidemic" (*TD*, 31). Purification, then, or death, is the answer to society's ills, expressed cosmically and catastrophically. Artaud wrote in a preparatory note to the essay, "If peoples, as the Proverb says, have the government they deserve, epochs also have the scourge they deserve, and not just anyone can get the plague!"[30] Olivier Penot-Lacassagne succinctly asks the question the statement provokes: "But why, then, would the people of 1930 deserve a scourge like that?"[31]

Rather than a specific outcome, *The Theater and Its Double* focuses on the violence called forth to create a crisis, the moment of exaltation, the frenzy of eruption that liberates us from "asphyxiating matter." Unleashing our dark powers; bringing us to a state of absolute agitation; annihilating society, physical constraints, and the self, the theater leads us to a continual revelation of chaotic, dangerous energies.

But, out of any chaos, a new power must ultimately emerge to give that eruption of energies a direction or a definition. Thus, the passage just quoted becomes even more disturbingly historically relevant when we read next, in the final paragraph of the essay, who will carry out this cosmic war: "a nucleus of men capable of imposing this superior notion of the theater" (*TD*, 32). This passage is worth considering in its full context—it is the culmination of the essay, providing the only mention of leadership and direction of the event:

> And the question we must ask now is whether, in this slippery world which is committing suicide without noticing it, there can be found a nucleus of men capable of imposing this superior notion of the theater, men who will restore to all of us the natural and magic equivalent of the dogmas in which we no longer believe. (*TD*, 32)

This "nucleus of men" (the designation resonates more militaristically than theatrically) will use the Theater of Cruelty to orchestrate a delirium of destruction, of which it, alone, determines the stakes, rules, and means. Artaud demands that the spectators give themselves over to the authority of the event without providing specifics of where it will lead them because the "nucleus of men" will "impose" the direction.

These, then, are the terms in which Artaud imagines his event will be "beneficial": "equilibrium" through "purification," the shaking off of "asphyxiating" matter, the revelation to "collectivities of men their dark power," hidden forces revealed through cataclysmic events, "a superior and heroic attitude" emerging in response to adversity, and a caste of superior men arising to guide these unleashed powers. This catalog of terms and ideas we have heard before in the context of another contemporaneously emerging set of ecstatic visions and images thriving on destruction. This contemporaneous mindset shaped not only an aesthetic but also the politics of the era. Individuals, in this world, will be immersed in an impassioned, aggressive pursuit of lost, magical dogmas; and a small number of men will guide them to either worldwide purification or death. The theater event as elucidated in "The Theater and the Plague" parallels, to an unnerving degree, the structures, images, and worldview of fascism, developing at exactly the same moment in time.

In this light, Artaud's image of the plague for his ideal theater appears more historically grounded—and more complex—than a reading through the lens of its later reception alone would reveal. Where the essay invokes liberation, it also invokes vengeance; when it seems to advocate freedom, it also sets up a caste of men in control. Further, it speaks not of humanity's goodness, but of its evil; not with sympathy for suffering, but with exaltation. When it appears to be locating itself out of time, in the middle ages, it is actually reinforcing its position among others frustrated, angered, and strangely exalted by the recent war. Finally, when it speaks of empowerment, it is not of individual empowerment, but the empowerment of a mass of dangerous energies: it will "revea[l] to collectivities of men their dark power, their hidden force."

The Theater of Cruelty, appealing to "collectivities of men," embraces de-individuation, asking the spectator to dissolve into something bigger than the self, to think in generalities and essences, to return to a "fragile, fluctuating center" (*TD*, 13) beyond or before civilization. The spectators Artaud imagines are liberated from the "tyranny" of logic and encouraged to give themselves over entirely to emotion and impulse, under dictatorial guidance. Their capacities for thought are short-circuited by the spectacle around them. They are, in this sense, members of a crowd, as we will see when we unpack, in section II, the vision of the audience and mass society that *The Theater and Its Double* contains. To call forth an event such as this reveals the desire to push people past reason and into a state initiated—and orchestrated—by something literally outside of their own minds.

It seems, then, that the scorpion swarm we encountered at the beginning of this essay is an image not only of a mythical, insect-like, "avenging scourge" but also of the new humanity. The million poisonous creatures unleashed in a worldwide catastrophe represent both Artaud's imagined agents of destruction as well as a new population. "The Theater and the Plague" conjures a mass of people, transformed by catastrophe and compelled by intoxicating dark powers, to jettison—recklessly, exaltedly, heroically, brutally—reason, laws, and individual choice in order to meet a new destiny. Artaud conjures something, then, that was unfolding in the world right beside him.

CHAPTER 2 : Reactionary Modern

In the long history of alternatives to rationality, Artaud's writing occupies a critical place. A vein of irrationalist and vitalist thought that had flowed through late nineteenth- and early twentieth-century Europe found a ferocious and climactic articulation after World War I, a war that had, in the words of Robert O. Paxton, "discredited optimistic and progressive views of the future, and cast doubt upon liberal assumptions about natural human harmony" (*Anatomy of Fascism,* 28). At the same time, a reaction against Western civilization manifested itself in a seeking out of inspiration in cultures as far removed from the one at hand as possible. While a strong revulsion against the cultural, intellectual, and political systems of Western civilization might have seemed to contain the potential for positive and emancipatory creativity in some avant-garde circles, destructive and reactionary tendencies were always deeply interconnected with this potential.[1] Indeed, intellectual and political historians have argued that reactions against positivism, liberalism, materialism, and Western culture—drawing on and developing trends established in the nineteenth century—set the stage for the rise of fascism.[2] A particularly aggressive rejection of rationalism and Western civilization drew from the urge for further destruction after World War I, the yearning for a connection with something bigger than the self, and the craving for a cataclysmic event to wipe out humanity's mistakes. This fueled Céline's hunger for "planetary conflagration" and Artaud's return to the Black Plague. This chapter examines Artaud's list of rejections—science, reason, discourse, individual psychology—and counter-propositions—vitalism, non-Western and "primitive" cultures, and occultism—that he shares with a darker set of doubles among the flourishing interwar opposition to the legacy of the rationalist Enlightenment and contemporaneous Western civilization.

The Controversions of the Counter-Enlightenment

The intellectual historian Isaiah Berlin established the term "counter-Enlightenment" as a way to analyze the reactions against rationality and social progress whose history extends back to the eighteenth century. This current of European thought, he argues, came to "a point of violent hysteria" in the 1930s and '40s with fascism (*Magus*, 52).[3] The Enlightenment represented faith in reason and the belief that intellect could lead to the eventual happiness of humanity; it situated logical systems against what it deemed "guesswork, tradition, superstition, prejudice, dogma, fantasy and 'interested error'" (Berlin, *Magus*, 28). Enlightenment thinkers and their heirs had worked—through the emerging fields of psychology, sociology, economics, and political science—toward the discovery of general laws governing human behavior that would replace intuition and myth. But this business of attempting to manage existence through quantifiable knowledge seemed not just distasteful but profoundly immoral (or sacrilegious) to those who did not set great store by mankind's intellectual powers and did not believe in the possibility of scientific or historical progress.

Counter-Enlightenment thinkers counter empirical science with vitalism, rationalism with irrationalism, putting belief not in man's powers of reason but in forces either more sublime (God) or more primitive (organic energies). Such thinkers oppose individual psychology with an extreme de-individuation, an emphasis on annihilation of self and union with a primitive, universal, or national spirit. History is countered by Myth with a capital "M," as discrete historical events, political negotiations, and the like, fall into insignificance compared to another order— fate, destiny, divinity—that reveals the true nature of events. Materialism is countered by mystery so that magic, religion, or essential forces can reclaim their primary places in the experience of the world.

Rainer Friedrich describes an "irrationalist vitalism" animating *The Theater and Its Double* that manifests itself in "Artaud's vision of an ecstatic liberation from the burden of reason, subjectivity, and autonomy, and his longing for primitive forms of life."[4] He is right to see in the book's worldview and vision for a live event a set of concerns directly related to intellectual and cultural currents flourishing in the interwar era. Artaud's privileging of force, power, and energy over intellect, reason, and science signifies an alliance with those who, in Berlin's phrase, regarded the Enlightenment as "a personal enemy" ("Joseph de Maistre," 110) and who yearned for a return to a state of being that would supposedly be more authentic and dynamic.

The first term of this reaction whose parallels to *The Theater and Its Double* we examine is the opposition to science. The late nineteenth and early twentieth centuries witnessed a major backlash against the encroaching compartmentalization and regulation of the conceptualization of *le corps* and *l'esprit* advocated by the new field of "science" (which replaced the old "natural philosophy" in the mid-nineteenth century). The move to establish boundaries between what was "scientific" and what was intuition or guesswork, to specialize and professionalize fields of knowledge relating to the body, mind, and spirit, led conservative skeptics to fear that the unified nature of existence was being partitioned and degraded by a scientific approach that had lost sight of the whole. Intuitive linkages between mind and matter as well as spiritual awareness of unseen forces and their observable manifestations lost credence in favor of empirical observation and deductive thinking. "Discredited" theories such as animal magnetism (i.e., mesmerism), alchemy, trance states, occult practices, and spiritualism generated interest among those arguing against alienated and strictly rational science.

The appeal of such systems lay in their promise of a conceptual reunification of observable material phenomenon and instinctual forces. To lend themselves more credibility, they introduced their mystical ideas of unified matter into a framework of scientific "legitimacy" by highlighting their use of techniques such as "controlled" observations, experimentation, and data collecting. Like animal magnetism and alchemy, Artaud's writings insist on the physical nature of intangible forces, while refuting the legitimacy of the enterprise of material science. The ideas in *The Theater and Its Double* clearly reflect the reaction against the perceived limitations of science—while appropriating the scientific framework emptied of its positivist principles.

Artaud's attitude toward science exhibits itself most clearly in his process of writing "The Theater and the Plague." Artaud immersed himself in researching the plague from a clinical and historical standpoint, something evident in his detailed description of the symptoms and general course of the disease.[5] However, this research and study led him to reject scientific interpretation of the epidemic, preferring to consider the plague more of a "psychic entity" than a virus, a "direct instrument or materialization of an intelligent force" rather than a physical cause of contagion (*TD,* 18). Poetic license plays a role in this decision, to be sure, but, more importantly here, such a move manifests *The Theater and Its Double's* attitude toward scientific phenomenon, utterly consistent in all of Artaud's works: material objects don't control things—invisible, willful forces do. With this predilection to see reality in energies rather than matter, Artaud denies the causal role of the microbe: "Personally, I regard this microbe only as a smaller—infinitely smaller—material element which appears at some moment in the development of the virus, but which in no way accounts for the plague" (*TD,* 21). In place of a scientific analysis resting on material forms, he wants to sketch "the spiritual physiognomy of a disease whose laws cannot be precisely defined" (*TD,* 22).

The idea of the microbe had just entered into scientific thinking in the late nineteenth century, and while Artaud explicitly dismisses the medical importance of the microbe's physical body, he adopts a viewpoint that the microbe made possible: that the world is at all times awash in *le mal.*[6] As Hewitt writes in *Les maladies du siècle:* "The Pasteurian theory of bacteriology . . . furnishes a scientific model for a Manichean universe, dominated by the notions of infection and plague. The very concept of all-pervasive, invisible bacteria is the scientific equivalent of the theological notion of evil, 'le Mal,' again all-pervasive and invisible" (50). This use of the idea of the microbe, in its most rigorously unscientific application, demonstrates how Artaud's engagement with scientific research provided him with a moral and mystical framework for his theater and his condemnation of the state of the world. If the "physiognomy" of evil corresponds to the physiognomy of physical viruses, then the plague metaphor enables Artaud to connect his dark metaphysics to the sensory effect of the theater on the spectators' bodies.

Unscientific thinking employing the clinical discourse of contagion flourished in right-wing and anti-Semitic thought between the wars, as Hewitt demonstrates through his study of Céline—a doctor and writer whose single-minded focus on cleansing made him one of the most notorious French anticipators of fascism. The use of anti-scientific science around the plague microbe to fuel violent reactionary thought is also documented by Robert O. Paxton, who links both Pasteur's and Mendel's discoveries to that part of fascism that imagined "whole new categories of internal enemy" (*Anatomy of Fascism,* 36). Constance Spreen discusses the bacillus as racial metaphor in the context of French right-wing thinking contemporaneous with Artaud's essay, pointing out that "the metaphors of contagion and bacillus were central to the Maurrassian articulation of a politics of culture."[7] Spreen, however, does not pursue the implications of the fact that Artaud's essay employs the same metaphors during the same time period with equal (if not heavier) doses of disgust and anger.

The Theater and Its Double teems with disdain for rational thinking and discourse ("our excessive logical intellectualism" reduces "primordial" energies to "useless schemata" [*TD*, 50–51]), a dismissive attitude toward professional specialization, and a refusal of scientific conclusions ("empiricism" must be done away with [*TD*, 79]).[8] The book rejects structured and institutionalized systems of knowledge as impediments to a full existence and as obstacles to experiencing the "truth." The intuitive biases underlying the work have important ancestors in Richard Wagner and the early Nietzsche, whose works had an influence impossible to overestimate on Western European artists and thinkers of the late nineteenth and early twentieth centuries. In particular, their opposition to established intellectual systems (we will investigate their artistic ideas in the next section) bear directly on the discourse of the counter-Enlightenment and speak to its popularity in the interwar era.

Richard Wagner's *The Art Work of the Future* (1849) ranks intellect as highly as religion among the "great instinctive errors of the People."[9] Once thought becomes detached from life, its products are nothing but "the exploitations, the derivatives, . . . the splinterings and disfigurements" of genuine intuitions (80).[10] Wagner's précis of the dangers of thought and its corollary, science, establishes the terms of this discourse:

> Could conscious autocratic Thought completely govern Life, could it usurp the vital impulse and divert it to some other purpose than the great Necessity of absolute life-needs: then were Life itself dethroned, and swallowed up in Science. (74)

For Wagner, analytical thought, "the egoistic spirit of Athenian self-dissection" (136), rips the heart from drama, which should come from a profound and secret source. Intellectual systems created and practiced by rationalist philosophers only obscure life's true energy. Art, which should spring directly from vital powers, suffocates under regimented systems and codified knowledge.

The Nietzsche of *The Birth of Tragedy* (1872), in harmony with Wagner's ideas at the time, elaborates this line of thinking in terms of the Apollonian and Dionysian, the rational and the mysterious. The despised Socratic principle—"knowledge is virtue"—combines with the "audacious reasonableness" of Euripides to culminate in the life-killing Euripidean aesthetics, which declares: "to be beautiful everything must be intelligible."[11] Both Wagner's *Gesamtkunstwerk,* or total artwork, and Nietzsche's idea of the rebirth of tragedy through music rest on the belief that science represents an act of hubris by man, who wrongly declares himself superior to Nature.[12] Music, which is non-discursive and, of all the arts, appears to have the least relation to scientific and logical systems, holds the key to transcending mankind's stifling, arbitrary systems.

One of the most damaging attempts to apply rational scientific systems in the theater was, in Artaud's eyes, individual psychology, which "works relentlessly to reduce the unknown to the known, to the quotidian and the ordinary," and "is the cause of the theater's abasement and its fearful loss of energy" (*TD,* 77). Theater, when overtaken by psychological drama, by attempts to analyze and systematize the workings of a life, to try to explain the fluctuations of passions or spirit, loses its power to connect us with the metaphysical and universal. Naturalist and commercial theaters appeal to spectators' desires to define themselves as individuals, to understand their inner workings, and thus they create a "closed, egoistic, and personal art" (*TD,* 79). Their preoccupations "stink unbelievably of man, provisional, material man . . . *carrion man*" (*TD,* 42). To Artaud, the application of such a rational system disfigures the theater's spiritual possibilities, leading toward egoistic introspection and away from collective primal energies.

In rebuffing science, individual psychology, and all established intellectual systems, Artaud positions himself as a thinker in line with those who believe that truths are inherently opposed to thought and articulation. What Berlin writes about the counter-Enlightenment thinker Joseph de Maistre (in "Joseph de Maistre and the Origins of Fascism") could just as easily have been written about Artaud:

> To classify, abstract, generalise, reduce to uniformities, deduce, calculate and summarise in rigid, timeless formulas is to mistake appearances for reality, describe the surface and leave the depths untouched, break up the living whole by artificial analysis, and misunderstand the processes both of history and of the human soul by applying to them categories which at best can be useful only in dealing with chemistry or mathematics. (114)

The Theater of Cruelty posits a spiritual reality whose depths cannot be sounded by calculations, deductions, or formal analysis, a truth with a living soul resistant to the rigid formulations of bounded, linear human reason. It is truly knowable only through invocation.

Artaud's writing fundamentally rejects logical systems and militates against scientific argument. Although *The Theater and Its Double* may wield logical discourse at times, it is an ancillary weapon, far less potent than the poetic, emotional, or spiritual spell it may cast on its audience through image-laden rhetoric and exhortation. Artaud's language seeks to convert rather than convince us into a view. It commands, damns, elevates, invokes, repeats, capitalizes, underlines, threatens, directs, alludes, and asserts, and never reasons. The essays of *The Theater and Its Double* sprawl in associative, self-contradictory, unsystematic pages, often circling around a central image or conceit, but never arguing a point by means of logical deduction. Language, in this usage, is gesture, not discourse. Its urgency, not its sense, determines its efficaciousness.

Artaud's "readings" of artworks in *The Theater and Its Double* demonstrate well the overall stylistic emphases of the book: assertion over demonstration, revelation over interpretation. They proceed by a kind of emotional and metaphysical impressionism that projects a vision of a dark, violent, and discarnate ruling life force onto whatever it encounters. It is fascinating to observe Artaud's distinctive and wholly consistent manner of engagement, so we will now follow one of his readings carefully. When describing the painting *Lot and His Daughters*, in "Metaphysics and the *Mise en Scène*" (*TD*, chap. 2), Artaud approaches the artwork as a manifestation of the kind of "mystic deductions" (*TD*, 33) one could glean from the Bible in the Middle Ages. His description of the image focuses on its mysterious nature, taking no notice of the explicit content (God destroying the city of Sodom; Lot's daughters' getting their father drunk in order to procreate).[13] The reading intentionally focuses on the work from "a distance" (repeated twice, 33, 34), as if one might comprehend it better unfocused. Without discerning the subject of the painting, Artaud writes, "you sense something tremendous happening" (33). The ideas of the picture are not clear, but its "grandeur" is (36). As for the actual painting, the technique is of no importance: "It matters little how this effect is obtained, it is real; it is enough to see the canvas to be convinced of it" (35). The painter, he states, possessed the secret of "affect[ing] the brain directly, like a physical agent" (35). Shunning the explicit content, history, method, and meaning of the work, Artaud arrives at his conclusion: he sees "intelligence and malice" (35) as the underlying force of the painting, a dangerous life energy that is, for him, both the substance of the painting and the desired effect of the work on its viewer. Artaud reads *through* the artwork to a truth he already knows is there. Consequently, he does not need to convince, but only to impress the meaning of the work upon the reader.

The same method is at work in Artaud's readings or reviews of plays and novels, any performance or artwork: he uses, for example, the Balinese theater and the Marx Brothers (both subjects of essays in *The Theater and Its Double*) as catalysts for a revelation of a pre-existing worldview. This view is articulated through Artaud not so much reading the artwork, but rather reading his fixation with catastrophe, evil, and universal correspondences onto external objects.

The major rhetorical feature of *The Theater and Its Double* is its gesturing toward an ineffable truth that can only be grasped by seeing past what you (the reader) can perceive on your own. There are no "facts" in this world, no field of objects to be interpreted by powers of deduction. We can only approach truth by hints and gestures by which the author steers us. This is irrationalism in its pure state. Rationalists believe that empirical observation combined with reasoned analysis can lead to correct interpretation. Further, this working toward meaning is a co-operative venture: discourse and engagement with external, material objects form an essential part of the search for truth. Irrationalists, on the other hand, assert that attempts to observe and logically deduce are fruitless and distracting, because everything has been decided already in an unknowable other sphere. The conclusion has been predetermined by powers beyond our own, and it is incomprehensible to us. It is left for us to be guided by one with higher insight to accept this truth.

What I have just described—a search for meaning operating outside codified human systems, pursued via an irrational, mystical, associative rhetoric by one who perceives himself as "not of this world"—can clearly be seen as one of the cultural legacies of Romanticism. It would perhaps not be worth dwelling on if we were simply pursuing, with Artaud, another inheritor of the Romantic belief in the neo-religious role of the artist and if we relegated *The Theater and Its Double* to an aesthetic realm removed from a context of intellectual history. But the work's links to the theatrical theories of Wagner and Nietzsche, and the discourse's striking parallels to a contemporaneously thriving current of irrationalism, make such a detailed consideration meaningful if we want to seriously examine Artaud's ideals for a live performance event in their context. In either case, we would have to take note of the striking way irrationalism plays out in *The Theater and Its Double* and how it signals a distinct shift in emphasis from the Romantics. As we saw in our previous discussion of the *nouveau mal du siècle*, Artaud's work lacks both the inner conflict and the melancholy serenity that normally operate in tandem with the darkness and destructive urges of the earlier Romantic movement. Further, the totalizing thinking, aggressivity, belief in the foulness of human nature, unsettling dynamics of power, and hatred of individuality (even individual creativity) manifest in *The Theater and Its Double* are all unsettlingly of a piece less with the early Romantic poets and more with the ominous rising culture of angry, irrational, mass politics in the interwar era.

Anywhere Out of This World

Artaud's antipathy to Enlightenment thinking stems in part from his craving for mystery. His impatience with rationalist systems of thought impels him to reach toward foreign beliefs and ideas that he only understands on the level of impulse. Christopher Innes argues that primitivism underlies the theatrical avant-garde project, that the exploration of dream states, myth, magic, and ritual forms a consistent thread throughout the avant-garde desire to "return to man's 'roots,' whether in the psyche or prehistory" (*Avant-Garde Theatre*, 3).[14] Here, we will see how *The Theater and Its Double*'s emphasis on a crisis beyond reason anchors itself in a distinctly reactionary conception of myth and non-Western cultures, one whose elevation of mystery and the mystical operates in violent opposition to the material and historical.

Artaud's fascination with "primitive," occult, and Eastern cultures is evident everywhere in his writing. In *The Theater and Its Double,* he devotes two chapters to Balinese theater; presents an original scenario dramatizing the conquest of (Aztec) Mexico; creates extended theatrical metaphors of "the Alchemical Theater" and "metaphysics and the *mise en scène*"; and proposes a breathing system based on the Kabbalah, Hindu *gunas*, and Chinese acupuncture. Amid these chapters we also find references to Mexican *manas*, Quetzalcoatl's serpent body, the ancient Egyptian concept of Ka, Hindu and Iranian cosmogonies, Chinese puppet theater, Buddhist philosophy, Orphic and Eleusinian mysteries, the Great Arcanum, and much more.[15] This wide-ranging embrace signifies Artaud's consummate rejection of what Western civilization was calling progress (rationalism, scientific materialism, an increasing secularism, etc.) and his glorification of cultures or ways of thinking whose only common trait is that they suggest a "way out."

Studies of Artaud's attraction to these other cultures abound.[16] Indeed, his exaltation of the Tarahumara Indians, the Balinese theater, and the resistance to the conquest of Mexico has endeared him to artists and scholars who find in these preoccupations support for the belief that he had a liberal attitude to culture, that he sympathized with the "other." In fact, however, works like "On the Balinese Theater" and "Voyage to the Land of the Tarahumara" are classic examples of orientalism, fetishizing the other precisely because Artaud does not—and does not attempt to—understand them.[17] The glory of not knowing how to decode the Balinese dancers' gestures (which he saw at a Colonial Exposition in Marseille), the determination to preserve the mystery of ancient Mexican rituals—these moves demonstrate that Artaud sought something beyond embodiment, beyond time and place. He was in search of Myth—with a capital "M"—and the indecipherability of these gestures, traditions, and codes could, he believed, bring him closer to it.

The Theater and Its Double draws on generalized conceptions of the mythic in its quest for essences. For Artaud, "Myths" reach toward the universal. They suggest a meaning beyond particulars: the stories in which they find themselves transmitted are merely functional. Myths exist as a truth that is more a force than a fact, an impulse rather than an object, a becoming. Artaud is not particular about the provenance of the stories he uses, as long as they have a pre-modern or non-Western point of origin. The wide variety of myths that *The Theater and Its Double* embraces demonstrates an attachment to the *idea* rather than the *form* of myth and a complete disinterest in their historical or cultural contexts. As far from a cultural anthropologist as Jung is from Levi-Strauss, Artaud embraces myths for what they appear to reveal about humanity's essence, for what he believes are the eternal truths manifest in them.

In this way of thinking, myth is bastardized once it is historicized. It is stripped of its timeless truth and separated from its essential life force. The materialization of its stories and characters reduces its significance to unpoetic provisionality. Saul Friedländer identifies this approach to myth as one of the cornerstones of an anti-rationalist aesthetic: "Myth is a footprint, an echo of lost worlds, haunting an imagination invaded by excessive rationality and thus becoming the crystallization point for thrusts of the archaic and of the irrational" (*Reflections of Nazism*, 49).[18] The idea of "excessive rationality" murdering myth leads us again to ideas latent in

Wagner's and Nietzsche's early ideas on the theater. Wagner calls for an art based not on the individual or the particular, but on myths that convey the universal structures of human desire. Similarly, Nietzsche accuses overly rational society of murdering myth by systematizing, particulariz- ing, and historicizing it: "He who recalls the immediate consequences of this restlessly progressing spirit of science will realize at once that *myth was annihilated by it*" (106).[19]

Artaud's approach to the mythic enlarges the bias against scientific knowledge, as if science, by working through nuance and phenomenon, worked against the true unknowability of things, against the mysterious and universal, and, ultimately, as we will see, against self-immolation. Ar- taud is the quintessential essentialist: in his writings, energies and powers matter more than history, characters, or specificity. *The Theater and Its Dou- ble,* in its search for a precedent for an "essential theater," turns to the Ba- linese theater, to ancient Mexican rituals, to the Mysteries of Eleusis. But these forms are effective only insofar as Artaud neglects (or rejects) their contingencies of time and place and their differences. His readings of them highlight the fact that his ideal "archetypal, primitive theater" works beyond space and time. The Theater of Cruelty will be a meta- physical "materialization or . . . exteriorization of a kind of essential drama which would contain . . . the essential principles of all drama" (*TD,* 50).[20]

Following this premise, the Theater of Cruelty does not want to rep- resent important historical moments or figures but to "extract the forces which struggle within" "famous personages, atrocious crimes, superhu- man devotions" (*TD,* 85). In the scenario for "The Conquest of Mexico" included in *The Theater and Its Double,* Artaud employs the exotic figures of Montezuma and Cortez as "forces" enacting their roles not in a histor- ical event, but in a predetermined cosmic battle:

> ["The Conquest of Mexico"] will stage events, not men. Men will come in their turn with their psychology and their passions, but they will be taken as the emanation of certain forces and understood in the light of the events and historical fatality in which they have played their role. (126)

Artaud uses myth to reach essences. Contingencies obscure the great truths, so the Theater of Cruelty aims to reveal these hidden truths by wiping out the details of history.

The Theater and Its Double repeatedly expounds a belief in hidden forces and energies. It is "vitalist" in the broad sense that it promotes an idea of life that cannot be traced to or located in chemical or physical origins. Artaud's conception of vital forces is not exactly that, however, of Henri Bergson, who described *élan vital* as an intuited but not scientifically verifiable force continuously shaping all life—a force deeply connected to individual will and mind. Artaud's writings put forth a more generalized idea of vital forces: his attitude is far less intellectual, less focused on the individual, and, as we saw with "The Theater and the Plague," more geared toward destruction than development.[21] Significantly, the nearest *The Theater and Its Double* comes to defining its eponymous "double" is in terms of this vitalism. The theater, writes Artaud, is the double of an "archetypal and dangerous reality," a "reality [that] is not human but inhuman" (*TD*, 48). The double is the shadowy dark force that drives everything. For Artaud, who always searches for the hidden reality, the double of theater is the essence of life itself. It is "dangerous," "evil" (*TD*, 51, 30, 103), and utterly beyond reason.

The theater and all its cataclysmic doubles, like the plague, reveal these vital forces, which make themselves felt in movement rather than in any particular manifestation. *The Theater and Its Double*—calling for paroxysm, exaltation, catastrophe—focuses on intensity of experience rather than form. "Everything that acts is a cruelty. It is upon this idea of extreme action, pushed beyond all limits, that theater must be rebuilt" (85). The content of the action is irrelevant; its sensational power is everything. Artaud wants to push past inconsequential particulars and achieve an eruption for the sheer visceral experience of it, and the theater is the instrument to bring us there: "I am searching for every technical and practical means of bringing the theater close to the high, perhaps excessive, at any rate vital and violent idea that I conceive of it for myself" (114). "Vital and violent": like a Dionysiac revel, the Theater of Cruelty strives for the annihilating force of life itself.

Nietzsche argues in *The Birth of Tragedy* that the genius of ancient drama arose from the combination of Apollonian and Dionysian elements, of order and chaos, reason and emotion. *The Birth of Tragedy* stresses the under-recognized role of the Dionysian, vividly depicting a fantasy of a pure experience of Dionysiac art: "We are really for a brief moment primordial being itself, feeling its raging desire for existence and joy in existence; the struggle, the pain, the destruction of phenomena, now appear necessary to us" (104). This idea of Dionysiac art, which occurs "not in phenomena, but behind them" (104), provided a focus for a vitalist interwar reception of Nietzsche's work that furthered an idea of life forces and energies that needed release from rationality and man-made restrictions in order to flourish, a release that could best be attained through the orchestration of sensorial experiences collectively imposed on a group of people.

Nietzsche at the time was writing in close proximity to Wagner, who had established theatrical terms for the rejuvenation of what Nietzsche would call the Dionysian element through his music dramas. A *Gesamtkunstwerk,* or total artwork, would rescue the arts from their overly formalized and compartmentalized existence. The immaterial, impotent, and lonely figures of poetry, music, and dance that populate *The Art-Work of the Future* suffer separation from their life forces, the *"inner natural necessity"* of each supplanted by "an *outer* artificial counterfeit."[22] Each form has been severed from its roots, and yet the husks continue to be circulated by a duped and ungrounded people. Wagner worked to combat the stultification of art by reconnecting its forms to the "plain and innate force of Life" (79).

Nietzsche's and Wagner's works obviously reach beyond the uses made of them by later political systems—both were eventually adopted, adapted, and championed by National Socialism—but *The Theater and Its Double* follows the same vitalist, myth-oriented, de-individuated, anti-scientific, anti-materialist lines of interpretation that were generating interest in interwar reactionary circles.[23] Artaud's idea of cruelty demonstrates what would happen if the Dionysian were freed of any dialectical balance with the Apollonian and left to rot, spread, and explode without constraints. Artaud exaggerates Wagner's objection to the inflexibility of existing artistic forms to the point that, in *The Theater and Its Double,* forms themselves are deemed inadequate for the task of conveying the emotional vitality art actually represents. The swell of feeling of communion, of loss of self, of heroic and tragic sentiments that Wagner's music dramas sought to evoke becomes, with Artaud, a goal to be reached not through reunited and rejuvenated art forms but through a new concept of theater that aspires to a completely formless state. "Beneath the poetry of the texts, there is the actual poetry, without form and without text" (*TD*, 78). *The Theater and Its Double* responds to the inadequacy of existing forms not by improving them but by searching for a pure poetry that has no form at all.

What Nietzsche sought through the "spirit of music" and Wagner through the combination of music, drama, and dance in the *Gesamtkunst-werk,* Artaud seeks through a sensorial assault of forces and "spirit" that takes as little material form as possible, a way to establish a direct connection to natural vitalism. A distinction between reality (forces) and reproduction (forms) underlies *The Theater and Its Double:* for Artaud, the sublime can be experienced but not represented, felt but not contained; we have confused the sublime with "one or another of its formal manifestations" (*TD,* 74). Art forms have been "castrate[d]" by a focus on their materiality, as if "to sever their ties with all the mystic attitudes they might acquire in confrontation with the absolute" (69). The theater must return us to "that fragile, fluctuating center which forms never reach" (13).

The ideal theatrical experience in Artaud's writing is an event and not a thing: "The theater, far from copying life, puts itself whenever possible in communication with pure forces" (*TD,* 82). There is no mimesis, no representation, no "as if": the event is not representing, it *is.* The event takes place in order to fundamentally affect the participants; it is not an object, but an influence. For Artaud, the theater "presents itself first of all as an exceptional power of redirection" (83): it is an action, a movement of forces.

Artaud reaches toward a vitalist unified theory, a "total life" supported by an intuitive understanding of the dark forces of the universe.[24] The emphasis on a unified life evident throughout *The Theater and Its Double* finds a double in an exemplary instance of modern reactionary thought: Madame Blavatsky's Theosophical Society. The Theosophist movement presents an illuminating context for Artaud's work. It found a warm reception as a secular-religious way of thinking in late nineteenth- and early twentieth-century Western Europe among prewar French artists, as well as early National Socialists in Germany. Madame Blavatsky mined "esoteric sources to discredit present-day beliefs," resulting in her work *Isis Unveiled* (1877), a mystical polemic against "the rationalist and materialistic culture of modern Western civilization."[25] Nicholas Goodrick-Clarke demonstrates that Madame Blavatsky's work owed its enthusiastic reception to its "appealing mixture of ancient religious ideas and new concepts borrowed from the Darwinian theory of evolution and modern science," creating a much-needed "syncretic faith" after the wave of European positivism had destroyed traditional spiritual beliefs (*Occult Roots of Nazism,* 22). Theosophy's central beliefs included

an electro-spiritual force at work in the universe and an essential unity between the micro- and macrocosm evident in correspondences between
observable matter and more difficult to define forces.

Theosophy, like most occult and mystical systems, tended to be eclec-
tic, drawing from a variety of unconnected sources. In this, Artaud takes
a page from Blavatsky's book; specifically, from the introductory pages of
her most famous book, *The Secret Doctrine* (1888), in which she articulates
the vitalist premise underlying Theosophy's eclecticism:

> But it is perhaps desirable to state unequivocally that the teachings,
> however fragmentary and incomplete, contained in these volumes,
> belong neither to the Hindu, the Zoroastrian, the Chaldean, nor the
> Egyptian religion, neither to Buddhism, Islâm, Judaism nor Chris-
> tianity exclusively. The Secret Doctrine is the essence of all these.
> Sprung from it in their origins, the various religious schemes are
> now made to merge back into their original element, out of which
> every mystery and dogma has grown, developed, and become mate-
> rialised.[26]

The Theater and Its Double reflects a similarly widely read but not entirely
well-read grounding. It tends to equate anything non-Western, "primitive," and occult, as they all seem to point toward lost truths. In 1936,
speaking of Chinese medicine, Paracelsus, the Mayas and Aztecs, Moslem
and Brahman esoterisms, the Judaic Zohar, the Mesoamerican *Popul Vuh*,
and more, Artaud wrote, as Madame Blavatsky had:

> Who does not see that all these esoterisms are the same, and mean
> spiritually the same thing? They express a single idea—geometrical,
> mathematical, organic, harmonious, occult—an idea which recon-
> ciles man with nature and with life. The signs of these esoterisms are
> identical. (*SW*, 364)

For Artaud, *gunas, mayas,* and *chakras* are essentially interchangeable. The
Theater of Cruelty represents a kind of scavenger ideology in which eclec-
tic beliefs are held together by a perceived underlying impulse completely disassociated from their specific points of origin or intention.

It is interesting to note that, among this spiritual eclecticism, one
source of spirituality, mysteries, initiated rites, and arcane symbology is
totally missing from *The Theater and Its Double:* that of Catholicism. France
has a native tradition of mystics and artists fascinated with the rituals and

imagery of Catholicism.[27] Fin de siècle Symbolists, decadents, and esoter-
ically minded avant-gardists embraced Catholicism as a fount of aesthetic
if not spiritual sustenance. J. K. Huysmans's protagonist Des Esseintes in
À rebours (1884) venerated Catholic works on equal footing with those
from Eastern and atheistic sources, and Alfred Jarry (1873–1907) drew no
line between the poetic and intellectual value of scientific, occult, ancient,
modern, or secular creations from those of Catholicism—in fact, his work
Caesar-Antichrist synthesizes Catholic images and rites with those of a
dozen other religious, scientific, and philosophical systems.[28] Yet while
The Theater and Its Double refers to medieval and Renaissance painters
who depicted biblical stories, Catholicism itself is absent from the book.
In fact, Artaud explicitly denounced Catholicism as working against the
unification he praises other religious and occult systems for promoting.[29]

On one hand, this can be seen as a clear temperamental preference.
Apocalyptic stories from the Old Testament do appear in *The Theater and
Its Double* (usually marked as "Judaic" or "occult"), but the New Testament—with the mildness of Jesus's preaching and its espoused virtues of
humility, forgiveness, and love—is patently irrelevant.[30] Artaud gravitates toward the violence of Old Testament stories, preferring to anchor
ideas about spirituality in catastrophe and an unforgiving higher order.
On the other hand, the omission is one more manifestation of the any-
where-but-here position of *The Theater and Its Double:* the rites of Catholicism are too familiar to excite interest. The further away a tradition is, the
more intimately it is invoked in *The Theater and Its Double;* what is the least
known promises to hold the greatest truth.

Irrational Affinities

Artaud is an absolutist, but the challenge with his work is to determine
what, exactly, he is an absolutist *about.* He is technically neither religious
nor nationalist, in the sense that he does not advocate adherence to any
single organized religion or state. But there is a religious, totalizing aspect
to Artaud's thought, and, while some of the mystical terrain covered earlier was shared by a broad range of thinkers in the early twentieth century, our analysis of *The Theater and Its Double* leads us to see that the
terms in which Artaud expresses it are even more consonant with the discourse of the reactionary Right between the wars than with the liberal
Left.

Artaud's hostility toward science, rationalism, materialism, and liberal individualism, his rejection of systems of knowledge that, in his view, attempted to reduce experience by limiting it to discrete, positive quantities, is part of an established cultural and intellectual trend that fed into reactionary politics in the interwar era. This trend has been articulated by historians and thinkers such as Isaiah Berlin, George L. Mosse, Zeev Sternhell, Roger Griffin, and Robert O. Paxton, who, by following the development of these tendencies, demonstrate that such challenges to the modern status quo, while potentially exhilarating, are not necessarily liberating. Berlin argues that the stances taken by the early irrationalists, including "anti-intellectualism" and "hatred of natural science and criticism," had a "powerful" and "fatal" "influence in the two centuries that followed" (*Magus*, 52). The historian and theoretician of fascism Roger Griffin writes, "In the inter-war period at least, fascism specifically repudiates the rationalist and political tradition of the Enlightenment."[31] He argues that fascism's rejection of Enlightenment values plays out in its discouragement of belief in individual responsibility and material progress. Instead, it "encourages the individual to subsume his or her personality unquestioningly *but willingly* within the greater whole" ("Staging the Nation's Rebirth," 15) and abolishes the idea of legal (rational) concepts of authority to clear the way for more charismatic ones.[32] We find in Artaud's writing patterns of denunciations corresponding to what Zeev Sternhell calls the tendency to aggressively espouse the "primacy of the spiritual" (rather than material facts and events), patterns that feature prominently in the early stages of the development of fascism.[33]

Since, as Paxton writes, "it seemed to many Europeans that their civilization itself, with its promise of peace and progress, had failed" (*Anatomy of Fascism*, 29) after the war, the space was open to a host of denunciations of that evidently failed civilization. This field of negativity, Paxton argues, led some intellectuals and cultural thinkers to "create a space for fascist movements by weakening the elite's attachment to Enlightenment values" (18). They themselves did not necessarily create actual political programs; however, "intellectuals then made it possible to imagine fascism" (18). While fully developed fascism did not necessarily have to follow from this (what Paxton calls the first stage of five stages of fascism), it is the stage in which artists and intellectuals did articulate its ideological underpinnings.[34] The very violence of marshaling negative forces in the early stages of fascism paved the way for its ascension. Alice Yaeger Kaplan refers to this as the "gathering" stage of fascism, the stage that "appealed most to artists and intellectuals" and that was actually dropped once the fascist state came to power (*Reproductions of Banality*, 53–54).[35] Sternhell looks toward the contribution of intellectuals in the early stages of fascism in terms of both the arguments they make against shared targets and the vaguely utopian dreams they just begin to articulate. "Neither right nor left": the desire for a "third way" proved compelling across traditional political affiliations.[36]

Many artists and intellectuals were caught up in what Paxton describes as the "mobilizing passions" of fascism. We have found many of these passions articulated by Artaud, including, as discussed in this section, what Paxton outlines as "a sense of overwhelming crisis beyond the reach of any traditional solutions," the strong move toward de-individuation, and the desire for immersion and domination in the face of otherwise unthinkable chaos.[37] Critics such as Susan Sontag, Saul Friedländer, and Mark Antliff have analyzed key features of a fascist aesthetic as evidenced in film, literature, and the arts, drawing from such mobilizing passions.[38]

So while irrationalism and vitalism had enormously important points of connection with spiritual and artistic trends in fin de siècle France, they took on a particular character of not just aesthetic but political urgency in the interwar era among proto-fascist artists and intellectuals. A furious rather than contemplative attitude, a rancor toward Western civilization rather than a liberal curiosity about "other" cultures, and a fundamental basis in violence rather than a search for beauty or peace underlay this interwar irrationalist resurgence. In his study of German fascism, George L. Mosse distinguishes between left-wing intellectuals' and reactionaries' characterization of this development, arguing that "unlike the fascists," the left-wing intellectuals "sought to transcend" the mutually despised materialist and capitalist systems "by emphasis on the triumphant goodness of man."[39] No such belief grounds the thinking of interwar irrationalists or of Artaud, who emphasized the persistent evil of the world and superior, mysterious energies. The reactionaries wanted to annihilate the legacy of the Enlightenment, humanity's faith in its own powers, and European traditions in order to allow the dark forces of true life to come forth.

While the Surrealists of the 1920s and '30s were reading much of the same esoteric, occult, and orientalist materials as Artaud was, they read this material with a sense of beauty, humor, discovery, and irony. Artaud's readings, in contrast, are absolutist and deadly earnest. And while the

Surrealists, as noted in the introduction, joined the French Communist Party, hoping to advance the prosperity of all people through the advancement of progressive social systems, Artaud, like their proto-fascist contemporaries, manifested a disgust with all political parties, feeling that the necessary revolution was beyond the reach of politics itself.[40]

The Theater and Its Double's commonalities with the maelstrom of ideas that fueled the early stages of fascism are substantial. But we could never think of Artaud as a citizen in a fully developed fascist system: neither nationalist nor explicitly racist impulses make any appearance in his work.[41] The first stage—the creation of the movement, the mobilizing passions, and its self-styled position against existing political systems—is what concerns us here.

Susan Sontag's famous description of a fascist "aesthetic" focused on that of Leni Riefenstahl and Albert Speer: austere beauty captured in the clean choreography of unified masses, crisp perfection, rigid order, masses made minimalist.[42] But there's another strain of aesthetics in fascism, which is less classical and more chaotic. It focuses on decadence, corruption, death, destruction (such as the kind of look we find popularized in *Cabaret* or epitomized in Hans-Jürgen Syberberg's film *Hitler*). Saul Friedländer describes this aesthetic in terms of "the yearning for destruction and death" (*Reflections of Nazism*, 75) and "the attraction to nothingness" (76) that was very much alive in the interwar era in groups of people whipped into a frenzy, driven by a desire for apocalypse, submission, and exaltation.

Curiously, in many ways, the aesthetic of *The Theater and Its Double* echoes this second strain of a German fascist aesthetic rather than any French one. This is, at any rate, what the French Right thought. The German Right flourished in a chaos, irrationality, and apocalyptic violence far removed from the rational, monarchist, often elitist tenor of the French Right. The highly conservative French Right was, at the time, working defensively against a large and vocal Left that was leaning toward international Communism. The Right's cultural journals, such as *Je suis partout* and *L'action française*, worked to fortify their nationalistic and traditional concerns against the strong presence of the Left.[43] The writers and art critics of *L'action française* advocated a classical aesthetic in explicit opposition to the corrupting influence of the nineteenth century and Romanticism more generally.[44] They, in fact, noted Artaud's apparent "German" decadence with some vitriol in their reviews of both his Theater of Cruelty manifesto (published in *La nouvelle revue française* in 1932) and his production of *The Cenci* (1935). As regards the former, André Villeneuve mocked Artaud's prose style, seeing it as an offense against the elegance and clarity of good French language.[45] As regards the latter, Robert Brasillach condemned *The Cenci* for confusing "power and bellowing," for being an exercise in bad taste that did not in any way transcend itself.[46]

The French Right saw in the ideas, aesthetic, and rhetoric of the Theater of Cruelty a kind of dark German Expressionism, a chaos of violent images and impulses, a "screaming Romanticism" (Dubech, "Chronique des théâtres") far better suited to the barbarians to the east than to France.[47] Lucien Dubech goes so far as to use the occasion of *The Cenci* production as a point of comparison between French and German national cultures and politics: "The romanticism unleashed by defeat amidst the anarchy natural to Germany was naturally the most vivid image one could give to the universal moral disorder."[48]

In addition, the way Artaud embraced occultism has more in common with the German 1930s and '40s than with French esoterism. What flourished in the 1880s in France took on a darker tone in interwar Germany. Mosse describes the peculiar national character of mysticism and occultism in Germany: "This German reaction to positivism became intimately bound up with a belief in nature's cosmic life force, a dark force whose mysteries could be understood, not through science but through the occult" (*Masses and Man*, 198). This articulates the foundation for Artaud's version of mysticism, precisely describing, notably, Artaud's interpretation of the plague.

The Theater and Its Double, as a whole, reveals an aggressive antipathy to society and civilization in its modern Western form. It extols the unknowable, primitive, imagined, or exaggerated customs of other cultures to such an extent that the quest for "liberation" or "freedom" takes on the tone of attack.[49] Artaud's rhetorical absolutism and extremism compel him to condemn as vigorously as he would praise—to elevate the Balinese theater to the heights he wishes, for example, he goes this far in his renunciation of the West, writing that the superiority of Oriental theater

> condemns us, and along with us the state of things in which we live and which is to be destroyed, destroyed with diligence and malice on every level and at every point where it prevents the free exercise of thought. (*TD*, 47)

Total freedom achieved through constant attack; malice in the pursuit of liberty: this sounds more like terror than liberty. Artaud's extreme ideal of purity leads him to a disgust with human activity so virulent and comprehensive it can only be expressed in terms of systematic, exhaustive annihilation.

Artaud sees decay on such a fundamental level that his writings do not distinguish between its artistic, moral, social, cultural, or material manifestations. Artaud's writings never address the actual wars of his lifetime, but they constantly invoke the idea of war. As Naomi Greene points out, Artaud's writing shares the stage with that of the fascists Marinetti and Drieu La Rochelle in its exaltation of violence and especially war: "War is bathed in an aesthetic glow, seen as apotheosis and apocalypse, as the triumph of warrior virtue and the eruption of 'latent cruelty'" (*Antonin Artaud*, 110).

Considering *The Theater and Its Double* in its historical context of the mid-1930s brings to mind Benjamin's formulation at the close of "The Work of Art in the Age of Mechanical Reproduction" (1936): "[Mankind's] self-alienation has reached such a degree that it can experience its own destruction as an aesthetic pleasure of the first order" (242). This was no metaphor. Jünger's ecstatic diaries from the Great War bring this home: as he ran through a deadly bottleneck in his first trip to the front and the "heavy sweetish" smell of scores of rotting bodies reached him, Jünger records, he experienced an "exalted, almost demoniacal lightness" (*Storm of Steel*, 93), a feeling that suffuses his entire chronicle. This apocalyptic, crazy elation, this destructive frenzy, flourished in the early stages of fascism and continued to mount until the beginning of World War II. As Paxton has read this moment: "Fascism's deliberate replacement of reasoned debate with immediate sensual experience transformed politics . . . into aesthetics. And the ultimate fascist aesthetic experience, Benjamin warned in 1936, was war" (*Anatomy of Fascism*, 17). Hannah Arendt, writing about "the German question" after World War II, makes a piercing observation:

> During the last war [World War I] this catastrophe [World War II] became visible in the form of the most violent destructiveness ever experienced by the European nations. From then on nihilism changed its meaning. It was no longer a more or less harmless ideology, one of the many competing ideologies of the nineteenth century; it no longer remained in the quiet realm of mere negation or mere skepticism or mere foreboding despair. Instead it began basing itself on the intoxication of destruction as an actual experience, dreaming the stupid dream of producing the void.[50]

Considering these contexts, we have to at least note that *The Theater and Its Double*'s constant repetition of the idea that "our present social state is iniquitous and should be destroyed" (42) has real resonance. The book's invocation of destruction and its ecstatic revelry in the contemplation of wide-scale devastation between two world wars are in direct dialogue with a violent and reactionary trend flourishing in the world all around it. Because the Theater of Cruelty aspires to reach far beyond the limits of theatrical and cultural forms, the "iniquitous" human society that needs to "be destroyed" is never marked as disinterested metaphor. Indeed, *The Theater and Its Double* issues explicit injunctions against taking its ideas metaphorically. The "Theater and Cruelty" essay closes, dramatically, with a passage not noted often enough, asking "whether a little real blood will be needed, right away, in order to manifest this cruelty" (88).

This was being written in 1933, shortly before its author traveled to Mexico to deliver tirades against rational Western civilization.[51] There are different ways to abjure Western civilization, and there were good reasons for wanting to do so after an event such as World War I. But if this repudiation is advocated in the context of eradicating that civilization—by the plague, apocalypse, blood, by embracing "a fundamental cruelty, which leads things to their ineluctable end at whatever cost" (*TD*, 103)—and presents no vision for the aftermath other than total submission to undefinable higher orders, we find ourselves in the darkest pit possible of mobilizing passions, prey to dreams of "producing the void."

While allowing for the uniqueness of Artaud's thought—that is, allowing that it is not directly in line with any other mode of thought, political or otherwise—it seems important to consider the doubles of his writing that are both more disturbing and more historically relevant than the ones we normally hear invoked. We have, in this section, focused primarily on contemporaneous cultural and intellectual trends, exploring the realm of ideas and the rhetorical and imagistic world in which *The Theater and Its Double* operates. In the next two sections, we move on to the performance principles articulated in the book, to investigate the implications of this worldview as it plays out in the dynamic of audience and performer, crowds and power, of an individual subservient to a leader's vision.

SECTION II : Audience, Mass, Crowd

What was needed was a new irruption of . . . healthy barbarian energies. . . .
The crowd was the bearer of those energies which had been tamed by progress
traditionally conceived. Progress was already old; it was holding back the new
world, just as the bonds of an old civilization were holding back the crowd,
which was the bearer of the new.
  —J. S. MCCLELLAND, *The Crowd and the Mob*

CHAPTER 3 : The Avant-Garde and the Audience

A theater audience, as it appeared in Paris by the time Artaud arrived in 1921, assumed the general form of an obedient group of spectators sitting silently in a darkened auditorium. The dynamic, noisy, and engaged audiences of centuries' worth of theatrical performances had metamorphosed, in the nineteenth century, into the restrained and domesticated audiences that predominate today, accomplishing one of the most profound changes in modern Western theater history. The question facing theater artists of the early twentieth century was what to do with that new group of well-behaved spectators: use its acquiescence to their advantage, or fight it?

This chapter situates the Theater of Cruelty's ideal spectator at the crossroads of shifting conceptions of the audience by examining Artaud's theatrical writings of the 1920s and '30s within the historical framework of the creation of a subdued bourgeois audience and the avant-garde's reactions to it. The technologies, organizations, and aesthetics of power that helped radically alter the conception of a theater audience provide the backdrop for *The Theater and Its Double* and elucidate its central concern: the effect of the theatrical event on its spectators.

Thus, we look back at the technical and theoretical antecedents to the Theater of Cruelty in nineteenth- and early twentieth-century theaters in order to more fully understand Artaud's conception of the audience. The categories within and against which Artaud worked were articulated in the course of this historical shift: in the late nineteenth century, the audience as recipient, consumer, or inductee; in the early twentieth, spectators to be activated or empowered, galvanized or shocked. The Theater of Cruelty draws from seemingly incompatible developments in the two periods to create its own audience/performance dynamic, unique among the avant-garde.

The Crisis of Bourgeois Theater

The domestication of the audience served as the essential condition for what widely came to be known among early twentieth-century theater makers, theorists, and politicians from widely different constituencies as the "crisis of bourgeois theater."[1] The taming of the audience was an objective that had been voiced for centuries, even millennia, but that only the late nineteenth century managed to definitively accomplish.[2] In the late 1800s, social and economic conditions combined with new technologies in such a way as to enable theaters to create an atmosphere in which previously noisy and mobile spectators would remain silent, seated, passive, and polite throughout the duration of a performance. This seismic shift came about because of a new decorum, group identity, consumer mentality, and need for class security imposed on the theater—deliberately and incidentally—by the bourgeoisie, accompanied by revolutionary innovations in stage technologies.[3]

Theater managers and spectators worked together to create a passive audience: the technologies and business practices of commercial theaters responded to the bourgeoisie's quest for comfort, stability, decorum, and hierarchy. They created a compromise between artistry and community, between the holy and the immediate, that satisfied a little of the need for community and a little of the need for art while radically altering the audience/performer relationship. Turn-of-the-century theaters sought increasingly to overwhelm, manipulate, or envelop their audiences. The key terms in the new configuration of the theatrical event that establish the foundation for Artaud's conception of the audience are: a stable hierarchy within the performance, enforced physical behavior, and immersion.

Since a theater could represent an ideal civic order, the bourgeoisie needed the theater event to be stable—both fixed socially and logistically orderly. Being economically new and feeling tenuously so, and being socially a new creation, the bourgeoisie sought to fortify themselves as a class by developing cultural and social systems that seemed to guarantee a sense of permanence.[4] Since they themselves were always afraid of slipping, bourgeois audiences longed for a theatrical performance that could be conceived of as a stable consumable unit—one that could be defined, purchased, and exhibited. The theater event, as it had been inherited, included too many uncontrolled elements for the new class.

Uncontrollable elements of traditional theater included, in particular, the unruliness of audience members. In the new order, the lower classes' active and noisy behavior was recharacterized by their superiors as "rowdy" and came to be seen as perhaps dangerous but certainly bad mannered. Commercial theater managers, eager for the patronage of the more moneyed classes, happily pushed the lower classes out of "legitimate" theaters and into music halls, puppet shows, and nickelodeons. These audiences retained their high activity levels, but in increasingly limited venues. Separating the classes removed an array of possible conflicts, tensions, and activity, helping to create definition, hierarchy, and fixity.

The audience/performer contract, which previously allowed for multiple kinds of activity in exchange for a minimum of violence, shrank to one rule: the audience will *behave*. Manners prevailed over participation: the domination of upper- and middle-class spectators led to corresponding changes in decorum and theater-going habits. Audiences, now much more homogenized and belonging to a single class that continually needed to assert its values and establish social codes, began to enforce an ethics of restraint within the theater building. "For most of western theater's history," as Neil Blackadder points out, "playgoers have routinely talked during performances, often shouted, and quite frequently responded in an even more forthright manner, particularly if they were displeased" (*Performing Opposition*, 2). Further, in many eras, spectators had argued among themselves and with the performers, arrived late, left early, moved around during the performance, eaten, booed, hissed, stamped, and even, in extreme cases of enthusiasm, called for a repetition of a speech, scene, or an entire act. All these activities vanished under the combined internal and external pressures of late nineteenth-century manners and their material enforcement. The latter included uniformed ushers, mandated silence, late-seating policies, and the removal of concessions sellers from the auditorium. Bourgeois decorum helped establish a notion of the audience/performer relationship that privileged the importance of an uninterrupted performance over the personal desires or caprices of the spectators.

This ethics of restraint and conception of the performance's stability encouraged and reflected a new consumer mentality. The performance itself now appeared more of a commodity than an event and the spectator more a customer than a participant.[5] Middle-class audiences bought the show with their hard-earned money, and thus, they expected to enjoy it unimpeded by noisy neighbors or distracting activities in the balcony.[6]

Consumer satisfaction formed the basis for a new order of sociability. The ability to observe and appreciate the product without interruption became a moral right, leading to arguments in favor of restrictions on disruptive modes of audience behavior, including bringing in security guards and even police. Audiences wanted to buy a good show, and they wanted to enjoy it as much as possible. In pursuit of this consumer goal, they traded in their rights to many types of activity and self-expression.

The new theater rested on the assumption that the performance was a thing in its own right, whether or not the audience received it. The performance now being a fixed entity, technical developments worked to enable the physical enforcement of the newly developed reverence for product (on the part of the audience) and a desire for more control (on the part of the theaters). The production became literally what the French call mise-en-scène: "putting in place."

New designs for theater buildings encouraged a passive audience. Separate entrances, comfortable chairs, assigned seating, and improved vestibules and coat checks answered the customers' desire to make theater going a predictable and hassle-free endeavor. Other changes—such as bolting the seats to the ground—worked more overtly to give the theaters increased regulatory power. The bourgeoisie's desire to be comfortable dovetailed with the theaters' move toward more control.

With the advent of gaslight in the 1810s, limelight in the 1830s, and the introduction of electric lights in the 1880s, theaters acquired the ability to physically control the audience's focus. The dimmed or extinguished house lights wrested the spectators' attention away from each other and on to the stage. With lights on the boards and not the auditorium, the stage achieved clear dominance over the people watching. In a reciprocal move, performers were increasingly less able to interact with audience members, as the once-illuminated faces of the spectators became increasingly obscure and unindividuated. The lights enforced separation. Thrust into darkness, the audience neither spoke nor saw itself but sat and contemplated the illuminated world on stage.

The stage rewarded this newly focused audience by creating absorbing, dynamic spectacles. As Blackadder writes: "In the nineteenth century more than ever before, . . . mass appeal of visual imagery influenced theatrical production, so that elaborate spectacle often dominated over drama involving actors" (Performing Opposition, 10). Audiences were made to feel that they were immersed in an event far larger than themselves.[7] This was true of the performance and also of the theater building's architecture. An exemplary instance of this is Charles Garnier's Opéra de Paris, opened in 1875, whose ornate structure reflected its architect's belief that the building's "sole purpose was to command a 'silent awe.'"[8] The Opéra's labyrinths of marble staircases, colossal gilt statues, and eight-ton chandelier prove that theaters wishing to hush their audiences into stillness could do with theater architecture what the church had been doing for centuries.

In sum, the late nineteenth century saw the emergence of the most restrained audience in theater history, one that reflected the new middle class's desire for stability, a new consumer mentality, and innovations in theatrical design and technologies that created a hierarchical performance event. The consolidation of systems of control in the theater made this possible: lights could be turned off, focus enforced, the audience's ability to influence the course of the play curtailed, and verbal and physical disruptions of the performance or others' experience of it minimized to nothingness.[9]

The strategies I have described in primarily economic, technological, and social terms were also being developed in the late nineteenth century in terms of artistic theory. The audience's increasingly prescribed participation options made possible an event that was immersive—aesthetically, psychologically, and physically. The very nature of the audience-performance relationship had changed around the most fundamental questions of control. The authority of the performance event and audience obedience emerged as key terms for subsequent theater artists to either embrace or resist. Should the audience be conceived of as an entity to be acted upon, a recipient of the event, or should the new characterization of its role be resisted?

The Avant-Garde and the Audience

The avant-garde's outpouring of spectatorial theories arose in response to the new bourgeois audience/performer relationship. Two distinct trends of the avant-garde's reaction bear directly on Artaud's Theater of Cruelty: that which capitalized on the new audience passivity by incorporating immersive techniques into their aesthetic visions, and that which reacted against these controls and sought to agitate and activate the audience. Both of these tendencies—spanning the pre- to postwar periods—profoundly inform *The Theater and Its Double*'s conception of the audience.

The Theater of Cruelty, as we will see, is unique in that it shares the pre-war movements' move toward immersion and control while speaking in the postwar movements' terms of agitation.

Immersion

Richard Wagner established the major terms of the immersive aesthetic, first in theory in *The Art-Work of the Future* (1849) and then in practice at the Bayreuth Festspielhaus (opened in 1876). At Bayreuth, Wagner anticipated, complemented, and advanced the innovations occurring in the bourgeois theaters described earlier, developing techniques to subsume the audience into his creation by the use of dimmed house lights, new seating arrangements that forced focus on the stage, sensory inundation, and a sunken orchestra pit.[10] He placed the performers behind a double proscenium so the action looked remote, creating what he called the "mystic gulf." Further, he theorized these audience-control techniques as artistically necessary. Wagner's *Gesamtkunstwerk,* or total artwork, conceptualizes the audience as a recipient or inductee: it requires the spectator to abandon individual subjectivity and choice in order to follow the mythical event on stage.

Elite avant-garde theaters in the late nineteenth century furthered this conception of the audience/performer relationship, augmenting the innovations in lighting, seating, architecture, and new illusionistic possibilities developed by Wagner and the popular theaters. Two of the first European avant-garde movements, Naturalism and Symbolism, produced artistically radical new works at the same time as they developed an aesthetics and technique to subsume the audience into their creations.

André Antoine's projects for the Théâtre Libre inextricably linked comfort, control, and an aesthetic program, theorizing the audience as something that needed to be subdued for its own good and for the good of the art. Antoine argued tirelessly in favor of making theaters more focused on the production and more regulated. His design for the Théâtre Libre theater building modeled itself explicitly on Wagner's theater at Bayreuth and implicitly on new bourgeois theater comfort innovations.[11] From Bayreuth, Antoine took the mandate that all spectators face the stage, eliminating the galleries and side seating areas, creating a seating "wedge" in order to force focus on the performance.[12] From the bourgeois theater, he took advancements in convenience, including wider vestibules, more efficient check rooms, and cozier seats. (One of his four main goals for the new theater was to create a "salle confortable."[13]) These developments did more than increase comfort levels: they gave enormous power to the theaters. Indeed, Antoine even had the idea to avoid the nuisances of noisy latecomers by creating an automatic device for locking the theater's exterior doors once the curtain had risen.[14]

The aesthetic program of fourth-wall naturalism depended on a restrained audience. By creating the illusion of a real event unfolding in a real room and by using new staging and lighting techniques to concentrate attention on the stage, the Théâtre Libre encouraged the audience to observe as a voyeur. Drawn into the rules that they must pretend as if they were watching a "slice of life," audience members internalized the directive to remain silent so as not to spoil the illusion. In a reciprocal move, the actors' concern for maintaining the fiction inhibited any activity that would solicit the audience's physical or vocal engagement.[15]

In an aesthetically opposite but structurally complementary move, Symbolist theaters also conceived of their audiences as recipients of the theater's offering, reviving a spiritual or neo-religious function for the theater event. Symbolist theaters, such as the Théâtre d'Art (1890–92) and the Théâtre de l'Oeuvre (1893–97), worked to plunge their audiences into enforced contemplation of the performance, creating an extremely hierarchical theater event. From Wagner, they took the idea that the space could be designed to immerse the audience in the universe of the play, creating a mythical, hypnotizing world, captivating in its visceral impact. From early twentieth-century British theorist/designer Edward Gordon Craig, they took the theorization of a performance hierarchy in which performers as well as audience members would be subordinate to the supreme will of the director.

Symbolist theaters insisted on the reality of the stage's alternate reality with every theatrical means available, including lighting, costumes, scrims, smoke, and even scents. They followed Wagner's goal of annihilating the actuality of the audience's world in favor of the ideal world on the stage. They employed the concept of synaesthesia—the correspondence of different senses, such as light with sound, color with touch, scent with emotion—as a theatrical principle in an attempt to more fully address the entire being of the spectator. Atmosphere—invoked by sensory rather than intellectual stimuli—reigned in the Théâtre de l'Oeuvre, and the appreciative audiences were the ones that desired to give themselves over to it.

Thus, in the prewar era, two of the foundational European avant-garde theaters conceptualized the audience as something to aesthetically seduce and physically control. The result was the artistic justification of a one-way communication between audience and performer.[16] In both theaters, the performance event attained a new level of autonomy. Even though it still unfolded as a live performance, mobility within the event was recharacterized and reduced. Audience members' participation shifted to reception: suspending their disbelief, giving themselves over to the atmosphere, and engaging with the performance on its own—increasingly comprehensive—terms. This is one line of Artaud's heritage: the theater event as something that could be imposed on a forcibly receptive audience; that regulates the audience for the good of the work; that seduces and absorbs individuals into its more powerful being.

Agitation

Later avant-garde artists railed against the domesticated audience and fought the new conventions of separation. They conceptualized active audience members instead of a group of decorous viewers and sought ways to incite them to revolt or revolution.[17] Two main types of activity emerge from this reaction: one created by shock, the other by reason.

In the first category, shock provided the means to activate the spectator. Alfred Jarry fired the opening salvo of this fight in 1896 with the premiere of *Ubu Roi*, beginning with the scandalous utterance of the play's very first word, "merdre" ("shit" with an extra "r") and continuing through the performance's implementation of popular puppetry techniques, props in the form of toilet brushes, and a barrage of linguistic vulgarities. The confrontation of lowbrow theater with the elite Parisian audience at a Symbolist theater led to one of the most famous riots in theater history, satisfying Jarry's wish to fight the new audience members (and the social order they reflected), who, "inert, obtuse, and passive," needed "to be shaken up from time to time so that we can tell from their bear-like grunts where they are—and also where they stand."[18] Dadaists and Italian Futurists followed the ideas of Jarry to disrupt audience expectations, insisting that, as the Futurist "Variety Theater" (1913) manifesto demanded, the audience not "remain static like a stupid *voyeur*, but [join] noisily in the action."[19] This desire manifested itself in audience provocations geared toward moving spectators out of a passive relationship to the stage and, more ambitiously, their own lives. This lineage of theatrical practices assumed the audience's inability to perceive reality outside of established codes of viewing, and it attempted to use the theater as an instrument of re-visioning. These theaters embody the phrase applied to all avant-garde movements but in fact applicable only to a few: *épater le bourgeois*. They imagined the theater as a catalyst for individual transformation in the audience members. Their audiences would, at the very least, react vocally to the event and, ideally, be imaginatively activated.

The use of shock revealed the artists' willingness to use any means to achieve their goal: to get the spectators out of their seats and stop simply spectating. Physical agitation with the Italian Futurists or the dadaists formed a central goal of the theatrical event, and it was so little linked to the plays' content that the Futurists could attempt to invoke it by putting glue on people's seats or giving away tickets to homeless people. When fisticuffs erupted at Italian Futurist *serate* (evenings of variety performance) or at the Cabaret Voltaire (where dadaists passed out whistles for the spectators to blow in disapproval), the point for the artists was to stimulate movement in the individual audience member. Revolt took center stage—revolt against the passivity of the audience, which they would ideally link to revolt against existing society as a whole. Anarchy would be more acceptable than passivity in this view, because any kind of movement would be better than compliance or stagnation.

These artists created a deliberately antagonistic relationship between the performer and the spectator. Futurists and dadaists provoked audiences to react against their passivity by inviting spectators to take it out on the performers themselves—the Futurists developed the capacity to revel in "the pleasure of being booed."[20] This willed antagonism—the offer to audience members to mistrust the performance, to question its designs on them—reflects a belief that the audience, as a group of individuals, should be active.

In the postwar years, a new branch of avant-garde performance called for an activated spectator, sharing the assumption that transforming the spectator's viewing habits could lead to a re-visioning of the world, but this branch worked toward stimulating the intellect rather than provoking anarchic creativity. This is the politically oriented experimental theater, articulated most clearly by Bertolt Brecht's and Erwin Piscator's ideas for an "epic theater" (1926). The theater, in this light, can intellectually empower the audience. The spectators will be active, thinking, physically free, engaged, debating artistic, social, or political issues. Here, the audience assumes, in the artist's mind, the identity of a collective rather than a crowd, a group of individuals encouraged, through the configuration of the new theatrical event, to think more rigorously. Its audience is not riotous, but at ease; it inhabits what Brecht referred to as a "smoker's theater"—one in which comfort and distance promote engagement and reflection. The audience is not arbitrarily stimulated, but invited to participate in the debate the performance presents. It will be intellectually engaged while physically relaxed.

Brechtian theater theorizes itself as revolution rather than revolt: it will empower the audience politically, intellectually, and, eventually, materially, when spectators become actors in political life. The individual empowerment conceived of broadly by the groups discussed earlier finds a pointed articulation in Brecht's theater, which works to stimulate considered, individual responses that may be antagonistic to, but certainly engaged in, a dialectical relationship with the performance.

This sampling of the most striking features of the changing audience/performer relationship and the reaction to it helps us establish Artaud's unique position among the interwar avant-garde circles in which he moved, and it provides the categories that help us understand more clearly his own conception of the audience, to which we now turn.

The Theater of Cruelty and Conceptions of the Audience

Artaud is indebted to the milieu of the avant-garde that reacted against the new bourgeois audience, but his experience is just as heavily influenced by techniques established by the late nineteenth-century theaters and the tradition of controlling the audience that drew from the commercial theaters and Wagner. The Theater of Cruelty borrows the rhetoric of revolt and revolution, of shock and agitation, from later avant-gardes, while building on earlier developments of a new hierarchy of power, immersion in the spectacle, and techniques designed to assert the performance's authority over the spectators.

In terms of the crisis of bourgeois theater and the question of what to do with its passive audience, *The Theater and Its Double* agrees with most of the later avant-gardes that "this conception of theater, which consists of having people sit on a certain number of straight-backed or over-stuffed chairs placed in a row and tell each other stories . . . is, if not the absolute negation of theater . . . certainly its perversion" (*TD*, 106). *The Theater and Its Double* argues in favor of a theater that erases separation, abolishing the structure of "the spectacle on one side, the public on the other" (76), advocating a more immediate involvement of spectator with performance. Like the agitational avant-garde movements, it revolts against the separated, formulaic, safe, aesthetic commodity that had become the established theatrical event.

The element of revolt embodied by *Ubu Roi* and its attendant riots held a great attraction for Artaud, and he named his first and only significant theatrical venture after its author. Artaud's Théâtre Alfred Jarry (1927–28) (examined in detail in chapter 5) attempted to provoke disturbances at its performances the way *Ubu Roi* had done. It performed a prohibited play and then insulted its author; it screened a banned film; it created a piece "with the deliberate aim of needling people";[21] and it insulted its beneficiaries in public. But the scandals that Artaud orchestrated always backfired on the theater: they called attention to the disruptions at the expense of the rehearsed and directed work. Ultimately, Artaud decided in favor of the integrity of his productions over active spectators— so much so that he called in police to guard one of the Jarry Theater performances against the entry of disruptive audience members.[22] The Jarry Theater's choice of artistic sovereignty over audience revolt demonstrates how Artaud's call for aggressiveness indicates aggressiveness on the theater's terms, not the spectator's. Artaud's theatrical manifestos advocate not anarchy, but a theater that finds its "true" form in what Artaud calls "organized anarchy" (*TD*, 51).

While anarchy enjoyed popularity as a concept in early twentieth-century avant-garde circles, from both the performance's point of view and the audience's, the oxymoron "organized anarchy" points to the unique dynamic at the heart of the Theater of Cruelty's ideal audience/performer relationship. Dadaists and Italian Futurists incited revolt in order to unleash destructive as well as creative energies that might pour out into the street or back into the individual's own imaginative process. Their ambition for the audience was to generate a questioning of the structure of the event, a reaction against its authority, and a liberation from entrenched systems. Among the Surrealists, anarchy found its place in paradox, startling juxtapositions, unexpected actions and effects, and all forms of surprise generated to stimulate individuals into a reinvigorated creative state. This creative state involved an individual lawlessness, a freedom from established codes.

Anarchy in these terms is anathema to the Theater of Cruelty. *The Theater and Its Double* insists: "randomness, individualism, and anarchy must cease" (79); it seeks to cure "our spiritual anarchy and intellectual disorder" with a theater "utilized in the highest and most difficult sense possible" (79). True anarchy signals decadence, an encouragement of individual expression that will operate outside and irrespective of higher laws. The Theater of Cruelty does not aspire to create a space for the unfettered freedom of individuals; in fact, it actively works against such freedom. The theater that, in Artaud's terms, "has the power to influence the aspect and formation of things" exists to impose order on our disordered world (*TD*, 79). Not generalized anarchy, then, but "organized anarchy." This term gives us a way to conceptualize the mixture of agitation and control at work in the Theater of Cruelty. Organized anarchy points to an orchestration of the feeling of breaking boundaries that unfolds within a predetermined structure.

There is likewise an important difference between the concept of shock deployed by the agitational avant-garde and by Artaud. The basic rhetoric of disrupting the spectator's complacency, so common among the avant-garde, is only the most superficial layer of the complex relationship to the audience these artists envisioned. Disruption among the avant-gardes in fact took on diverse forms, each growing from the movements' underlying impulses. Artaud borrows the avant-garde's vocabulary of shock and audacity primarily in writings promoting his theatrical productions. The Jarry Theater, for example, publicized one of its productions widely (as several identical press notices testify) as a new endeavor that would disrupt audience expectations: "This production comprises three unpublished pieces which, we have been assured, introduce a new and audacious theatrical formula."[23] A 1927 Jarry Theater manifesto, written with the theater's co-director, Roger Vitrac (as were most of the theater's publicity notices and manifestos), promises that its audience will be "shaken and irritated by the inner dynamism of the production taking place before their eyes" (*CW*, 2: 18). Artaud also uses this language, albeit less lightheartedly, in promoting his 1935 production of *The Cenci:* "There *isn't anything* that won't be attacked among the antique notions of Society, order, Justice, Religion, family and Country. I therefore expect very violent reactions on the part of the spectators."[24] In this sense, Artaud was very much a product of his time in advertising his work within the rhetorical framework of shock. The stated goal to shake up spectators, cause a commotion, confound people's expectations, is one of the most visible features of the avant-garde, but it is also one of the least informative about the actual substantive work of which it is a part.

When looked at through the lens of how theaters conceived of the intended effect of this shock on the audience, a difference emerges between familiar avant-garde impulses and those of the Theater of Cruelty. Alfred Jarry's ideal audience member was an imaginatively engaged proto-pata-physician who would address the impossibilities, surprises, and contra-dictions the performance presented with the application of his/her own newly invigorated and idiosyncratic logic. The dadaists attempted to shock audience members out of their acceptance of social and cultural constructs in order to inspire a state of constant questioning. The Surreal-ists sought the shock of the *merveilleux*—such as the revelation inspired by the uncanny juxtaposition of an umbrella and a sewing machine on an op-erating table (an image taken from Lautréamont)—to provoke renewed aesthetic creativity. In these cases and more, a common denominator is clear among the various usages in the avant-garde: shock is the first step toward a reawakening of the spectator's creative or intellectual sensibility.

Artaud applies the trope of shock, but his use of it outside of public-ity pamphlets is more punishing than provocative. His characterization is distinctive: it is primarily physical, nervous, sensual. It returns most fre-quently to descriptions of the anticipated immediate visceral effect, the "intense and sudden shocks" on "the organs" of the spectator (*TD*, 86). These far outnumber descriptions of any hoped-for result of the stimula-tion; instead, the manifestos dwell on the experience of the shocks them-selves: the theater will "g[o] as far as necessary in the exploration of our nervous sensibility" (87). Jean-François Lyotard aptly describes this goal as that of an "energetic theater," a theater of "forces, intensities, present affects," with no representational or intellectual value.[25] This is a theater in which energies "no longer mean anything" (Lyotard, "Tooth, the Palm," 109), and it brings us directly to the frequently reconnoitered chasm between Artaud's theater and that of Brecht.

It is clear that with the Brechtian idea of engaging the spectator intel-lectually and politically, Artaud shares nothing. Artaud's vision for which part of the spectator to activate and which to stimulate is the inverse of that of Brecht's and of all politically engaged theater. Bodily and emotional processes are what matter in the Theater of Cruelty—not their meanings, contexts, or projected future consequences. Seen through the lens of how Artaud conceives the audience, the terminology of *The Theater and Its Dou-ble* opens up for us a startlingly clear view of this chasm: where Brecht sees a group of individuals with minds, Artaud sees a mass of "organisms."

The word *organisme* recurs in Artaud's manifestos in the place of a referent for the spectator, as does the idea of acting on *les organes*. The The-ater of Cruelty seeks to create an event that will "directly affec[t] the organism" (*TD*, 81); its spectacle is "addressed to the entire organism" (87); its new concrete language will "fascinate and ensnare [*sert à coincer, à enserrer*] the organs" (91). We will explore further implications of this in depth in the next chapter; for now, the striking thing to note is the difference between the conception of the spectator as an individual with a brain to be stimulated and that of a collection of organs to be acted upon.

(It is worth noting here that readers of *The Theater and Its Double* in English see the word "mind" frequently on its pages. This results from the translator's choice to use "mind" in the impossible task of translating *esprit*. *Esprit* means both mind and spirit in French: it is a way of referring to the abstracted elements of a person, including thought, attitude, a general way of being, acting, and perceiving. "Mind" is not exactly wrong, but its repeated translation as such throughout the book gives the impression of a more intellectual presence than Artaud posits. There is a good argument to be made for choosing "spirit" in most cases in *The Theater and Its Double* or, perhaps best, simply keeping *esprit*.)

The other key point of difference here between the Theater of Cruelty and Brechtian theater is that Artaud's theater is characterized by immediacy. Its conspicuous lack of articulated objectives for the aftermath of the performance event relates directly to its lack of thought about the audience members as people with lives beyond and after the present moment. Whereas Brechtian spectators are people who will ideally be stimulated to subsequent action in social and political spheres, Artaudian spectators are ruthlessly non-abstracted organisms, existing in the present moment. The Theater of Cruelty's focus on the immediate sensation of the event rather than a desired, subsequently materializing goal—its "gratuitousness"— separates it definitively from this second branch of avant-garde conceptions of the audience. The performance is an act in and of itself.

Overall, Artaud does not build on avant-garde notions such as that the audience should creatively awaken, intellectually reflect, or develop an antagonistic attitude toward or dialogue with the performance. Perhaps the most striking difference of all between the Theater of Cruelty and the agitational avant-garde is that it does not encourage the creative input of the spectators: it requires that it alone establish the rules and flow of communication. The Theater of Cruelty doesn't posit that spectators have good ideas or instincts. It holds all the authority and will use it to "reinstruct" (*TD*, 81), "redirec[t]" (*TD*, 83), and "*take hold of*" (*TD*, 140) the audience members.

Seen in the light of the conception of the audience, the late nineteenth-century theaters move to occupy a central place in our understanding of *The Theater and Its Double*'s audience/performer relationship. The Theater of Cruelty develops the early avant-gardes' conception of the audience as something to be submersed in the artist's vision, manipulated by the theater layout, and behaviorally controlled by new technologies. Its methods of orchestration build on the creation of a radically controlled space in Naturalism, the use of synaesthesia in Symbolism, and the desire to subsume the audience in the artistic creation that found theoretical and technical footing in both the bourgeois theaters and in a different but related way in Bayreuth.

Artaud embraces the idea that the performance's rights are stronger than those of the audience. The Theater of Cruelty is a hierarchical, fixed event that can be imposed on its spectators. Because its goal is "redirection" and "reinstruction," because it possesses all the authority in the event, individual spectators must internalize restrictions on their behavior for the good of the performance and for their own good—as conceived of by the performance.

The Theater of Cruelty's ideal theater space draws from and further develops the immersive framework inherited from the nineteenth century. *The Theater and Its Double* describes a use of space that would physically force absorption into the spectacle. The late nineteenth-century theaters developed methods to enforce focus and curtail the audience's ability to influence the event on a proscenium-style stage. The Theater of Cruelty takes the possibilities of this dynamic further by actually encircling the audience: "The spectator, placed in the middle of the action, is engulfed and physically affected by it" (*TD*, 96). To enable the action to unfold around the audience, Artaud calls for a performance space such as a barn or hangar, whose expansive, non-designated space would not be bound by fixed seating areas and stages.[26]

Within this space, the individual's immediate reality is erased in favor of the performance's by means of the staging area, the dynamic deployment of objects, and light and sound design. Artaud describes the staging as an overwhelming, ceaseless onslaught of sensory stimuli. The Theater of Cruelty creates a space in which there will be "an intensive mobilization of objects, gestures, and signs," "space thundering with images and crammed with sounds" (*TD*, 87), and in which "sonorisation is constant" (81). In one vision of the performance area, "the spectacle will be extended, by elimination of the stage, to the entire hall of the theater and will scale the walls from the ground up on light catwalks, will physically envelop the spectator and immerse him in a constant bath of light, images, movements, and noises" (125).

The Theater of Cruelty envisions sets, lights, sounds, and new technologies encompassing the entirety of the spectator's sensorial perception: "We shall introduce into the spectacle a new notion of space utilized on all possible levels and in all degrees of perspective in depth and height," adding "the greatest possible number of physical images" (*TD*, 124). This theorization occurred in the context of a reaction against the proscenium stage that had been in development since the latter part of the nineteenth century. Arnold Aronson points out that Artaud's scenographic ideals were very much in line with these anti-proscenium scenographic innovations, but that they were notable because they "synthesized the ideas and tendencies of the post-war era" and made "a definitive statement about environmental scenography."[27] Aronson notes that artists who reacted against the proscenium spanned a wide range of rationales but shared a common trait: they all represented "conscious attempts to alter the spectator's relationship to the performance" (29). As part of the reaction against the proscenium, artists including Max Reinhardt, Erwin Piscator, the Italian Futurists, Walter Gropius, and the Bauhaus theorized a "total theater."[28] Total theater theorists, excited by the possibilities of new media and moving architecture, advocated the invention of new spaces and new staging techniques that would create an encompassing theatrical event. One of the best-known designs—never realized, like most of them—is that of Gropius, who, in 1926, designed a "total theater" for Piscator, a space able to convert into three types of stages, including one in the round, with the walls and ceiling covered with screens for projections and lighting effects.[29]

The fundamental feature of the encompassing theatrical ideals expressed in *The Theater and Its Double* distinct from other "surrounding space" or "total theaters" is the desired effect of the event on the spectator. Total theater advocates of the avant-garde theorized their new theaters with the intention that such developments would stimulate audiences, make them active, create participants rather than spectators. This idea was conceived within the social ideal of increased individual engagement.[30] As the Bauhaus member Laszlo Moholy-Nagy put it, "It is time to produce a kind of stage activity which will no longer permit the masses to be silent spectators, which will not only excite them inwardly but will let them *take hold and participate*."[31] It theoretically provided a means of waking up, invigorating, activating the spectator. Piscator, for example, staged total theater pieces that surrounded the spectators and included multiple areas for film, projections, and actors, bombarding the audience with information and sensory stimuli with the goal of inciting them to think about a given issue. The multilevel or surrounding spaces were used to encourage audience members to react to the information and to participate in a debate—in some productions, spectators were called upon to make speeches, argue, and even vote on the outcome.[32]

The Theater of Cruelty will surround the spectators, but to what end? "In the 'theater of cruelty,'" writes Artaud, "the spectator is in the center and the spectacle surrounds him" in order to "conduct them [the spectators] *by means of their organisms* to an apprehension of the subtlest notions" (*TD*, 81). This idea is repeated several different ways:

> It is in order to attack the spectator's sensibility on all sides that we advocate a revolving spectacle which, instead of making the stage and auditorium two closed worlds . . . spreads its visual and sonorous outbursts over the entire mass of the spectators. (86)

Far from waking up, empowering, calling for co-creation or participation, *The Theater and Its Double*'s language of attack, immersion, and seizure points us toward the conception of the spectator as an organism to be worked upon. The Theater of Cruelty's staging is organized in such as way as to claim the utmost dominance over spectators.

There is a notion of synaesthesia at work in *The Theater and Its Double*'s descriptions of the use of sensory stimuli that reveals a heritage from Symbolism, which celebrated the sensorial "correspondences" sought after by Rimbaud, Baudelaire, and Huysmans. Symbolist theater artists orchestrated mises-en-scène around correspondences of word, music, color, and scent to create the perfect synthesis of arts in the service of a poetic text. The Theater of Cruelty also seeks to find and utilize such sensorial interconnections in its mises-en-scène: "From one means of expression to another, correspondences and levels of development are created" (*TD*, 95). Sounds, lights, objects, motions, emotions, shapes, are all conceived of as working together. Effects will not "orbit . . . a single sense"; rather, the theater will "cause them to overlap from one sense to the other, from a color to a noise, a word to a light, a fluttering gesture to a flat tonality of sound" (125).

The impulse behind manifesting these correspondences differs greatly in its intended effect on the audience. The Symbolists encouraged meditative or contemplative states to reflect and promote a tranquil harmony. The onslaught of corresponding sensations in the Theater of Cruelty enacts, on the contrary, a kind of forced synaesthesia, in which the correlation of the senses operates within a framework of aggression. The language makes this difference clear: the Theater of Cruelty will "crush [*broyer*] and hypnotize the sensibility of the spectator seized by the theater as by a whirlwind of higher forces" (*TD*, 83). It will summon up "a bloodstream of images, a bleeding spurt of images in the poet's head and in the spectator's as well" (82). The Symbolists had conceived of the audience as a beneficiary of the event, spectators to be brought into an experience of reflection, beauty, and elevation. In the Theater of Cruelty, the audience is conceived of as a victim.

The Italian Futurists advocated the deployment of synaesthesia in more aggressive and more dynamic staging plans than those of the Symbolists, calling for tactile, olfactory, simultaneous, sound-producing, media-filled, surrounding-space theaters powered by the latest technological inventions. But even in their most exuberant scenic design ideas, in which the spectator would be placed in the middle of this multilayered sensory performance, they encouraged the spectators to intervene and interact dynamically.[33] The idea of "crushing" the spectator never appears as a goal in their work. Indeed, for the Futurists, the combined sensory elements would ideally function as stimuli, igniting the spectator's ultra-modern and ultra-fast sensibility.

The Theater of Cruelty, in sum, embraces two extreme trends in the evolving early twentieth-century relationship to the audience: immersion and agitation. The former shows itself in the theorization of a spectacle that "engulf[s]" (*TD*, 96) the spectator, that captures and "crush[es]" the sensibility (83), of "directly affecting the organism" (81). The latter manifests itself in the feeling of breaking out of all boundaries, a "contagious delirium" (26), a sense of "the agitation of tremendous masses . . . pour[ing] out into the streets" (85). The combination of the two—control and ecstasy, direction and agitation—is what gives the Theater of Cruelty's ideal audience/performer relationship its unique character.

Artaud's envisioned theater resists incorporation into identifiable audience/performer discourses of the avant-garde. It consists of a startling yet revealing combination of the desire for the spectator to feel revolutionary while submitting, to stir up the audience while harnessing its energy. Artaud's spectators will not be inert while they absorb the performance; nor will they be spurred to flights of their individual imagination;

nor will they be activated by reason—in no way does the Theater of Cruelty call for intellectual engagement or individual empowerment. This is the disturbing crux of the issue: Artaud does not ask his audience members to remain calm, but neither will he empower or engage them as individuals.

We have looked at the features of the historical avant-garde through the lens of the conception of the audience: as either an entity to be pacified or a group of individuals to be agitated. Michael Kirby, in his 1987 *A Formalist Theater*, examined the historical avant-garde movements from the viewpoint of the production. Kirby distinguished between "hermetic" and "antagonistic" productions, between theaters that saw themselves as producing aesthetic totalities and theaters that required active audience participation in order for their performances to be complete.[34] Hans-Thies Lehmann, more recently, discusses the move from hermetic to antagonistic performance in terms of the "fundamental *shift from work to event*," arguing that the two categories are antithetical, because antagonism "is incompatible with the idea of an aesthetic totality of theatre 'work.'"[35] These are insightful categories and observations, but it is impossible to locate the Theater of Cruelty within them. Artaud's theater is a hierarchical, fixed work, an "aesthetic totality," but it *also* seeks to aggressively agitate the spectators sensorially, mentally, and physically, antagonizing them without requiring their active input. To situate the Theater of Cruelty within this discourse, we would have to describe it as its own category: the antagonistic-immersive ideal, one that seeks to immerse without contemplation, to assail without response.

The Theater and Its Double emerges from its author's engagement with the historical avant-gardes, as well as his work in some of the most important French theaters of the 1920s and '30s.[36] Regarding both, it seems, in many ways, out of its time. Artaud's points of connection with the historical avant-gardes are at their final days: by the time he was designing, directing, and theorizing his own theater, the era of riotous avant-garde theater performance was largely a thing of the past in France. Accustomed to the idea that they might be the targets of deliberate provocation, Parisian audiences in the late 1920s and '30s greeted agitational pranks with either partisan approval or yawns, but rarely with surprise. Alfred Jarry, dadaism, Surrealism, and Italian Futurism had essentially prepared audiences for such assaults, and, although some small venues—including Artaud's Théâtre Alfred Jarry—attempted to re-create their impact, these efforts provoked far fewer repercussions than their predecessors.

The Theater and Its Double's conception of the audience/performer relationship is in many ways jarring within its immediate French context. Interwar theater in Paris was turning away from the groups and the haphazard performances of avant-garde movements and toward the works of the acclaimed directors Jacques Copeau, Charles Dullin, Georges Pitoëff, Gaston Baty, Louis Jouvet, and Jean-Louis Barrault. These directors developed beautifully stylized works within theater spaces that, while innovative compared to the bourgeois theaters, were still more traditional than those of the total theater artists. At Dullin's Atelier or Copeau's Vieux Colombier, the dreams of breaking out of theatrical structures and creating a total event held less sway than a desire to create aesthetically invigorating theater appealing to a wide range of the public. These theaters, excelling at what Barthes called "une sorte de clarté passionnée" (a kind of passionate clarity), formed the "Cartel"—a directors' association comprised of Baty, Jouvet, Pitoëff, and Dullin—in 1927, as a kind of safety net for these directors, ensuring their ability to continue developing their artistic visions for the public.

The Theater and Its Double expresses no sympathy with the passionate clarity of French theater or with the ideals of confederation and community the Cartel stood for. Although Artaud had worked at several of these theaters and initially responded to the ardent devotion they brought to the art and the advancement of the importance of the mise-en-scène,[37] their privileged aesthetic experiments ultimately appeared irrelevant to the kind of total performance event he was envisioning.[38] The perfection of a "craft" is something Artaud gestures toward in his manifestos, but vaguely, and he does not make it the centerpiece of his work (in fact, Artaud is drawn to incomplete works, pieces full of imperfections, that give his imagination room to expand).[39] Artaud was attempting to theorize not one aspect of a theatrical performance, not one piece of an aesthetic structure, but an entire affective event.

Other ways that the Theater of Cruelty's ideals are out of synch with those of the avant-garde are also revealing. Artaud's project was not driven by the need to make the audience contemplative, as were many late nineteenth-century experimental theaters, and no move toward social justice motivates his theater, as it did for many interwar avant-gardes. Artaud was in the milieu of the Parisian avant-garde without participating in its humanist spirit. His work did not engage in the communal ethos of contemporaneous avant-garde movements—a fact most evident in his heated relations with the Surrealists, but also in the absence of talk of collaboration and community in *The Theater and Its Double*.

The Theater and Its Double describes a new theater that will shatter existing conventions on terms it defines and executes itself, with no help from the spectators. The Theater of Cruelty has no problem with the domination of the audience by the artist. Its imaginary spectator achieves exaltation rather than enlightenment or awakening—an exaltation carefully orchestrated by the performance. Thus, Artaud's theater calls for an event with the authority of Wagner's Bayreuth but the agitation of a Futurist *serate*. *The Theater and Its Double* explicitly argues in favor of spectators who are physically and emotionally agitated and intellectually disabled. The Theater of Cruelty's antagonistic-immersive ideal places the spectator in an event designed to submit her/him to an order previously unknown, but supplied by the performance. That spectator will be compelled to assent to the performance's authority after visceral agitation forecloses intellectual reflection.

We have seen that, like almost everyone in his milieu, Artaud execrated the new consumer-driven theater and its complacent spectators, and *The Theater and Its Double* participates in the avant-garde's denunciation of the bourgeois audience. But the Theater of Cruelty's unique situation in this complex discourse of the changing audience/performer relationship comes into clearer focus when we examine its kindred spirits in the *solution* to the "crisis."

All purely aesthetic responses to the question of the audience/performer relationship, all performances "that never transcen[d] the realm of art," fall short of the Theater of Cruelty's objective (*TD*, 78). Further, performance that conceives of the audience as a gathering of individuals is also inadequate. *The Theater and Its Double* draws from a different well to find answers to the question of the audience's role, one that leads it to a quasi-political zone that we examine in the next chapter, one where the whole concept of "audience"—within which the avant-garde was still working—is abandoned in favor of a "mass" or a "crowd." Immersed and agitated, sensorially overwhelmed, these other groups of spectators that are plunged into a hierarchical event and treated as organisms demonstrate the real historical doubles of the Theater of Cruelty's audience/performer relationship.

CHAPTER 4 : Theaters for the Masses

Artaud conceived of his theatrical project in the aftermath of World War I, when feelings of alienation and a deep yearning to belong to something larger than the self organized the social and aesthetic dimensions of much of European mass culture. The change in the relationship between the individual and the community was heralded as both alienating and empowering, atomizing and unifying, and it was manipulated by political systems on both the left and the right. While Marxists explained the rise of the masses in economic terms, fascists looked on it as a biological phenomenon, one that auspiciously heralded the demise of the hated bourgeois individual and the birth of a new communal identity. In the war between the religions of matter and spirit, the Theater of Cruelty, as we will see, is certainly not on the side of the class theorists. It embraces the mass as an organic entity that can bring us closer to an essential spiritual state—a state that materialist concerns had obscured and enfeebled.

The history of the Great War combines with the history of the theater in a striking manner when viewed through the lens of the audience. Some saw in the new bourgeois theater and its audience/performer relationship an embodiment of the separation and alienation being experienced across the continent on a wider scale. Developing their aesthetic ideas in opposition to bourgeois theater, they attempted to eliminate that feeling of alienation through what we could best describe as crowd-manipulation techniques, and they did so concurrently with Artaud. The new set of doubles to the Theater of Cruelty revealed in this chapter is the theorists of people's theaters in interwar fascist Italy and Germany. My approach to these theaters foregrounds their ideals of interaction between the performance and the spectators—specifically, methods that productions attempted to employ to work against individual responses and toward an immersive, communal experience. The Theater of Cruelty's kinship with the practices of people's theaters reveals a relation between spectator and performer that succeeded far better in *entre-guerre* politics than inside theater buildings. While avant-garde theaters were still conceiving of an "audience," these theaters, instead, conceived of a "crowd."

People's theaters make us think about the implications of engineering a crowd in contrast to performing for an audience.[1] (We will investigate this concept through the lens of crowd theory in the next chapter.) People's theaters share common features across countries and decades: they work with myth, archetype, and broad strokes of plot and character. They aim to arouse the passions; they are for "the people" conceived of as a unit. They draw from public festivals and athletic events, and they look a lot like rallies. They attempt to channel the energy of a crowd into a revolution of identity that would occur not on the individual but on the communal level. People's theaters advocate the dramatic use of essentialized elements of history and the classics; they elevate emotions over dialogue, text, and reason; they emphasize the "real" in terms of bodies in space; and they aspire to engineer, by technical and performative means, a total spectacle.

In France, the notion of a *théâtre du peuple*—a mass performance *for* and *by* the people—took hold during the French Revolution, as Robespierre, Jacques-Louis David, Danton, and others developed ideas drawn from Jean-Jacques Rousseau, Denis Diderot, and Louis-Sébastien Mercier to promote spectacles such as the Festival of Unity and Indivisibility (1793) that would unite the entire French people. At the turn of the next century, the people's theater impulse—nationalist, with an anti-elitist bias—became more pacifist and concentrated on cultural decentralization. In 1895, Maurice Pottecher created the first official French Théâtre du Peuple in remote Bussang, performing on a hillside for two thousand spectators. In 1902–3, Romain Rolland advocated a *théâtre du peuple* drawing from ideals of community celebration and equality he found in Rousseau, the Convention, and Jules Michelet. Firmin Gémier created the Théâtre National Ambulant in 1911–12, which literally brought the theater (a structure of 1,650 seats) on trains and trucks to the non-Parisians of France. In each incarnation, the artists called for performances with thousands of performers and spectators that would establish a collective identity through mythologized history, archetype, and elevated passions. They banked on the feelings of belonging inspired by being in a crowd of one's fellows to improve citizens. Rolland approvingly cites Michelet: "What is the theater? It means the resigning of oneself, the abdication of egotism and aggrandizement in order to assume a better role."[2] By the 1930s, the revolutionary ideals associated with mass theater had subsided, and French artists and theoreticians turned to the more modest goals of establishing conventional theaters that might be financially accessible to all.[3]

In the early twentieth century, the desire to create a populist mass theater flourished in Germany, notably seen in the work of Max Reinhardt in Berlin and Vienna from about 1902 until 1933.[4] Reinhardt was the acknowledged master of directing crowds, known across Europe for his ability to artistically manage thousands of performers. But the people's theater impulse took a turn in interwar Germany—and also Italy—distinct from that of France: it continued to grow in scale after the war, increasingly interested in larger and larger masses, and it became aggressively right-wing, reactionary, and apocalyptic in tone. The idea of a people's theater in the frustrated atmosphere of post–World War I Germany and Italy took off as both countries developed national theater initiatives in the 1920s and '30s that exploited the prevalent feelings of social isolation and longing for community.[5] Interwar people's theater theorists sought to create an identity for the masses of people World War I had bereft of one. Rejecting the idea of finding a self through an interior focus mirrored by a discrete theatrical event onstage, they reacted against bourgeois individuality—an expression of alienation, they argued—by encouraging the dissolution of the self into the crowd.

My focus in this section is on conceptions of the audience; the next section of the book analyzes the Theater of Cruelty from the other side—the point of view of the performance creator. However, it is worth remarking now on an observation made on the performance side by Erika Fischer-Lichte in her important study of several early twentieth-century mass theaters. Whereas people's theaters before the war (such as Max Reinhardt's) theorized their event apolitically, Fischer-Lichte argues that people's theaters after the war used similar techniques but with a specific agenda of helping "to shape and establish a lasting collective identity."[6] Putting aside for the moment the larger question of whether or not it is possible to apolitically orchestrate masses of people together in time and space, Fischer-Lichte's demonstration of the similarities in strategies, despite differences in stated agendas, usefully indicates that, nevertheless, the prewar mass theaters—especially including Reinhardt's—turned out to be the very theaters that the fascists wanted to use.[7] In fact, much of fascist theater was, in the words of Victoria de Grazia, "deceptively apolitical," preferring to appeal to seemingly universal truths that roused a specific set of feelings—truths that could be found in spectacles such as those of Reinhardt.[8]

In this context, we can say that Artaud did not pursue a nationalistic agenda, and the Theater of Cruelty did not support any extant political system. However, *The Theater and Its Double* clearly outlines an event that belongs to a performance discourse that emerging fascist theaters and fascist regimes theorized and implemented: Artaud developed an approach to theater that is inherently fascistic in its relationship to and effect on the audience. Examining the Theater of Cruelty alongside contemporaneous people's theater theorists, we see that, in addition to their significant thematic overlap, the use of similar theatrical techniques reveals shared conceptions of the audience-as-crowd. A parallel structure underlies both: a kind of fascist performance template. Although we cannot fully answer it here, the following discussion necessarily raises the question of whether the very structures we examine—a transformation of a group of individuals into an exalted crowd through the use of immersion, unreason, emotion, and myth—can, in any case at all, be separated from an implicit politics.

This chapter first introduces the aims and strategies of people's theaters in interwar Italy and Germany. Then we compare the theatrical techniques shared by the fascist theaters and the Theater of Cruelty that treat people not as individuals, but as crowd members—that is, people to be manipulated, not reasoned with. The shifting conceptions of the audience discussed in the previous chapter found another iteration with these theaters, one that promotes an ideal of immersion and agitation.

Working on the Masses

The abolition of the passive bourgeois theater audience was as fervently desired and theorized in fascist circles as it was by the progressive avant-garde. The best expression of the widespread interwar aggravation with the "crisis" of bourgeois theater, in fact, came from Benito Mussolini, in a speech he made in 1933 during the fiftieth anniversary of the congress of the Italian Society of Authors and Publishers:

> Enough with the notorious romantic "triangle" that has so obsessed us to this day! The full range of triangular configurations is by now long exhausted. Find a dramatic expression for the collective's passions and you will see the theaters packed.[9]

His solution to this problem paired a profound loathing of the prevailing contemporary theater with an equally profound belief in the theater's potential power. In this speech, Mussolini called for a *teatro del popolo* (theater of the people), saying:

> Theaters . . . must be designed for the people. . . . They must stir up the great collective passions, be inspired by a sense of intense and deep humanity, and bring to the stage that which truly counts in the life of the spirit and in human affairs.[10]

Collective passions, intense and deep humanity, a vague assertion of "that which truly counts," the life of the spirit—here is one approach to the hated prevalence of bourgeois drama, presented clearly and succinctly: reach beyond the bounds of the individual, bypass thought and reach directly for sentiment and spirit. The way to find the essential humanity assumed in this approach is by creating a theater that breaks through artificial aesthetic boundaries inherited from liberal, individualist nineteenth-century forms.[11]

Mussolini's call for a *teatro del popolo* in 1933 was followed by several attempts to fulfill his request. Many of them failed, and our discussion will focus on the theories and ideals as much as representative productions. Among the attempts to realize his vision was the extraordinary production entitled *18BL,* a drama of three thousand performers and twenty thousand audience members that played for one night in 1934 in Florence with a truck—the eponymous 18BL, the first mass-produced Fiat truck—as the lead character. This production, like all the fascist theater projects, was designed to bring the people together in a mass spectacle of mythic impact and import.[12] In Germany, Hitler called for a revolutionary, unifying theatrical form, spurring the *Thingspiel* movement (1933–36), which resulted in hundreds of new dramas that played in at least sixteen specially built outdoor stages (*Thingplätze*) to audiences of thousands.[13] *Thingspiel* takes its name from a medieval assembly (*Thing*), connoting a public sphere and the political participation of the people. The project embodied the reactionary modernism characteristic of fascism. In addition to *18BL* and the *Thingspiele,* Italian and German theaters went about producing their often "deceptively apolitical" works for the masses, which drew from the principles we will now examine.[14]

Mussolini said, "Theatre is one of the most direct means of reaching the heart of the people."[15] (Both Mussolini and Hitler harbored dramatic aspirations of their own: Mussolini wrote several plays, and Hitler, influenced by seeing Wagner productions in Vienna, had ambitions to be a dramatist, as well as to design and write an opera.) The "heart of the people" was, here, assumed to be uncivilized, emotional. The rational, schematic nineteenth-century commercial theater had taken all the majesty, heroism, and larger-than-private-life feelings out of drama. Realism had killed grandeur—a quality that the fascist state needed in large doses in order to promote and sustain a new national identity and imperial mission. In the task of creating a collective self, the government made every effort to harness the combined energies of live theater and crowds.

To achieve this objective, Nazi and fascist theaters sought to create a total theater: "As a total art form, they felt, [the theater] alone could perform the work of integration once performed by religion" (Schnapp, *18BL*, 4). The new total artwork would appeal to the masses by combining elements of drama with those of dance, music, sport, and festival. This was the explicit goal of the *Thingspiel* movement. Its "conceptual totality" corresponded intimately with its purpose to address the entire people: "the new drama was to be the ultimate in art, a syncretic experience of inimitable immensity" (Niven, "Birth of Nazi Drama?" 59). Fascist theaters in Germany and Italy would use every possible theatrical means to create a visceral, physical, and emotional experience for the spectator in an attempt to address all parts of the human—all parts, that is, except the critical faculties. These theaters mobilized and put into dramatic form all the biases and beliefs of the counter-Enlightenment.

A total artwork had been, since the nineteenth century and Wagner's idea of a *Gesamtkunstwerk*, the "holy grail," as Modris Eksteins puts it, of modern artists (*Rites of Spring*, 25).[16] It was essential to fascist theaters, which were attempting to create a "charismatic community" (Schnapp, *18BL*, 78) as well as a revolution. Schnapp observes that the creators of *18BL* wanted to "forge a hallucinatory dramatic form not unrelated to the Wagnerian *Gesamtkunstwerk*, at once hyperreal and superreal in character" (77). In Germany, *Thing* plays aimed to create "a kind of total artistic and aesthetic spectacle, both visual and aural" (Niven, "Birth of Nazi Drama?" 59). Both turned to theater for its ability to awaken the kind of physical excitement evoked by athletic events and parades while being sensorially seductive and in control of the spectator.

Fascist theater initiatives emphasized the "real" in theater. The fact of bodies together in mass audiences forms one part of the real: bodies on stage in close proximity to one another, merging into a higher unity. Physical presence is what leads fascist leaders to the art form: people mass together "in order to stand before one another in actual time and space," to create "an instinctual attraction" that can provoke a "contagion" like that of athletic events or rallies (Schnapp, *18BL*, 78). Bodies, material presence, sensory experience: these qualities drew political leaders to "single out theater as the privileged fascist art" (Schnapp, *18BL*, 78). They would provide the means to reconnect with an essentialized whole distorted and forgotten by middle-class individualism.

National Socialists and Italian fascists promoted theater as an essential tool in the project of de-individuation. The theater, argued Reichsdramaturg Schlösser, one of the most powerful figures in interwar German theater, must become a communal experience. It must not be an event for a collection of individuals: "The German should no longer experience himself as private person and isolated individual."[17] Realizing that mass psychology is a totally different science than individual psychology, Italian and German interwar people's theaters played upon the likes and dislikes of crowds. Breaking down boundaries between people was meant to liberate citizens from their individual identities and merge them into a fascist whole.

These theaters elevated communal over private identity, in both the audience member and the dramatic characters. Both became dynamic potentialities—totalities lacking nuance or difference. This mass-over-individual principle resulted in larger-than-life figures that would definitively abolish particulars in favor of type. The Italians took this to such an extreme that the protagonist of *18BL* actually was an 18BL itself: a Fiat truck they named Mother Cartridge-Pouch. She was, in the words of one of the reviewers of the drama, "a truck as protagonist; as single and collective personage."[18] In Germany, *Thing* plays featured huge choruses that "represent[ed] the German people synecdochically" (Niven, "Birth of Nazi Drama?" 67). For fascist theaters, individual psychology encouraged decadent prurience on the part of the performers and the spectators; the new theater must, in contrast, focus only on essences.

The quest for essence led to generalizations of plot as well as character. Myth was invoked—or invented—to serve the theater's purpose of creating new works and new interpretations of works that would slough off old traditions. The classics and the past were distilled into "drama which raised historical events to a mythical level *above* reality" (Niven, "Birth of Nazi Drama?" 57). History could be employed but only if mythologized. "The great events of history," one writer before the premiere of *18BL* anticipated, would be, in the new theater, "reconstructed

along essential lines."[19] As a result, *Thingspiel* performances were held together, in the words of one critic, by "insupportable distillations of classical history, mythological acts of Teutonic heroism, speculative signifi-
cances of hoary relics of a prehistoric age, vague interpretations of
medieval drama and, in particular, the culled dramatic theories of both
Wagner and Nietzsche" (Zortman, *Hitler's Theater*, 13). Fascist theater relied on "a mythicised version of national history [and] the invention of
new heroes, traditions and ceremonies," a theatrical tradition inherited
from Wagner (Griffin, "Staging the Nation's Rebirth," 17). The paradoxical aim of creating new forms to attain a more authentic, primordial tradition that had gone missing with modernity is embedded in the process
Eric Hobsbawn has called the "invention of tradition."

Distillations of plot and character led to plays that worked with
"myths and symbols" that intended to shape a "mental attitude which embraced each and every aspect of life" (Cavallo, "Theatre Politics," 122).
New fascist dramas, as Pietro Cavallo writes, "never present political pro-
grammes or precise and articulate aims, but rather a set of symbols" (122).
These symbols operate on the level of archetype in fascist drama. Fascist
theaters would "replace the primacy of individualism and reason" with an
"all-pervasive use of myths, symbols and rituals" that would foster a sense
of "belonging to a supra-individual reality."[20] Archetypes—another kind
of invented tradition (they were named by Carl Jung around 1919)—if exploited dramatically, effectively shape mental attitudes, ensuring that the
spectator focuses on what connects rather than differentiates.

For fascist people's theaters, true drama resides in the heart of things,
not the details; thus, performance must obliterate separation, definition,
and contingency in order to raise people out of material concerns. As one
commentator on *18BL* phrased it: "The Mass Theater . . . [aspires to raise]
up the mass of spectators to partake of unmediated sensations and meanings, the fusion of thousands and thousands of souls within a single
framework of ideas and events."[21] The *Thingspiel* movement claimed that
the theater could "liberate" people from "the politics of self-interest"
(Niven, "Birth of Nazi Drama?" 58). Fascist plays dramatized the anti-materialist attitude that "living by instinct" had to triumph over rationalism
and its relatives. The real fascist had "felt what it meant to be part of a
whole" through World War I; the war provided a "unique opportunity to
overcome the alienation, egotism, and materialist thinking that characterized human life in the industrial age" (Cavallo, "Theatre Politics," 120).

Even though they were to serve a propagandistic purpose, fascist theaters eschewed didacticism and, even more completely, logic. Their plays had no recourse to detailing explicit political programs. Even plays depicting characters converting to fascism did so in terms of faith over reason, instinct and sentiment, rather than explicitly political, rational motivations. This is because conversions to fascism occurred due to a "motivating force" that "was more than a political doctrine; it was life experience elevated almost to the status of religion" (Cavallo, "Theatre Politics," 123). As one converting character describes the blackshirts: "Their belief has religious significance. It stands for something that is far more than a method: it is a way of life, mystical in its sources, palpitating, restless, and heroic in its deeds."[22] The fascist theaters instilled revolutionary ideals on a nonrational level (and also on the level of complete earnestness; as the fascist dramatist Salvator Gotta stated: "In a work of art, nothing is more anti-fascist than irony!").[23] They asked for faith in something not argued, but assuredly known by the leaders.

Intellect and reason came under intense fire by the fascists in their theaters, accused of being at the root of much of what was wrong with modern society—its fragmentation, individualism, and anarchic separation from "what truly matters." The Nazi dramatist Hanns Johst made the case for experience over intellect in his plays, representing, in George L. Mosse's words, "an organic view of the world, which was supposed to take in the whole man and thus end his alienation" (*Masses and Man*, 168). The cultural and political circumstances that led to the opposition to reason being so welcome in fascist dramas is found in the shattered postwar mindset. Gerwin Strobl writes:

> Anti-intellectualism worked in the Nazi's favour. Their celebration of instinct and feelings was peculiarly suited to the emotional needs of a traumatised public. The politics of reason—democracy—had, after all, twice presided over mass destitution. . . . The lesson seemed clear: "The rape of life by the intellect" had to stop. (*Swastika and the Stage*, 42)

The appeal to a non-intellectual "experience" thus became the favored basis for fascist performance, both as a principle on the part of the dramatists and as a desire on the part of the spectators.

Italian and German interwar people's theaters elevated images and emotion over dialogue or reason. As Mabel Berezin writes of fascist theater projects in Italy: "Fascist aesthetic education aimed to arouse the emotions, not stimulate the intellect. Rather than drawing intellectual distinctions based upon content, it used the theater's power of spectacle to engender feelings of community" ("Cultural Form," 1260). Schnapp describes the new Italian drama's goal this way: "The poetic word is subordinated to the mysterious play of image and rhythms. Physical actions, optical tricks, acrobatics, magic, fireworks . . . in short, *external* effects and affects occupy the place of honor once held in the theater by the values of individuality and interiority" (*18BL*, 78).

The "unmediated sensations" these theaters desired arose from an onslaught of visceral effects. Advertisements for new Italian play contests in 1934 emphasized the selection committee's interest in promoting spectacle and keeping dialogue to a minimum. In dialogue's stead: sensory assaults, "because nothing that speaks to spectators' sensory organs and emotions is precluded in this new theater."[24] The Italians, especially, enthusiastically employed new war technologies as well as innovative stage effects in their performances, the most extreme example being the truck-protagonist of *18BL*. They also included machine guns, artillery, searchlights, and even airplanes in their outdoor performances.[25] As Berezin writes of Italian fascist dramas: "Spectacle was the vehicle of feeling . . . which educated the heart" ("Cultural Form," 1260).

Finally, rhetoric of cosmic upheaval dominated Italian and German people's theaters. The dramas traded in "apocalyptic motifs, symbols, and structures" (Niven, "Birth of Nazi Drama?" 79). Their rhetoric was that of Judgment Day, of triumph and overcoming, of the promise of rebirth after an agonizing age of decay and decline. The secularism of Mussolini and Hitler made no difference in the deeply religious terms in which fascism expressed itself theatrically. Mother Cartridge-Pouch herself, after trucking through war and revolution, is eventually buried in the mud with the prophecy that "in three days she will return to her duties anew" (Schnapp, *18BL*, 76).

People's theaters in Italy and Germany between the wars were clearly theorized but basically unrealized or abandoned in favor of other performance methods being perfected by the government. *18BL* was unrepeated and largely a failure. The too-large audience (with twenty thousand spectators, some people were simply too far away to hear or see much) and the non-human protagonist failed to capture the spectators' imaginations. *Thing* plays enjoyed some noticeable successes during their three years, building on—and building—an artistic base more interested in spiritual than material needs, more essence than particulars, more culture than politics. The fascist theaters aspired to create a theatrical event stripped of bourgeois theatrical conventions, one that would unite the people in an ecstatic, but carefully orchestrated, experience. Overall, however, their strategies—sensory assault, appeal to emotions, capitalizing on a press of bodies, elevating myth—worked more effectively once they discarded all elements of theater as fiction and simply operated directly on crowds.[26]

Mythical, Total, Real

In the fight against bourgeois theater, the fascist theaters' list of enemies is quite distinct from that of the avant-garde. Fascist theaters denounce, equally, Naturalism and psychology; dialectical exchange and logic; and, crucially, anarchy and the individual. This striking grouping is, term for term, *The Theater and Its Double*'s list of enemies. Even more importantly, the Theater of Cruelty also shares most of these theaters' solutions to the crisis: the use of mythologized characters and plot that lead to the uncovering of a common essential identity; the invocation of heroic attitudes; the elevation of sensation over intellect and feeling over reason; a hugely visceral assault on bodies and senses; total theater aimed at "total" man; the use of the theatrical event as a "real" event; and a reliance on mystical, apocalyptic motifs. In both cases, the unfolding of the performance event is articulated in terms that reach beyond an aesthetic solution to the problem of the unengaged spectator. This combination of strategies promotes a concept of the audience as a group of undifferentiated spectators to be acted upon by theatrical techniques designed to treat people not as individuals but as a mass.

What Artaud and the fascist theater theorists hated about the inheritance of bourgeois theater was not its firm hierarchy of power, but its use of this power to encourage psychological introspection or aesthetic contemplation, its tight focus on psychology and individuals, and its lack of ecstatic states. Introspection and individual psychology are portrayed in *The Theater and Its Double* as hallmarks of theatrical decadence and irrelevance: "Once and for all, enough of this closed, egoistic, and personal art" (*TD*, 79). To find a dramatic way to sweep us out of this individualistic, psychological interiority, these theaters turn to the mythic. The Theater of Cruelty counteracts the indulgence and triviality of the new theater with a theater that harnesses the power of "Myth":

The theater must make itself the equal of life—not an individual life, that individual aspect of life in which CHARACTERS triumph, but the sort of liberated life which sweeps away human individuality and in which man is only a reflection. The true purpose of the theater is to create Myths, to express life in its immense, universal aspect. (116)

The Theater of Cruelty turns to epics and myths to bypass the narrowness of psychological understanding and bourgeois individuality. Here, myth is a non-historical collection of archetypal images and symbols, presented as a product of the harnessing of universal laws. History, analysis, and individuality get in the way of the grandeur and cosmic import sought. A mythic approach leads to dramatic characterizations and approaches to plot that both the Theater of Cruelty and the fascist theaters employ.

The strong influence of Wagner's and Nietzsche's ideas on myth and drama helps elucidate the shared ground of the Theater of Cruelty and the fascist theaters. Reaching toward the mythic creates the dramatic characterization strategies we saw earlier, stemming directly from Wagner and his attitude toward historical accuracy. Wagner depicts history as a clutter of facts that obstructs seeing the essence of a character: to reach "*Man,* in all the freshness of his force," the true artist must "unloose" the "swathing[s]" of history that cramp and disguise "the real naked Man . . . the type of the true *human being*" (*Art-Work,* 358). In the same spirit, *The Theater and Its Double* invokes "the terrible lyricism of . . . Myths" (85) to sweep away contingencies of time and place that obscure man's essence: "Myths" are there to "express life in its immense, universal aspect" (*TD,* 116), not its details. Fascist theaters were drawn to Wagner's use of mythical dramatic characters: their own embrace of essence in theatrical character reflects their desire to reach a type of pure humanity theorized aesthetically, socially, and politically. Such character types reflect an essentialist mindset: a "pure" human is theorized. However, it is theorized not in a spirit of universal acceptance, but in one of exclusion: positing one "pure" type of human suggests there might be less pure versions of it in existence.[27]

The kinship between the Theater of Cruelty's approach to theatrical characterization and that of the fascist theaters is also seen in their mutual accord with Nietzsche's ideas on dramatic character in *The Birth of Tragedy.* Artaud's hatred of bourgeois introspection parallels Nietzsche's condemnation of the "un-Dionysian myth-opposing spirit" that he claims overtook drama via Euripides. This spirit wrongly favors *"character representation* and psychological refinement in tragedy," the unique over the universal, the individual over the eternal, and imitation over reflection (Nietzsche, *Birth of Tragedy,* 108). As we saw in the earlier quotation, Artaud writes (with exactly the same emphasis) that theater must move us beyond "an individual life, that individual aspect of life in which CHARACTERS triumph." Nietzsche demonstrates how myth opposes psychologically defined individual character by deriding Euripidean drama, which instead of "expand[ing the character] into an eternal type," develops character "individually through artistic subordinate traits and shadings, through the nicest precision of all lines, in such a manner that the spectator is in general no longer conscious of the myth" (108). Euripidean drama, according to Nietzsche, wrongly privileges "the phenomenon over the universal and delights in a unique, almost anatomical preparation" (108). *The Birth of Tragedy* denounces the psychological theater's "atmosphere of a theoretical world, where scientific knowledge is valued more highly than the artistic reflection of a universal law" (108). The Theater of Cruelty likewise rejects and derides all anatomical, scientific, psychological approaches to character and reaches toward that "liberated life" mentioned earlier that "sweeps away human individuality and in which man is only a reflection" (*TD*, 116). The fantasy of instigating a Dionysiac dissolution, of mythic scope and eternal, universal import, inherited from *The Birth of Tragedy,* underlies both Artaud's and the fascist theaters' conception of what they would accomplish on their spectators.

For Artaud, as for Nietzsche and Wagner and the fascist theaters, the deployment of myth is the key to dramatically instigating the Dionysiac dissolution. "May it [the theater] free *us,* in a Myth in which we have sacrificed our little human individuality, like Personages out of the Past, with powers rediscovered in the Past" (*TD*, 116). A "liberated life" is one whose specificity has been annihilated, one that surrenders itself to dissolve into a higher state of being. Évelyne Grossman writes concisely of Artaud's approach to characterization:

> What Artaud seeks in myths . . . is a force that dissolves individual particularities, a "unitary" and collective position that doesn't separate subject and object, matter and spirit, man and animal—in other words, the continuities and analogies through which the limited contours of human "characters" are effaced.[28]

Dramatically, by its mythic approach to character, the Theater of Cruelty will model the dissolution of individual particulars that it wishes for its spectators.

A chart of *Thingspiele* dramaturgical principles distinguishes "Individualistic" from "People's" theaters, creating columns of corresponding characteristics and decrying the traits in the Individualistic column.[29] The list advocates replacing "Individual" with "Relative type" in terms of characters. Strobl describes the consequences of this in the *Thing* productions: designed with the express goal of having clearly typed characters, "all ambiguity, all scope for individual interpretation had been removed. Audience responses seemed calculable in advance. Here was the promise of a truly totalitarian theatre."[30] Totalitarian because the production asserted higher truths unknowable in any terms other than those put forward by the spectacle. Their "essences" were subjective choices presented as the highest principles, compelling to the audience because of their confident, sweeping grandeur.

This mythic approach to characterization draws us—as most clearly seen in Wagner's operas—toward the heroic. Fascist theaters bear witness to this, and Artaud uses heroic characters relentlessly—his use of Cortez and Montezuma in the "Conquest of Mexico" scenario in *The Theater and Its Double* is exemplary. They are forces of nature, but also heroes; they are universal, but exceptional. This combination of traits exemplifies what Hal Foster sees as one of several characteristic tensions of fascism, a movement "caught between the contradictory imperatives of the new mass subjectivity and the old heroic individualism, of the new mythic homogeneity of the people and the old elitist heterogeneity of the leader."[31] In this conception of character, we find a yearning for individual dissolution combined with an absolute addiction to heroic types.

The essentialist approach to character works in tandem with a mythic deployment of plot. Artaud suggests plot in all of his dramatic proposals, but essentialized ones. What "No More Masterpieces" (*TD*, chap. 6) argues is not that we should do away with classics, but that we should get past their particular language, their historically determined style, everything that marks them as part of their time or a construct, and uncover their essence. The real thing to show is "without form and without text" (*TD*, 78), without historical context and without material limitations. Myths are particularly well-suited to this task. The use of mythic plot was forcefully advocated by Wagner, who wrote of "History's unsuitedness to Art": history is "an unsurveyable conglomerate of pictured incidents, entirely crowding out from view the real and only thing [necessary to show]" (*Art-Work*, 360, 359). Asserting that history clutters essence allows one to create—as Hal Foster notes the fascist theaters did—a "phantasmagorical presentation of history as myth" with a truth truer than mere fact ("Foreword," xv). Fascist dramatists embraced Wagner's dismissal of historical facts and used mythic imagery to sound universal while in fact promoting their own context-bound ideas. To employ myth is one dramatic way of bypassing the analytical brain in order to enlist believers. As Mosse writes, apropos of crowds and fascism: "Myth is always more important as a persuader than sober analysis of reality" (*Masses and Man*, 192). The list of *Thingspiele* dramaturgical principles, in addition to advocating "Relative Type" over Individual" characters, also substitutes "Being" for "Knowing," "Reality" for "Illusion," and "Guiding and Following" for "Free." In each case, a truth outside of individual "knowing" is advocated and, ideally, brought into being through the guidance of the theatrical event.

Artaud's need to infuse the spectators with grandeur and cosmic import is bound up with the idea that there are keys to interpreting and channeling these cosmic forces—keys that the creators of the performance alone hold. This attitude gives an occult aspect to the performance: "These gods or heroes, these monsters, these natural and cosmic forces will be interpreted according to images from the most ancient sacred texts and old cosmogonies" (*TD*, 123). The performance will present truths outside the audience's independent ability to know, but that the creators of the performance can interpret for them.

Grandeur, in both the fascist theaters and the Theater of Cruelty, is conceived in aggressive opposition to historical-materialist uses of the theater, including didacticism. Fascists urged their playwrights to dramatize higher truths and to consider their goals beyond any material concerns. In this, they felt themselves superior to the socialists, who had resorted to crass propaganda in their art. What Schnapp writes about fascist theater's answers to leftist dramaturgy also speaks directly to the Theater of Cruelty's vision:

> Socialism, it was claimed by many, had confused propaganda with art, the material context with the spirit of the artwork. Fascism would promote *a more exalted art*, an art conjoining the real and the ideal, *total in its scope* and *transformative in its impact on the audience*,

an art free from the obligation to educate or to persuade, *so that it could educate and persuade on a higher/deeper spiritual plane.* The precise formula would be worked out. . . . It would conjoin an elemental form of "realism" with something more: *magic, mystery, myth, a sense of secular, but nonetheless sacred, rituality.* (*18BL*, 32; emphasis added)

Much of fascism's appeal lay in its promotion of the idea that it operated on "a higher/deeper spiritual plane" and that the revolution it promised would be "exalted," "transformative," even if its exact terms were unclear. The main thing in performance was to exalt the spectator by any means possible and to portray materialist concerns and the specificities of political agendas as beneath the spiritual realm in which the audience should be operating. Artaud's dislike of material politics and his emphasis on a total transformation of the audience on a plane that is simultaneously sacred and secular double these theaters' attitudes. This kinship results in corresponding dramatic strategies. Real and ideal, total and transformative, persuasive but not argumentative, sacred and secular: in each case, terms of myth and essentialism serve as the groundwork for a new kind of theater "total in its scope" and total in its impact on the assembled spectators.

A look at the case of "total theater" and its inherent power dynamics merits a brief discussion here to illustrate the comparisons at hand from another angle, that of a different set of interwar artists developing similar strategies. Piscator, Reinhardt, Bauhaus artists, and other nonfascist total theater theorists envisioned their productions as mechanisms to stimulate and liberate the spectator. They wrote of participation, awakening, cocreation, and empowerment. But spectatorial *initiative* does not necessarily—or even naturally—follow from the implementation of devices they advocated, such as surrounding spatial and technical effects. Fischer-Lichte writes of total theater theorists' goals: "The passivity of the audience in the bourgeois theatre . . . had to be overcome by devices that worked on the spectators' senses, overwhelming them and, thus, spurring them into action" (*Theatre, Sacrifice, Ritual*, 136). The second part of this sentence, "thus, spurring them into action," only seems possible when the action the spectators are spurred to is one put forward by the spectacle itself. "Overwhelming" points to a loss of agency and self-determination, to being driven out of your senses. Engineering such a state is not likely to generate individually considered action. It may be less of-

ten than not that such techniques successfully inspire an individually empowering response, one that actually opposes the politics of power embedded in the bourgeois audience/performer relationship.

The dubiousness of the idea of "overwhelming" spectacle being in
any way a positive force for individual progress is brought into stark re-
lief when we note that such innovations in "total theater" theories appealed greatly to the fascists and, ultimately, suited their ends far better
than those of the Marxists. The context for Fischer-Lichte's statement is, in
fact, this: the Nazi attempts to adopt the ideas and innovations of Piscator
and Reinhardt. The new "epic" and "total" theatrical techniques appealed
to the Nazis to such a degree that Goebbels sent an invitation—through
another total theater theorist, Edward Gordon Craig—to Piscator to attempt to enlist him and his theatrical techniques in the service of the
Thingspiele. Goebbels also tried to woo Reinhardt back to Berlin to participate in the *Thing* movement by offering the director "honorary Aryan
status."[32] These offers were rejected with horror by both directors, who
saw their politics and social goals as directly opposed to those of the fascists. But their ideas had a profound impact on fascist theater and spectacle: Strobl points out that Reinhardt's "influence on the Nazis is unmis-
takable. . . . His effort to break down the barriers between audience and
players and the emotionalism of his productions were all taken up by the
Nazis in one form or another" (*Swastika and the Stage,* 53). After Reinhardt
left Berlin, the Nazis adopted his Grosses Schauspielhaus for their own
theatrical projects.

The Theater of Cruelty strives to be a total theater in three fundamental ways: it addresses what it perceives as "total man," it concentrates
on maximizing sensory stimulation through new and existing techniques
and technologies, and it completely controls the unfolding of the event.
While *The Theater and Its Double,* informed by the ideas of a variety of contemporaneous total theater theorists, conceives of itself as apolitical, Artaud's power dynamic within the spectacle and his conception of what
will happen to the individual spectator align with the "total theater" motivations of the fascist theaters.[33]

The crucial difference to note here between the deployment of similar
techniques revolves around the conception of what the theorists wanted
to *do* with or to the spectator within this total theater event. Fascists
quickly recognized the potential dynamic power of total theater: it could
overwhelm the audience with space and spectacle, batter it out of its individual mind and into an ecstatic, unified mass. Artaud's ideal audi-

ence/performer relationship allies him with these artists working to harness the energy of the unindividuated spectators, to use the anti-reason of
the crowd in the pursuit of an emotionally driven, image-based experience of ecstatic liberation from social systems and bourgeois individuality.

The total theater ideas of the Theater of Cruelty—surrounding the
spectator with the playing area, creating a space in which sensory stimuli
could be launched from all sides, in which the audience would be "engulfed and physically affected" (*TD*, 96) by the work—aim to break down
the spectator with mythic, universal powers mobilized by the event.
Combining visceral aggressiveness and mysticism, the Theater of Cruelty
will attack the spectator "by physical means it cannot withstand" (81); a
"whirlwind of higher forces" (83) will sweep away the individual in its elemental fury. What these "forces" actually are signifies little outside of
their general contours. Artaud believes in higher powers, but they remain
cosmically and physically indeterminate (he describes the idea he sees expressed in *Oedipus Rex* as that "there are certain unspecified powers at
large . . . call them *destiny* or anything you choose" [74–75]). The main
point is to convince the spectators such forces *exist* in the manner the theater presents, and that the performance can channel them in order to dissolve the individual.

The Theater of Cruelty's total artwork presumes a "total man" like
the one envisioned in fascist theaters—a being whose totality specifically
and aggressively excludes intellectual and individualistic aspects of
"man's" being. *The Theater and Its Double* announces this clearly: "Re-
nouncing psychological man, with his well-dissected character and feelings, and social man, submissive to laws and misshapen by religions and
precepts, the Theater of Cruelty will address itself only to total man"
(123). Artaud associates thought with the individual, and thus he seeks to
activate something he considers more profound than either in the imagistic, visceral, and universalist terms of the spectacle.

Sensation over intellect: the Theater of Cruelty insists on affecting
people through their bodies, nerves, and energies, with visual spectacle
"utilized on all possible levels and in all degrees of perspective in depth
and height" (*TD*, 124). The "resuscita[tion of] an idea of total spectacle"
works in conjunction with a less active intellect:

> Thus, on the one hand, the mass and extent of a spectacle addressed
> to the entire organism; on the other, an intensive mobilization of ob-
> jects, gestures, and signs, used in a new spirit. The reduced role

given to the understanding leads to an energetic compression of the
text; the active role given to obscure poetic emotion necessitates concrete signs. Words say little to the mind . . . new images speak.
(86–87)

The Theater and Its Double aims to affect the spectator's "entire organism"
by a sensorial assault "mobilized" by the theater. Theatrical dialogue
gives way to visceral stimuli, intellect to emotion, as the drama is conceived of as a physical event for the immersed audience, with the need to
develop new technologies, new instruments to assail the spectator's body.

The use of ultra-modern technology within non-modern spaces—
such as the outdoor performances of the Italian fascists, the Nazi *Thingplätze*, or Artaud's barn or hangars—reveals another parallel tension between these theatrical projects. As Foster writes, fascist spectacle brought
to light a fascism "ambivalent about media spectacle, eager to exploit its
technological advances but reluctant to sacrifice the communal basis of
archaic arts" ("Foreword," xvi). The Theater of Cruelty's fascination with
new technologies employed in stripped-down spaces reminiscent of ritu-
alistic sites reveals a similar ambivalence about modernity. It is modernism with a base in primitivism, certainly, as Christopher Innes has argued of the avant-garde in general, but it is also particular to the fascist
moment: the natural theatrical space speaks to simplicity and community,
while new technologies are employed to act directly *on* the spectators. The
combination strives to create a feeling of primitive togetherness within a
technologically advanced manipulation of the senses.

This, then, is the "real" event so frequently invoked by both the fascists and Artaud, a real event theorized in a time when cosmic change
seemed necessary and theatrical *illusion* a betrayal of the potential power
of a live gathering. The *Thing* plays are emphatically *events*: "no writer is
being played, no play presented" in them (Willett, *Theatre of the Weimar
Republic*, 186); "cult, not 'art'" was their motive (Niven, "Birth of Nazi
Drama?" 58), as it was with the Italian fascist theater theoreticians. Fascist
theaters decried the aesthetic artifice that kept spectators from feeling
they were experiencing a "real" event. Artaud's repeated insistence that
the theater be a real event demonstrates that he, too, saw these theatrical
techniques as having real consequences on the assembled people. The
idea of the events being entertainment, "as if," does not apply here.[34] The
Theater of Cruelty is "a true act" (*TD,* 114); it will "influence the aspect
and formation of things" (79); theater is "the perfect and most complete
symbol of universal manifestation" (137).

The "real" consequences of the Theater of Cruelty's "universal manifestation" are a "fiery purification" for the world that has gone wrong. Rhetoric of cosmic upheaval, as we saw in chapter 1, dominates Artaud's work, in the tone of apocalyptic retribution against the failures of humanity. This tone leaves no room for discussion, for dialogue, for collaboratively conceived solutions. It is the tone of one who conceives of the masses as in need of redemption—masses who are not able to find it on their own.

The heroic attitude summoned by the fascist theaters in the face of a perceived apocalypse underlies the Theater of Cruelty. The theater, in Artaud's view, will force us "to take, in the face of destiny, a superior and heroic attitude" (*TD*, 32). The Black Plague, the destruction of Sodom and Gomorrah, the Fall of Jerusalem, the Conquest of Mexico . . . *The Theater and Its Double* operates in an atmosphere of end-time cataclysms that demand of people a loss of self-interest in favor of giving themselves over to "higher" battles.

George L. Mosse describes "the mystical and millenarian dynamic" of fascism that articulated itself in its language of "overcoming," of being at a "threshold of fulfillment," speaking in a "language of faith," of "blood and soil" (*Masses and Man*, 167). He argues that "the appeal to apocalyptic and millenarian thought" gave fascist rhetoric a religious tenor (167). But in France, the kind of frustrated, apocalyptic anger that *The Theater and Its Double* manifests was almost entirely absent from the writings of the highly structured, politically conservative French Right. Again, strikingly, we find imagistic, rhetorical, and thematic doubles to the Theater of Cruelty among the German and Italian fascist writers.

By looking at developments happening simultaneously with the writing and conception of the Theater of Cruelty, by examining the ideas fueling the ideas of neighboring people's theaters, we move beyond different kinds of ideal audiences to another concept that we need to examine in this context in order to develop a fuller picture of the Theater of Cruelty's ideal group of spectators: that of the crowd. As the fascist theaters show, it is possible for a group of people to be engaged without being empowered.

CHAPTER 5 : Crowds and Cruelty

Stephen Koch argued persuasively in 1966 that Artaud's theater is non-dialogic, that it proposes a one-way communication between the controller of the event and its participants. As opposed to Jarry's theater, which launched its assault with the goal of engaging the audience member's own capacity for action, Artaud's theater represents a "graver development of the modernist relation between spectacle and spectator":

> The audience is obliged to be far more passive than it is with Jarry. It is acted upon. Artaud does not regard his spectator as a thinking man, to be instructed, cajoled, seduced. Rather, the spectator is an organism, an exalted nervous system to be set free of itself through shock. In the Theater of Cruelty, the spectator is a hieratic victim. ("On Artaud," 30)

Not a thinking human, but an organism: Koch is right to point out that Artaud's theater seeks to "free" the perhaps unwilling audience member, who is conceived as an unthinking "victim." Koch calls this audience member "passive," and *The Theater and Its Double*'s construction of a theater space that envelops the audience and its staging techniques, which "seize" and "assault," does support a general notion of passivity. But this is not the same kind of passivity found in a Naturalist or Symbolist audience, so we must be more precise with this term. Passivity in *The Theater and Its Double* represents the complex kind found in crowds—specifically, the kind of crowd being cultivated at the same time elsewhere in Europe: the spectator remains agitated and even ecstatic, while her/his individual intellect or will is immobilized under the overwhelming coercion of other forces.

The crowd is one way of conceptualizing both artistically and politically the pairing of alienation and desire for the loss of self in the interwar period. This theoretical model sheds light on Artaud's ideal spectator and its social implications. Crowd theory helps us see that the Theater of Cruelty envisions the audience in many of the same ways people's theaters in

Italy and Germany did, and as demagogic political leaders elsewhere in Europe were also doing: as a group of people they would make feel liberated and exalted while keeping it under tight control. The means of affecting the audience that Artaud shares with fascist theaters become clear in the vocabulary of crowd theory and its place in the interwar era.

This chapter examines the effects of these methods from the point of view of the audience member and, crucially, his/her *receptivity* to such techniques. We close with a reading of Artaud's conception of his spectators, centering on the dissolution of the individual as seen through the powerful image he articulates of "The Nerve Meter."

The basic premise of crowd theory—that individuals behave differently in a group than they do when alone—has been noted (disparagingly) since ancient times.[1] But the crowd only took its place as a subject of serious critical inquiry in the late nineteenth century, with the belief that, as Gustave Le Bon wrote in his influential *La psychologie des foules* (1895), the modern era is "the Era of Crowds."[2] It reached a peak in the interwar era, with Mussolini, Sorel, and Hitler reading Le Bon, and books on the social, political, and psychological aspects of crowds appearing in the 1920s and '30s by Sigmund Freud, William McDougall, Karl Jaspers, and José Ortega y Gasset, among others.

After World War II, crowd theory took on a new urgency, after the horrific possible outcomes of mass politics became known. Le Bon's analysis had served (literally) as a handbook for fascist leaders to control crowds. Studies by Theodor Adorno, George L. Mosse, and Serge Moscovici examined the functions of crowds in modern political movements.[3] In 1960, Elias Canetti's *Crowds and Power* investigated the composition and function of crowds, creating a cultural, anthropological, and even aesthetic history of crowds and the structures and figures of power that control and define them.

The picture that emerges from a cumulative look at this body of thought presents the following basic characteristics of crowds. They are violent, contagious, and extraordinarily powerful; they operate by emotion rather than reason; they respond to images and archetypes rather than arguments; they will gladly surrender themselves to higher powers and forceful figures. In a crowd, suggestion replaces discussion; crowds are "given to excesses of both violence and idealism";[4] things become possible in crowds that otherwise individuals never would or could achieve.

For the participant, crowds promise reversal and a kind of permanent carnival, the unleashing of what's been controlled or repressed. A person in a crowd craves intensity and thus is given to excesses of both a constructive and a destructive nature. Crowds are essentially amoral; their tremendous energy can be directed to an unlimited number of ends.

A crowd grows without a sense of where it will stop or what it will achieve. One of Canetti's most powerful crowd images, among his many symbols drawn from the natural world, is a fire. A fire, like a crowd, "is multiple; it is destructive"; at the root of all crowd symbols, Canetti argues, is "the human urge to *become* fire."[5] The fear of fire is always coupled with an attraction to its "contagion" and "violence" (Canetti, *Crowds and Power*, 77). A crowd breaks boundaries and collapses distances, propelled by the furious desire to "experience for itself the strongest possible feeling of its own animal force and passion" (22). A crowd craves sensation and fights any limits on its desire.

People in crowds *feel* free. This is essential to thinking about the concept of freedom in our discussion. To be without boundaries—and to be among others without boundaries—signals both the highest goal and the deepest fear of the modern individual. Someone caught up in a crowd experiences a particular kind of freedom. It is the freedom to do things otherwise forbidden or out of reach, although these actions are in fact undertaken under the inexorable influence of others. Crowd theory demonstrates that to be part of a crowd is both an unimaginable ability to free oneself from laws and also the experience of unfreedom because one is following the inescapable impetus of the crowd.

People in crowds are emphatically *not* individuals.[6] The individual's "conscious personality vanishes" in a crowd (Le Bon, *Crowd*, 2). This has always been the case, but the implications of this vanishing took on a special political import in the modern era, when, as Le Bon wrote, "one of the principal characteristics of the present age" was "the substitution of the unconscious action of crowds for the conscious activity of individuals" (iii). By the interwar era, further possible uses and abuses of the emerging knowledge of crowd psychology came into view, as a sense of meaninglessness seemed to overtake this creature Gasset designated "mass man."[7]

Crowd Feeling in the Theater of Cruelty

The 1920s and '30s found much of Western Europe in what Gasset described as a state of spiritual unemployment (*Revolt of the Masses*, 136).

The Great War seemed to have butchered, along with millions of soldiers and civilians, what faith there had been in God, liberal democracy, and Enlightenment belief in mankind, with nothing arising to the fill the void. Céline cursed, "We're dying from being without legends, without mystery, without grandeur."[8] The modern individual seemed more adrift than ever, uncertain even of himself in an age of mechanization and increasing individual anonymity.[9] Eksteins writes of the 1920s: "A profound sense of spiritual crisis was the hallmark of that decade" (*Rites of Spring*, 257). Serge Moscovici has argued that, ever since, the modern individual has been defined by the search for "an ideal or a belief . . . a model which will enable him to restore his longed-for wholeness" (*Age of the Crowd*, 5). The "age of the masses" had managed to make an individual a part of a crowd in which s/he experienced no crowd feeling. It created membership in a group of people without a meaningful sense of belonging.

The fascist theaters discussed earlier sought to fill—or manipulate— the desire for communal sensation and union by taking advantage of the energy of bodies next to bodies, of the contagious property of crowds, aiming to intensify the spectator's emotional experience while continuing to develop more sophisticated means of control. In order to forge a sense of unity, they employed every possible theatrical means to dissolve the individual, because only in the destruction of the bourgeois self could they attain the higher super-personal unity that was supposed to overcome the "modern condition." It is in this sense that these people's theaters treated their audiences as crowds: they demanded of their viewers not spectatorship, but absolute involvement; not anarchy, but participation in carefully orchestrated ecstasies.

Likewise, Artaud's reaction against the bourgeois audience seeks not to encourage it to go wild, but to intensify its emotional experience while keeping it under tight control. Artaud exalts emotions while calling for "liberation": his rhetoric champions the idea of intense overturning, of reacting against the perceived injustices of restriction, tradition, and order; it advocates the theater to embrace "everything that is in crime, love, war, or madness" (*TD*, 85). As we have seen, however, the actual theatrical event he envisions does not advocate physical anarchy—only an exalted emotional and psychological state. What he aims for is a kind of crowd being cultivated in the interwar era: ecstatic and controlled.

The experience of being in a crowd entails characteristics prominent in the Theater of Cruelty's vision for the spectator, which we now examine. These traits include the visceral excitement of bodies pressing against bodies; the loss of rationality; the susceptibility to suggestion, hypnosis, and trance; contagion; the elevation of sensation over reason; the fear and attraction to de-individuation; and, as we will see, the death of discourse.

Crowds fulfill the desire to be uninhibited but in company, to run free while belonging, to break taboos en masse and therefore without fear of repercussions. Moscovici describes their amoral passions, their revelry in exaltation, this way:

> A crowd or mass is the social animal which has broken its leash. Moral prohibitions loosen their hold. . . . Men express, in action which is often violent, their dreams and their passions and all the heroism, brutality, delirium and self-sacrifice they contain. (*Age of the Crowd*, 4)

This image of an animal unchained is the dream expressed in "The Theater and The Plague," as we saw in chapter 1, and it lies at the heart of the Theater of Cruelty:

> The Theater of Cruelty proposes to resort to a mass spectacle; to seek in the agitation of tremendous masses, convulsed and hurled against each other, a little of that poetry of festivals and crowds when, all too rarely nowadays, the people pour out into the streets. (*TD*, 85)

Artaud proposes in place of the complacent audience descended from nineteenth-century bourgeois theater something that is turbulent, heroic, exalted, and imposing. He wants to create the feeling of intense freedom, the kind that—like the plague, which "liberates possibilities" (*TD*, 31)—is created best in a crowd. This feeling of freedom derives even more power from the fact of people being together in time and space with shared energy. People in crowds press together in pursuit of an ecstatic turmoil that cannot be achieved in isolation.

The reaction against intellect, logic, and reason we've seen in *The Theater and Its Double* and interwar counter-Enlightenment thinking is innate to a crowd. Crowds are motivated not by logic but by suggestion. As Moscovici puts it, "Individuals have to be convinced, masses have to be swayed" (*Age of the Crowd*, 33). Emotions rule, and the capacity for nuanced thought disappears:

> Once men have been drawn together and fused into a crowd, they lose most of their critical sense. . . . Individuals forming a crowd are

borne along by limitless waves of imagination and tossed about by
emotions which are strong but have no specific object. The only language they understand is one which bypasses reason, speaks directly to the heart and makes reality seem either better or worse than
it in fact is. (Moscovici, *Age of the Crowd*, 31)

Critical reflection would hinder the crowd's move toward fusion. Instead,
the group imagination seeks to expand on suggestive images, visceral
stimuli, icons, and archetypes. These stimulate an exalted expansive-
ness—one that is totally unaware of its originating impulse. In the Theater
of Cruelty, the road to understanding avoids reason (seen as only of use
for individuals) and instead is marked by suggestion, contagion, hypnosis, and shared hallucination.

Freud writes that when in a crowd, "[the individual's] liability to affect becomes extraordinarily intensified, while his intellectual ability is
markedly reduced."[10] Affect comes about through suggestion, that which
"is aroused in another person's brain which is not examined in regard to
its origin but is accepted just as though it had arisen spontaneously in that
brain."[11] Moscovici describes how influence works on a member of a
crowd: "Individuals have the illusion that they are making their own decisions" under the power of suggestion (*Age of the Crowd*, 17). Thus, contagion and suggestibility play crucial roles in changing an individual into
a crowd member. Both of these qualities are of "a hypnotic order" (Le
Bon, *Crowd*, 7); the individual, once immersed in a crowd, is "no longer
conscious of his acts" (7). The individual deprived of conscious selfhood
is quick to act on suggestion: "He is no longer himself, but has become an
automaton who has ceased to be guided by his will" (8). Immersion in a
crowd means loss of consciousness and openness to suggestion; the consequences can be violent or heroic, but they are, in all cases, unrational
and uninitiated by the individual.

For Artaud, hypnosis and trance structure the ideal audience/per-
former relationship. *The Theater and Its Double* speaks of "throwing the
spectator into magical trances" (140), as well as "treat[ing] the spectators
like the snakecharmer's subjects."[12] Artaud admires the snake charmer
for his ability to "conduct [the spectators] *by means of their organisms*" (*TD*,
81) via reverberations sent through the earth. These vibrations touch the
subject on a physical yet subliminal level, "like a very subtle, very long
massage" (81). The theater that succeeds in incorporating such powers
would be, literally, irresistible. Contagion works as a function of both
body and spirit.

Artaud calls for "rhythmic repetitions" of sounds to "arouse swarms of images in the brain, producing a more or less hallucinatory state" (*TD*, 120–21). This hallucinatory state is an essential condition for his conception of a total theater. To bring spectators into your hallucination is to get them out of their thinking selves, to make them forget their immediate reality and identity in favor of the world you have created.

Crowd feeling is always infectious: an eruption spreads with the force and rapidity of a conflagration, overtaking each individual it encounters and transforming him/her into part of the larger whole. Artaud's theater will erupt in "paroxysms" that "will flare up like fires in different spots"; the "direct and immediate influence of the action on the spectator" will spread like a fire (*TD*, 97). A crowd gains power through its own energy, exponentially magnifying the energy of the initial impetus and exceeding the sum of its own parts. Le Bon writes: "In a crowd every sentiment and act is contagious, and contagious to such a degree that an individual readily sacrifices his personal interest" (*Crowd*, 7). For Canetti, a true crowd advances with the force of an epidemic; it is "contagious and insatiable" (*Crowds and Power*, 76). Freud develops the idea of the "uncanny and coercive characteristics of group formations" to theorize why "we invariably give way to . . . contagion when we are in a group" (*Group Psychology*, 59, 21). In each theoretical model, the effect of the crowd is coercive—a sensation so strong that self-interest vanishes under the thrill of experiencing it.[13]

Contagious qualities are possible because of the proximity of bodies and energies. The press of bodies creates that "instinctual attraction" discussed earlier in the context of the fascist theaters (Schnapp, *18BL*, 78): the crowd experience works on visceral rather than intellectual levels. Artaud's imagined theater returns repeatedly to bodies in space, the effect of visceral stimuli on the *organisme*.

Crowds represent a particular and potent mixture of submissiveness and strength. The former element, seen in their unthinking nature, the fact that they are easily led, emotional, and respond readily to symbols and images, suits them perfectly to manipulation by a charismatic leader. The latter element, their force, points toward the possibility for violence they embody. The Theater of Cruelty wants to exploit these qualities in the same measure, attracted to a mass of people's submissiveness and to its power.

The crowd's desire to grow at all costs, its destructiveness, its ability to unleash what crowd theorists name either primitive urges, a biological condition, or the return of the repressed—gives it the potential, in all cases, to bring forth the hidden in man. Crowd theorists acknowledge that the hidden can be very dark—Le Bon writes: "In consequence of the purely destructive nature of their power, crowds act like those microbes which hasten . . . dissolution" (*Crowd*, xiii). In Artaud's worldview, the hidden is always dark, violent, evil. *The Theater and Its Double* extols this element: it embraces the destructive, epidemic nature of a crowd, as seen in the plague essay. The Theater of Cruelty would be "the exteriorization of a depth of latent cruelty"; it functions in the image of "carnage" (*TD*, 30, 31). It encourages the wholesale unleashing of this energy of a crowd, a plague, a contagious event of cruelty.

Artaud wants the theater to achieve the "contagious delirium" (*TD*, 26) of the people in a city hit by the plague. A will to danger, to destruction, manifests itself in this delirium. "The Theater and the Plague" describes in vivid detail how, as the (former) citizenry senses the inescapable eruption of the deadly disease, it begins to behave en masse, feeling the group's power expand as they erupt into a crowd. Artaud aims to dismantle hierarchies: the plague breaks down classes; the not-yet-infected exult in the collapse of boundaries, their new equality, their freedom. The now-liberated citizens range over the city as one exalted unit, which seeks only, to use Canetti's phrase, to experience "the strongest possible feeling of its own animal force and passion" (*Crowds and Power*, 22). What is contagious is an amoral extremity, a kind of unreasoned intensity, a "gratuitousness" of action:

> The dregs of the population . . . enter the open houses and pillage riches they know will serve no purpose or profit. And at that moment the theater is born. The theater, i.e., an immediate gratuitousness provoking acts without use or profit. (*TD*, 24)

The plague represents the force of dissolution the Theater of Cruelty aims at the spectator.

In 1936, in Mexico, Artaud stated, "The destruction of individual consciousness represents the highest notion of culture."[14] In his 1933 scenario "The Conquest of Mexico," included in *The Theater and Its Double*, he proposed a theatrical event that would achieve the mass extinction of individual viewpoints:

> The spirit of the crowds, the breath of events will travel in material waves over the spectacle, fixing here and there certain lines of force,

and on these waves the dwindling, rebellious, or despairing consciousness of individuals will float like straws. (127–28)

This persistent thought in Artaud's writings of the 1920s and '30s—to harness the power of essential forces in order to wipe out the individual consciousness—forms the heart of his idea of "theater." The key to achieving
this ideal is, as Artaud instinctively knows, through the body. The feeling of
closely packed intensity dominates the crowd's allure: "*The crowd loves den-
sity. It can never feel too dense. Nothing must stand between its parts or di-
vide them*" (Canetti, *Crowds and Power*, 29). Artaud taps into this desire by
aiming at an overpowering concentration: "And just as there will be no un-
occupied point in space, there will be neither respite nor vacancy in the
spectator's mind or sensibility" (*TD*, 126). Crammed in by each other and
the event, members of the crowd will surrender their individual autonomy
and give themselves over: "the spectator must be allowed to identify himself with the spectacle, breath by breath and beat by beat" (140). Physical
overpowerment leads to complete submission: body, intellect, and self lose
their autonomy and identify—merge, even—with the spectacle.

The individual with an immobilized sense of self in the Theater of
Cruelty is sacrificed—yearns, even, to sacrifice itself—to the higher
power of the spectacle. Crowd theorists address the phenomenon of desiring absorption into an overwhelming whole from the aspect of the
pleasure internal to a crowd experience. William McDougall gives an exemplary account of the heightened emotions associated with giving oneself over to a crowd:

> This is for most men an intensely pleasurable experience; they are, as
> they say, carried out of themselves, they feel themselves caught up in
> a great wave of emotion, and cease to be aware of their individuality
> and all its limitations; that isolation of the individual, which op-
> presses every one of us . . . is for the time being abolished.[15]

As Artaud calls for the spectator to be carried out of itself on the waves of
emotion conjured by the performance, he also appeals to a desire to be
free of the isolation of individuation. The Theater of Cruelty will create
the extreme conditions required in order for this desire to manifest itself.
All the pummeling of the spectator called for by the Theater of Cruelty
promotes not inertia but frenzy, exaltation, and a giving over of the self.
The ideal spectator is someone reduced to a being with no agency, but
who feels enormously powerful.

Loss of self and submission to a higher power leading to an almost orgiastic excitation and exaltation: *The Theater and Its Double* recalls the Dionysiac revelers of Nietzsche's imagination in *The Birth of Tragedy*. As Nietzsche envisions the Dionysian celebration, a fever of passion and excitement—an epidemic—passes from the inspired performers to the observers, perfectly combining the will to frenzy with that of self-annihilation:

> Here we have a surrender of individuality and a way of entering into another character. And this phenomenon is encountered epidemically: a whole throng experiences the magic of this transformation. (64)

The participant is driven to frenzy by equal and opposite desires. Artaud taps into the longings of the crowd, in which the individual is only too happy to negate him/herself in the yearning for annihilation in others.

Rainer Friedrich has argued that Artaud attempts to re-ritualize theater, to turn it into a pre-individuation participatory ecstatic experience, freed from "consciousness and reason," that goes even further than Nietzsche's anti-Socratic polemic in *The Birth of Tragedy*:

> Just as Nietzsche and Heidegger tried to cancel the history of Western metaphysics by going back to the Presocratics, Artaud tried to cancel the history of Western drama by going even farther back: to the rituals of tribal man, to a totemistic culture in which man is still *homo naturalis* and at one with his instincts—the blissful regression to a pre-reflective and pre-rational age, before individuation, according to Nietzsche the *fons et origo* of all suffering, set in. (Friedrich, "Deconstructed Self," 287, 286)

The Theater of Cruelty will cancel the individual and return humans to an imagined undifferentiated state. Whether they condemn it as primitive or see sublime possibilities in the fact, crowd theorists point to human desires that can not be satisfied in the individual; they make us aware of basic needs that can only be fulfilled in a group.[16] Artaud's manifestos tap into the individual's hunger for expansion and exaltation, with the attendant loss of self.

The Nerve Meter

Artaud's wish to treat the spectators like snake charmers' subjects, to throw the audience into trances and orchestrate every breath, emotion, and act in the theatrical event, is an aspiration not to awaken the individual but to transmit a vision directly into another human being.[17] This idea occurs early in Artaud's oeuvre: in a 1925 poem, he articulates a communicative fantasy that would bypass all the imperfections of language, works, and separation: "Le Pèse-Nerfs"—"The Nerve Meter":

> And I have already told you: no works, no language, no words, no mind, nothing.
> Nothing but a fine Nerve Meter.
> A kind of incomprehensible stopping place in the mind [*l'esprit*], right in the middle of everything. (*SW*, 86)

The Nerve Meter connects people on the most essential level, one that is both and neither physical and spiritual. It is not logical or even definable; it transcends understanding. The Meter would replace all discrete entities and actions with pure being.

Artaud's Nerve Meter rests on the idea of nerves of different organisms being in absolute sympathy with one another, across space, time, and matter. It calls to mind that blurred boundary between the will and the body, which, as we have seen, was so strongly in evidence in the between-wars resurgence of hostility toward rationalist science. In particular, the Nerve Meter poetically re-envisions the idea of animal magnetism, or Mesmerism, which had been popular, in different forms, in the late eighteenth and nineteenth centuries. Mesmerism was the belief that being was composed of "animated matter." It rested on an underlying conception of the identity of the physical, mental, and spiritual realms. The theory of animal magnetism purported that animated matter could be manipulated by one person—the Mesmerist—who had comprehended the co-existence of these realms and thus harnessed the power to control them. The practice of Mesmerism itself, the production of phenomena by the "physical force or subtle organic emission from one body into another," provides us with a way to envision Artaud's call to "directly affec[t] the organism" (*TD*, 81).[18] It can easily stand with the Nerve Meter as an image for how the Theater of Cruelty would operate in three aspects: the image of being, that is, the identity of physical, mental, and spiritual realms; the unified totality (via the loss of the self) it demands; and the element of absolute control by one exceptional person that this view makes possible.

The Nerve Meter posits the simultaneous transfer from one person to another of will, physical forces, and a more ineffable life force. It conflates all levels of being and blurs lines between the material and immaterial. It is "incomprehensible" because it operates outside of these categories, or, more precisely, encompasses them; it *is* all categories. The Meter represents the dissolution into pure being. To communicate via the Nerve Meter would be to bypass any perceived distinction between the mental and the physical, as well as between the self and the other.

The ultimate end of this kind of dissolution can be seen as enrapturing or terrifying. Artaud's vision is to return us to a primordial sludge. "In ten years," ends the poem, people

> will see all language drain away, all minds run dry, all tongues shrivel up, human faces will flatten and deflate as if sucked in by hot-air vents, and this lubricating membrane will continue to float in the air, this lubricating caustic membrane, this double-thick, many-leveled membrane of infinite crevices, this melancholy and vitreous membrane, but so sensitive, so pertinent itself, so capable of multiplying, dividing, turning with a flash of crevices, senses, drugs, penetrating and noxious irrigations,
> then all this will be accepted,
> and I shall have no further need to speak. (*SW*, 86–87)

This is the ideal state to which Artaud's theater aspires: an undifferentiated membrane, all nerves and no mind, pre-humanity, post-civilization—a vision of noxious energies that spread themselves out in the amorphous infinity into which the theater wants to lead us.

The universe, made of animated matter that differentiates itself at great cost, will be manifested in its entirety by the theater. Artaud envisions the totality of the Theater of Cruelty as an "essential drama" (*TD*, 51). It operates on the level of being, undivided, absolute, manifesting "one Will":

> in the image of something subtler than Creation itself, something which must be represented as the result of one Will alone—and *without conflict*.

"Subtler than Creation itself": the event is not artifice, but existence. It comes into being by way of a controlled event. The Theater of Cruelty will first expose seething, undifferentiated existence, then, beyond the powers of thought and articulation, control it:

> Only poetically and by seizing upon what is communicative and
> magnetic in the arts can we . . . evoke . . . states of an acuteness so in-
> tense and so absolute that we sense, beyond the tremors of all music
> and form, the underlying menace of a chaos as decisive as it is dan-
> gerous. (50–51)

As we have seen, Artaud thinks in totalizing terms, and this is where his
essentialism leads us: to a single membrane that expands and summons
controls over all life, a membrane defined by menace, "penetrating and
noxious irrigations," danger, and intense and absolute "states of acute-
ness." All of this "must be represented as the result of one Will alone—
and *without conflict.*"

Koch argues that Artaud's work represents "a violent negation of the
discursive spirit through paranoia" ("On Artaud," 37). There is no possibility of dialectical exchange with Artaud's writings, Koch argues, because there is no possible connection with the impulse (which, according
to Koch, is madness) that drives them.

> They are not discourse, for they don't participate in any kind of di-
> alectic. This means two things. They are entirely un-self-aware—
> many are, simply, ravings. Secondly, their ideas are unstable, unas-
> similable. (36)

Susan Sontag concludes her discussion of Artaud similarly: "It is not a
question of giving one's assent to Artaud. . . . What is there to assent to?
How could anyone assent to Artaud's ideas unless one was already in the
demonic state of siege that he was in? . . . Not only is Artaud's position not
tenable; it is not a 'position' at all" (*SW,* lvi–lvii). No discourse is possible
with someone in a "demonic stage of siege." And yet Artaud wanted to
create a total event that would intimately involve the very "senses and
flesh" of others.

In the final chapters of *Crowds and Power,* which discuss the fantasies
of Judge Daniel Paul Schreber in his asylum cell, Canetti implies that
when you pursue the monomaniacal non-logic of the insane or power-
hungry, you end up subservient to his vision. You cannot actually see the
world through his eyes, but you can, with loss of agency, follow. What
happens by giving one's self over to the event that *The Theater and Its Double* describes? You agree to lose yourself, to—as Artaud writes in his
praise of the clairvoyant—become "without limits or boundaries" (*SW,*
129), to dissolve into the whole, and what does the theater promise in re-

turn? An early English critic asked, in 1964, of the Theater of Cruelty: "The spectators are to be induced to rise and to throw aside their own inhibitions in a crescendo of mass—well, mass what?"[19] Artaud never provides an explicit answer to this vital question; he only speaks of his desire to orchestrate that ecstatic state. To correctly analyze what his ideal event is, we cannot simply supply our own notions of what the crescendo would consist in or be in service of. We must take our cue from the worldview grounding the ideas for a Theater of Cruelty—including the fetishization of violence and destruction, the fantasy of individual dissolution, and the vision of the Nerve Meter—in order to come to the clearest view possible of the proposition for the spectator embedded in *The Theater and Its Double.*

In this chapter, we have looked at the conception of the audience found in *The Theater and Its Double* and have found a mass of *organismes* that the spectacle can agitate and manipulate to unspecified ends. What we have been examining is one side of the dynamic of power at work in the Theater of Cruelty. Returning to crowd theory, we find the idea that following the leader is not neutral, that excitation for excitation's sake cannot be harmless: the crowd, once agitated, will always be eager for instruction. The crowd—desperate to grow once formed—needs a direction. Its desire is so strong, in fact, that it will accept *any* goal. The crowd "is the slave of the impulses which it receives" (Le Bon, *Crowd*, 11). As we have seen, it is essentially amoral: it can be worked up for noble or destructive causes, depending on its external cues. But the crowd does not exist in isolation: its partner—power—always determines its direction. We now need to examine the implications of that source of direction in terms of the way the controlling force behind the event is articulated in *The Theater and Its Double.*

SECTION III : Visions of Power

Every great leader is a fanatic.
 —SERGE MOSCOVICI, *The Age of the Crowd*

CHAPTER 6 : The Artist of the Theater

"In my view," Artaud writes, "no one has the right to call himself author, that is to say creator, except the person who controls the direct handling of the stage" (*TD*, 117). "Director"—or *metteur en scène*—is the primary theatrical term in which we should think of Artaud. Even when separated from practice—as he was for most of his life—he expressed his theatrical ideas from the perspective of the creator of the event, where he employed the discourse of seer, shaman, demiurge, and so on. In this, he was taking to an extreme a language that had just been born: that of the director.

The theater director—or *metteur en scène* (French), *Regisseur* (German)—is a surprisingly modern figure, only taking definite form in the late nineteenth century. As the audience's experience altered, a new figure emerged as the controlling force of that experience, and of an increasingly large number of production elements. This is an often-overlooked, but essential, context for reading Artaud's works.

The rise of the director has been situated as part of a broad historical narrative that sees Western civilization moving from unity to fragmentation, from shared values to atomization. Helen Krich Chinoy, in her influential introductory essay to *Directors on Directing*, argues that a fundamental disunity arose in English and European theater around the Renaissance.[1] People lost sight of the raison d'être of theater, both in terms of how it was produced (increasingly professionalized) and why people went (diminished civic and religious function). Theater moved from being integrated by what has been referred to by German writers as an *innere Regie*, or inner direction, to an *äussere Regie*, or outer direction. As a French critic argued in 1929, no "outer direction" was needed before the modern period: "In Greek tragedy, in medieval mystery plays, in the *commedia dell'arte*, under Elizabeth, under Louis XIV, . . . one could do without this hidden direction. Mythology, Christian faith, popular delight or the tastes that form the intangible aesthetic of a closed society—these things were the true *metteurs en scène*."[2] The late appearance of the director in the theater can be explained, in this framework, as a response to omnipresent societal fragmentation. The director arose to impose order.

The director's advent also, and even more relevant to our examination, corresponds to the rise of mass culture and politics. "The modern director . . . was born with a congenital interest in crowds," writes Frederick Brown in his study of early twentieth-century France through the lens of its theater directors.[3] Early directors shared an interest in orchestrating fictional crowds on stage and also expanding their directorial powers over masses of spectators. The very different directors Vsevolod Meyerhold and Max Reinhardt, for example, both strove for social integration through mass theaters, and several of the earliest French directors, including Maurice Pottecher, Romain Rolland, and, later, Firmin Gémier, were concerned almost exclusively with directing large people's theaters. In "the era of the crowd," the question of who would lead the crowd had equal urgency in the world of theater and the world of politics.

The director quickly became the visionary behind the artistic event, as poets and visual artists had been previously in their domains. Unlike the poet, however, the director creates his or her work directly with and on a body of people. Directors have the power to frame the audience's experience, to establish the power dynamic between live bodies within the event. Given this power, we may naturally be curious to know directors' motivations for orchestrating the event—do they seek community (Reinhardt, Pottecher), the development of knowledge and reason (Piscator, Brecht), the perfection of an art (Craig, Appia)? Whatever the inciting motive, the structure of the audience/performance relationship directly determines the event's social and political potential. One example illustrates this point succinctly: Erika Fischer-Lichte argues that Reinhardt, famous for orchestrating crowds on and off stage, "was opposed to any kind of politics and propaganda in art": he wanted his pageants to join people in a pan-human spirit without any political agenda attaching to the events (*Theatre, Sacrifice, Ritual*, 169). However, there could be no denying the potential of Reinhardt's mass spectacles to serve as effective tools for arousing nationalistic and ideological sentiments—as the fascist leaders' fervent desire to appropriate his work (discussed in the previous chapter) demonstrated.

The act of directing—even on scales smaller than Reinhardt's pageants—has consequences on a body of people. Brown demonstrates that, more often than not, the desires driving the major French directors fed into systems that reached beyond the theater's bounds, whether in the context of the director's ability to orchestrate and rally huge crowds (Gémier), to inspire individual self-abandonment (Gémier, Copeau), or to search for an "essential soul" (Dullin, Barrault). Jean-Louis Barrault's idea of using the theater to find an "essential soul," to take one example, drew from Rousseau, the French Revolution, and occult theories such as animal magnetism. This combination of essentialism, populism, and strategic manipulation also served as an effective mixture for totalitarian performances and pageants between the wars. The point was brought home by the fact that Barrault wound up staging mega-spectacles for the Youth Festival for Vichy, guaranteed employment, as Brown notes, by his "weakness for spectacles incorporating men in an heroic myth" and his "dream of fusion whose inherent grandiosity compelled him to manipulate ever-larger masses on ever-bigger stages" (*Theater and Revolution*, 428). He then produced the same kind of spectacles for the Resistance.

The director was not always a dictator, but he was a missionary figure with unusual skills in manipulating crowds of people. Consequently, in the interwar era, the ideas and strategies he developed could readily be appropriated by, exploited, or lead seamlessly to uses that went beyond "mere" aesthetics or the fantasy of being politically neutral.[4]

This chapter first looks back at the historical rise of the director in order to see the milieu from which Artaud draws the basis for his rhetoric and ideas, highlighting the trends that make the most impact on Artaud's thought. The second part of this chapter traces how Artaud developed, in his work for the Théâtre Alfred Jarry, an extreme version of formulations, tendencies, and impulses common to early theater directors in his directorial theory and practice. These include a drive toward artistic synthesis and the centralization of power in one figure, a move toward a theater without texts, and the use of a quasi-religious language to describe the performance experience and its effect on the audience. Ideas latent in many other directors' discourses are dragged into the open by the extremity of their articulation in Artaud's work—work that stretches our understanding of the function of the theater as "art." His ideas on directing combine with the dark worldview evident throughout *The Theater and Its Double* to create the Theater of Cruelty's singular vision.

Artaud organized his own theater projects twice: once for the Alfred Jarry Theater in 1926–28[5] and once for his production of *The Cenci* in 1935. In both instances, he was the sole director. For the Jarry Theater, which comprises the bulk of Artaud's theatrical practice, Artaud created theatrically effective works on stage that provide a crucial focus for our examination of Artaud's work as a director, and thus it is the subject of the second part of this chapter. *The Cenci,* however, which we examine in the following chapter, was a failure by all accounts. Artaud attempted to co-ordinate every aspect of the work himself, and his artistic skills slipped away as the "menace" he imagined started to be about power, not about what he was calling the "lazy, unserviceable notion" known as "art" (*TD,* 10). Between the two projects, a visionary yet effective theater artist collapsed into an isolated theorist whose writings betrayed extreme fantasies of power centered on the absolute artist of the theater.

The Rise of the Director

The first *Regisseur* was an aristocrat. When Georg II, the Duke of Saxe-Meiningen, arrived with his theater troupe in Berlin in 1874, he brought the peculiarly modern phenomenon of the director into being.[6] The Meiningers' tour of Western Europe and England inspired a wave of admirers, critics, and followers that included a diverse range of artists, including the soon-to-be directors Konstantin Stanislavski, André Antoine, and Max Reinhardt. Discussion of Saxe-Meiningen's work centered on theatrical unification. As one commentator has noted, the duke's work revealed

> the necessity for a commanding director who could visualize an entire performance and give it unity as an interpretation by complete control of every moment of it; the interpretive value of the smallest details of lighting, costuming, make-up, stage setting; the immense discipline and the degree of organization needed before the performance was capable of expressing the soul of the play.[7]

To a theatrical system in which, until that point, rehearsals had been minimal, scenery was pulled indiscriminately from stock, actors chose their costumes from their own wardrobes, and star performers often determined the arrangement and style of the entire production, the arrival of this *Regisseur* was a revelation. In addition to bringing all these elements under his control, the duke revolutionized crowd scenes: he massed previously haphazard supernumeraries on the stage in great numbers and with unprecedented precision. Their visual and rhythmic harmony, their ability to control focus, and their interaction with the scenery changed the overall appearance and effect of the spectacle. Saxe-Meiningen's "complete control of every moment" in organizing the entirety of production details conferred material form, in the eyes of contemporaries, to a "true" interpretation, to the "soul of the play." This "commanding director" (as the commentator referred to him with rather militaristic terminology) exerted strict control over the performance and the other artists involved.

The fact that Saxe-Meiningen was an aristocrat tells us something about the power it took to create the role of the theatrical director. As a wealthy duke, Saxe-Meiningen had the resources to unify production elements, and he had the power to not only run his theater but also tour it all over the continent for seventeen years. In other words, it took a manifestation of superior power (financial and political) to integrate the theater.

Saxe-Meiningen's expertise in directing crowd scenes is a parallel manifestation of the principle of leadership he exercised as a nobleman. Directing provided the duke with the ability to exercise his authority within a controlled realm. Brown argues:

> When a crowd cluttered the stage, leaving no part of it inert, or "dead," when the director's eye resolved every nook and cranny of his domain in some design, then his authority became absolute. The crowd functioned as an ideal audience supplanting the real one, as a perfectly responsive choral instrument by means of which the director could manipulate spectators and, in manipulating them, abolish their externality. (*Theater and Revolution*, 289–90)

The director directs the stage crowd with a view to directing the audience: the first is a microcosm of the second, and both are representations of a larger social sphere. Other artists were drawn to imitate, then, not only an artistic innovation, but also the embodiment of sovereign will on stage.

An essential fact of theater history bears emphasis here: the rise of the director parallels the changing role of the audience. Indeed, it is its necessary counterpart. At precisely the same time as the audience was silenced, restricted, and thrust into darkness, the director arose to become the all-important conceptualizer, organizer, and overseer of a given performance. Thus, theaters placing the director at the helm of their newly consolidated resources elevated the director's activities over the audience's. Because he interpreted the play as well as orchestrated its staging, the director assumed the role of intermediary between the spectator and the play. The audience/performer relationship transformed into the audience/director relationship.

The director became indispensable within a very short period of time. In 1887, just over a dozen years after Saxe-Meiningen's Berlin debut, André Antoine established himself as a *metteur en scène* at the Théâtre Libre, promoting the necessary, new, "exciting but obscure work" of directing—"an art that has just been born."[8] In 1905, Edward Gordon Craig was fantasizing about the advent of a single theater artist who would design, organize, compose, and build everything needed for a production and, eventually, completely eliminate the need for other artists.[9] By 1913, Jacques Copeau had elevated the director's authority over playwrights and actors to these towering levels:

> The science of the past, it is I who will absorb it, who will direct it, who will clarify it and who will transmit it to you little by little, all fresh, all new, pell-mell with the personal godsend of my unpublished science. No substitution. A creation. Life.[10]

We will return to the implications of this messianic language shortly; the point now is that within a matter of decades, the structure of the theater event had changed radically, the director's rise operating as practical and theoretical counterpart to the shift in the role of the audience.

Several traits common to all theater directors command special attention in a discussion of Artaud: centralized control over the mechanics and aesthetics of productions (over both other artists and the audience), a shift from textual to directorial authority, and the development of a Romantic and mystical terminology to describe the director's role and the synthesis he would achieve.

Early directors across styles and genres, from Naturalists to the most experimental artists, organized productions in much the way earlier producers or actor-managers had done, with a key difference: they structured them in line with their specific and all-encompassing artistic visions. In other words, directors combined economic with creative control. Saxe-Meiningen chose the repertoire, prepared the texts, assembled his company and cast the roles, designed scenery and costumes and oversaw their construction, and blocked the piece. In the Meiningen theater, "offstage control of the production was, in short, comprehensive and overwhelming."[11] The combination of mechanical and artistic control impressed artists such as Stanislavski and Antoine, who similarly sought a unity of style and effect in their directing through fitting acting methods, set and costume designs, and stagings to the tenor of the play itself.

The director's integration of production elements mobilized the Wagnerian conception of the *Gesamtkunstwerk,* answering a Romantic ideal of a unified work of art prevalent in the mid-nineteenth century. (In fact, Wagner and Saxe-Meiningen watched each other's work with interest, developing parallel ideas on how to implement a unified vision for performance.)[12] Saxe-Meiningen's practical and conceptual command of theatrical production and Wagner's ideals stimulated theorists such as Edward Gordon Craig and Adolphe Appia, who advocated that one person alone control the entire performance event. In the idea's most radical form, the director no longer directs a play, but creates a work. Craig complained of the theater having "seven masters instead of one" and called for "one brain" to create the work of art.[13] This person is the director—although Craig refers to him not so often as "director" but simply "artist of the theater." Appia argued that productions must be controlled by an author-director, the only real artist of the theater, who must be entrusted with "the entire interpretation of the drama."[14] The ideal of integration—of sets, lights, movement, acting, sound, text, interpretation, and orchestration—signifies a shift in thinking away from a production as a collection of discrete parts and toward an organic totality arising from a single source.

This kind of grand-scale directorial thinking contributed to the displacement of the play as the hallowed core of a production.[15] Some directors began using production plans—detailed outlines of how the play would be staged, including blocking, design, rhythms, and more—that subordinated the dramatic text to a single party's vision. Developed before the rehearsal process, production plans extended the director's power by cementing his conception of the piece and ensuring control over its interpretation and unfolding. Such plans led to a conclusive shift in power in the hands of both experimental directors such as Meyerhold and Gaston Baty as well as Naturalist directors such as Antoine and Stanislavski. Even directors known for their commitment to new plays were far from immune to the attraction of directorial power—Stanislavski, for example, wrote that in an early (1896) production, he staged the play "not as it was written but as my imagination prompted me."[16] Antoine committed the Théâtre Libre to presenting the works of new playwrights, but his writing reveals a desire for the director's interpretation to determine every facet of production: "The director must . . . understand the author, feel his work, transcribe it, transpose it, and interpret to every one of the actors the part assigned to him."[17] In planning the production ahead of time, the director "must perform the same function in the theater as descriptions in a novel"—the director becomes the author alongside the playwright.[18] Copeau's methods with his acting school in 1913 demonstrate this vividly: he began each day with extensive textual exegeses, so that, as Brown writes, "a play would have been drenched to its last indefinite article with *his* thought before rehearsals even began" (*Theater and Revolution*, 196). At the era's furthest stylistic extreme, Meyerhold's 1926 production of *The Inspector General* was determined by one commentator to have more accurately been called "Meyerhold's mental associations apropos *The Inspector General*," and, indeed, Meyerhold listed himself on the program not as director but as "author of the spectacle."[19]

Some directors deliberately sought incomplete texts to stage because it gave them more creative leeway. Reinhardt embraced rough or nontheatrical works that provided him with ample room to create the production himself.[20] In this way, a text could serve as a pretext for a director's ideas. Baty, often cited as less respectful of the playwrights' "intentions" than his contemporaries, justified his practice this way:

> A text cannot say everything. It can only go as far as all words can go. Beyond them begins another zone, a zone of mystery, of silence, which one calls the atmosphere, the *ambiance*, the climate, as you wish. It is that which it is the work of the director to express.[21]

Craig predicted that when one person would be able to master "actions, words, line, colour, and rhythm . . . then we shall no longer need the assistance of the playwright—for our art will then be self-reliant" (*On the Art*, 148). To his imaginary interlocutor who asks if the play won't be missed, he responds: "There will not be any play in the sense in which you use the word" (179). This synthesis of creative elements and centralization of power shifted the theater away from the playwright's dominance.

All of this led to a discourse—both appreciative and condemnatory—on the possible dictatorship of the director. As John Osborne points out in his study of the Meiningen theater, the duke's theater gave the impression of "firm and unwavering authoritarianism. For the members of the Meiningen company . . . Georg II was not just the director, he remained the ruling prince" (*Meiningen*, 141). Stanislavski referred to the Meininger's methods of leadership as a "despotism" that, because of the unified results, "seemed justified."[22] In France, Copeau elicited similar sentiments: in the early 1920s, an actor in his company reported that, while exhilarating, Copeau's total control over the work and belief that he alone could find the answers made them think "we were witness to something very like the birth and flowering of a dictatorial will" (Brown, *Theater and Revolution*, 249).

Some theorists believed that a strong enough director could theoretically make other artists unnecessary. Appia called for a "despotic drillmaster" who would eventually dominate the actor.[23] Craig's ideal theater would replace the imperfect human performer, full of individual passions and personality, with a performer he called an "über-marionette," capable of incarnating the "spirit" of the production more fully than a traditional actor could. Until these über-marionettes could be realized, the director/artist would have to function as a ship's captain, requiring "obedience" from all others (*On the Art*, 171).

If the discourse of the director was always a discourse of authority, many directors invested it with a nearly religious significance, as well.[24] More than managerial power and more than artistic guidance, in its extreme forms, the power wielded by the director neared that of a divine leader. Religious terminology applied to the theater situates the director as the person uniquely able to channel higher truths; he can lead the audience to nothing less than revelation. In particular, Edward Gordon Craig's ideas of an artist of the theater exerted an enormous influence over the conceptualization of the director—including that of Stanislavski, Reinhardt, Copeau, and, later, Artaud. In Craig's way of thinking, theater is a secular religion: it has a moral, social, and spiritual function that requires a seer to fulfill it. Art is, in his terms, "an expression of spiritual life. And artists are but the instruments of the gods."[25] To orchestrate all the elements of production, one has to discover "the Laws of Art." Few are equipped to make this discovery:

> The Laws must be discovered and recorded. Not what each of us personally takes to be the law, but what it actually is. . . . If all of us fail to find the thing and one comes along who makes it clear, who will there be to deny him? . . .
> How then can [the theater] obtain [its true] form? Only by developing slowly under the laws. And these laws? I have searched for them, and I believe I am finding some of them. (*On the Art*, 111)

Craig asserts that he works not for himself or for his own idea of theater, but for the absolute Laws of Art, which he—as a kind of aesthetic Moses figure—will discover and record. Other directors, such as Copeau—who wrote that the director "does not invent new ideas, he recovers them"—likewise contributed to the sense of a sacred mission involved in creating theater.[26] Reciprocally, Copeau inspired his followers with the impression of having the power to "marshal them around a sacred cause" (Brown, *Theater and Revolution*, 195). With attitudes such as these, the director emerged as a new role for the Romantic poet. But the consecrated artist of the theater differs in one significant way from the visionary poet: instead of containing the poetry, being himself a vessel for revelation, the theater director enacts his vision with and upon others. To believe in theater as a place of revelation and the director as the illuminated one necessitates accepting the power of one over a collective.

The late nineteenth and early twentieth centuries, then, consolidated power in the figure of the director, whose orchestration of the acting, design, and production of a play seemed to represent a possibility of unification not just within but also beyond the theater's bounds. The co-ordination of crowds of people—both those on stage and the audience—attempted to counter a widespread sense of fragmentation. Humanist, nationalist, and populist ideals swelled the sails of many theater directors; others spoke of achieving harmony and communion through the perfection of the theater event. They worked to perfect the craft of the theater because they believed their theatrical efforts would ultimately benefit the theater audience. Within the diverse range of ideas and styles that flourished within the first fifty years of theater directing, we find many points of origin for the directing strategies developed and expanded—albeit with a very different character—by Artaud.

Artistic Power in the Jarry Theater

The emergence of the director—firmly established by the beginning of the twentieth century—is the essential theatrical context for Artaud, who stepped directly into the era of the great French *metteurs en scène* when he began working in Paris in 1921. The milieu in which Artaud was trained was the apogee of a furiously concentrated period of directorial innovation. Pioneer figures such as André Antoine and Paul Fort were on everyone's mind. The directors Aurélien-Marie Lugné-Poe, Firmin Gémier, Jacques Copeau, the "Cartel des quatre"—Charles Dullin, Gaston Baty, Louis Jouvet, and Georges Pitoëff—and Jean-Louis Barrault were practicing and defining the art in France. Artaud saw the work being done in Berlin by Max Reinhardt and Erwin Piscator, and he also was exposed to the work of Constantin Stanislavski and Vsevolod Meyerhold when they toured from Russia. He was directed by Lugné-Poe, Dullin, Pitoëff, and the influential Russian émigré director Theodore Komisarjevski.[27] Finally, Artaud knew the work of Appia and Craig, whose ideas about a unified vision behind a production present many parallels to his own. Total theater theories, experiments with stripped-down stagings, technological innovations, directors who believed their job was to interpret a text and directors who considered themselves the "authors" of a piece, actors' directors and non-actors' directors . . . Artaud's ideas on directing arise from a comprehensive familiarity with the contemporary discourse and practice of directing.

Gathering ideas from these artists, Artaud latched on to the idea of a single authority over a theatrical production early in his career. Artaud's points of connection to the strategies and theories of directing outlined earlier include consolidation of aesthetic and practical theatrical authority over both other artists and the audience, a shift away from text, and the development of a messianic language to describe the director's role.

In an emerging discourse of a synthetic theater, Artaud distinguishes himself from his peers and predecessors by the extremity of his vision, as well as the worldview that propels it. Artaud theorizes complete control over both the other artists and the audience. He is one of the first theater artists to take the idea of being "author" of the spectacle literally, envisioning creating performances solely from his own ideas. He also theorizes being the "author" of the spectator's intimate experience in a way unmatched by the directors we have just surveyed. For his first theatrical project, the Jarry Theater, Artaud conceived of a theater free from texts or any other authorities, where sinister visions materialize, higher truths are evoked by dissonances and distortions, and the director adopts the role of an all-powerful leader who motivates through fear.

For a short period of time, Artaud was an artistically (although not commercially) successful director—a fact often overlooked by followers as well as scholars. This is due in part to the extremely short runs of his pieces (generally one or two performances) and also to the interest aroused by their attendant scandals (provocations staged from both inside and outside the theater). Artaud's techniques in the theater developed over a short period of time and reveal a great deal of internal consistency. Examining his ideas and their practical implementations in the

Jarry Theater provides us with a way to discuss Artaud's identity as a director and the discourse of control he articulated over his collaborators and his audience.

The Jarry Theater, which Artaud ran with Roger Vitrac and Robert Aron between 1926 and 1928, managed, with scant resources and borrowed actors, to mount four separate productions, which included six plays and a film screening.[28] Artaud directed, designed, coproduced, acted in, and wrote manifestos, productions plans, and scenarios for the Jarry Theater. He exercised control in all areas of the theater's four productions, including directing each play and designing almost everything on stage.[29] His work in theory and practice advanced the ideal of theatrical integration—"*integral theatre*," "*total theatre*"—which, in line with the ideas of Craig and Appia, involved making the director or "artist of the theater" the new organizing principle, responsible for the entire production.[30]

A 1926 Jarry Theater manifesto states the visionary importance of the *metteur en scène* to this "integral theatre":

> The director, who does not work according to any principle but who follows his own inspiration, may or may not . . . find the *disturbing element capable of throwing the spectator into the desired state of doubt [élément d'inquiétude propre à jeter le spectateur dans le doute cherché]*. Our whole success depends on this alternative. (*SW*, 158)[31]

The director's inspiration works outside of existing laws and is uniquely capable of negotiating between the material world and the invisible one. The manifesto extends the discourse of artists such as Craig and Copeau, but it adds two distinctive elements. For one, the goal of throwing the spectator into "doubt" implies a new power relation, a hierarchy based on the ability to create uncertainty and fear. The other, more immediate to our discussion of artistic authority, is that the "whole success" of the event rests in the unrestricted imagination and inspiration of the director.

Jarry Theater performances would, ideally, achieve theatrical synthesis by unfolding under the hand of the director without the restriction of another authority. A *metteur en scène* himself embodies "total" or "integrated" theater. Everything emanates from his vision, "his own inspiration," which encompasses the entire spectacle. He guides the production with a view to a physical and spiritual whole.

Artaud longed for an end to the reign of the playwright, as other directors had, and he adopted the strategy of using production plans to shift authority away from plays. Production plans limit the influence of a given text and throw control back to the director. Artaud conceived of works not as distinct parts coming together under his guidance, but as whole creations springing from his insights (imagination would be the wrong word).

Although the Jarry Theater manifestos proposed to perform established plays by authors such as Cyril Tourneur, Shakespeare, and Jarry, as well as contemporary playwrights such as Vitrac, Strindberg, and Claudel, Artaud denounced "subservience to the author, dependence on the text" as a "dismal tradition" (SW, 53). This seeming contradiction is explained by his use of the production plan, which allowed him to produce plays, as he wrote, in "freedom and independence" while working with a script that entailed "a certain number of directions" (CW, 2: 20), by emphasizing the directorial vision over those scripted instructions. Artaud used the production plan to insert the maximum amount of his ideas into the performance of a written play. When Artaud outlined the mise-en-scène in a production plan, he turned the play into a pretext for performance, not a finished work.[32]

Artaud's use of the production plan reflects a further extension of directorial agency from that of contemporaneous directors. Charles Dullin (with whom Artaud worked from 1921 through 1923) believed that the director was indeed a creator, but he objected when directors chose scripts they knew they would not adhere to. Dullin articulated a kind of spiritual middle ground: "The director is the spiritual representative [mandataire] of the author."[33] "The director must bring to light the original spirit" of the text, Dullin wrote; he must "manifest [extérioriser] all that there is in and behind the text."[34] Dullin made an exception to this for Meyerhold, whose productions of The Inspector General and The Forest came to Paris in 1930, igniting discussion about the "supremacy of the mise en scène."[35] Meyerhold, as Edward Braun points out, adhered to the dictum: "Chaque texte n'est qu'un prétexte" (Each text is nothing but a pretext), asserting that "the art of the director is the art not of an executant, but of an author—so long as one has earned the right."[36]

Artaud, articulating a belief in "the spirit of the text, not the letter!" (SW, 53), combined Meyerhold's "pretext" attitude with the spiritual language of Dullin. Artaud took stage directions, dialogue, costumes, and the order of events only as indications of the play's underlying truth, not the necessary actual mechanics of production. Here Artaud's ideas draw closer to Copeau's, who wanted to strip away all "temporal accretions" that had piled up around a text to find its "timeless core," as he called it (Brown, *Theater and Revolution*, 196). Although the text might serve as a point of origin, in this view, only the director could articulate the "spirit" of a piece.

Artaud's production plans articulate his interpretation of the play and then meticulously detail his ideas for the lights, sound, set, movements, acting style, and overall atmosphere of the staging. His mise-en-scène for Strindberg's *Ghost Sonata*, for example, rests on the idea that the "real and the unreal merge" in the play:

> The mise-en-scène must be inspired by a kind of double current running between an imaginary reality and something that has come into contact with a given moment of life.[37]

His conception of the piece unfolds through staging ideas such as abrupt changes of tone and rhythms; mysterious doubles of characters; echoes and amplifications of sound; slow motion; alternately blinding, mysterious, and shadowy lighting effects; and skewed set pieces. Artaud describes what he sees as the spiritual presence of the characters as "always seem[ing] on the point of disappearing, to be replaced by their own symbols" (*CW*, 2: 98). He translates that interpretation into theatrical terms, such as the suggestion that "beside each character appears a sort of double dressed like him. All these doubles are disturbingly motionless, at least some of them being represented by dummies. They slowly disappear, limping" (*CW*, 2: 102). These doubles, appearing as slow-motion manifestations of the characters' underlying symbols or gestures, would create the sense of the shifting layers of reality that Artaud sees merging on stage. The production plan aspires to give form to the invisible, spiritual, and metaphysical universe Artaud sees in Strindberg's piece and that he wants to bring into being.

Artaud also wrote scenarios, which go even further than production plans in giving control to the visionary artist, or director. In this, Artaud exceeded his contemporaries, who, with their detailed production plans and stylized mises-en-scène, might have recharacterized or devalued but still did not completely abandon literary texts as bases for production. Artaud wrote several scenarios for the stage between 1925 and 1932. Scenarios sketch the framework of a theatrical event, including broad strokes of plot, atmosphere, and decor and indications of possible bits of dialogue and stage directions. As opposed to a narrative, which is extensive, a scenario is intensive. It allows unrestricted exploration of one moment. The scenario manifests Artaud's desire for integration and immanence: it lives through physical enactment and investigation. A striking proof of this interpretation of the use of the scenario is the fact that the only written scenarios we have left that Artaud wrote were never actually produced in his lifetime: the ones that *were* produced are lost.[38]

Artaud's use of scenarios shifts the improvisatory power away from its traditional location in actors. *Commedia dell'arte* scenarios of the Italian Renaissance—outlines of the basic plot and key moments of the performance—relied on the performers' skills to create the piece. *Commedia* scenarios were, in fact, enjoying a renaissance among interwar French directors as exercises for their acting companies. Jacques Copeau, for one example, used them as training tools to free his performers from habit and to encourage a flexibility and readiness to actively respond to new situations. In conspicuous contrast, Artaud used scenarios—which he wrote with minute attention to acting and design details—not to give the actors more freedom, but to give the director more power. In a letter to Jean Paulhan (eventually included in *The Theater and Its Double*), he made this clear:

> My plays have nothing to do with Copeau's improvisations. . . . They are not . . . left to the caprice of the wild and thoughtless inspiration of the actor. . . . I would not care to leave the fate of my plays and of the theater to that kind of chance. No. (*TD*, 109–10)

For Artaud, scenarios necessitate that the theatrical event unfold on stage under the control of the director. The resulting event is neither circumscribed by a written document nor realizable outside of the director's theatrical terms.

All of Artaud's scenarios reveal unified theatrical thinking in the service of manifesting catastrophic visions. They are comprised of extensive stage directions; little to no dialogue; and sounds, lights, and movement designed along synaesthetic principles. The opening sequence of *Il n'y a plus de firmament* (*No More Firmament*), an unfinished scenario conceived with the composer Edgar Varèse around 1931 as a piece with music, describes the collapse of the heavens—the elimination of space itself—through a detailed orchestration of a whirlwind of lights, music, voices, movements, and sounds. Artaud's 1925 play *Le jet de sang* (*Jet of Blood*) also describes an apocalypse in synthetic theatrical terms; in fact, it stages several cosmic cataclysms, enacting a condensed version of the world's disasters from the Fall to Revelations. Its opening sequence orchestrates the collapse of all we know—civilization, nature, human bodies, and our selves—in an inverse tornado that deposits the remnants of the world (body parts, architectural pieces, insects) on the stage floor one by one. In the midst of the universal chaos ongoing since the opening scene, a brothel keeper reacts to an abusive Almighty: "Leave me, God," she says, with an act of anger that gives the play its title: God's blood spurts across the stage when she bites his wrist. Lightning then flashes to reveal a fresh pile of dead bodies, a divine massacre soon to be followed by a plague of scorpions. With more stage directions than dialogue, the short play reads like a scenario. It demonstrates, with its integrated theatrical thinking, how synthesis and apocalypse combine in Artaud's vision: the moment everything comes together is the moment of destruction. Always circling around images of comprehensive devastation, Artaud's works invoke the recent horrors of the world, finding its end not in the peaceful joining together of humanity (as many of his contemporaries sought, at least spiritually and rhetorically), but in a catastrophe that reveals its innate degeneracy.

Artaud's first scenario staged for the Jarry Théâtre, *Ventre brûlé, ou la mère folle* (*Burnt Belly, or the Mad Mother*), created another version of an apocalypse in synthetic theatrical terms. *Burnt Belly* developed from a minimalist scenario Artaud created, which scarcely involved any writing at all (the sound designer said he couldn't remember ever having a text between his hands). Collected memories of spectators and participants paint the picture of a "short hallucination, without any (or barely any) dialogue," in which a king rocked back and forth in a chair, uttering strange chants, until he was killed by a jet of violet light.[39] Other characters entered the stage only to be assassinated by the violet jet, piling up in front of a "curtain of light" (*OC,* 2: 281). The atmosphere of the piece was what was most memorable, including its orchestrated use of light and sound.[40] Benjamin Crémieux described the piece as a "condensed . . . synthesis of life and death," which left "a strong and lasting impression of strangeness."[41]

Artaud's writings reveal a desire to incorporate and arrange everything—performers, texts, lights, sounds, movements, and more. He was encouraged in this direction by critically favorable assessments of his directing, always more positive than the reviews given to the plays themselves.[42] An open letter to Artaud by the author Benjamin Fondane (who saw all the performances of the Jarry Theater) provides a clear articulation of how Artaud's ideal of integration could lead to a theatrical event envisioned, embodied, and manifested by one person. In his 1930 "Lettre ouverte à Antonin Artaud," Fondane (who rated Artaud's directing more highly than that of Jouvet, Baty, and Dullin) encouraged Artaud to take the next step in centralizing theatrical power: do away with texts entirely and create a piece wholly from the director's vision. "Here it is twenty years since Craig, Tairoff [a Russian director sympathetic with Craig's ideas, and] . . . Copeau created the modern miracle that is the director, the rediscovery of the theater, its only possible modern form, and for all that none of them has dared to deliberately *break* with the text."[43] Fondane saw in Artaud's stagings the possibility of a theater without texts, fully developed by the director. However good the plays were in the Jarry Theater productions, he writes, Artaud's direction exceeded them: "To realize a new theater, only you are called to create it" (89). His urgings that Artaud become the new artist of the theater rested on the idea that Artaud's mises-en-scène were more valuable than any plays, that the theater would necessarily succeed "[if] your décors, your lights, your costumes, your staging were the very material of the text, were the text itself."[44]

Fondane was articulating a route Artaud himself had been pursuing. In 1928, Artaud had proposed a "manifesto-play" for the Jarry Theater that would "demonstrat[e] every possible method of production" (*CW*, 2: 28). It would "synthesize all desires and all agony" (2: 28), springing from conception into integrated being with no intervening text. The realization of this would have revealed Artaud's worldview in pure theatrical form: "Everything which stems from the mind's . . . sensory illusions," Artaud proposes, "will be shown from an extraordinary angle, with the stench and excreta of unadulterated cruelty, just as they appear to the mind" (2: 26). (One wonders if Fondane, who admired the austere, transcendental beauty of Copeau and Craig greatly, would have admired Artaud's aesthetic in its full articulation.)

This is one dimension of directorial power: the control over the unfolding of a production, manifest in the decisive move away from playwright-based theater and in claiming the initial as well as final say over other artists. Artaud draws from previous directors in their strategies to unify the vision behind a piece, and he goes even further than his contemporaries by theorizing a performance springing entirely from the director's intuitions, insights, and ideas. The other dimension of directorial control that Artaud develops in an equally radical manner is that of developing new means of power over the audience.

The Direction of Menace

We have seen how the figure of the director arose at the same time as avant-garde and commercial theaters developed strategies to subdue unruly or inattentive audiences. Artaud manifested the most extreme extension of that discourse in both its practical and aesthetic dimensions, taking the one-way communication of the audience/director relationship to heights not matched before or after. Artaud's directing projects in the Jarry Theater reveal an aesthetics of domination, seen in his theoretical conception of the director's meta-theatrical superiority and influence over the spectators, as well as in his stagings.

A distinctive feature of Artaud's stagings was their shadowy invocation of menace, their ability to create an atmosphere of fear and impending violence in an animistic framework, where objects pointed to mysterious universal forces. The world of the Jarry Theater was characterized by an atmosphere of de Chirico–like eeriness punctuated by jarring props or set pieces that one reviewer called "objets violemment vrais"—"violently real" objects whose obtrusive materiality signified a powerful immaterial world at work.[45] The Jarry Theater was populated by puppets, masks, dummies, piercing sounds, and striking lighting effects. Governing rules included slow motion, violence, disproportion, and what Alain Virmaux has discussed in terms of *décalage*—a gap or lag, a temporal disruption between things.[46] *Décalage* is a useful term in analyzing Artaud's stagings, in which objects were positioned to create such a gap so that the universe's inhabitants might crawl between the material world and the frightening invisible one. The effect of his stagings was to create an atmosphere of "mystery," of the "irréel";[47] as one reviewer wrote, "The universe M[onsieur] Artaud succeeds in conjuring up is one where everything assumes a meaning, a secret, a soul."[48]

Artaud's directing developed strategies to push the pre-existing world aside in favor of a dangerous one known only in its contours, but to which he, the director, alone could lead us. In the Jarry Theater, Artaud realized what he later formulated in *The Theater and Its Double*: "*Mise en scène* properly speaking . . . must be regarded solely as the visible signs of an invisible or secret language" (*SW*, 160). Emphasizing the secrets they will unveil, his manifestos highlight the elect nature of those who can reveal them. His rhetoric emphasizes the unknowable and the mysterious in hierarchical terms akin to those of religious figures, political conspirators, leaders of cults or magic. "We are totally dedicated to unearthing certain secrets," he wrote, and the Jarry Theater's mises-en-scène would point to "the invisible" (SW, 160). Individuals would find truth in Artaud's theater by granting authority to the director, the seer of the invisible.

The Jarry Theater represents a medium through which higher "truths" can be attained: "We are creating a theater not in order to put on plays but so that all that is obscure, hidden, and unrevealed in the mind will be manifested in a kind of material, objective projection" (SW, 160). This echoes the spirituality in the rhetoric of Craig and Copeau, but Artaud's language of mystery and transcendence combines with that of physical violence in his calls for a total assault on the spectator. His director emerges as a ruthless holy man who commands the audience in the name of a "secret" goal, using the theater as a means to a revelation that operates beyond the bounds of the theater. The Jarry Theater writings and staging techniques put forward the idea that theater is an "event" (SW, 157) whose "terrible task" (161) is to return us to a devastating truth, a discovery that must be experienced through suffering. As is always the case in Artaud's work, the notion of revelation, the idea of total understanding brought about by a privileged seer, animates his writing, while the nature of these truths, mysteries, and revelations is only intimated.

A picture of the "truth" emerges, however, through recurrent characteristics of Artaud's mises-en-scène and manifestos, which theatrically manifest the vision later described in "The Theater and the Plague" of dark forces, invasion, and catastrophe. Unlike Craig, whose vision for theater culminated in beauty and harmony, or Barrault, who believed "only a boundless love of mankind" could, through its discovery of a "common heart," create a theater that "succors" (Brown, *Theater and Revolution*, 359), Artaud's vision for the Jarry Theater culminates in the audience perceiving a dark "fatality" (SW, 157) through threats, confusion, and mystification. His stagings evoke this through shadows, doubles, punishing lights and sounds, a world of fear and certain suffering, of—as he wrote of his staging of a Claudel piece—"disorder, anxiety, menace."[49] Artaud describes the process the spectator will undergo in excruciating terms. The spectator must feel a kind of "*human* anguish . . . as he leaves our theater. He will be shaken and antagonized by the internal dynamic of the spectacle that will unfold before his eyes" (SW, 157). The director envisioned for the Jarry Theater is a master of magical ceremonies, a leader to truth, but his ceremonies strive to lead spectators not to peace, beauty, or insight, but to a wracking revelation of the true awfulness of existence.

The attitude toward the spectator in the Jarry Theater is consistently expressed in terms of physical as well as psychological aggression. At the end of Vitrac's *Les mystères de l'amour* (*The Mysteries of Love*), which Artaud directed in 1926, a spectator was "shot" and "killed" at the end of the performance. The imagistic, metaphorical, and fictional aggression reflects an underlying attitude we have seen throughout his writings, enacted theatrically. Anaïs Nin, in her diary in 1933, put it simply and effectively: "The theater, for him [Artaud], is a place to shout pain, anger, hatred, to enact the violence in us. The most violent life can burst from terror and death" (*Diary*, 187).[50]

In an earlier work, "The Umbilicus of Limbo," Artaud had envisioned for writing what he now envisioned for directing; in both cases, the artwork serves as a means rather than an end: "I would like to write a Book which would drive men mad, which would be like an open door leading them where they would never have consented to go" (*SW*, 59). This calls to mind Mallarmé's project to write a "Book" that was an event, an experience of truth, synthesis, and completion. In contrast to Mallarmé's goals, however, Artaud did not seek to attain harmony, but to "drive men mad" with his work. In this, he draws closer to a goal articulated by Edgar Allan Poe that was eagerly taken up by the creators of the Grand Guignol, a theater genre specializing in horror thriving in certain circles in Paris in the 1920s and '30s. Poe wrote that he would like to create a work that would be so terrifying that people would run screaming from the theater the minute the curtain rose. André de Lorde, a writer of the Grand Guignol, agreed, except he said he wanted to make the audience so compelled by the horror that they wanted to *stay*. The Jarry Theater clearly connects to the Grand Guignol in the aesthetic of horror, and yet there is an element of playfulness, of entertainment value, of aesthetic boundaries, evident in Grand Guignol that is strikingly absent in Artaud's work.[51]

The clearest articulation of the theoretical, rhetorical, and strategic vision for the Jarry Theater event comes at the close of a 1926 brochure and is worth quoting at length for the vividness of its description of the performance's ideal relationship to the audience:

> With each performance we put on we are playing a serious game.
> . . . The whole point of our effort resides in this quality of seriousness. It is not to the minds or the senses of the spectators that we address ourselves but to their whole existence. Their existence and ours. We stake our lives on the spectacle that unfolds on the stage. If

we did not have the very clear and very profound sense that an intimate part of our lives was involved in that spectacle, we would see
no point in pursuing the experiment. The spectator who comes to
our theater knows that he is to undergo a real operation in which not
only his mind but his senses and his flesh are at stake. Henceforth he
will go to the theater the way he goes to the surgeon or the dentist. In
the same state of mind—knowing, of course, that he will not die, but
that it is a serious thing, and that he will not come out of it un-
scathed. If we were not convinced that we would reach him as
deeply as possible, we would consider ourselves inadequate to our
most absolute duty. He must be totally convinced that we are capable of making him scream. (*SW*, 156–57)

No matter how metaphorically one takes such passages (and note the passage insists on *not* being taken metaphorically), we must be alive to the
aggressive power dynamic screamingly evident in the imagery. The Jarry
Theater frames the spectators as surgery patients and the director as the
person performing this operation. The manifesto stresses the "serious-
ness" of the event, the fact that the performers "stake [their] lives on the
spectacle" and the audience members must entrust their "whole existence" to the performance as they would to a surgeon. Formulations such
as "the spectator knows that his . . . senses and his flesh are at stake" recur
throughout the Jarry Theater manifestos, pointing to the violent, one-way
directionality of the event. They create a sweeping sense that the director
of the event holds the power to reveal hidden truths through the suffering
he inflicts.

A sadistic quality pervades this passage and many others. "He must
be totally convinced that we are capable of making him scream"—this
line ends the essay, focusing on the event of pain and its administration,
not on its outcome. Availing itself of the menacing apparition of a dentist
and an incapacitated patient, the manifesto establishes a power dynamic
in which the reasons for the "real operation" are only known to one party.
It is easy to pursue the idea of sadism in the manifesto: the sadist per-
forms superiority on weaker beings in order to see his power. The direc-
tor/audience relationship of Artaud's ideal theater proposes just this: not
a cure, but an enactment of power.

Artaud's mises-en-scène dramatized menace with remarkable theatrical effectiveness. All the Jarry Theater projects deal in dissonances and
denatured objects, in elements hugely disproportioned, such as enormous
dummies, oversized set pieces, and blinding lights. Dissonant elements

open the space for the unknown, but, unlike the surrealist vision of using juxtapositions to reveal *le merveilleux*, Artaud uses them to reveal *la menace*. In his production plan for Strindberg's *Ghost Sonata*, the frightening character of the cook, who, as one character says, "won't go [away]! No one has any control over her!" is played "by a dummy, her lines being delivered by a monstrous, monotonous voice amplified by several loudspeakers so no one can tell its exact source."[52] This kind of sonic *démesure*—a term Virmaux employs to describe Artaud's disproportioned props and dissonant and distorted effects—disorients the audience, manipulating it into an atmosphere of uncertainty.[53] In the same production plan, an old man's crutches "knoc[k] rhythmically" as he calls to a group of beggars; their cries merge with the tap of his crutches, both of which "are punctuated towards the end by a bizarre sound, as if a monstrous tongue were violently slapping against the teeth."[54] The Jarry Theater sound elements—radically out of proportion to their ostensible causes—disrupt the present reality to evoke a menacing, deformed parallel one. While such extremes of scale were also employed in some of the highly stylized productions of the Cartel, Virmaux notes that, in contrast to their goals, Jarry Theater stagings seek in their creation of "disequilibrium and dissonances" to "deprive the spectator of his/her habitual refuges."[55]

The use of mannequins and dummies contributes to Artaud's theatrical atmosphere of deformation, disproportion, and a threatening hidden truth. Dummies haunt the Jarry Theater productions, allowing for the irruption of the fantastic, to create the *décalage* between living actor and mannequin, between moving flesh and immobile object.[56] The disconcerting doubles in Artaud's *Ghost Sonata* production plan, which mysteriously appear next to each character and then slowly disappear, create a world of creeping, menacing objects alongside feeble living things that ideally will invade the viewer's reality.

A dummy is a physical and theatrical representation of the hidden world, as Artaud sees it, and the nature of Artaud's dummies—always hypertrophied, temporally dissonant, accompanied by either disturbing silence or horrible, ear-splitting noise, disfigured—gives us an idea of the composition of that hidden reality. Artaud employed a variety of artificial extensions or replacements of the human in his work. In *No More Firmament*, once the sky has fallen and thrown the world into the disarray of perpetual night, dark creatures ascend to earth. They reveal the evil that has been lurking underneath:

> Hideously deformed creatures steal on, oozing on at first, as if breathed up out of the lower depths. Yellow, green, cadaverous, over-large or over-long faces appear scattered, then suddenly the stage is full of them. (*CW*, 2: 87)

The faces of the creatures "grow larger and larger," representing vice, sickness, and menace in the "gross artificial features" of their masks and prosthetic limbs (*CW*, 2: 88). Such devices give us the dark parallel to visible life. Oozing from the depths, these creatures manifest Artaud's ideal articulated shortly afterward that the theater, like the plague, "is the revelation, the bringing forth, the exteriorization of a depth of latent cruelty by means of which all the perverse possibilities of the mind, whether of an individual or a people, are localized" (*TD*, 30).

Artaud's production of Vitrac's *Victor; ou, le pouvoir aux enfants* (*Victor, or, Power to the Children*), a play rife with both physical and metaphysical violence, concentrates these dissonant elements in the figure of a nine-year-old boy.[57] Victor is a child whose physical *démesure*—he is six feet tall and growing fast—matches his mental state. He is a divided being: materially grotesque, he physically embodies the ugly realities of life; mentally, he has an intellectual awareness of the world that disgusts him. He manifests the discord between flesh and spirit, disliking the universe as he incarnates it. The child, unable to live in the world as it is, dies on his ninth birthday. This boy is an incongruous being, physically disjointed and manifestly superior because of his embodiment of the perverse nature of his universe. The play represented for Artaud an opportunity to dramatize an apocalypse in a degraded domestic world. Oversized props, empty picture frames, and cacophonic sounds comprised his staging for this piece, which he described as a play with "a terrible desire to be truthful, a spotlight trained on the foulest lower depths of man's unconscious."[58] Artaud's mise-en-scène for *Victor* attempted to bring his catastrophic vision into immediate being, to "shak[e] and antagoniz[e]" the spectator through the vision he manifests.

Jarry Theater productions and scenarios brim with violence, and puppets and mannequins enable the execution of this violence on doubles of the human body. *La pierre philosophale* (*The Philosopher's Stone*), an unproduced 1931 scenario, stages a nightmare version of a *commedia dell' arte* story line with the aid of dolls and artificial limbs. The mad Doctor Pale is discovered "in the midst of a veritable massacre of dummies," hacking mannequins to pieces in a furious search for the philosopher's stone (*CW*, 2: 74). A two-sided harlequin offering his body up for the search presents a grotesque hunchbacked shape to the doctor and a suave young appearance to the doctor's wife, Isabella.[59] Doctor Pale dismembers him with an axe, hacking off all his arms and legs.[60] The gruesome torso manages to make its way to the wife, and they engage in violent sex, immediately producing a kind of baby/homunculus/puppet identical to Doctor Pale. Monstrous and artificial replicas of humans present the hideous double of visible reality, enabling the spectators to witness the degradation of their likenesses.

Artaud returns repeatedly to slow motion in his staging ideas, a tempo stretched so far that it becomes punishing. In his 1925 *Le jet du sang* (*Jet of Blood*), for one example, stage directions call for objects—including human flesh, heads of hair, scorpions, and a scarab—to fall with "a dispiriting, a vomit-inducing slowness."[61] Events that unfold in Artaud's theatrical world at this excruciatingly slow speed, keep, as Artaud envisions for the production of *Victor*, a "spotlight trained on the foulest lower depths of man's unconscious" (*CW*, 2: 65). Since everything on stage is intended to disturb the audience, slow motion would force spectators to engage the violent events on stage as fully as possible, as if submitting them to an endurance test of the mind and body. It also represents a temporal *décalage*, another means of creating the dissonances that will reveal the dark double of what is visible on stage. In his production plan for *Le songe*, a "slow-motion effect" allows characters and their doubles to "arrive on stage without anyone having noticed it" (*CW*, 2: 104). This production plan aimed to break down the dividing line between material being and its double by using dummies, temporal disruptions, and sonic *démesure*.

In its theatrical context, then, the Jarry Theater demonstrates Artaud's move toward artistic consolidation that was occurring around him. In his writings and practice, Artaud extended the move toward control over the elements of the performance through the notion of the director as an author/creator with a unifying vision, his use of production plans, and his further extension, with scenarios, of the move away from text. In his stagings and manifestos, he conceptualized extreme control over the audience, with a distinct emphasis on menace and a one-directional affect realized by the director. All of this unfolds in the language of the seer, controller, privileged one, the one who can reveal universal truths—truths that reflect the dark worldview that permeates Artaud's writing.

Alain Virmaux concludes a brief discussion of points of theatrical similarities between Artaud and the Cartel by pointing out that there is one "untraversable frontier that separates Artaud from *all* the great directors of his time."[62] That frontier is made clear by comparing a 1921 announcement for Baty's theatrical enterprise, "Les Compagnons de la Chimère" (The Companions of the Chimera) and an announcement for the Jarry Theater in 1928. The former declares: "La Chimère ne se sert pas de l'art; elle le sert" (The Chimère does not serve itself to art; it serves it). Artaud precisely inverts Baty's mission statement, declaring, "Le Théâtre Alfred Jarry a été créé pour se servir du théâtre et non pour le servir" (*OC*, 2: 29) (The Jarry Theater was created to serve itself to the theater and not to serve it). The irreconcilable difference between the two is, then, what their enterprise's final goal really is. Unlike the Chimère, the Jarry Theater is "[pas] un but, mais un moyen" (*OC*, 2: 26) (not an end but a means). Artaud wanted to push the theater out of theatrical boundaries altogether. As Artaud wrote to Jean Paulhan in 1928, "The Jarry Theatre has nothing to do with the theatre" (*CW*, 3: 111).

Even if he emphatically theorized them as "real," Artaud's ideas were, at this stage, still attempting to take form theatrically, and in a theater building. But his frustration with the restrictions of the event being considered simply "art" was violently evident. Artaud repeatedly organized disruptions of his own productions at the Jarry Theater, taking the stage in order to try to antagonize the audience on a "real" level, even though these disruptions—such as insulting the author (as he did Claudel) or the audience (as he did Swedish patrons at his Strindberg production)—always detracted from the goals of the piece he was staging.[63] His stagings aimed to immerse; his disruptions did the opposite. Artaud held two ideals during the Jarry Theater, both ideals of power: one, to create a whole world that would immerse the spectators; and, two, to physically antagonize and agitate them. Artaud attempted to be a provocateur and a total theater artist at the same time in the Jarry Theater. Such an ideal—the antagonistic-immersive—would only have succeeded if the two goals were not placed at odds with each other, but substantively combined. Artaud's later push out of the theater building and into the mythical, essentialist, "total" theater event envisioned in *The Theater and Its Double* attempted to achieve this combination more fully.

Artaud had studied at Dullin's Atelier in the 1920s, and he was familiar with the prevalent tendency among French theater directors such as Dullin, Baty, and Copeau to form schools, creating ensembles of actors whose combined energies determined much of the productions' distinctive character. However, Jarry Theater manifestos do not articulate an interest in pursuing a creative ensemble—instead, they promote the authority of the director. It is worth briefly noting in this context Artaud's actual process of directing to see how he carried out his ideals as a director in rehearsals. Although Artaud's writings expressed the fantasy of one figure creating and controlling everything in the performance event from the conception to the implementation, the Jarry Theater performers and designers testified to the freely creative atmosphere in his rehearsals.[64] The evidence demonstrates that during the Jarry Theater project, people worked enthusiastically toward Artaud's goals, citing Artaud's compelling presence ("his contact was stimulating," remembers one actress).[65] The act of material collaboration seemed to keep Artaud's ideas in contact with others.

After the collapse of the Jarry Theater, however, Artaud's writing reveals an intensification of the belief that he, alone, as director, or artist of the theater, needed complete control over the event, that nothing could be left to the whims or initiative of either the performers or the audience. Following his next and last theatrical production, *The Cenci,* he wrote to Barrault in 1935, "I do not believe in collaboration" (*SW,* 343). Once separated from actual production, his theorizations about the director developed more and more mystical and absolutist aspects—describing the director in terms such as "Creator" (his capital) (*TD,* 94), "demiurge" (114), and "master of sacred ceremonies" (60)—that combined the extremes of control over production and audience. The next chapter examines the disastrous effects of this attempt to control everything as it played out in the production of *The Cenci* and charts how Artaud's ideas about the director moved even further away from the theater. The Theater of Cruelty—as we will see as we tie together its vision of spectators as crowd members and the director as leader—is, at its core, not so much a work of art, but an exercise of power.

CHAPTER 7 : Controlling Forces

Michel Foucault invokes Artaud in *Madness and Civilization* as a visionary artist whose "courage" in the face of his "ordeal," as Foucault frames it, represents a personal and poetic protest against the absence of a coherent reality and the inability to create. Coming as it does near the end of his study of the institutionalization of the insane, Foucault's passage on Artaud's words "hurled" against the "void"—"all that space of physical suffering and terror" (287)—also suggests a social and political protest against the way the insane have been restricted, pathologized, and institutionalized. But Artaud's work is not just a protest; it is also a program. If Artaud's "ordeal" expresses a horror of authority, it is not because he wants to eliminate power, but because he wants to wield it. As if in an attempt to counteract the chaos and powerlessness that Foucault describes, Artaud constructs his own kind of limiting structure—the Theater of Cruelty—that aims to shape and control.

The Theater and Its Double proposes a theatrical experience in which the performance "imposes" (28) itself upon its spectators. The terms Artaud uses to describe the goals of the new theatrical event reinforce this in every essay. The Theater of Cruelty aims to "fascinate and ensnare," "arrest," "benumb" (91), "hypnotize" (83), and "immerse" (125). It works toward a "genuine enslavement" (92), a "magnetism" (91). It is "hallucinatory" (121), "spellbinding" (91); it will "impel" (31), "engulf" (96), "attack" (86), and "crush" (83). It seeks to know, as an acupuncturist, "at what points to puncture in order to regulate the subtlest functions" (*TD*, 80). It wants to "enchain" the spectator, and to do so, the production must know *"where to take hold of him"* (*TD*, 140). These terms and images are not synonyms, but they point toward the same fundamental conception of the performance as a one-directional event, a system of control and coercion. The Theater of Cruelty would be the realization of an apparatus that would make people experience the vision of the world its creator had. Enacted in the space of his imagination or on the stage, Artaud's ideal theater represents the convergence of the pathological and the political in a single vision of power.

This is not the place to delve into Artaud's madness or his personality—as porous as the boundaries become when speaking about him as a director—but to examine *The Theater and Its Double*'s ideas about the controlling figure of power. We do this first through a discussion of Artaud's directing practice. Second, through crowd theory, we see the political implications of such a discourse that, in 1930s Western Europe, was promoting itself as "beyond" politics. Artaud employs the most autocratic language articulated by early directors and goes even further: his discourse finally moves outside of "art" altogether. As we have seen, the double of Artaud's audience is the crowd. This chapter uncovers the double of his director: the demagogic crowd leader.

While Artaud's rhetoric unfolds within the context of a theatrical event, examining its underlying gesture brings us to an understanding of the impulse propelling that event. This chapter demonstrates how Artaud's staging goals for *The Cenci* and his description of the function of the director in *The Theater and Its Double* parallel a discourse on leaders and crowds with specific echoes in the interwar era. What Artaud calls for with the Theater of Cruelty is the re-creation of the dark maelstrom that the director sees as the truth of life, enacted on the bodies of others. The Theater of Cruelty is, at its heart, an exercise of power.

Directing *The Cenci*

Artaud's writings, particularly those of the 1930s, are marked by their preoccupation with sanguinary figures of power.[1] In 1931, Artaud adapted Matthew Lewis's novel *The Monk*, the story of a depraved man of the cloth who satisfies his brutal desires on the bodies of others with literally satanic force.[2] *Heliogabalus*, Artaud's 1934 fantastic account of the ruthless Roman emperor, overflows with extravagant descriptions of sexual debauchery, political manipulation, and grisly murders. And in 1935, under the aegis of the Theater of Cruelty, Artaud produced his adaptation of *The Cenci*, in which he himself played the lead character of Count Cenci, a historical figure notorious for terrorizing his family, defying the pope, and considering himself above any law: "I believe myself to be and I am a force of nature. For me, there is neither life, nor death, nor god, nor incest, nor repentance, nor crime. I obey my own law."[3]

This exaltation of tyrannical, merciless power is repeated in Artaud's rhetoric on directing. "Cruelty . . . means doing everything the director can to the sensibilities of actor and spectator," Artaud stated in an interview before the premiere of *The Cenci*.[4] He publicized the production in interviews, pamphlets, and essays using a wide range of aggressively autocratic language: the event would overpower, immerse, hypnotize, compel; it would make spectators submit, bring them to their mercy, and plunge them into a bath of fire.[5] The production also attempted to employ many of the staging ideas developed in the Jarry Theater to facilitate an eruption of a menacing, hidden reality. By analyzing the staging of *The Cenci* in conjunction with the intentions and structuring notions behind it, we can bring into clearer focus the conception of the director's role as it developed in Artaud's work. Although Artaud did not write as often and as explicitly about the *metteur en scène* as he did about the concrete theatrical language the Theater of Cruelty would create, the conception of such a figure underlies the entire event. And, as we will see, the concrete language Artaud envisions *itself* gives power to the director, reinforcing his singular importance.

The only show produced under the name of the Theater of Cruelty was *The Cenci*, which opened on 6 May 1935. The production marked the first and only time in Artaud's career that he had comprehensive control of a theater production, that he could attempt to create a piece wholly from his own, undivided vision. Artaud was the author, director, and lead actor of the piece; he was its main publicist and producer; he had a strong voice in the sound design; and he did the lights.[6] Artaud was writing the manifestos for the Theater of Cruelty (which were eventually published in *The Theater and Its Double*) as he was planning *The Cenci*. Some of these manifestos were published contemporaneously (approximately 1931–35) in *La nouvelle revue française,* in the hopes (harbored by Artaud) of garnering enough support to establish a full-time theater. The threads of Artaud's thought we have been following come together in the ideas for this production: a revelation of dark forces, heroic attitudes, myth and destiny, unreason, fear and menace, catastrophe, universal correspondences, and the dynamic of one singular figure who wields total and precise control over a group of people. Far from being an embodiment of the Theater of Cruelty, however, or the beginning of a theater venture, the production was an aesthetic failure and a financial "catastrophe" that had to close after a mere seventeen performances.[7] A series of serious miscalculations led to this failure, including the casting of wealthy and connected but unsuitable actors in lead roles and the use of the Folies-Wagram operetta theater.[8] The utter unsuitability of the Folies-Wagram illustrates the failure of the production's goals vividly and succinctly: Artaud's vision of immersion, menace, and revelation was cramped onto a decorated proscenium stage, where, from the comfort of ample gallery seats, the *beau monde* audience viewed the performance as a distant and unthreatening work of "art."

These well-documented miscalculations, as interesting and instructive as they are, however, are not the focus of this analysis of the production.[9] We will look at only two, undiscussed missteps, for the light they shed on underlying conceptions of power: the dramatic adaptation and Artaud's attempt to control everything himself. The rest of our discussion of the production focuses on the way Artaud's "ambition totalitaire" of a performance event tried to manifest itself; how his theatrical ideas, even though they did not succeed in this instance, stemmed from a desire to enact his vision on the bodies of the spectators.[10]

Artaud's *Cenci* is an adaptation of a verse play by Shelley and a prose chronicle by Stendhal. It draws almost the entirety of its plot, structure, and dialogue from Shelley's play, resulting in a fairly conventional linear narrative drama.[11] Artaud's most significant alteration is a dramatic shift in thematic and character emphasis. Other treatments of the story tend to focus on the figure of Beatrice Cenci, the outraged daughter forced to choose between succumbing to incest and committing parricide. Choosing the latter, she dies a brutal death at the hands of the corrupt authorities, an execution that confers on her a legendary moral purity. Artaud minimizes the investigation into Beatrice's character and principles by eliminating most scenes after she murders her father (which dramatize her reaction to the act, the investigation, and her trial). In the process, he shifts more of the drama to Count Cenci, who dominates many of the early scenes. While other authors had dismissed the count as too one-dimensionally evil to be dramatically interesting, Artaud attempted to highlight and embody the fatality and dark energies he saw the character as representing.

The Cenci employs the dramatic strategies examined in chapter 4: it elevates forces over people, operates in the realm of "Myth," exalts heroic figures and cataclysmic events, and aims for a sensorially immersive experience. By eliminating almost every monologue (the outstanding feature of Shelley's drama), Artaud rids the piece of its individual, psychological elements—what he calls, in a letter to André Gide explaining his choices before the production, "nuances humaines" (*OC*, 5: 178):

> By remaining in the realm of pure ideas, I have not taken into consideration at all a mass of human nuances that would only constrict me and paralyze all action. . . .These human nuances . . . generally paralyze action and prevent men from doing anything or even attempting anything. (*TDR* 16, 92)

The "pure ideas" the piece conveys are those of domination; specifically, of one dominating presence—a "destroyer," as Artaud describes Count Cenci (*TDR* 16, 104)—who exercises his will on others. Count Cenci is not a dramatic character who wants things in recognizably human ways. Like the characters in Artaud's scenario *The Conquest of Mexico*, Count Cenci is envisioned as a "force" as opposed to an individual character. He exists, in Artaud's interpretation, solely to channel the dark forces of life: "I can't resist the forces that burn to burst out of me."[12] This characterization reflects a desire to create an anti-hero, Wagnerian in scope, who takes us out of discrete human individuality and historical fact and into the more nebulous realm of the unified dark energies that drive life itself. Artaud writes of *The Cenci:* "I have tried to make beings speak instead of men; beings, each of whom are like great forces incarnate" (*TDR* 16, 104). People, in this view, are not historically situated individuals, but vessels for essences.

With *The Cenci*, we are again in the realm of "the Great Myths" (*TDR* 16, 104). And, as Artaud writes in "The Theater and the Plague," "All the great Myths are dark," because life itself is dark (*TD*, 31). So dark, in fact, that at the end of *The Cenci*, where Beatrice is customarily shown radiating purity, nobility, and righteousness, she is, in Artaud's version, led off stage with the insinuation that she, too, has become a vessel for the dark forces, fearing that "I have ended by resembling him."[13] She is no longer the virtuous heroine of the melodramas to which the play at times seems akin, nor the classic Antigone-like heroine that other versions of the story promote. She is more a character from a Jacobean tragedy, a vessel of pollution in a rotten world; more like the character of the same name—Beatrice—from Middleton and Rowley's *The Changeling*, shown to be depraved through the act of attempting to live in life.

By stripping the play down to one destructive current, Artaud attempted to affect the audience with the power of the drama's violence, bypassing reason and nuance with "energies." Artaud wrote to the director Louis Jouvet before the play (in an attempt to secure a theater for the production): "Count on arousing the masses by energies, by pure forces, with which this play has been proven to be abundantly provided, and don't count on reasonable calculations anymore" (*TDR* 16, 95). Jouvet had read the play and apparently expressed some hesitations about its clarity. Artaud wrote back, emphasizing the sense of catastrophe required by the script: "There is no longer time to retrench behind a reproach of insufficient clarity with a text like this one where it is only the dynamism that counts and exists above all" (*TDR* 16, 94). The state of crisis in which Artaud sees the world leaves no time for the luxuries of "reasonable calculations" or clarity. Movement, energy, is all that's necessary.

Dramatically, Jouvet's hesitations were warranted. Artaud excised the poetic, human, and rational elements from the drama to find its "dynamism," because he believed the play's power was distinct from its actual writing. As he had written in an earlier essay, Artaud strove to stage "the spirit of the text, not the letter!" (*SW*, 53). But the uniformly negative critical reactions to the text point to a fatal dramaturgical miscalculation.[14] The Shelley play could not withstand such a cut. The impact of Shelley's drama resided in the very development of its "nuances humaines" and in its poetic language: its writing, its craft, gave it its power. As we have seen, Artaud, to an extraordinary degree, reads *through* works to his own preoccupations: this was the case with his reading of Shelley's *The Cenci*, and a reason why the resulting text could not convey any of Artaud's theatrical gifts. For the premiere of the Theater of Cruelty, it would have been more theatrically effective for Artaud to have developed one of his own scenarios, a piece that he devised in rehearsal—a goal Artaud had articulated and was working toward in the Jarry Theater. A scenario would certainly have freed him from some of the limitations imposed by having a text, and Artaud was a more accomplished scenarist and director than playwright. Even then, however, such an approach had more chance of success when Artaud worked with other artists.

The period of writing the essays for *The Theater and Its Double,* including the Cruelty manifestos, and the efforts Artaud put into adapting, directing, designing, and acting in *The Cenci* constitute a very different creative framework than that of the Jarry Theater. This was a phase of Artaud becoming more isolated from the milieu of ensembles and schools around him (such as Dullin's Atelier and Baty's Les Compagnons de la Chimère) and group activities. In this period, Artaud's ideas were no longer tempered by collaboration with others. He attempted to give concrete shape to his fantasies of power and its enactment on others, with disastrous effects. What is revealed in Artaud's theater work of the 1930s is the corrosive influence of his own ideas on his practice. The more he was left to his own devices, the more he unilaterally followed his own impulses, the worse his work became. One reviewer of *The Cenci* observed (as did others) that it was a "mistake" for Artaud to act the lead, in a comment that elucidates the pitfalls of the entire undertaking quite effectively: "He abandoned himself to his interior demon too much, he was not moderated and restrained by the activities of a stranger" (*TDR* 16, 133). The visionary possibilities that seemed promising in his work with the Jarry Theater turned into something else when combined with unrestrained authority during the production process.

Actors did not respond enthusiastically to working with Artaud as director of *The Cenci* as they had in the Jarry Theater. For one illustration, his lead, Iya Abdy, after having rehearsed her final scene with her hair tied to a wheel suspended from the ceiling, insisted that the wheel be moved to the floor, even though this made little sense for the depiction of torture. She feared Artaud was going to overturn the stool on which she stood on opening night "so that her expression would become more true, more striking."[15] Whether or not her fears were justified, the anecdote reveals the very different directorial effect Artaud had on his actors at the time.

This anecdote—one of several such from the production—is here not so much to tell us about a personality as to illustrate a director's modus operandi in the theater.[16] These are difficult to separate: because the concrete materials with which a director works are other people (and objects created and controlled by other people), whose contributions unfold in meetings and rehearsals, the art of directing includes one's methods of interaction, one's interest in the creative work of others, and one's sense of hierarchy. Contemporaneous directors ranged from being very actor-centered to more authoritarian in their directing, but most of the directors around Artaud, notably Copeau, Dullin, and Barrault, saw a reformation of the performer as essential to the new direction of theater. Artaud, having been a member of Dullin's Atelier, had been trained in an ensemble/acting school environment in which the actors were put front and center. The Atelier focused on the performers' development first of all, and the ensemble was so closely knit that others acted with them with difficulty, and they were likewise at their best when performing with each other. Artaud's directing practice reflects how his theorizations of the role of the director moved away from the ensemble and toward a one-person hierarchy.[17]

It is revealing in this regard to note the importance Artaud placed on being the sole creator of the piece. It can be seen in the way he used his assistant, Roger Blin. Blin was to transcribe his directing in every manner possible: "Make a note of everything I say," Artaud instructed him: "Make notes on everything I say, make *careful* notes on what I say and even on what I *don't* say. You must act as a medium and be able to perceive what I think and what I'm going to say."[18] Artaud wanted to elevate the documentation of his work beyond production plan, blocking notes, or rehearsal record, into a transcription of divination. The result was a highly detailed record of the precision and specificity of Artaud's staging. Scene one of Act III alone was divided into seventy-six movements. Each scene and each movement were precisely delineated by Blin in color-coded pencils, including the gestures, steps, attitudes, and tempos of the characters; the length of crosses pinpointed down to seconds; the directions the characters faced, and so on. This corresponds to Artaud's desire articulated in the first Cruelty manifesto: "New means of recording this language [of the stage] must be found, whether these means belong to musical transcription or to some kind of code" (*TD*, 94). Inspiration, he writes in *The Theater and Its Double*, can be found in "hieroglyphic characters, not only in order to record these signs in a readable fashion which permits them to be reproduced at will, but in order to compose on the stage precise and immediately readable symbols" (*TD*, 94).

Outside of some acknowledgment (both positive and negative) of the innovative staging and sound design (more on these later), the reviewers of *The Cenci* were largely unanimous in their response: the text was awful, the acting incomprehensible, and the production as a whole disastrously ineffectual. Colette wrote in her review of the production, "*Les Cenci* of Artaud drive a train from hell that does not affect us" (*TDR* 16, 134.) Although this was just a few years after the artistic promise shown in the Jarry Theater productions, little of that skill was still in evidence. The one thing one could take from the performance was the tremendous force of will of its creator. Colette went on:

> The worst actor, Artaud, is not the least interesting. Hoarse, dark-haired, angular, agitated, hacking his text that cannot take it, he is intolerable and we tolerate him. It is because his insight is that of faith.[19]

The sheer force of Artaud's personality carried all the fascination, exuding urgency, faith, catastrophe, and will in his portrayal of the depraved count. We go along with him, reviewers reveal, because of the intensity with which he conveys to us that there is a crisis. *Paris-Soir* recorded:

> M. Artaud is a deplorable actor. And yet, with absurd violence, his eyes bewildered and his passion scarcely pretended, he carries us with him beyond good and bad into a desert where the thirst for blood parches us. (*TDR* 16, 133)

Artaud's intensity, "scarcely pretended," was the compelling event of the performance, moving us beyond artistic judgments, "beyond good and bad."

The miscalculations of Artaud's adaptation and his desire for comprehensive creative control (including the acting) notwithstanding, *The Cenci* production reveals much about what the Theater of Cruelty aspired to do to its audiences, especially in its implementations of Artaud's theatrical strategies and theories. In the essay "Le théâtre de séraphin" (1936), originally intended for inclusion in *The Theater and Its Double,* Artaud describes a dream he had of a scream, a scream so forceful that it called forth lost secrets. He writes of the need to give life to this scream through the theater, "to make it pass not into the ear but into the chest of the spectator" (*SW*, 275). While dreaming, he writes, his inner consciousness directs this scream, but the theater would be "one long waking state in which it is I who direct the fatality" (*SW*, 275). The idea of the director/visionary penetrating the spectator with his divinatory scream recurs throughout *The Theater and Its Double,* in part through its emphasis on the necessary power of sound and other physical effects. The idea also finds an articulation in Artaud's staging ideas for *The Cenci.*

The production attempted to engineer the manifestation of lost secrets and energies through its dynamic blocking and innovative special effects. Artaud had already experimented with some of these staging strategies in the Jarry Theater, such as slow motion, dummies, and a novel use of sound and lights.[20] Conceived around the image of a whirlwind or vortex, the blocking aspired to the vertiginous via the use of choreographed, constantly moving spirals. Large, orchestrated groups circled around smaller groups in whirlpools of movement. Artaud also wanted to implement ideas he was writing about concerning the visceral effect the piece could produce on the audience through sound and light.

The sounds from the *Cenci* production were a haunting series of knocks, creaks, voices, shouts, whispers, tolling bells, mechanical noises, winds, and thunder.[21] The effects were produced by flutes, anvils, screws, metal files, percussive instruments, amplified metronomes and echoing footsteps, and the first theatrical use of a Martenot—an early electronic instrument close in sound to the theremin, producing eerie, wavy tones, which Artaud employed for its "hypnotic effect."[22] The score is striking for the menacing yet desolate atmosphere it creates—somewhere between *musique concrète* and haunted house. A recording of these sounds is one of the few remaining traces—outside of reviews and interviews—of the special effects that preoccupied Artaud as a director. On tape, it all has a haunted quality, an echo, a sense of distance—the bells are far off, the tempest is elsewhere.

To read Artaud's goals behind the sound design gives us another view. "I believe in the necessity of using physical means to bring the spectator to submission," Artaud wrote in an interview before the play (*TDR* 16, 97). Artaud worked with sound designer Roger Désormière to surround the audience with sound. He lamented not being able to use real cathedral bells for the tolling effect, which, he wrote, would have "enveloped the spectator and brought him to our mercy in a network of vibrations" (*TDR* 16, 97).[23] However, the production did employ a recording of the Amiens cathedral bells that assaulted the audience with their tolling at earsplitting volume.[24] The effect was made possible by the placement of four speakers in each corner of the auditorium in what was perhaps the first use of surround sound in the theater.[25]

These effects draw directly from Artaud's ideas in his Cruelty manifestos. *The Theater and Its Double* discusses the need for technical innovation to create a theatrical use of sounds and lights with penetrating qualities. Sound needs "to act directly and profoundly upon the sensibility through the organs," requiring "research . . . into instruments and appliances which, based upon special combinations or new alloys of metal, can attain a new range and compass, producing sounds or noises that are unbearably piercing" (*TD*, 95). New lighting methods, also, would be developed to "sprea[d] the light in waves, in sheets, in fusillades of fiery arrows," to achieve "the particular action of light upon the mind," to directly "produc[e] the sensations of heat, cold, anger, fear, etc" (*TD*, 95). For *The Cenci*, Artaud wrote that he wanted to experiment with light because "I think it is certainly capable of direct activity on the spectators' nerves" (*TDR* 16, 107). The Theater of Cruelty attempts to work directly on the body of the spectator. Its aim is an event in which to speak of "the direct and immediate influence of the action on the spectator will not be hollow words" (*TD*, 97). In *The Theater and Its Double*, Artaud calls for advanced technologies in pursuit of engaging primal sensations. The modern enabled the archaic: in another instance of the modern atavism theorized throughout his theatrical ideals, Artaud employed, in *The Cenci*, "noises that would be at home in a medieval torture chamber."[26]

We have already seen how Artaud envisions the spectator: as a victim (of an operation or attack), as a mesmerized or charmed subject, as a body that must be assaulted by all available means. He writes of *The Cenci*: "Through my play I . . . want the public to be plunged into a bath of fire, moved by the action and encircled by the spectacular and dynamic movement of the work."[27] The Theater of Cruelty advocates bypassing dramatic devices entirely in favor of spectacular ones in order to work on spectators' bodies, using lights and sounds as instruments: "In our present state of degeneration it is through the skin that metaphysics must be made to re-enter our minds [*les esprits*]" (*TD*, 99). To achieve this, *The Theater and Its Double* proposes changing the stage space so that the spectators are "engulfed" by the spectacle that happens "all around them" (96), enabling an inescapable onslaught of stage effects that the "spectator will undergo" (97). Elevating the role of the mise-en-scène and focusing on violent physical effects enable the director to mentally immobilize the audience and agitate its emotions. While he did not achieve it in this production—with the stage so far away from the spectators and the inability to physically surround and engage, the theater event remained very much an artistic performance for an "audience"—his writing about it gives us a clearer view of how Artaud's staging ideas revolve around how he will control and affect the spectators. This allows us to return to *The Theater and Its Double* and see how its staging ideas illuminate Artaud's theory of directorial control.

Concentrating Control

Theoretically, Artaud's belief that the director needed to have complete authority had been prepared for in his previous writings on the theater. His 1924 call to eliminate "subservience to the author, dependence on the text" (*SW*, 53), led to giving complete control to the director. One of *The Theater and Its Double*'s most influential ideas was the creation of a "pure theatrical language" (69) that would replace the authority of text and the theatrical preponderance of rational, spoken language with intuitive and physical directness. The Theater of Cruelty emphasizes, as did the Jarry Theater, the mise-en-scène as "the point of departure for all theatrical creation" (*TD*, 94). This elevation of the mise-en-scène represents several things: the triumph of the director over other artists; the move beyond text and the intellectuality it represents; and, consequently, the rise in importance of viscerally affective staging devices. The creation of a purely physical language replaces the author/director duality with "a sort of unique Creator upon whom will devolve the double responsibility of the spectacle and the plot" (94). Its unfolding on stage necessitates granting the *metteur en scène* comprehensive authority: "And this immediate and physical language is entirely at the director's disposal. This is the occasion for him to create in complete autonomy" (119).

To achieve an extreme version of the displacement of textual authority that other directors had advocated in more moderate terms, *The Theater and Its Double* outlines a theatrical language composed of rhythm, movement, sound, light, and music that would make the "discursive, logical aspect of speech disappear beneath its affective, physical side" (119). Artaud attributes what he sees as the superiority of the Balinese theater to the director's ability to create a purely theatrical language: "They victoriously demonstrate the absolute preponderance of the director (*metteur en scène*) whose creative power *eliminates words*" (53–54). His attribution is not accurate—the specificity of the Balinese theater's staging derives from tradition and the performer's craft, not from a director (in fact, there is no director at all to speak of in most Balinese theater)—but it is revealing that Artaud interprets the authority this way. The Theater of Cruelty envisions the director, with his access to higher truths and his ability to perceive hermetic laws, constructing such a language. The spectacle using these methods will produce its effects via "a technique which must not be divulged" (87), that the director controls.

The Theater and Its Double's fight for the disappearance of text and discursiveness replaces literary with spectacular authority, substituting one kind of language with another. The essay "On the Balinese Theater" interprets the Balinese actors' gestures, rhythms, costumes, and sounds as "animated hieroglyphs" (*TD*, 54); in other words, a complex code of mystical symbols. The reaction against "language" repeated throughout *The Theater and Its Double* is, very pointedly, a reaction against *literature,* not against all language. *The Theater and Its Double* promotes a rhythmic and concrete language that will ultimately be as codified as the literary one. "Everything is thus regulated and impersonal," Artaud writes admiringly of the Balinese performers' movements (58). In contrast to the traditions of Western theater, all of the Balinese gestures, as he interprets them, "seem to belong to a kind of reflective mathematics which controls everything and by means of which everything happens" (58). Artaud's reading reveals his desire for a systematic coding of the invisible forces of the universe.

As far from anarchy or improvisation as imaginable, a mania for fixing, for pinning down precise movements and meanings, runs through Artaud's ideas on directing. This is reflected in his use of Blin and the extraordinarily detailed *Cenci* rehearsal notebook; it also is stated many different ways in *The Theater and Its Double*. The "ten thousand and one expressions of the face . . . can be labeled and catalogued, so they may eventually participate directly and symbolically in this concrete language of the stage" (94); "even light can have a precise intellectual meaning" (95); "the spectacle will be calculated from one end to the other, like a code (*un langage*)" (98); all of the new language's findings "will culminate . . . in a work *written down*, fixed in its least details, and recorded by new means of notation" (111). The work of cataloging, specifying, and recording will control and name the forces the production calls forth. Anarchy only consistently emerges in Artaud's work insofar as it is "organized anarchy"; that is, hidden forces called forth and organized by one with superior powers and access to secret techniques.

Artaud elevates the prevalent directorial rhetoric of unification to a new level. His conception of a world in which matter, soul, mind, and flesh all obey the same rules leads Artaud to believe that the theater director can affect and control the entirety of the spectator's being. His idea of power is nothing less than omnipotence—in a world that equates physical, mental, and "cosmic" levels of existence, he envisions affecting them all simultaneously through the theater event. The following passage from *The Theater and Its Double* is worth considering at length for the implications about the kind of event and type of envisioned power it reveals:

> The director, having become a kind of demiurge, at the back of whose head is this idea of implacable purity and of its consummation whatever the cost, if he truly wants to be a director, i.e., a man versed in the nature of matter and objects, must conduct in the physical domain an exploration of intense movement and precise emotional gesture which is equivalent on the psychological level to the

most absolute and complete moral discipline and on the cosmic level
to the unchaining of certain blind forces which activate what they
must activate and crush and burn on their way what they must crush
and burn. (114–15)

Artaud's definition of a director is "a man versed in the nature of matter
and objects." It takes a "demiurge"—a being responsible for the creation
of the universe—to direct, because what is sought is a "consummation" of
"purity." Although we clearly see in this quotation familiar elements of
the discourses of his contemporaries, including the spiritual language
and totalizing theatrical vision that Artaud shared with other directors,
Artaud's language reaches toward a synthesis of "blind forces" in which
"art" is never mentioned. He strives for a uniquely aggressive mobilization of forces that will achieve an "implacable purity." The forces that "activate what they must activate and crush and burn on their way what they
must crush and burn" are blind, controllable only by the demiurge. The
passage posits a world of equivalencies the director must command, including the physical, mental, and cosmic. These realms are manipulated
by the director's mastery of precise rhythmic and emotional gestures,
complete "moral discipline," and the "unchaining" of higher forces.

Complete manipulation of the spectator is justified in Artaud's cosmic terms by the director's status as a divinely privileged being. What Artaud reads into the Balinese theater, as described in the following quotation, is his own ideal—one viewpoint imposed on the production with the
highest authority possible:

It is a theater which eliminates the author in favor of what we would
call . . . the director; but a director who has become a kind of manager
of magic, a master of sacred ceremonies. And the material on which
he works, the themes he brings to throbbing life are derived not from
him but from the gods. They come, it seems, from elemental interconnections of Nature which a double Spirit has fostered
What he sets in motion is the MANIFESTED. (*TD*, 60)

Artaud was not alone in viewing his job as a "master of sacred ceremonies." This language of priesthood, as first applied to the artist by the
Romantics and later adopted in the theater by Craig, Copeau, and others,
focuses on the artist as a seer with the power to clear away false appearances and reveal absolute truths, an avatar of the divine work. Artaud's
language sometimes is that of a divine intermediary (and this passage

echoes Craig very strongly), but it also sometimes appears that he envisions the director not so much as a Moses figure—a privileged intermediary—but as the lawmaker himself. In all instances, Artaud's writings about the director demonstrate an impatient desire to leave the realm of "art" behind—they strive upward, to control the "interconnections of Nature," to "[set] in motion the MANIFESTED."

These passages aim beyond the "laws of art," which Craig sought. André Veinstein observes that the difference between Artaud and other totalizing theater visionaries is that "the primary concern of Appia and Craig is theater itself—to give the theater back to itself," whereas only "one central preoccupation guides all of Artaud's reflections: to arouse in the spectators a true passion for salvation by means of the theater."[28] Taking the work of the theater out of the realm of theater, Artaud imbues his writing with an extraordinarily exhilarating quality: the rhetoric elevates the theater to the status of a redemptive medium and promises a rigorous, all-consuming salvation.

The widespread tendency among theater artists and critics to think of Artaud as a liberator has led to inaccurate interpretations of his relationship to power. Instances of this tendency are, as discussed in the introduction, legion, centered in England and America in the 1960s with the translation of *The Theater and Its Double* into English and the substitution of that era's politics for Artaud's interwar mindset. One recent example highlights the way that Artaud's theatrical strategies are still being interpreted in the light of an emancipatory attitude. David Graver asserts that Artaud de-centers authority as a director, when in fact the opposite is true. Graver argues against Artaud's authority by pointing out, "Artaud wants the director to give the text of the performance over to powers greater than any of the human participants" ("Antonin Artaud," 49).[29] But the only person who can do that is a prophet or priest, someone in a privileged relationship to these powers. Graver writes that Artaud's director is a self-effacing artistic co-ordinator who will orchestrate the revelation and manifestation of "extraordinary spiritual and earthly powers" (50). But Artaud actually posits himself (for he is always the director) as a chosen one who has unique access to spiritual forces and truths and who, moreover, *defines* these truths. To claim to be the sole privileged instrument of higher powers (which you yourself name) is the very opposite of self-effacement.

Craig had asked why, if one person can find the Laws of Art, everyone should not obey him. In 1932, Artaud asked André Gide why he shouldn't be entrusted with the entire production of works in his new theater, for which he asked Gide's support:

> And why shouldn't people have complete confidence in me, why shouldn't they believe me capable of inventing and manifesting a theatrical reality? (*SW*, 299)

Artaud wanted Gide to translate *Arden of Feversham*, but Artaud wanted to "create" it on stage himself, in the new theatrical language he was inventing:

> The interest that will be aroused a priori by the spectacles that I will put on will be tied to the confidence that is placed in me, the credit that will be accorded to me as creator, inventor of an absolute and self-sufficient theatrical reality.[30]

Artaud had, at that point, not directed anything in four years; he was asking Gide—the highest artistic authority in many Parisian circles at the time—to translate a text and support a venture in which the *metteur en scène* (Artaud himself) would become "author," that is to say, "creator," of the piece (*SW*, 299). The letters to Gide reveal Artaud's desire to create a reality entirely from his own vision, superseding the authority of even the author he was soliciting.

Artaud's writings reflect the widespread urge to "liberate" the director from the ideas and restrictions of established texts and conventions. Ultimately he theorized liberating the director from any other ideas at all. Writing to Jean-Louis Barrault in 1935 (and blaming him for some of the failures of *The Cenci*, for which Barrault had rehearsed some of the actors), Artaud announced his refusal to collaborate with anyone ever again:[31]

> I WON'T HAVE, in a spectacle staged by myself, so much as the flicker of an eye that does not belong to me.
> I do not believe in collaboration . . . because I no longer believe in human purity. No matter how highly I regard you, I believe you to be fallible and I do not want to expose myself again even to the shadow of a risk of this sort.
> I am not the man who can stand to work closely with anyone on any kind of material. . . . If there are animals to be led in my play I'll lead them myself in the rhythm and attitude that I impose on them. (*SW*, 343)

To direct means to be infallible, to be able to control every "flicker of an eye," every "rhythm and attitude." This is the most total view of directing ever articulated. It goes well beyond the rhetoric of Artaud's contemporaries, in terms of both scope and purpose. It demands that nothing happens outside the director's vision and control.

Artaud's writings at this stage do not speak in terms of art but speak, almost exclusively, in terms of morality, truth, and power. We do not have to speculate about where such language leads. We need, in fact, only to look three years after *The Cenci* at the publication of the work carrying the title *Les nouvelles révélations de l'être* (*The New Revelations of Being*). The work proceeds as a transcription and interpretation of revelations and coming destruction, with Artaud as the interpreter of the visions. It is not presented as theater, fiction, anything other than a revelation. Artaud signed the work as "Le Révélé." The work begins with the warning that the reader must have complete belief in the author:

> Je dis ce que j'ai vu et ce que je crois; et qui dira que je n'ai pas vu ce que j'ai vu, je lui déchire maintenant la tête. (*OC*, 7: 119)

> [I say what I've seen and what I believe; and whoever says that I haven't seen what I've seen, I now rip off his head.]

The arrogance, violence, and threats found throughout Artaud's theatrical writings move entirely outside the realm of fiction and aesthetic formulations and into the realm of prophecy here. Artifice and pretense are absent: there is no self-consciousness about these revelations being anything other than the unmediated writing of the author's visions. Artaud positions himself, as "Le Révélé," as an oracle, but also as the originator and substance of the revelations—the name "Le Révélé" can mean both "The One Who has Received Visions" and "The Revealed One." As with his directorial language, Artaud is both the vessel and the vision itself. The prophecies of *The New Revelations of Being* are typically apocalyptic, although here they focus not only on natural upheavals but also on the necessary violence of Man. They announce the terrible fact that we will only be able to find our true nature by destroying ourselves, and they predict a coming war: "Mankind will re-find its stature. And it will re-find it *against* Men."[32] This was written in 1938. It should be little surprise, then—in light of its disdain for individual "Men," its focus on a superior vision being forced on the masses, and its announcement of the necessity of worldwide war—that this is the work that, when it was being republished during his internment at an asylum in Rodez in 1943, Artaud dedicated to Hitler.[33]

Artaud was incarcerated for mental illness at the time of that dedication, to be sure, but his attitude and thinking up until this point were entirely consistent with such a culmination: his ideas of grandeur were always bound up with violent, totalitarian figures. As we will see in the conclusion, examinations of Artaud's biography, non-theatrical writings, and products of his madness all reveal further manifestations of these strands of thought that thread their way throughout his theatrical works. For now, in terms of his theatrical writings, we can say that Artaud's dark, totalizing worldview makes itself felt in the way he moved to incorporate all elements of production into his control, how he spoke about wielding this power, and the nature of the "truth" he sought to disclose. His theater aims to dominate the audience physically, mentally, and spiritually by overriding reason with violent sensory assaults and fear. All of this is justified because the event the Theater of Cruelty strives to bring into being is not art, but a Revelation.

One final look at the image of the mesmerist will help synthesize how Artaud's vision of a world of physical, mental, and spiritual correspondences, as seen idealized in the image of the Nerve Meter, lead to a uniquely powerful view of the role of a leader figure. The idea of hypnosis and magnetism recurs throughout Artaud's writing.[34] *The Theater and Its Double*'s proposed stage effects reflect a belief in laws of "universal magnetism" (73) that the director can manipulate. The director's role appears as that of a kind of Mesmer of the theater. The Theater of Cruelty's effects "will not exercise their true magic except in an atmosphere of hypnotic suggestion in which the mind is affected by a direct pressure upon the senses" (*TD*, 125). The connections to mesmerism, or animal magnetism—which rested on the belief in "animated matter" as the one substance of existence—are striking in this context. Mesmerism revolved around the idea of control. Because of its foundation in the belief of the identity of matter and mind, this control equaled complete domination of one human over the will and body of another. Such a totalizing belief system—which Artaud shares with mesmerism—creates the unique possibility of a figure of total power.

Franz Mesmer, whose works were well-known in French Surrealist circles as well as right-wing occult circles farther east, had written in his 1779 *Animal Magnetism:*

There exists among celestial bodies, the earth, and animate bodies a mutual influence. What conveys this influence is a fluid spread throughout the universe continuously so as to suffer no void . . . a fluid susceptible of receiving, propagating, and communicating all the impressions of movement.[35]

Artaud's Nerve Meter, which we examined in chapter 4, poetically re-envisions this magnetic fluid. He envisions a "lubricating membrane" whose function and composition exactly correspond to Mesmer's idea. Artaud describes how this "lubricating membrane" will "float in the air, this lubricating caustic membrane, this double-thick, many-leveled membrane of infinite crevices, this melancholy and vitreous membrane, but so sensitive, so pertinent itself" (*SW*, 87). The membrane, like Mesmer's fluid, represents an ideal of intimately and wholly connected cosmic being.

Given this totality of being—this unifying membrane or fluid—some are more able to manipulate it than others. Franz Mesmer himself was "expelled from Vienna for propagating the notion that there resided within himself an occult force by which he could influence others" (Brown, *Theater and Revolution*, 370). The mesmerist engineers a trance situation in order to clearly distinguish between stronger- and weaker-willed people. Mesmerism occurs when one person controls animated matter and directs it; his nervous system activates a power that would "excite the requisite action in the propagating medium, which, being conveyed to a distance, may affect the nervous system of another animated being."[36] This would then produce "corresponding mental perceptions and emotions" in the other being (Winter, *Mesmerized*, 54). What started out as a popular parlor game (animal magnetism trances for the elite and curious) led naturally to the public sphere and assemblies, given "the will to exercise unlimited power over those with unlimited aptitude for self-abandonment that characterized its discoverer" (Brown, *Theater and Revolution*, 371). The mesmerist demonstrates his superior mind or will by manipulating energy-matter in such a way as to influence another person's movements, thoughts, emotions, and desires. The mesmerist has recognized and mastered the totality of being.[37] Artaud, as the visionary of the Nerve Meter, theorizes, in his directorial language, artistic power wielded over an entire audience as animal magnetism was wielded over individuals. The one person who retains power in the "hypnotic" situation is the one giving orders.

Artaud differs from his directing predecessors who also envisioned strategies of domination, agitation, and/or a mystical, shamanistic role for themselves in that Artaud's "truth," unlike that of other directors who believed they were going to find "truth" through the theater event, is very clearly his own, horrific version, which he needs to enact, through a kind of mesmerism, on the bodies as well as the minds of the spectators. The Theater of Cruelty requires its audience to submit in order to manifest its vision. Artaud accepted the element of control attendant on the rise of the director on his own unique terms: he wanted reason to remain dormant, but he insisted on the agitated activity of the emotions and senses. Strikingly, the *Theater and Its Double*'s vision of the experience spectators would have contained no happiness, health, or collaboration—in short, no benefit to them other than the opportunity to undergo the experience it conceives. This is why the director needs complete control over the theater event—so he can impose the theater's revelations on the lives of others.

Contrasting the productions of the Jarry Theater to that of *The Cenci*, we see that Artaud was an effective director when he had constraints placed upon him, such as those necessarily imposed by collaboration with other artists. As a singular artist—simultaneous author, director, lead actor, and designer—he failed. But this is what reception of his work has focused on—Artaud as a singular, visionary theorist—and this is what he looks like through that lens: a self-proclaimed prophet who dreams of wielding total power over a group of de-individuated spectators. Examined in the light of charismatic leaders and the regressive sensibility coming to the fore in interwar mass politics, Artaud's vision, as articulated in *The Theater and Its Double*, appears less a liberating aesthetic program than a warning lesson about the dynamics of crowds and power. This intensifies when we return to our discussion of crowds and the element of control over them: the leader.

Power by Charisma

Brecht's Epic Theater and Artaud's Theater of Cruelty are often held up by theater scholars as opposite theater experiences representing two extremes of twentieth-century theater theory. But we don't often consider the parallel in terms other than performance theory. Almost no one would talk about Brecht's theater as if his work were divorced from a political motivation, as if it were an aesthetic program with no humanistic political impulses propelling it. Brecht's theater is driven by a Marxist view:

knowledge leads to informed action; through knowledge, men can become more reasonable; the "triumphant goodness of man" (Mosse) will win out. It rests on the fundamental belief that the theater can construct a situation of awareness that can make manipulation—the enforced implementation of attitudes on people, especially through non-rational and emotional means—impossible. But we have passed over the obvious parallel in Artaud's work. We talk about the Theater of Cruelty as if it were divorced from politics, as if it could be purely metaphysical, spiritual, universal, essential, or any number of the words Artaud and many critics and followers have used to argue for its apolitical function. But when we look at the event called forth by *The Theater and Its Double,* we see an orchestrated space of physical, mental, and spiritual manipulation. All performance events are, of course, to some degree, a product of orchestration and engineering, but some are engineered to create a space in which examination or new self-knowledge can flourish. Artaud orchestrates the opposite kind of space, as far removed from the goal of heightened material awareness as conceivable. This is because he does not want to encourage individual reflection, only immersion in his world. He wants to enact power on a crowd of *organismes*. One may reasonably object that Brecht is explicit about his politics; Artaud isn't. Brecht announces that he is "political"; Artaud announces that he is not. Yet the complete inversion of their methods of orchestrating a live event stems from an inherent and equally complete inversion of ways of thinking about manipulation, power, and individuality.

Artaud's rhetoric of directing inhabits a realm between poetic metaphor and literal prescription, between artistic fantasy and desired material reality. He protests emphatically against taking his performance event as "art"; he also rejects material political action. Yet *The Theater and Its Double* has everything to do with the enactment of power. Insofar as the fantasy of power the book describes is about administering the collective life of a group of people, it is political. Although it never attained material realization, that fact does not negate the extraordinary structural likeness between it and the contemporaneously emerging power dynamics of mass politics. Artaud proclaimed that he wished to abolish the artificial boundaries between different spheres of life, and if the Theater of Cruelty remained "theoretical," it was not due to lack of effort to make it otherwise.[38]

Historically, directors have been inclined to blur boundaries between art, social action, and politics. Helen Krich Chinoy notes that the great synthetic, visionary directors Reinhardt and Meyerhold "both went on to attempt a new social integration—Reinhardt in the Theater of the Five Thousand, Meyerhold in the Theater of the Revolution" (*Directors on Directing*, 53). If, as we saw in the previous chapter, certain features of the directing mindset naturally lent themselves to autocratic rhetoric and even actions, both Reinhardt and Meyerhold tempered these with their strong humanistic impulses and anti-fascist political convictions, which dictated the content, if not the form, of their work.

Frederick Brown's study of early French directors highlights how several of them felt a strong desire to control crowds—a desire that manifested itself in calls for theaters "of the people" that drew from the French Revolution's ideals and spectacles. Romain Rolland, the author of the treatise *Le théâtre du peuple* and the most vocal proponent of mass festivals and popular performances in early twentieth-century France, tied his love for such spectacles (which he explicitly anchored in the Committee for Public Safety's charter for a people's theater established under Robespierre during the Terror) to a human need to experience a sense of belonging.[39] As Rolland wrote in a 1927 letter to Freud—which became the basis for the opening passage of Freud's *Civilization and Its Discontents*—people have an "oceanic" feeling that ties us to others; we need to feel we are connected, in some way, to something "limitless, unbounded," to "eternity": "We cannot fall out of this world" (Freud, *Civilization and Its Discontents*, 1–2). This sentiment, Rolland argues, is the basis for all religious feeling. It is also the basis for political feeling in the era of mass politics. This can be seen through the work of Rolland and his staunchest supporter, the actor turned director of people's theaters, Firmin Gémier.

As Gémier was one of the first people Artaud met in the Parisian theater scene and shares many commonalities with Artaud's directing ideals, his work merits a brief discussion here. In 1911, after a successful acting career (including the lead role in the 1896 premiere of Jarry's *Ubu Roi*), and after having directed the Théâtre Antoine (formerly the Théâtre Libre) for several years, Gémier founded and ran the Théâtre National Ambulant, a mobile theater that brought plays to the French countryside on collapsible stages that could hold sixteen hundred audience members. He was animated by a desire to create and satisfy those "oceanic feelings" described by Rolland (whose plays, among others, he produced). For Gémier and Rolland, the theater's purpose was to engineer crowds, to promote collective emotions and movement. "There is perhaps nothing more captivating in reality and in art than the spiritual communion of a crowd," Gémier wrote. "It seems at times that the crowd is a colossal person in whom thought runs untrammeled across a thousand brains. . . . That is what must be translated in the theater."[40] Brown points to the implications of this conception of the crowd from the standpoint of its leader: "Organized around a protagonist or a director . . . the crowd, in Gémier's conception of it, translates what its leader says into physical evidence" (*Theater and Revolution*, 293). Eventually, Gémier's vision for performance became one of a *culte extérieur* (outdoor cult) that would manifest itself in festivals. As Brown reads this utopian dream of collectivity, the principle of political power is all too evident:

> Held out-of-doors, in nature, the *culte extérieur* promoted by Gémier set physical against intellectual culture, a quasi-divine mass or racial "soul" against the individual psyche, and a *raison d'être* embedded in holy soil against the otherwise fortuitous course of human affairs. . . .
>
> What he could hardly admit—that the externalization of this ideal was inherently belligerent, that the apotheosis of the collective body sanctioned individual violence even in rendering it impersonal—became evident in 1914. (297)

Gémier's "dramatic enterprise was predicated on feelings that abolish any sense of duration and selfhood" (Brown, *Theater and Revolution*, 302), just as Jacques-Louis David's orchestrated spectacles for the French Revolution were designed "with a view to exorcising from *le peuple* singular thoughts, hidden events, private allegiances" (Brown, *Theater and Revolution*, 295). The "violence" done to the individual sees its inverse in the strength of the leader, who has organized the crowd in his image, and who revels in the self-immolation occurring all around him.

In order to discuss the leader figure who directs *le peuple*'s self-immolation, we need to first return to the characteristics of crowds as established by crowd theory: specifically, why a crowd is drawn to a leader. An individual loses his/her characteristic powers of judgment when in a crowd. The crowd operates according to emotion, force, and desire and does not sift through multiple options or intellectual arguments before acting. Rather, its force heaves and surges in the most compelling direction given. A crowd leader, then, exerts force through irrational and emotional rhetoric. Tapping into the exaggerated feelings of a mass of people, a leader manipulates the crowd's overwhelming desire for heightened sentiments, as Gustave Le Bon describes:

> An orator wishing to move a crowd must make an abusive use of violent affirmations. To exaggerate, to affirm, to resort to repetitions, and never to attempt to prove anything by reasoning are methods of argument well known to speakers at public meetings. (*Crowd*, 23)[41]

Reasoning is of no use to the crowd leader, as Le Bon writes: "The laws of logic have no action on crowds" (69). Serge Moscovici observes that "individuals succeed in their aims by using analysis . . . [the masses, however,] are passionately enamoured of an ideal and a man who is its incarnation" (*Age of the Crowd*, 33). Reason belongs to the individual, whereas faith, emotion, and leader worship characterize crowds.

All crowd leaders share this knowledge, whether by intuition or by study. As the crowd is inherently amoral, it can be led to any number of outcomes. It craves direction. As Moscovici writes: "[Crowds] cannot bear very much reality. . . . The only language they understand is one which bypasses reason, speaks directly to the heart and makes reality seem either better or worse than it in fact is" (*Age of the Crowd*, 31).

As we have seen, Artaud's rhetoric naturally turns in these directions. The Theater of Cruelty abolishes the idea that reason will lead the spectator to understanding; it seeks to forcefully sway rather than convince. To do this, *The Theater and Its Double* intuitively upholds hypnosis, suggestion, emotion, rhythm, sensory effects, and broad, epic strokes of plot and character as primary tools of influence.

What is a crowd drawn to in a leader? Crowd theory demonstrates that leaders are always driven by an idée fixe; their obsession makes them "necessarily beings apart" (Moscovici, *Age of the Crowd*, 123). This fixed thought could be a specific desire, the plain desire to lead, or a belief in themselves. They are "madmen of faith" (Moscovici, *Age of the Crowd*, 123), characterized by a desire so strong it can compel by its intensity rather than its reason. The leader may desire only to lead; to exercise power even when there is no logical agenda put forward, no clear outcome of this exercise of power other than power.

In the context of the interwar era, the political ascendancy of fascism owed much to the people's desire for and attachment to a strong leader figure, regardless of specifics of political agendas. Robert O. Paxton, in *The Anatomy of Fascism*, discusses how banking on this desire formed a key feature of the fascist leader: the dynamic of desiring to control even without a specific agenda to advance. "Fascist leaders made no secret of having no program. . . . The will and leadership of a *Duce* was what a modern people needed, not a doctrine" (17). In "the era of mass politics," fascism "sought to appeal mainly to the emotions by the use of ritual, carefully stage-managed ceremonies, and intensely charged rhetoric. The role programs and doctrine play [was minimal]" (16). As one early fascist wrote, the truth of the ideology lay "in its capacity to set in motion our capacity for ideals and action" (Paxton, *Anatomy of Fascism*, 16). Ideas gave way to charisma, as Paxton succinctly summarizes: "Power came first, then doctrine" (17). Theodor Adorno, in a discussion of the discourse of fascist propaganda, notes that "one of the most conspicuous features of agitator's speeches" was "the absence of a positive programme and of anything they might 'give,' as well as the paradoxical prevalence of threat and denial" ("Freudian Theory," 141). Power, even political power, can be exercised without a clear agenda, if the will and need to follow is strong enough.

The case of the Italian playwright Luigi Pirandello is illuminating in this context. Pirandello publicly celebrated Mussolini's rise to power after the March on Rome, saying, "A great man's role is to construct reality for the weak who cannot construct these realities themselves."[42] Pirandello promoted the notion that a "great," creative act in the political world could be the consummation of an artistic impulse. During the Ethiopian campaign, Pirandello proclaimed: "The Author of this great feat is also a Poet who knows his trade. A true man of the theater, a providential hero whom God granted Italy at the right moment, he acts in the Theater of the Centuries both as author and protagonist."[43] This helps us contextualize Artaud's 1943 dedication to Hitler (mentioned earlier) and also a previous letter to Hitler Artaud wrote in 1939, in which he proffered his support in attacking Paris: "Parisians," he wrote to the chancellor of the Reich, "have need of gas."[44] Both letters—however dramatic, confused, or rhetorical—reach out to a man whose political acts represented the power to manifest a vision, to, returning to Pirandello's words, "construct reality."

The leader of the crowd positions himself as more than an individual: he must have the ability to present his own ideas as not being his, but coming from something much larger. Hannah Arendt discusses this feature of the leader in terms of the totalitarian dictator, who is concerned with the "imitation" or "interpretation" of "the laws of Nature or of History."[45] In contrast to the tyrant, he "does not believe that he is a free agent with the power to execute his arbitrary will, but, instead, the executioner of laws higher than himself" (Arendt, "On the Nature," 346). Artaud, to return to an earlier citation, writes that the director "brings [themes] to throbbing life . . . derived not from him but from the gods. They come, it seems, from elemental interconnections of Nature which a double Spirit has fostered" (*TD*, 60). Again, this is far from a self-effacing claim: he is always the one determining these terms and appointing himself the medium.

Artaud's belief that the Theater of Cruelty will act according to higher laws is evident on nearly every page of *The Theater and Its Double*. He never frames his ideas as personal desires in this work—he writes as if his ideas are channeled directly from metaphysical, mythic, and universal powers. His own "elemental interconnections" grant him the power to "interpret" truth for his audiences. These claims have resulted in him being hailed as "prophet," "shaman," "mystic," and so on. His claim to interpret, to be "Le Révélé," has been accepted by those exhilarated by his infectiously passionate writing.

Artaud wrote to Jacqueline Breton from Ville-Evrard in April 1939: "I'm not mad. I'm a fanatic."[46] This was a few years after the period under discussion, after he was, in fact, mad, but the traits of fanaticism make themselves known in his earlier works, as well as in the way people have received them. His oeuvre conducts all the force of fanatical writing; his presence exerts such a fascination over those who encounter or study him that his charisma is inextricably intertwined with his writing and practice (as we saw in the introduction). A body of work such as his—part rant, part poetry, part theory, part vision, but mostly exhortations and sensibility—compels by, as Derrida admitted, its force rather than its ideas ("Artaud, Oui . . . ," 26).

Theodor Adorno strikingly notes that fascist leaders resemble "ham actors and asocial psychopaths" ("Freudian Theory," 142). They lead, he argues, because they speak without inhibitions what is latent in others:

> The famous spell they exercise over their followers seems largely to depend on their orality; language itself, devoid of its rational significance, functions in a magical way and furthers those archaic regressions which reduce individuals to members of crowds. (148)

The power of nonrational language is immense: when speech or writing writhes under the weight of too much passion to crystallize into neat phrases, all audiences face the choice either to dismiss or to give in to its seductions, forging their own paths through the tortured field of signs. Artaud's writing (and, evidently, his speech and presence) exerted this force; the very labyrinthine nature of his oeuvre invites fascination.

The eye for the crowd Artaud evidences is intuitive; I am not sug-gesting that he was a political mastermind or that he ever articulated a dream for power in those terms—the power he theorized over other bod-ies in his directing strategies and his writings remained theoretical. But the monomania of his vision, the ferocity of his expression, and the charisma of his presence combined to create a strong leader figure. Ar-taud writes that he himself is his son, his father, his mother, and himself; that he levels the need for a "papa-mama" (*SW*, 540); that he is going to "have done with the judgment of god."[47] In other words, Artaud an-nounces in no uncertain terms that he is the manifestation of a new world order.

For Elias Canetti, the "higher truths" the leader believes he is inter-preting stem from the individual's desire for power. In his analysis of the Dresden judge Daniel Paul Schreber in his asylum cell—as Schreber envi-sioned heaps of celestial scribes connected to him through his nerves—Canetti names the longing for catastrophe as an essential feature of the leader. The paranoiac and the despot share the same urges: "No-one has a sharper eye for the attributes of the crowd than the paranoiac or the despot who . . . are one and the same" (*Crowds and Power*, 447). But one en-acts his urges on the intimate space of his powerless self, and the other en-acts it on a public field.[48] Religious or insane fantasies of power operate structurally identically—is it too much to suggest that aesthetic fantasies for power may share this structure? Artaud's goal was never wholly artis-tic; his writing speaks of theater as a means to an end, an end that he never fully articulates. His driving urge is that of conducting a crowd, not of creating an artwork.

Here, then, is the explanation for the impassioned and often wor-shipful reception of Artaud we discussed in the introduction: he exerted a commanding charismatic force, and he claimed the right to the most pow-erful titles and the most absolute power. He envisioned the theater as an event in which the individual is battered out of his or her mind, over-whelmed with sensory stimuli, worked on with image and myth, and en-gineered to an ecstatic state controlled not by narrative, political agenda, or any kind of impulse to self-expression or self-exploration, but by the desires of the leader, who, occupying a divine status, does not need to ex-plain or even articulate his goals. He imagines stripping the individual at the Theater of Cruelty of his or her previous identity and imposing new terms on that body. A "bloodstream of images" (*TD*, 82) structures this process: cosmic upheaval, slaughter, rape, dismemberment, plague, self-annihilation. What pleasure does Artaud promise in return for participation? What benefit does he envision? The answer is only self-loss: he orchestrates an experience in which we are given the space to lose ourselves. *The Theater and Its Double* proposes nothing for the spectator, society, or mankind except for the opportunity to submit. The Theater of Cruelty concerns itself above all else with the exercise of power, with what a director—filled with messianic zeal—can do.

The language of power Artaud wields, while it has traditionally been seen as that of a unique visionary, shares very much, in fact, with an all-too-familiar language of the historically nascent totalitarianism. It echoes that wielded by others who believed their violent directives to have cosmic force, that possible negative consequences of their ideas needed to be accepted without question, who assumed that the positive program they never articulated (outside of the vaguest terms) would be filled in by the listeners themselves, that followers would create individual justifications for the direction given. People have turned to images of martyrs, shamans, and even Christ to explain the force of Artaud's influence, but his language is neither focused on shared goals, nor spoken on behalf of others, nor compassionate. Taking him out of divine terms and setting him in his historical context allows us to see that *The Theater and Its Double* speaks not, as has usually been assumed, in the aesthetic or empowering language of the avant-garde, progressive politics, or sympathetic seers, but always in the decidedly illiberal language of power and violence entirely of a piece with a reactionary, frustrated, interwar discourse.

Artaud's work has been described as "impossible" theatrically; it is said that there is no practical component with which to realize his vision. What I think is actually impossible is to grant his wish, which is very far beyond theater. It is not so much a practical element that is missing, but a vision for what comes after the sensory assault on the audience. It seems to me that there is, quite simply, no "after" posited in *The Theater and Its Double*. The Theater of Cruelty is, as I said at the beginning of this chapter, more than anything else, a vision for an exercise of power. It might not be that the event Artaud describes is impossible, but to what end would one realize it?

What I have attempted to do is examine Artaud's works at the height of his career and look at what they actually *say*. They don't say they want to be read as poetic texts or metaphors; they say they want to enact their truths on our bodies. We might dismiss Artaud as a madman, but we might also consider that madmen, as Canetti reminds us, flourish under many circumstances, not just literary ones. The systems of power that were coming into being in the 1920s and '30s followed a similar template: one "terrible truth," its enactment, faceless followers fused together without a clear knowledge of why or for what, and a figure who sought to inspire not by reason but by force of will alone. Structural parallels such as this rarely make it into the history books if they never attained material reality, but taking them seriously and examining them may be worthwhile—if that examination can make us more attuned to the possibilities that our own ideas, experimentations, and enthusiasms may bring about. This possibility is the subject of the conclusion.

CONCLUSION : Longing for Nothingness

A détruire, à ne pas exister.
—ARTAUD, *"Enquête"*

If World War I had shattered many Europeans' belief in the promise of their civilization, Artaud responded by continuing to attack those beliefs, as if to prove, over and over, that the worst fears about our civilization were correct. His theater aimed for a revolution based on pulling down structures and not, as has often been assumed, constructing better ones to take their place. Artaud never joined a political party because he had no hope for actual fulfillment or happiness in the material world: "I have too much contempt for life to think that any sort of change that might develop in the realm of appearances could in any way change my detestable condition" (SW, 141). If his writings articulate a goal for humanity, it is a vague, aggressive surge called forth by an ecstatically imposed revelation of annihilating dark powers.

All of this we have seen demonstrated abundantly throughout this study, through Artaud's dark, vitalist, worldview; through his performance events that seek to crush, hypnotize, and overwhelm the spectator; and through his conceptualization and exaltation of occult figures of total power. The company he keeps in formulating his ideas is consistently that of those who nourished irrationalist, totalizing worldviews between the wars, fueled by a belief in a superior Will and a bleak vision of—and for—humanity.

And yet Artaud, as we discussed in the introduction, for all his anti-rational, anti-individual, anti-democratic thinking, has been canonized—sanctified, even—by artists and intellectuals who strive toward a more progressive, liberal, and democratic society in which informed, empowered, and tolerant individuals play a key role. There is no simple explanation for the puzzling reception of this profoundly reactionary thinker, but one part of the answer comes clear when we consider how Artaud's place in theater history was fixed in the 1960s, a time when all limits were considered bad limits, and the urge to lose oneself in something bigger paradoxically accompanied a dedication to self-discovery. A generalized notion of "freedom" attached itself to Artaud's work in the pursuit of political and cultural revolutions during this time. But Artaud's ideas about liberation do not really suit the liberal culture or progressive politics embraced by this generation—he is a fellow-traveler only insofar as his opposition to existing systems sometimes coincides with theirs. Any kind of "freedom" he may have envisioned keeps him traveling much farther down another road, with very different people.

Opposition and liberation are not the same things, but the destructive urge of the former in Artaud's work appealed strongly enough to those seeking revolution that they conflated the two. Artaud's theatrical event promises the collapse of societal boundaries and the experience of self-loss, an experience in which destruction boomerangs back into the thrill of non-being. Is this the fascination exerted by his oeuvre to such a degree that it could be misread as constructively liberating?

To honestly examine Artaud's particular kind of freedom—a dismantling of the self and the social order against a backdrop of generalized, "gratuitous" violence—requires not making general assumptions about the inherent goodness of freedom. For such generalizations do not apply to Artaud's completely unbalanced universe. His works articulate a one-sided worldview that reveals a spiritual pessimism on the scale of, for example, the eighteenth-century irrationalist thinker Joseph de Maistre, whose unadulterated distrust of mankind and its freedoms begat a dogmatic belief in the superiority of a world controlled by a triumvirate of pope, king, and hangman. In place of a traditional religious divinity organizing his thought, Artaud posits a Will or life force that can be channeled (as we saw in his theories of directing) by a superior human. Readings of Artaud that optimistically superimpose benevolent community feelings on the dissolution of order he advocates, that interpret self-liberation as self-articulation, or that treat his idea of "cruelty" as an existential metaphor, miss the entire spirit of Artaud's oeuvre, especially its dynamic of power.[1] In Artaud's world, violence is the governing principle, and it is wielded by powerful men: "Each stronger life tramples down the others, consuming them in a massacre which is a transfiguration and a bliss" (TD, 103). The equation of these two terms—"transfiguration" and "bliss"—in the instance of a "massacre" takes us back to the image of

Dionysiac frenzy this study has previously invoked, an image that greatly appealed to other, non-progressive thinkers in the interwar era, who also brandished the words *liberation, revolution, unification,* and *freedom.*

The catastrophic imposition of liberty described in Euripides's *The Bacchae* provides a powerful illustration of the dangers of the total loss of inhibitions lauded by the Theater of Cruelty. *The Bacchae* demonstrates an equation of ecstasy and violence and a perilously thin line between liberation and vulnerability to total domination. In the play, Dionysos returns to his hometown to avenge himself on those who don't believe in his divinity. He inspires a Bacchic frenzy in the women of the town, including Agave, the mother of the most intransigent unbeliever, Pentheus. Agave hunts, sings, and dances in the woods with the other Bacchantes in total freedom from the restraints of her position, of codes of civilization, of an individuated sense of herself. And when, in this Dionysiac state, she believes that her son is a beast of prey, she joins in the ecstatic frenzy of ripping him limb from limb, tearing his flesh and rejoicing in the warmth of his blood. She returns parading his head on a stick, exultant up to the moment the spiteful god restores her to her own sight, at which point recognition completes her downfall. The blissful dissolution of the self results in butchery and horror.

Two different kinds of loss are at work in Euripides's text: the loss of the individual self and the loss of order among individuals. From both losses arise ecstasy and devastation. The image of Dionysian revelry expressed by Euripides compels and disturbs because it insists that in the moment of complete liberation—of loss and freedom—fulfillment and horror are inextricably bound together. Freedom, in fact, signifies loss: it is not a tangible entity, but an absence. It signifies the loss of those restrictions or boundaries that were originally established to give order to something threatening in its limitlessness—either the chaos of a group of people or the void of a self with no definition. In either case, the loss of those boundaries provides an exhilaration of a limited duration . . . limited until the moment of "freedom" becomes oppressive.

The Euripidean image, so crucially linking liberation, ecstasy, violence, and domination, provides a point of similarity to the kind of freedom found in Artaud's vision; namely, the effects of ordained total liberation that culminate in catastrophe. It also illuminates, through a difference, a unique point of Artaud's oeuvre. The rewards of Dionysos are extraordinary, but they come in a package. Artaud's vision, in contrast, conspicuously omits the pleasures of Bacchus—no drinking milk from the ground; no gleeful singing and dancing; and, importantly, no physical release. Even the temporary rewards Artaud promises are, unlike those of the inebriated Bacchantes, extraordinarily joyless.

What, then, is the appeal? The thrall and danger of "freedom" at work in equally extreme manifestations in Artaud's writing lead us both to self-immolation and to power. As Terry Eagleton recently illustrated in a dissection of the notion of terror, which he accomplished by dissecting the notion of the sublime, nothingness rests right on the edge of a feeling of omnipotence. The sublime, represented by the Bacchic frenzy, restores as well as destroys: "By identifying ourselves with the boundlessness of the sublime, we cease to be anything in particular, but thereby become potentially everything. . . . It is for this reason that feeling utterly inconsiderable can tip over into a sense of omnipotence."[2] This is the reason for the exalted and dangerous nature of crowds, for their feeling of power that is, in fact, orchestrated from above. It is also the situation invoked throughout *The Theater and Its Double*. As Artaud dreams of self-annihilation for the participants in the Theater of Cruelty, he dreams of unleashing fury, violence, and power through the simultaneous acts of loss and destruction. The ignited crowd is a self-consuming fire that exalts because it is both everything and nothing, all-powerful and annihilating, with nothing stable at its center.

"I have an appetite *for not existing*" (*SW*, 103). Artaud's theater seeks a freedom based on loss of self. The most positive text Artaud ever wrote is "Letter to the Clairvoyant," in which he expresses a profound satisfaction at feeling the annihilation of his individuality, at gaining "the sense of the uniformity of all things. A magnificent absolute" (*SW*, 126). Destruction of difference and the stupor of unreason define Artaud's notion of the absolute: "My mind, exhausted by discursive reason, wants to be caught up in the wheels of a new, an absolute gravitation. For me it is like a supreme reorganization in which only the laws of Illogic participate" (*SW*, 108). The "uniformity" he craves and envisions for mankind can only come about by crushing individuality. An unreasoned reorganization of de-individuated organisms: it is a striking vision to have wound its way into the art and thought of the radical artists and intellectuals of the 1960s.

A brief look at a recurrent critique of postmodernism is instructive here. Postmodernist and post-structuralist thinking posit a de-centered self, and many critics have argued that deconstruction and antihumanism have been a boon to liberalism, providing alternate possible ideas of the self that make room for non-normative identities and non-totalizing concepts of "man."[3] But others have critiqued the de-centered subject—as emblematized in Michel Foucault's striking image of man, on the verge of extinction, being a face drawn in the sand—as paving the way for totalitarianism.[4] The de-individuation of our selves encouraged by post-modern art and post-structuralist ideas might, in this view, lead to a totalitarian political basis, a preparedness for mass politics that takes advantage of the deaths of the self, author, and character that we have celebrated.[5] Rainer Friedrich argues, in the context of Artaud's work, that "the negation of the subject is indelibly inscribed in the ideology and praxis of twentieth-century totalitarianism," reminding us that "this century has given rise to powerful historical forces that are predicated on depersonalisation and dehumanisation" ("Deconstructed Self," 293–94).[6] The possibility of such a consequence is present all the way back in Euripides: *The Bacchae* demonstrates how dismantling identity can verge dangerously close to totally liquidating the self and falling prey to another's monolithically destructive plans. "You don't know what you're doing," Dionysos taunts Pentheus, whom he has "liberated" from his own status, his own gender, his own convictions: "You don't even know who you are."[7]

On the surface, one can readily see why Artaud's call to break with "the system" would have appealed to revolutionaries, intellectuals, and radical artists in the 1960s. His opposition to existing institutions suits the goals of the counter-cultural revolution; the sensibility of experimental theater practitioners; and critiques of capitalism such as those articulated by Herbert Marcuse and Norman O. Brown, whose ideas were hugely influential among radical activists of the period, and who posited resistance as the first step in change. But the unfocused ecstasy resulting from such a grand-scale opposition is exactly what something like fascism capitalizes on. Félix Guattari, in his essay "Everybody Wants to Be a Fascist," articulates how the search for the right revolutionary approach to totalizing political systems invites this very danger: "The minute you stop facing it head-on, you can abruptly oscillate from a position of revolutionary openness to a position of totalitarian foreclosure: then you find yourself a prisoner of generalities and totalizing programs."[8]

"Dionysus' presence can be beautiful or ugly or both," wrote Richard Schechner in 1968, thinking about the contemporary emphasis on liberation both inside and outside the theater.[9] It is instructive to see how key figures in theater theory raised cautionary flags about this very issue without explicitly pursuing its implications in Artaud's oeuvre. Schechner, at the end of his 1968 essay "The Politics of Ecstasy," wondered briefly if we could really handle Dionysiac energies or if, by charging the theater with creating them, we weren't risking getting our own heads on a stick:

> There are many young people who believe that an unrepressive so-
> ciety, a sexualized society, is Utopia. . . . But this same ecstasy, we
> know, can be unleashed in the Red Guards or horrifically channeled
> toward the Nuremberg rallies and Auschwitz. . . . The hidden fear I
> have about the new expression is that its forms come perilously close
> to ecstatic fascism. (228)

This reservation did not stop Schechner from seeking the "right" kind of theatrical ecstasy at the time, as he was committed to exploring communal ritual theater and finding positive Dionysian transports. A similar reserva-tion about the wholesale opposition to restrictions and reason was articu-lated, but only hypothetically, by one of the most influential readers of Ar-taud, Peter Brook. Brook dedicated much of his chapter "The Holy Theatre" in *The Empty Space* to what he believed was the constructive side of Artaud's liberation through boundary-breaking. As a counter to his own interpretation, Brook mentions that, in thinking of Artaud's "dragging us back to a nether world" before the constraints of civilization and logic were established, one might ask: "is there even a fascist smell in the cult of unreason?"[10] He quickly answers no, stating that "Artaud applied is Ar-taud betrayed" (*Empty Space*, 54) and reinforcing his own commitment to bringing forth a constructive, "holy" theater from such new freedoms.

Susan Sontag herself, in the essay discussed in the introduction that established the language of Artaud's divinity, began to articulate one way that Artaud's "freedom" differs from the freedom found in liberal thinkers among the avant-garde: "To be spiritually liberating, Artaud thinks, theater has to express impulses that are larger than life. . . . Theater serves an 'inhuman' individuality, an 'inhuman' freedom, as Artaud calls it in *The Theater and Its Double*—the very opposite of the liberal, sociable idea of freedom" (*SW*, xlviii). This stands, she notes, in clear opposition to the thinking of his contemporaries such as the Surrealists. Someone like Breton was sensitive and "loyal to the limits that protect human growth and pleasure." But Artaud "is enraged by *all* limits, even those that save" (*SW*, xlviii). This is an excellent point, but Sontag uses it to take Artaud out of the Western artistic tradition altogether and relate his thinking to

Gnostic philosophy, effectively keeping him in the realm of the spiritual "other" and reinforcing the sense of him being uniquely out of time.

Strikingly, Sontag's conception of fascist aesthetics as articulated in her critical essay on Leni Riefenstahl—"Fascist art glorifies surrender, it exalts mindlessness, it glamorizes death"—certainly fits Artaud's writing, although she never makes the connection.[11] And her warning that overlooking the fascism at work in Riefenstahl's art "do[es] not augur well for the keenness of current abilities to detect the fascist longings in our midst" is equally applicable here ("Fascinating Fascism," 97). But Sontag's elevation of Artaud's otherness leads her to place him in a fundamentally different category than Riefenstahl—a separation that precludes her from pursuing fascist underpinnings that are evident in Artaud's indiscriminate war against limits, articulation, and individuality, and in his glorification of surrender, mindlessness, and death.

Such an assessment was clearly made, however, in observation of some of Artaud's more conspicuous disciples. Robert Brustein voiced his objections to what the young radicals of the 1960s saw as the ideal of Artaudian ecstatic liberation through his controversial critique of the practices of the Living Theatre. Brustein thought *Paradise Now* overwhelmed the spectator in a manipulative, Wagnerian way, and he thought the "freedom" with which audiences sometimes responded represented repressive chaos and not the beautiful liberation the Living thought it did. Two dangers are articulated in his critique: first, that lack of order means simply that—and not freedom. The "limits that save," Brustein thought, came perilously close to being totally annihilated in this Living Theatre performance. Second, unthinking frenzy in such a state, Brustein argued, invites the imposition of an order from above: "in the face of excessive freedom people might swerve to fascism."[12]

In the United States, the threat of fascism and the threat of communism have taken turns in the national imagination as the worst possible outcome for a land of free people; individualism has always been the mainstay of American political identity. American fears and anxieties repeatedly project onto the same phantasm of being subsumed into an anonymous mass. It is curious, then, to say the least, that the fight for "freedom" through artistic practice has so strongly embraced and drawn from Artaud, who yearns for the annihilation of the self. How could his vision for the loss of the individual get so exalted in such a climate?

The longing for incorporation into something higher than the self—

the pull of "oceanic feelings"—is what moves us to relinquish our individuality. This desire for self-loss—both terrifying and sublime—is obviously not necessarily progressive. In fact, its extreme versions are why people join cults, crowds, and rallies. Elias Canetti argues that in forming crowds, we simultaneously surrender to and liberate ourselves from our oldest terrors, the fears of seizure and incorporation; we yearn for "the moment when all who belong to the crowd get rid of their differences and feel equal" (*Crowds and Power*, 17). But we created those "differences" to begin with, to define ourselves and to create order. So there's a "self-destructive fusion" at work in the dynamic of crowds and power, which could be described as a dialectical synthesis: we lose ourselves, disintegrate, in order to be reborn into an experience without limits—the sublime.[13] Members of the crowd drive themselves to self-annihilation, preserving themselves in a new form: they sublimate themselves. In Artaud's ideal theater, the individual might destroy him- or herself in order to be united with a higher unity, but, far from envisioning a positively resolved dialectic, the Theater of Cruelty draws on the darkest possible versions of this urge.

Could we view the "unity" among people that Artaud invokes as a constructive community rather than a crowd, a collective rather than a mass?[14] Marxists continue to theorize an empowered collective;[15] contemporary liberal culture strives to attain a community of tolerant difference; experimental theater practitioners have attempted to realize this vision through ensembles and, in the case of the Living Theatre (among others), communes. On the other hand, the field of crowd theory provides some compellingly dismal prognoses about the ability to make social progress within the framework of mass politics.[16] The question of the possibility, in any event, lies outside the scope of this book. What I've attempted to do is to situate Artaud's crowd where it belongs historically, conceptually, and socially: not with a dreamed-of liberal collective, but with a crowd motivated by fear, frustration, and disgust that yearns for a loss of individuality, leaving its members open to the most manipulative dynamics of crowd formation.

Schechner concludes his thoughts on unleashing Dionysiac freedom this way: "Liberty can be swiftly transformed into its opposite, and not only by those who have a stake in reactionary government" ("Politics of Ecstasy," 228). It is easy to see the reactionary possibilities in the fervid reach for "liberty" in light of Artaud's universe of negative energies. To return to a point Roger Shattuck made in 1984:

Artaud was prepared to renounce the social transactions of language, to renounce reason itself. He did not fear violence, bombs if necessary, against poets who did not submit to their true mission. All this in the name of "myth," "being," "collectivity." . . . Over the long haul and in his most crucial writings, Artaud is prepared to surrender individual consciousness and even individual life to a higher collectivity. ("Artaud Possessed," 186)

Recognizing that the liberal framework equates happiness and freedom provides one answer to the puzzle of Artaud's reception. The violence of the ecstatic experience has been considered beautiful and never ugly by those such as Judith Malina and Julian Beck; the force of life itself always worth activating. If everyone were committed to others' well-being, and if a belief in the goodness of man prevailed, perhaps this would, at least in theory, be imaginable. But how would this play out in Artaud's worldview, in which "all true freedom is dark" (*TD*, 30)? In which everything is evil, rotten, betrayed? In which violence and aggression are the rule; in which the "rigor" of life is never the joy of orgasm but always the exhilaration of menace, cruelty, and annihilation?

As this book has shown, there can be no question of the attitude toward humanity underlying Artaud's theatrical vision. Artaud believes that "good is desired . . . evil is permanent" (*TD*, 102); "evil is the permanent law" (103); "It is cruelty that cements matter together, cruelty that molds the features of the created world. Good is always upon the outer face, but the face within is evil" (104); evil will only be reduced when everything is reduced to "chaos" (104). The selection of quotations used throughout this study reflects my focus on Artaud's theatrical writing, confined almost entirely to the 1920s and '30s. The argument of this book has been made in terms of the theatrical experience of "cruelty," but it could have been made using thousands of different pages drawn from Artaud's poetry, novels, letters, and asylum notebooks. His writings always evinced a belief in the foulness of mankind, and they increased in ferocity as time went on:

And now,
   all of you, beings,
I have to tell you that you have always made me shit.
   Go form
   a swarm
   of the pussy

of infestation,
crab lice
of eternity. (SW, 544)[17]

Artaud's vision of the world eventually congealed into one expressed exclusively in terms of scatology and hatred of the body, hatred of god because of the filth of man:

The groume makes things.
And what is it, this nose-groume?
The excavation of the birthing belly
scraped red and despairing,
a vaginal hemorrhoid screaming in its shitty smack against god,
 who makes it stink.[18]

Is God a being?
If he is one, he is shit.
. . . .
But he does not exist,
except as the void that approaches with all its forms
whose most perfect image
is the advance of an incalculable group of crab lice. (SW, 561–62)[19]

And these sentiments are expressed not only in poetry, but in every form of writing and in reported conversations. Exchanges such as the following conversation with Jacques Prevel make any claim that such expressions are intended as poetic metaphor hard to swallow:

Seven to eight hundred million human beings . . . should be exterminated; what is that to the three or four thousand million who inhabit the earth. Most human beings spend their life in doing nothing.[20]

The purpose of this final onslaught of unpleasantness is to reinforce that this book has not cited quotations opportunistically but, in fact, chosen rather mild representatives of the substance of Artaud's worldview itself, the one that underlies his works from beginning to end, the one that the Theater of Cruelty seeks to "impose" on its audiences.

In a few sentences tacked on to the end of his book, Artaud made a case for his proposed title, "The Theater of Cruelty," that eventually convinced his reluctant editor, Jean Paulhan, to agree to use the phrase. Artaud wrote, in response to Paulhan's objections: "This Cruelty is a matter of neither sadism nor bloodshed, *at least not in any exclusive way*" (*TD*, 101; emphasis added). "From the point of view of the mind, cruelty signifies rigor, implacable intention and decision, irreversible and absolute determination" (*TD*, 101). "Cruelty is above all lucid, a kind of rigid control and submission to necessity" (*TD*, 102). "Implacable intention," "rigor," lucidity—all this sounds more palatable than chopping up bodies and has been presented by numberless interpreters as the exclusive, correct way to read Artaud's choice of words, to read "cruelty." But then what do we do with all those chopped-up bodies? All the blackening organs, the rape of the dying, the wholesale slaughters, the hearts on daggers, the machine guns, the bombs, the "real" blood? Isn't it disingenuous to insist that Artaud's "cruelty" refers only to an existential abstraction? And even within that abstracted thought, whose determination, whose necessity, whose rigid control must we submit to?

Artaud inserted just enough sentences in his work to placate Paulhan's anxieties, and these sentences have been quoted far more often than the surrounding ones to which they were proposed as a corrective. They enable us to write off the disturbing parts of Artaud's exhortations and supply our own constructive determination in place of his reactionary nihilism. But extract these few sentences, and look at what remains. A body of work that says everything to the contrary.

NOTES

INTRODUCTION

1. Antonin Artaud, *The Theater and Its Double*, trans. Mary Caroline Richards (New York: Grove Weidenfeld, 1958), 86 (hereafter *TD*). [Throughout the book, works will generally be cited in the text proper after their first mention in the notes.]

2. "Fragments d'un journal d'enfer," published originally in *Commerce* 7 (Spring 1926). It can be found in *Oeuvres complètes d'Antonin Artaud, nouvelle édition revue et augmentée* (Paris: Gallimard, 1976, 1*: 111–20 (hereafter *OC*).

3. Gilles Deleuze and Félix Guattari evocatively call this kind of writing a "schizo flight" in, among other places, *Anti-Oedipus*, trans. Helen R. Lane, et. al. (Minneapolis: University of Minnesota Press, 1983).

4. Originally published under the title "Une correspondance," in *La nouvelle revue Française*, no. 132 (1 Sept. 1924). In Oct. 1927, it was published as *Correspondance avec Jacques Rivière* by Éditions de la Nouvelle Revue Française in the collection "Une oeuvre, un portrait," with a portrait of Artaud by Jean de Bosschère (see *OC*, 1*: 21–46)

5. Antonin Artaud, *Selected Writings*, trans. Helen Weaver, ed. and intro. Susan Sontag (Berkeley: University of California Press, 1988), 45 (hereafter *SW*).

6. A recent biography provides more details on his activities during this period: Florence de Mèredieu, *C'était Antonin Artaud* (Paris: Fayard, 2006). Also see Alain Virmaux, *Antonin Artaud et le théâtre* (Paris: Seghers, 1970).

7. This was driven home to me at the 2006–7 Bibliothèque Nationale Artaud exhibit. The section devoted to his film work projected excerpts from the films he acted in on about a dozen screens. Because of the angles of the exhibit and the reflective surfaces, you could, from at least one point in the room, see Artaud's face on eight screens simultaneously, including close-ups of him inciting riots and revolutions, being burned at the stake and strangled, praying and preaching, and more.

8. "Auréolé de l'image du poète 'fou' ou maudit, il est devenu pour beaucoup un symbole du combat pour la liberté" (as phrased in the Quarto Gallimard edition, *Artaud: Oeuvres*, ed. Évelyne Grossman [Paris: Quarto Gallimard, 2004], in the chronology on p. 1764).

9. Martin Esslin's widely read monograph on Artaud was published the same year and similarly stressed Artaud's "presence" and "suffering." See *Antonin Artaud* (London: John Calder, 1976), 2 and *passim*.

202 : NOTES TO PAGES 8–12

10. He has been called a "Martyr of Illogicality," "Saint Artaud," a prophet, and much more. For "martyr of illogicality," see Wallace Fowlie, *Dionysus in Paris* (New York: Meridian, 1960), 207. "Saint Artaud" served, more recently, as the title of Philippe Sollers's review of Artaud's collected works in *Nouvel observateur*, no. 2080, Sept. 16–22, 2004: 57–58.

11. "La tendance générale était au lyrisme et à la vénération fanatique" (Alain Virmaux and Odette Virmaux, *Artaud: Un bilan critique* [Paris: Belfond, 1979], 119). Virmaux and Virmaux cite a list of extracts taken from journals soon after his death exhibiting this tendency, such as: "Il est l'homme le plus beau, l'homme le plus vrai, l'homme le plus généreux, l'homme le moins homme," by Florence Loeb (Virmaux and Virmaux, *Artaud: Un bilan critique*, 120). This style created a myth of its own, as well as its backlash. Special issues of the periodicals *K* (nos. 1–2) and *84* (nos. 5–6) in 1948 consecrated to Artaud in this tone were countered by a controversial issue of *La tour de feu* (nos. 63–64, Dec. 1959) that attempted to "désacraliser" Artaud. This effort was met with an even more fervent counterattack: the issue itself garnered almost two hundred responses, some calling it, for example, "l'obscène repas" (Daniel Briolet, "Antonin Artaud et *La tour de feu*, une prédiliction de longue date," in *Artaud en revues*, ed. Olivier Penot-Lacassagne [Lausanne: L'Age d'homme, 2005], 81–101, at 94).

12. Paule Thévenin, cited in Virmaux and Virmaux, *Artaud: Un bilan critique*, 120.

13. "Artaud n'était pas fou, il était juif. Comme Jésus-Christ" (Sylvère Lotringer, "Artaud était-il chrétien?" in *Fous d'Artaud* [Paris: Sens and Tonka, 2003], 13–38, at 38). My comments on Lotringer's essay assume that his argument is meant in earnest.

14. "Est-ce que souffrir serait, finalement, penser?" (Maurice Blanchot, "Artaud," *La nouvelle revue française* 4, no. 47 [1956]: 873–81, at 881).

15. "Artaud est la souffrance même" (Jacques Derrida, "Artaud, oui ...", *Europe: Revue littéraire mensuelle* 80, nos. 873–74 [2002]: 23–38, at 28).

16. The appeal of his tortured persona is not limited to English and French academic and artistic circles. Novels, plays, and poems inspired by "Artaud" proliferate, and his iconic image appears in punk, metal, and rock music, as well as throughout visual and performance art. Alain Clerc and Olivier Penot-Lacassagne have written an overview of Artaud as icon in music circles in "Artaud dans la presse alternative: L'exemple des fanzines rock," in Penot-Lacassagne, *Artaud en revues*, 177–88.

17. Guillaume Bridet writes: "S'impose ainsi, dans la grande tradition de la malédiction romantique, la figure d'un poète génial et souffrant—génial parce qu'ayant souffert plus qu'aucun autre poète ou aucun homme avant lui" ("Retour sur l'histoire d'une malédiction poétique et éditoriale," in Penot-Lacassagne, *Artaud en revues*, 153–75, at 160).

18. Eric Sellin: "His unwavering conviction that the art of the theater is the loftiest of arts and in direct contact with primal forces has lent an aura of aesthetic sanctity and martyrdom to many of the more impassioned but less explicable utterances in *The Theater and Its Double*" (*The Dramatic Concepts of Antonin Artaud* [Chicago: University of Chicago Press, 1975], 101).

19. Artaud's violent rejections, in this thinking, can be transformed into

springboards for liberal projects with little to support the assumption: "It is as if his negations clear a space for us in which we may exist, and even if we do not inhabit that space the contemplation of its pure emptiness from a distance is enough to effect both a degree of self-knowledge and inner peace" (Timothy Wiles, *The Theater Event* [Chicago: University of Chicago Press, 1980], 124).

20. "À la grande nuit" (In Total Darkness) (*OC,* 1**: 59–66) was a June 1927 pamphlet published in response to the May 1927 pamphlet "Au grand jour" (In Broad Daylight), in which the Surrealists announced Artaud's expulsion from the group and their adherence to the Communist Party.

21. See Geoffrey Baker, "Nietzsche, Artaud, and Tragic Politics," *Comparative Literature* (Winter 2003): 1–23, for the idea of an engaged Artaudian art stemming from a reading of Adorno.

22. Another major branch of Artaud reception in the English language also operates within the countercultural project: that of the mystical/spiritual questers seeking alternatives to Western aesthetics, culture, and civilization. In this vein, Artaud's references to non-Western, non-modern cultures, metaphysics, and parascientific avenues of exploration such as alchemy take center stage. See Sellin, *Dramatic Concepts,* which analyzes Artaud's works in terms of "solar" and "lunar" drama; Jane Goodall's *Artaud and the Gnostic Drama* (Oxford: Clarendon Press, 1994); and abundant essays on Artaud's encounters with the Balinese theater and Tarahumaran Indians.

23. Peter Brook provides an exemplary instance of allegorizing "cruelty": "Artaud used the word 'cruelty' not to invoke sadism, but to call us toward a theatre more rigorous" (*The Shifting Point* [London: Methuen, 1988], 56).

24. Julian Beck, quoted in John Tytell, *The Living Theatre: Art, Exile, and Outrage* (New York: Grove Press, 1995), 248.

25. The translator, Mary Caroline Richards, brought the book to their attention while it was still in proofs. See Julian Beck, "Storming the Barricades," in *The Brig,* by Kenneth H. Brown, with an essay on the Living Theatre, by Julian Beck, and director's notes by Judith Malina (New York: Hill and Wang, 1965), 3–35, at 24.

26. Judith Malina, "Directing *The Brig,*" in Brown, *The Brig,* 83–107, at 106.

27. *Paradise Now,* written down by Judith Malina and Julian Beck (New York: Random House, 1971), 5.

28. The imagistic power of "revolution" separated from any real historical awareness is seen especially clearly in some contemporary youth cultures. Today, neo-Nazis are always calling for "revolution" and "resistance"; in fact, one of the major neo-Nazi record labels is "Resistance Records."

29. The one extensive exception to this is the work done by Alain Virmaux and Odette Virmaux over the course of many books and articles devoted to Artaud's theatrical work. See esp. Virmaux, *Antonin Artaud et le théâtre,* and Virmaux and Virmaux, *Artaud: Un bilan critique.*

30. "L'écrit d'Artaud, la sensation d'excès qu'il donne, servent bien plutôt d'impulsion à un positionnement subversif, à la négation de l'ordre social existant" (Olivier Penot-Lacassagne, "Vérités de *Tel Quel,*" in Penot-Lacassagne, *Artaud en revues,* 102–23, at 120).

31. Julia Kristeva, "Le sujet en procès," in *Artaud* (Paris: Union Générale d'Éditions, coll. 10/18, 1973), 43–108.

32. Jacques Derrida, "La parole soufflée," in *Writing and Difference*, trans. Alan Bass (Chicago: University of Chicago Press, 1978), 169–95, at 169.

33. Michel Foucault, *Madness and Civilization*, trans. Richard Howard (New York: Vintage Books, 1988), 287.

34. Derrida, "Artaud, oui . . . ," 26–27.

35. Text taken from "Ci-gît," *OC*, 12: 77.

36. These disputes are covered well in Virmaux and Virmaux, *Artaud: Un bilan critique*, and throughout the essays in Penot-Lacassagne, *Artaud en revues*.

37. "Shit to the spirit"; "All writing is pigshit"; "For nothing appears to me now more dismal and mortally malevolent than the stratifying and inflexible sign of the cross,/nothing more erotically pornographic than Christ, ignoble sexual concretization of all false psychic enigmas" (*OC*, 9: 31). The translation of the last quotation might be something like: "To beat to death and fuck the face, to throw it in the face is the last language, the last music I know" (quoted in Mireille Larrouy and Olivier Penot-Lacassagne, "Antonin Artaud: 1943–1948," in Penot-Lacassagne, *Artaud en revues*, 59–79, at 73).

38. "Le privilège écrasant accordé aux dix, et surtout aux deux dernières années de la vie d'Artaud" (Bridet, "Retour sur l'histoire," 161).

39. "Après la mort d'Artaud, le mythe du poète maudit s'amplifie. Publier Artaud devient un impératif éditorial" (Larrouy and Penot-Lacassagne, "Antonin Artaud: 1843–1948," 77).

40. "Ne pas publier Artaud, c'était rester en marge de polémiques fructueuses; le publier, ce n'est que répondre aux sollicitations du moment" (Penot-Lacassagne, "Vérites de *Tel Quel*," 110).

41. The edition in question is the 2004 Quarto Gallimard collection. Derrida wrote the letter a few days before he died. As this is going into proofs, I have just seen the new *L'affaire Artaud*, by Florence de Mèredieu (Paris: Fayard, 2009), which is a seven-hundred-page overview of the publication disputes over Artaud's works.

42. Bridet observes that, in the midst of all the agenda-driven appropriations of his works, Artaud's oeuvre itself "resta finalement largement absente des débats" ("Retour sur l'histoire," 154).

43. "Un homme . . . qui s'est sacrifié sur l'autel de révélations surhumaines" (Bridet, "Retour sur l'histoire," 160).

44. "L'oeuvre d'Artaud quitte le domaine de la création et de l'art pour se révéler ce qu'elle est aussi: un phénomène essentiellement social pris dans les rivalités qu'occasionne l'économie des biens symboliques" (Bridet, "Retour sur l'histoire," 168).

45. This attitude being one she herself encouraged, something evident in the earlier quotation and in her editing practices.

46. "Tous les gens qui touchent à Artaud sont paranoïaques. . . . Ça a posé des problèmes pour tout, pour tout. C'est cette attitude que les gens prennent par rapport à Artaud. Ça a même frappé l'éditeur. Il n'a jamais vu ça" (Paule Thévenin, "Faux-Témoins: Entretien avec Paule Thévenin," in Lotringer, *Fous d'Artaud*, 261–69, at 265).

47. It's more than possible that the continued study of Artaud makes the studier mad. Susan Sontag is said to have reported as much after "living with" Artaud for years while compiling the *Selected Works*. In her introduction to that work, she writes, "To read Artaud through is nothing less than an ordeal" (*SW*, lvi).

48. Artaud also wrote two texts that speak of theater in 1947.

49. George L. Mosse, *Masses and Man: Nationalist and Fascist Perceptions of Reality* (New York: Howard Fertig, 1980), 18.

50. Robert O. Paxton discusses how a new fascism could appear as a "functional equivalent and not as an exact repetition" of the familiar fascisms in *The Anatomy of Fascism* (New York: Vintage, 2005), 175.

51. Roger Shattuck, "Artaud Possessed," in *The Innocent Eye* (New York: Farrar Straus Giroux, 1984), 169–186, at 186.

52. Rainer Friedrich, "The Deconstructed Self in Artaud and Brecht: Negation of Subject and Antitotalitarianism," *Forum for Modern Language Studies* 26, no. 3 (July 1990): 282–97; Naomi Greene, "'All the Great Myths Are Dark': Artaud and Fascism," in *Antonin Artaud and the Modern Theater*, ed. Gene A. Plunka (Cranbury: Associated University Presses, 1994), 102–16; Stephen Koch, "On Artaud," *Tri-Quarterly*, no. 6 (Spring 1966): 29–37.

53. When mentioned, such concerns are quickly explained away in light of Artaud's suffering or in light of some assumed liberal framework. Martin Esslin's final chapter in *Antonin Artaud* is exemplary. He dedicates several pages to possible dangerous outcomes of Artaud's ideas but brushes them aside in his last few paragraphs, claiming that "what Artaud himself felt, thought and stood for" was irreconcilable with violent applications of his ideas. He makes the self-defeating and insupportable argument: "Precisely because Artaud's ideas are totally incarnated in Artaud's life and personality, they only make sense in the context of his own experience, above all his own suffering. His rage and aggressiveness are, ultimately, merely poetic metaphors for his suffering and can only be understood as complementary to it" (113).

54. As Thomas Nipperdy wrote: "It is a rather petty endeavor to stretch Wagner or Nietzsche or Max Weber on the Procrustean bed of our concept of democracy and to examine them for 'pre-Fascist' tendencies or results. This is the tyranny of suspicion" (quoted in Steven E. Aschheim, *The Nietzsche Legacy in Germany, 1890–1990* [Berkeley: University of California Press, 1992], 318).

55. Georg Lukács, *The Destruction of Reason*, trans. Peter Palmer (London: Merlin, 1980), 4.

56. In Alice Yaeger Kaplan's study of fascism, she examines her chosen authors not only in their "fascist pronouncements and 'engagements,'" but also in their attitudes toward life reflected in their writings, even most usefully so in their writings that did not explicitly address political events (*Reproductions of Banality: Fascism, Literature, and French Intellectual Life* [Minneapolis: University of Minnesota Press, 1986], 46). Saul Friedländer's *Reflections of Nazism: An Essay on Kitsch and Death* (Bloomington: Indiana University Press, 1993) approaches Nazism less through "ideological categories," but by "rediscovering the durability of . . . deep-seated images, the structure of these phantasms"; thus, he traces "associations of imagery," because they reveal a "latent discourse" carried within them (15).

206 : NOTES TO PAGES 28–35

57. As Paxton points out: "In France . . . the richness, fervor, and celebrity of the intellectual revolt against classical liberal values in the early twentieth century would seem . . . to make that country a prime candidate for the successful establishment of fascist movements" (*Anatomy of Fascism*, 76).

CHAPTER 1

1. The original leaves some ambiguity as to whose "sex" is exploding: the scorpions who "se mettent à pulluler dans son sexe" could also be swarming on the Knight's penis. See *Le jet de sang* in the collection *L'ombilic des limbes* (*OC*, I*: 76).

2. *Heliogabalus* is Artaud's fantastic novel on the Roman emperor. These images proliferate in his writings—early poetry pairs "women with pretty cunts" with their own "miniature corpses" (*SW*, 71), among numerous other examples.

3. Artaud's writings almost never advocate self-slaughter; only one work, the screenplay *Eighteen Seconds*, explicitly depicts a suicide—a remarkable fact in light of the romanticization of suicide rampant in Paris at the time.

4. Egon Friedell, *A Cultural History of the Modern Age*, trans. Charles Francis Atkinson (New York: Alfred A. Knopf, 1964).

5. As Christopher Innes argues in *Avant-Garde Theatre 1892–1992* (London: Routledge, 1993).

6. Paxton notes that the Great War was "at the root of much . . . that was violent and angry in the postwar world," including Bolshevism, expressionist painting, and fascism: "Four years of industrialized slaughter had left little of Europe's legacy unaltered and nothing of its future certain" (*Anatomy of Fascism*, 28–29).

7. Freud: "I can at least listen without indignation to the critic who is of the opinion that when one surveys the aims of cultural endeavor and the means it employs, one is bound to come to the conclusion that the whole effort is not worth the trouble, and that the outcome of it can only be a state of affairs which the individual will be unable to tolerate." Freud concludes that in "the present time" the "human instinct of aggression and self-destruction" may be more powerful than our attempts to master it, which could have serious consequences: "Men have gained control over the forces of nature to such an extent that with their help they would have no difficulty in exterminating one another to the last man" (*Civilization and Its Discontents*, trans. Joan Riviere [London: Hogarth Press, 1982], 81–82). See André Malraux, *The Temptation of the West*, trans. and intro. Robert Hollander (New York: Vintage Books, 1961), 97.

8. Modris Eksteins, *Rites of Spring: The Great War and the Birth of the Modern Age* (Boston: Houghton Mifflin Company, 2000), at 328.

9. Louis-Ferdinand Céline, *Bagatelles pour un massacre* (Paris: Denoël, 1937), 289. Translated in Norman Cohn, *Warrant for Genocide* (London: Serif, 1996), 277–78.

10. The dadaists exemplify this obsessive destructive drive with no positive program well, but they were politically committed pacifists who had

seen the trenches firsthand. We find the pro-war version of this impulse expressed much more widely and frequently in Germany and Italy. In France, we find it in the art and politics of a smaller number of artists and thinkers, such as Céline, rather than in the majority of the French avant-garde.

11. Friedell connects the comprehensive physical destruction of the epidemic with periods of prolonged mass psychoses in which, he argues, worldviews are so shaken that metaphysical doubts and fear reign throughout the long period following the event.

12. For Friedell, who committed suicide at the onset of World War II, the possibility that a great new era would arise from the ashes of World War I never materialized. Artaud never enjoyed the optimism that manages to inflect Friedell's writing, and since he spent the second war in asylums, he certainly never saw a new age dawn, either.

13. Nicholas Hewitt, *Les Maladies du Siècle: The Image of Malaise in French Fiction and Thought in the Inter-War Years* (Hull: Hull University Press, 1988).

14. Hewitt traces the development of the Romantic vision of "intellectuality, youth, neurosis and sickness" (*Maladies du Siècle*, 10) into a "morbid pathological state" (24) after World War I.

15. Stephen Koch discusses Artaud's early writings (from the 1920s) similarly. He argues that one enters into proximity with Artaud through his writings, but not into logical discourse: "Their words embody an esthetic of action as experienced in shock" ("On Artaud," 36).

16. Artaud never entered the battlefield himself, having been released from training in 1917 for reasons of health and, subsequently, spending much of the war in sanatoriums. But he could not avoid direct knowledge of it in such a situation. Many men in Artaud's circles had been wounded; many more had fought; the images were everywhere. Additionally, Artaud had acted in two films that rigorously restaged—one in the trenches in Verdun themselves—the experience of French soldiers in the trenches: *Verdun, visions d'histoire* (1928) and *Les croix de bois* (1932).

17. Walter Benjamin's formulation comes to mind: "[Mankind's] self-alienation has reached such a degree that it can experience its own destruction as an aesthetic pleasure of the first order" ("The Work of Art in the Age of Mechanical Reproduction," in *Illuminations*, ed. Hannah Arendt, trans. Harry Zohn [New York: Schocken Books, 1968], 217–51, at 242). But even more apropos is Hugh Trevor-Roper's observation: "The prospect of universal destruction may be exhilarating to some aesthetic souls, especially to those who do not intend to survive it and are therefore free to admire, as a spectacle, the apocalyptic setting of their own funeral. But those who must live on in the charred remainder of the world have less time for such purely spiritual experiences" (*The Last Days of Hitler* [New York: Collier Books, 1970], 137).

18. He draws on information from the fourteenth-, sixteenth-, and eighteenth-century (the most extensive) Western European plagues.

19. Artaud's interest in correspondences during this period echoes that of Paracelsus, who sought proofs in the natural sciences for a philosophy based on a macro- and microcosmic system. In 1921, Artaud's doctor and friend René Allendy wrote a book on Paracelsus's ideas vis-à-vis alchemy, astrology, and the Kabbalah: *Symbolisme des nombres, essai d'arithmosophie.*

For an exhaustive study on how Artaud's worldview relates to Gnosticism, see Goodall, *Artaud and the Gnostic Drama*. Gnosticism had been enjoying a revival of interest among artists since the late nineteenth century in France, and it also was a major influence on Madame Blavatsky's Theosophical Society.

20. Stanton B. Garner notes that Artaud's writing evoked another "recent demographic trauma": "the influenza pandemic of 1918 and 1919," which "had given the term 'plague' more viscerally immediate meanings." See Garner's description of the pandemic's parallels with the Black Plague in "Artaud, Germ Theory, and the Theatre of Contagion," *Theatre Journal* 58, no. 1 (2006): 1–14, at 8–9. This parallel is also never mentioned by Artaud.

21. On the necessity of bodily violence: "or whether a little real blood will be needed, right away, in order to manifest this cruelty" (*TD*, 88).

22. Cited and translated in Eksteins, *Rites of Spring*, 144.

23. Ernst Jünger, *Storm of Steel*, trans. Michael Hofmann (London: Penguin Books, 2004), 128.

24. A point of dramatic comparison here is Artaud's co-written (with Edgar Varèse) scenario *Il n'y a plus de firmament* (*No More Firmament*), ca. 1931 (unfinished). In this scenario, underworld inhabitants, monstrous and depraved, stream out into the streets once the sky has collapsed, heightening the terror already rampant because of the natural cataclysm.

25. Greil Marcus's *Lipstick Traces: A Secret History of the Twentieth Century* (Cambridge: Harvard University Press, 1989) paints a vivid picture of the dadaists' multifaceted relationship to the war.

26. Tzara moved to Paris and became a Surrealist, Hugo Ball retired to a religious life, and Huelsenbeck eventually practiced Jungian psychoanalysis in New York City.

27. For an examination of the complicated and varied political affiliations of the Italian Futurists, most significantly, those with fascism, see Günter Berghaus, *Futurism and Politics: Between Anarchist Rebellion and Fascist Reaction, 1909–1944* (Oxford: Berghahn Books, 1996).

28. Many theater scholars have read it in an Aristotelian sense, although Artaud shares little else with the ancient Greek drama critic. The notion of theatrically engineered catharsis itself is also politically problematic.

29. It might be of interest for those wanting more biographical facts on this point to investigate the works of Dr. Edouard Toulouse, Artaud's friend and doctor, with whom he worked closely on the journal *Demain*. Toulouse was a leader in mental health reforms and also a leftist eugenicist: he advocated a "biocracy" that would prevent mentally challenged people from procreating. See William H. Schneider, "The Scientific Study of Labor in Interwar France," *French Historical Studies* 17, no. 2 (1991): 410–46.

30. "Si les peuples, comme dit le Proverbe, ont le gouvernement qu'ils méritent, les époques aussi ont le fléau qu'elles méritent et, n'a pas la Peste, qui veut!" (*OC*, 4: 221).

31. "Mais pourquoi donc les hommes de 1930 mériteraient-ils pareil fléau?" (Olivier Penot-Lacassagne, *Antonin Artaud: "Moi, Antonin Artaud, homme de la terre"* [Croissy-Beaubourg (France): Éditions Aden, 2007], 149).

CHAPTER 2

1. Aschheim clearly demonstrates this idea throughout his study of the reception of Nietzsche in *Nietzsche Legacy in Germany*, particularly the postwar segments.

2. See, e.g., Isaiah Berlin's writings on irrationalism and counter-Enlightenment thinking, esp. "Joseph de Maistre and the Origins of Fascism," in *The Crooked Timber of Humanity*, ed. Henry Hardy (New York: Alfred A. Knopf, 1991), 91–174, and *The Magus of the North: J. G. Hamann and the Origins of Modern Irrationalism*, ed. Henry Hardy (London: John Murray, 1993). See also George L. Mosse, *The Culture of Western Europe: The Nineteenth and Twentieth Centuries* (Boulder: Westview Press, 1988) and "The Mystical Origins of National Socialism," in *Masses and Man*, 197–213. An underlying premise of Zeev Sternhell's book on the formation of fascism is: "The growth of fascism would not have been possible without the revolt against the Enlightenment and the French Revolution which swept across Europe at the end of the nineteenth century and the beginning of the twentieth" (*Birth of Fascist Ideology* [Princeton: Princeton University Press, 1994], 3). Perhaps the most exhaustive and controversial work in this vein centers on Germany: Lukács's *Destruction of Reason*. For Lukács, irrationalism was inherently reactionary, as it uncritically elevated intuition at the expense of understanding, exalted unjustifiable "natural orders," refuted historical progress, and extolled vitalism and myth. For him, the embrace of irrationalism led directly to National Socialism.

3. Counter-Enlightenment thought began flourishing in the mid-eighteenth century in Western Europe (with figures such as Johann Georg Hamann), then again in the early nineteenth century (with Joseph de Maistre and the widening influence of Romanticism), then erupted with great vigor among artists and intellectuals in France and Germany in the 1880s and '90s, coming to a violent climax in the 1930s and '40s with early fascist thinkers in Germany.

4. Friedrich, "Deconstructed Self," 287.

5. Artaud took detailed notes while researching the plague (see the notes to the plague essay and discarded fragments in *OC*, 4: 219–22, 277–78, 366–67); he clearly desired, as the *OC* points out, that "sa description de la peste soit du point de vue clinique tout à fait exacte" (277), while drawing his own, non-clinical conclusions. His friend and doctor René Allendy was researching the plague and its history in the 1930s. A contextualized study of its contemporary significations and Artaud's later attitude toward the subject can be found in Olivier Penot-Lacassagne, "Au commencement était la peste," in *Antonin Artaud*, 147–60.

6. Garner situates Artaud's essay in contemporaneous medicalized discourse in "Artaud, Germ Theory." This useful study does not reach to the political implications of the discourse, but Garner rightly notes that Artaud's plague discourse is clinical while not at all epidemiological (10) and that, "through a logic at once assertive and self-repudiating, contagion and the body become the animating centers of Artaud's medical metaphysics at the very moment their clinical meanings are superseded or bracketed from consideration" (11).

7. Constance Spreen, "Resisting the Plague: The French Reactionary Right and Artaud's Theater of Cruelty," *Modern Language Quarterly* 64, no. 1 (2003): 71–96, at 72–73. Spreen, in an otherwise fascinating essay, attempts to distance Artaud's plague metaphor from that of the French Right, asserting that, in Artaud's hands, it represents "a positive force" (73), but she supplies no support for this interpretation, no differentiation between their uses of the metaphor.

8. Artaud's hatred of science is stated even more clearly in a series of lectures he delivered in Mexico in 1936 that largely centered on condemnations of Western civilization:

> Everything that science has taken away from us, everything it isolates in its alembics, its microscopes, its scales, its complicated mechanisms, everything it reduces to numbers, we aspire to win back from science, which is stifling our vitality. (*SW*, 361; translation modified)

His opposition is grounded in a belief that our real life force is not intellectual and not to be found in specialization, but in intuition alone:

> Europe has dismembered nature with her separate sciences.
>
> Biology, natural history, chemistry, physics, psychiatry, neurology, physiology, all those monstrous germinations which are the pride of the Universities . . . are to enlightened minds [*les esprits éclairés*] merely a *loss of understanding* [*connaissance*]. (*SW*, 359; translation modified)

9. Richard Wagner, *The Art-Work of the Future and Other Works*, trans. William Ashton Ellis (Lincoln: University of Nebraska Press, 1993), 74.

10. In his Mexico lectures, Artaud echoes this sentiment exactly, adding a strong anti-European bias: "Reason, a European faculty, exalted beyond measure by the European mentality, is always an image of death" (*SW*, 358).

11. Friedrich Nietzsche, *The Birth of Tragedy* and *The Case of Wagner*, trans. Walter Kaufmann (New York: Vintage, 1967), 83–84.

12. For Wagner, it's an assumption of arrogance over the Folk; for Nietzsche, existence itself is under attack.

13. He also describes something not in the painting: a "parade" of daughters "strutting about, some as mothers of families, others as amazons, combing their hair and fencing" (*TD*, 34), when in fact there are only two daughters depicted, not doing any of those things.

14. An excellent collection of essays on the topic of primitivism and modern art can be found in Elazar Barkan and Ronald Bush, eds., *Prehistories of the Future: The Primitivist Project and the Culture of Modernism* (Stanford: Stanford University Press, 1995).

15. Artaud mentions "The Great Arcanum" in the context of the Kabbalah, although the term has meaning in alchemical traditions and the Tarot as well. It generally signifies the true, secret knowledge underlying any occult system.

16. See Monique Borie, *Antonin Artaud, le théâtre et le retour aux sources: Une approche anthropologique* (Paris: Gallimard, 1989); Florence de Mèredieu,

La Chine d'Antonin Artaud/Le Japon d'Antonin Artaud (Paris: Blusson, 2006); Kathy Foley, "Trading Art(s): Artaud, Spies, and Current Indonesian/American Artistic Exchange and Collaboration," *Modern Drama* 35, no. 1 (1992): 10–19; and Julie Stone Peters, "Artaud in the Sierra Madre: Theatrical Bodies, Primitive Signs, Ritual Landscapes," in *Land/Scape/Theater,* ed. Elinor Fuchs and Una Chaudhuri (Ann Arbor: University of Michigan Press, 2002), 228–51. For an excellent overview of Artaud's connection to alchemy, see Ann Demaitre, "The Theater of Cruelty and Alchemy: Artaud and *Le Grand Oeuvre,*" *Journal of the History of Ideas* 33, no. 2 (1972): 237–50.

17. Nicola Savarese researches Artaud's experience at the Balinese exposition and concisely concludes: "Artaud was in fact not interested in Balinese culture; he used the Balinese performance because its extraneousness to his own culture made it possible for him to delineate a difference. Artaud, finally, did not want to increase knowledge about Balinese dance but to use it to create a short-circuit. For Artaud, exoticism no longer represented, as it had done for 19th-century artists, a moment of friction with the familiar order but provided a way to react against the beautiful, the normal, of the Occident" ("1931: Antonin Artaud Sees Balinese Theatre at the Paris Colonial Exposition," *TDR* 45, no. 3 [2001]: 51–77, at 71).

18. Friedländer follows this trajectory through a lineage of Nazi-ist art, locating it in the desire to be free from the emerging scientism and materialism.

19. For Nietzsche, myth is perhaps invented but certainly essential; it is part of the aesthetic justification of the universe.

20. In all Artaud's writings, historical accuracy appears as an obstacle to engagement with deeper truths. A revealing contemporaneous example is found in a letter to Jean Paulhan in 1934 about Artaud's manuscript *Heliogabalus,* in which Artaud rejects Paulhan's questioning of the book's factual basis: "I am simply astonished that when confronted with a book written with my heart and with the skin of my entrails you dare . . . to ask me whether it is true. I think that this is either felt or not felt" (*SW,* 337). The "Superior Reality" of the book, its truth beyond truth, should be above question:

> A great many details are invented; the Esoteric Truths which I wanted to be true in *spirit* are frequently and deliberately FALSIFIED in form: but form is nothing; there is excess, exaggerations of images, wild statements; but then an atmosphere of madness is established in which the rational loses its footing but the spirit advances fully armed. In the last analysis a desperate sincerity underlies it, even under the apparent distortion. (337)

The impassioned explanation of an artistic commonplace (using a historical event as an impetus for a fictional work) reveals something more than artistic principle in this instance. History, for Artaud, is beyond irrelevant ("History, which records facts, is an image of dead reason" [*SW,* 358]): it is an obstacle to truth.

21. A striking example of how Artaud conceives of this force can be found in his infamous reading of a draft of the "Plague" essay at the Sorbonne in March 1933. As Anaïs Nin recounts, Artaud did not want to give a talk

"about" the plague but, instead, he said, "I want to give them [the audience] the experience itself, the plague itself, so they will be terrified" (*The Diary of Anaïs Nin, Volume One, 1931–1934,* ed. and intro. Gunther Stuhlmann [New York: Harcourt Brace and Company, 1994], 192). So he attempted to enact dying of the plague:

> His face was contorted with anguish, one could see the perspiration dampening his hair. His eyes dilated, his muscles became cramped, his fingers struggled to retain their flexibility. He made one feel the parched and burning throat, the pains, the fever, the fire in the guts. He was in agony. He was screaming. (192)

Writhing on the ground at the end of his "talk," with no one left in the hall except a handful of friends, Artaud showed that his interest in the plague was as a way to initiate others into the terribleness of his perception of the true life force. As Nin wrote on first meeting Artaud and hearing him speak about his ideas for "The Theater and the Plague": "No talking. No analysis. Contagion by acting ecstatic states" (187).

22. Wagner, *Art-Work,* 71.

23. See a detailed overview of Nietzsche's reception by the Nazis in Aschheim, *Nietzsche Legacy in Germany,* esp. the chapters "Nietzsche in the Third Reich," "National Socialism and the Nietzsche Debate," and "Afterword: Nietzsche and Nazism." George L. Mosse covers the influence of Wagner on the fascist theater well in the chapter "Public Festivals: The Theatre and Mass Movements," in *The Nationalization of the Masses* (New York: Howard Fertig, 1975), 100–126. An exhaustive, if controversial and certainly very speculative, argument about the extent of Wagner's influence on Hitler is made in Joachim Köhler, *Wagner's Hitler* (Cambridge: Polity, 2000).

24. Emilio Gentile argues that the search for a "total life," a secular religion, was common to "all the avant-garde movements that arose in Italy prior to fascism." They "constituted a polemical attack against rationalist political ideologies, . . . the theoretical systems of understanding and defining the course of history which had dominated the political culture of the nineteenth century" (*The Struggle for Modernity: Nationalism, Futurism, and Fascism* [Westport, Conn.: Praeger, 2003], 52–53).

25. Nicholas Goodrick-Clarke, *The Occult Roots of Nazism: Secret Aryan Cults and Their Influence on Nazi Ideology* (New York: New York University Press, 2004), 18.

26. Helene Petrovna Blavatsky, *The Secret Doctrine: Synthesis of Science, Religion and Philosophy, Part I* (Whitefish, Mont.: Kessinger Publishing, 2003) (orig. published 1888), 8.

27. This endless and endlessly interesting topic is explored at some length in Stephen Schloesser's recent *Jazz Age Catholicism* in terms of the cultural attraction of Catholicism after World War I. See *Jazz Age Catholicism: Mystic Modernism in Postwar Paris, 1919–1933* (Toronto: University of Toronto Press, 2005).

28. Indeed, Des Esseintes is based on the real Comte de Montesquiou, whose apartment, with its secular-religious combination of altar railings, bearskins, sleds, a pulpit, a gold-encrusted tortoise, and choir bells, allegedly

made a huge impression on Mallarmé. See Robert Baldick, *The Life of J.-K. Huysmans* (Oxford: Clarendon Press, 1955). Montesquiou also inspired Proust's Baron de Charlus.

29. See *La révolution surréaliste*, no.3, 15 Apr. 1925, which Artaud edited and for which he wrote most of the articles. He subtitled it "1925: Fin de l'ère chrétienne." This issue contains three letters to three spiritual leaders: the pope, the Dalaï-Lama, and the Buddha. Artaud addresses the latter two as spiritual gurus ("Nous sommes tes très fidèles serviteurs, ô Grand Lama" [*OC*, 1**: 42]) and the first as a fraud, traitor, and dog ("Nous n'avons que faire de tes canons, index, péché, confessional, prêtraille, nous pensons à une autre guerre, guerre à toi, Pape, chien," [*OC*, 1**: 41]).

30. Artaud's contempt for Christianity is evident throughout his life's writings, alternating with periods of fervent belief, in which he at times identified himself as Jesus.

31. Roger Griffin, "Staging the Nation's Rebirth: The Politics and Aesthetics of Performance in the Context of Fascist Studies," in Günter Berghaus, ed., *Fascism and Theatre: Comparative Studies on the Aesthetics and Politics of Performance in Europe, 1925–1945* (Oxford: Berghahn Books, 1996): 11–29, at 15.

32. Mark Antliff also describes in *Avant-Garde Fascism* how fascists wanted to erase democratic materialism, which was "associated with a political tradition grounded in Enlightenment rationalism; the national socialists therefore turned to the antirationalism of figures such as the sociologist Gustave Le Bon, or philosophers Henri Bergson and Friedrich Nietzsche, to justify their theories of political transformation." See Mark Antliff, *Avant-Garde Fascism: The Mobilization of Myth, Art, and Culture in France, 1909–1939* (Durham: Duke University Press, 2007), 7.

33. Zeev Sternhell, *Neither Right nor Left: Fascist Ideology in France*, trans. David Maisel (Berkeley: University of California Press, 1986), 214.

34. Paxton discusses the history of fascism in five stages: "Creating Fascist Movements," "Taking Root," "Getting Power," "Exercising Power," and "The Long Term: Radicalization or Entropy?"

35. Historians of fascism struggle with the difficulty of establishing a "fascist minimum"—a set of terms that would provide a basic commonality that a definition of fascism might rest on. This is nearly impossible because, while it manifests specific traits that different analyses can almost consistently identify, fascism does not, in fact, have a clearly definable program, either internally or across different manifestations. In fact, scholars of fascism do not agree if we can call what happened in Italy and Germany before World War II even remotely the same politics. (The opening pages of most studies of fascism attest to the enormity of this challenge.) Where analyses tend to find more agreement is in different fascisms' rejections and repudiations.

36. "Neither of the Right nor of the Left" was first used in reference to the Falange in Spain. The phrase "the third way" was frequently used to describe fascism. It's a kind of definition by exclusion that creates what Paxton calls a "catch-all party." A revealing point of comparison here are the German Expressionists, who yearned for cataclysmic change with "a spiritual and artistic momentum which led some Expressionists toward socialism but others into the arms of the Nazis who themselves emphasized a revolution of the

spirit rather than social and economic change" (Mosse, *Culture of Western Europe,* 223). In other words, this yearning went both right and left.

37. These mobilizing passions can be found in Paxton, *Anatomy of Fascism,* 41.

38. Saul Friedländer politically contextualizes the kind of language we explored earlier, arguing that fascism replaced "the linear language of interconnected argument [and] step-by-step demonstration" with "the circular language of invocation" (*Reflections of Nazism,* 50).

39. Mosse, "Toward a General Theory of Fascism," in *Masses and Man,* 159–96, at 164.

40. See the discussion in the introduction. In his letter condemning the Surrealists' move to join the Communist Party, Artaud denounces "all real action," any revolution in the material world, especially including politics, because of his "deep-rooted sense of the profound futility of any action whatsoever" (*SW,* 145).

41. However, Naomi Greene points out that "in his very rejection of overt politics, [Artaud] may have been akin to those 'true fascists' who, in Sternhell's words, 'hated politics' and rejected capitalism and communism alike'" (*Antonin Artaud,* 107). The quotation is from Sternhell, *Neither Right nor Left,* 225.

42. See Susan Sontag, "Fascinating Fascism," in *Under the Sign of Saturn* (New York: Farrar Straus Giroux, 1980), 73–105. Other examples of "fascist art" include, for Sontag, works by Walt Disney, Busby Berkeley, and Stanley Kubrick.

43. Divisions between the French Right and Left in the 1920s and '30s were pronounced and even violent, marked by the rise of the Popular Front and the right-wing riots surrounding the Stavisky Affair.

44. A clear overview of this can be found in Spreen, "Resisting the Plague."

45. André Villeneuve, "La chronique des spectacles: Le théâtre de la cruauté," *L'action française,* Oct. 14, 1932.

46. Brasillach advises Artaud that "il ne faut pas confondre la puissance et le hurlement" ("La chronique des théâtres: Les Cenci," *L'action française,* 17 May 1935). Spreen notes that Brasillach himself was not immune to the aesthetics of full-blown fascist spectacle. A few years later, he was moved by the "poetry" of National Socialism when watching the choreography of light and sound in the Zeppelinfeld ceremony: it inundated the crowd with "the harshest ideas on the value of life and death" (quoted and translated in Spreen, "Resisting the Plague," 95).

47. Lucien Dubech, "La chronique des théâtres," *L'action française,* 24 May 1935. In return, as Sternhell notes, "The total lack of any real will to action in the Action Française, its flavor of a literary salon, its royalism could only be repellent to the genuine fascists" (*Neither Right nor Left,* 100).

48. "Le romantisme déchaîné par la défaite parmi l'anarchie naturelle à la Germanie était tout naturellement la plus vive image qu'on pût donner du désordre moral universel" (Dubech, "Chronique des théâtres").

49. Rhetorically, the work reminds one of nothing so much as the pamphlets issuing from the pens of the Jacobins. Simon Schama concisely de-

scribes the rhetoric of the French Revolution: "Revolutionary rhetoric was tuned to a taut pitch of elation and anger. Its tone was visceral rather than cerebral; idealistic rather than realistic; most powerful when it was dividing . . . most stirring when it was most punitive" (*Citizens: A Chronicle of the French Revolution* [New York: Vintage, 1989], 292).

50. Hannah Arendt, "Approaches to the 'German Problem,'" in *Essays in Understanding: 1930–1954* (New York: Schocken Books: 1994), 106–20, at 110.

51. Greene discusses Artaud's Mexico lectures in the context of his denunciations of Marxism, pointing out that it was obvious at the time that fascism was setting itself up as the alternative not only to Marxism but to all other political systems of the time (*Antonin Artaud*, 109).

CHAPTER 3

1. The phrase "crisis of bourgeois theater" was being used by figures as far apart as Benito Mussolini, Max Reinhardt, and Firmin Gémier for different political or social agendas.

2. Moves toward a quieter, more controlled audience had previously been championed, in varying forms, in the eighteenth century by Lessing and Voltaire; in the medieval period; and even, it could be argued, by Plato.

3. For two excellent analyses of this history, see Richard Butsch, *The Making of American Audiences: From Stage to Television, 1750–1990* (Cambridge: Cambridge University Press, 2000), whose study reflects trends equally applicable to England and Western Europe, and Neil Blackadder, *Performing Opposition: Modern Theater and the Scandalized Audience* (Westport, Conn.: Praeger, 2003). An examination of the role of the theater building itself in the evolution of the audience/performer relationship can be found in Michael Hays, *The Public and Performance: Essays in the History of French and German Theater, 1871–1900* (Ann Arbor: UMI Research Press, 1981).

4. This is one reason why innovation usually met great resistance among the new, conservative bourgeoisie. In these circles, as Peter Gay has noted, "originality implied unpredictable and not always welcome changes of unknown dimensions" (*Pleasure Wars* [New York: W. W. Norton and Co., 1998], 47).

5. Blackadder describes "the shift from theatregoing as participation to theatregoing as observation" (*Performing Opposition*, 13); Baz Kershaw writes in terms of the new consumer economy of the shift from "patron, to client, to customer" ("Oh for Unruly Audiences! Or, Patterns of Participation in Twentieth-Century Theatre," *Modern Drama* 44, no. 2 [2001]: 133–56, at 135).

6. Kershaw argues that this translates into coercive sessions of applause. The thinking is that the product needs to be good to justify the purchase, and clapping will make it so: "The standing ovation becomes an orgasm of self-congratulation for money so brilliantly spent" ("Oh for Unruly Audiences!" 144). In this vein, the *New York Times* ran an article on the now-mandatory standing ovation on Broadway: "The Tyranny of the Standing Ovation," *New York Times*, 21 Dec. 2003.

7. As Richard Sennett puts it, nineteenth-century spectators at the new

Paris (1875) and Bayreuth (1876) opera houses knew that they were to become "witness to a rite, 'larger' than life; the role of the audience is to see, not to respond" (*The Fall of Public Man* [New York: Knopf, 1976], 209).

8. Quoted in Sennett, *Fall of Public Man,* 208.

9. Truly, nothingness: today, recorded messages instruct audience members to unwrap any cough drops they might want before the curtain rises.

10. A richly contextualized study of Wagner's staging innovations can be found in Patrick Carnegy, *Wagner and the Art of the Theatre* (New Haven: Yale University Press, 2006).

11. The influence of Wagner on Antoine is often overlooked. Antoine devotes several pages in *Le théâtre libre* to Wagner's innovations and reproduces a plan of the Bayreuth theater building as a model for his own.

12. "On a donc été amené à supprimer les galeries et toutes les places de côté, loge, baignoire ou pourtour. C'est le principe même du théâtre de Bayreuth" (André Antoine, *Le théâtre libre, mai 1890* [Paris: (unknown), 1890], 50).

13. Antoine writes: "Les quatre réformes suivantes sont devenues indispensables: *Pièces nouvelles, salle confortable, places tarifées à bon marché, troupe d'ensemble*" (*Théâtre libre,* 27).

14. Antoine, *Théâtre libre,* 53.

15. There is a striking irony here: one of the first populist avant-garde movements in theater—one that made history for its scandalous productions of social realist plays by Hauptmann, Ibsen, Tolstoy, and Zola—played a decisive role in drastically reducing the kinds of agency its spectators might exercise. In the name of social freedom, physical conformity was enforced.

16. Interestingly, riots at Symbolist and Naturalist theaters did not necessarily signify efforts on the part of the artists to agitate, empower, or deliberately engage audiences in participation or discussion. In fact, they often demonstrated the opposite: that audience members were being asked to watch performances that were alien or offensive to them while being told keep their intellectual or aesthetic objections to themselves. Blackadder's chapter "'This Is Not Irish Life!': Defending National Identity: Synge's *Playboy of the Western World,*" in *Performing Opposition,* 69–108, shows how this was disturbingly evidenced when Yeats called in police to enforce silence at a performance of *The Playboy of the Western World* at the Abbey Theatre in 1907. Blackadder suggests that riots were particularly pronounced in this era because of the new restraints on audience members: controversial material was presented to spectators at the same time as they were instructed to not respond.

17. Susan Bennett's *Theatre Audiences: A Theory of Production and Reception* (London: Routledge, 1997) analyzes the myriad ways subsequent theater artists have conceived of what she terms a "productive and emancipated spectator" (4).

18. *Selected Works of Alfred Jarry,* ed. Roger Shattuck and Simon Watson Taylor (New York: Grove Press, 1965), 84.

19. Michael Kirby and Victoria Nes Kirby, *Futurist Performance,* with manifestos and playscripts translated from the Italian by Victoria Nes Kirby (New York: PAJ Publications, 1986).

20. This is the title of a 1909 manifesto by Marinetti.

21. As described by Roger Vitrac and Artaud in "The Alfred Jarry Theatre and Public Hostility," *CW*, 2: 34.

22. The Surrealists, led by Breton, threatened to disrupt the second performance of Strindberg's *A Dream Play*, and the Jarry Theater kept them out by hiring police.

23. "Ce spectacle comprend trois pièces inédites dont on assure qu'elles apportent une formule théâtrale audacieuse" (unidentified newspaper clipping, 18 May 1927, Bibliothèque Nationale de France (hereafter BNF), Département des Arts du spectacle, Théâtre Alfred Jarry box, RT 3800).

24. Antonin Artaud, Roger Blin, and others, "Antonin Artaud's *Les Cenci*," *The Drama Review* 16, no. 2 (1972): 91–145, at 91.

25. Jean-François Lyotard, "The Tooth, the Palm," trans. Anne Knap and Michel Benamou, *SubStance* 5, no. 15 (1976): 105–10, at 109. Lyotard succinctly poses the question of the possibility of such an energetic theater: "The business of an energetic theater is not to make allusion to [sensory events]. . . . Its business is neither to suggest that such and such means such and such, nor to say it, as Brecht wanted. Its business is to produce the highest intensity (by excess or by lack of energy) of what there is, without intention. That is my question: is it possible, how?" (110).

26. This idea also drew from the work of Reinhardt, who, in 1919, adapted a former circus building into a theater, the Grosses Schauspielhaus. It eliminated the barrier between audience and performers and seated three thousand people. The next year, in France, Firmin Gémier used a circus for his production of *Oedipus Rex*, with a cast of hundreds. We examine Artaud's connections to these directors in section III.

27. Arnold Aronson, *The History and Theory of Environmental Scenography* (Ann Arbor: UMI Research Press, 1981), 54.

28. For a history of innovations in "total theater" design, see Aronson, *History and Theory*, esp. the chapters "Reactions against the Proscenium" (29–46), and "Surrounding Space Theatres" (47–66).

29. Artaud was at least somewhat familiar with the theories of the major international total theater artists, mentioning Appia and Craig in correspondence, and he was enthusiastic about the work of Reinhardt and Piscator, whose productions were being staged in Berlin when he was there. Christopher Innes notes similarities in Artaud's staging ideas to those of contemporaneous German artists, including Jessner, Piscator, and Gropius ("Antonin Artaud and the Theatre of Cruelty," in *Avant-Garde Theatre*, 59–94, at 92).

30. This idealist conceptual basis is seriously questionable, however: see the discussion in the next chapter of how Goebbels and fascist theater theorists were eager to adopt these very strategies.

31. Laszlo Moholy-Nagy, "Theater, Circus, Variety," in *The Theater of the Bauhaus*, ed. and intro. Walter Gropius, trans. Arthur S. Wensinger (Middletown, Conn.: Wesleyan University Press, 1961), 49–70, at 67–68.

32. As in Piscator's 1929 production #*218*, about the criminal code on abortion.

33. This "circular total theater," "*synthetic—multisensational—simultaneous—multiple stages—aeropoetic—aeropictorial—cinematographic—radiophonic—*

tactile—olfactory—sound-producing," is described in the 1933 manifesto "Total Theater: Its Architecture and Technology," translated in *F. T. Marinetti: Critical Writings,* ed. Günter Berghaus, trans. Doug Thompson (New York: Farrar, Straus and Giroux, 2006), 400–407.

34. Michael Kirby, *A Formalist Theatre* (Philadelphia: University of Pennsylvania Press, 1987), 100.

35. Hans-Thies Lehmann, *Postdramatic Theatre,* trans. Karen Jürs-Munby (New York: Routledge, 2006), 61.

36. These connections are examined in detail in chapter 5.

37. For a discussion of points of overlap in this regard, see the context provided in David Graver, "Antonin Artaud and the Authority of Text, Spectacle, and Performance," in *Contours of the Theatrical Avant-Garde: Performance and Textuality,* ed. James M. Harding (Ann Arbor: University of Michigan Press, 2000), 43–57.

38. Artaud's early admiration for these directors, evidenced in many letters and reviews of their work, gave way to absolute frustration with the limitation of their vision. See his letter to Jean Paulhan about the work of the Cartel: "Ces pourritures branlantes, . . . ces fantômes anti-représentatifs qui sont Jouvet, Pitoëff, Dullin, voire Gémier, etc. Quand aura-t-on fini de remuer de l'ordure" (*OC,* 3: 124).

39. Artaud's passionate readings of artworks throughout his oeuvre are wonderfully illustrative of how he is drawn to pieces that are either massively difficult or surprisingly minor—from the *Zohar* to automatic sketches by André Masson. These readings reveal his attraction to works with the highest number of rough edges—tidier, well-crafted pieces almost never engage his interest.

CHAPTER 4

1. By "people's theaters" I refer to theaters meant to be performed for, and usually by, large numbers of "the people." The name "people's theaters" has also been applied to theaters that were not necessarily aimed at crowds, but which sought to produce smaller-scale social-realist plays *for* the people, such as the Freie Volksbühne in Berlin in 1892. The most accessible introduction to the many definitions and complex history of people's theaters is David Bradby and John McCormick, *People's Theatre* (London: Croom Helm Ltd., 1978).

2. Romain Rolland, *The People's Theater,* trans. Barrett H. Clark (New York: H. Holt and Company, 1918), 80.

3. In this, they resembled the German popular theater movement begun in 1890, which emphasized affordability for all citizens.

4. John Willett discusses how Reinhardt's interest in theater by and for the masses led to his establishing a "people's theater" at the Grosses Schauspielhaus (*The Theatre of the Weimar Republic* [London: Holmes and Meier, 1988], 150), a theater that was eventually used by the Nazis.

5. This was especially the case in Germany and Italy because they had literally or practically lost the war. Italy, although technically a "victor," lost six hundred thousand men in its short engagement with the war and did not

emerge with much to show for it, and Italians felt deeply betrayed by the Allies because of the Versailles Treaty.

6. Erika Fischer-Lichte, *Theatre, Sacrifice, Ritual: Exploring Forms of Political Theatre* (London: Routledge, 2005), 96.

7. Both Italian fascists and the National Socialists asked Reinhardt to direct for their new theater initiatives.

8. Victoria de Grazia, *The Culture of Consent: Mass Organization of Leisure in Fascist Italy* (New York: Cambridge University Press, 1981), vii.

9. Translated in Jeffrey T. Schnapp, *Staging Fascism: 18BL and the Theater of Masses for Masses* (Stanford: Stanford University Press, 1996), 33.

10. Translated in Schnapp, *18BL*, 33.

11. This impulse was taking on different forms in Russia. An overview of revolutionary and mass theaters there can be found in Robert Leach, *Revolutionary Theatre* (New York: Routledge, 1994).

12. Schnapp's detailed examination of the production of *18BL* is accompanied by a study of other Italian fascist theatrical projects in their political, social, and theatrical contexts. Other sources of information on Italian fascist theater in English include the collection *Fascism and Theatre,* edited by Günter Berghaus, and Mabel Berezin, "Cultural Form and Political Meaning: State-Subsidized Theater, Ideology, and the Language of Style in Fascist Italy," *American Journal of Sociology* 99, no. 5 (1994): 1237–86.

13. For English-language overviews of this phenomenon, see Gerwin Strobl, *The Swastika and the Stage: German Theatre and Society, 1933–1945* (Cambridge: Cambridge University Press, 2007), esp. chaps. 2 and 3; William Niven, "The Birth of Nazi Drama?" in *Theatre under the Nazis,* ed. John London (Manchester: Manchester University Press, 2000), 54–95; Bruce Zortman, *Hitler's Theater: Ideological Drama in Nazi Germany* (El Paso: Firestein, 1984); and Erika Fischer-Lichte, "Producing the *Volk* Community: The *Thingspiel* Movement, 1933–36," in *Theatre, Sacrifice, Ritual,* 122–58. In addition to *Thing* plays, the cultural backdrop of Nazi theater is explored throughout George L. Mosse's *Nationalization of the Masses.*

14. For an overview of a range of state-supported Italian fascist theater projects, see Patricia Gaborik, "Italy: The Fancy of a National Theatre?" in *National Theatres in a Changing Europe,* ed. S. E. Wilmer (New York: Palgrave Macmillan, 2008), 138–50.

15. Translated in Pietro Cavallo, "Theatre Politics of the Mussolini Régime and Their Influence on Fascist Drama," in Berghaus, *Fascism and Theatre,* 113–32, at 113.

16. For a study of a wide range of inheritors of the idea of the *Gesamtkunstwerk,* see Matthew Wilson Smith, *The Total Work of Art: From Bayreuth to Cyberspace* (New York: Routledge, 2007).

17. As Wilhelm von Schramm, another important voice in interwar German theater, put it (translated in Niven, "Birth of Nazi Drama?" 56).

18. Translated in Schnapp, *18BL*, 51.

19. Translated in Schnapp, *18BL*, 68.

20. Griffin, "Staging the Nation's Rebirth," 17.

21. Translated in Schnapp, *18BL,* 212, n10.

22. Translated in Cavallo, "Theatre Politics," 123.

23. Translated in Cavallo, "Theatre Politics," 118.

24. Florentine theater critic Cipriano Giachetti, translated in Schnapp, *18BL*, 68.

25. The play *18BL* alone "brought together two to three thousand amateur actors, an air squadron, an infantry brigade, a cavalry brigade, fifty trucks, eight tractor plows, four field and machine-gun batteries, ten field radio stations, and six photoelectric units in a stylized Soviet-style representation of the fascist revolution's past, present, and future" (Schnapp, *18BL*, 7–8).

26. John Willett cites a Nazi "aesthetician" writing that the "annual Nuremberg Rally [was] 'the *Thing*-concept made blood and spirit'" (*Theatre of the Weimar Republic*, 186). Strobl writes that interwar Germans found their "greatest" "true works of art" in the party rally, in "Hitler's highly theatrical *Gesamtkunstwerk* of uniforms, music, lighting and carefully chosen settings" (*Swastika and the Stage*, 27).

27. Strobl points to this lineage in late nineteenth-century Germany: "Wilhelmine attempts to explore the mystical 'essence' of people, nations or the universe led to the pseudo-religious plays of the Third Reich" (*Swastika and the Stage*, 46).

28. "Ce qu'Artaud cherche dans les mythes . . . c'est une force de dissolution des particularismes individuels, une posture 'unitaire' et collective qui ne sépare pas le sujet et l'objet, la matière et l'esprit, l'homme et l'animal—autrement dit, des passages et des analogies qui effacent les contours limités des 'caractères' humains" (Grossman, *Artaud: Oeuvres*, 403).

29. The whole list is translated in Zortman, *Hitler's Theater*, 38.

30. See Strobl, *Swastika and the Stage*, 75–76, for a fuller discussion.

31. Hal Foster, "Foreword," in Schnapp, *18BL*, xiii–xviii, at xvi.

32. Fischer-Lichte, *Theatre, Sacrifice, Ritual*, 136.

33. Artaud was familiar with and enthusiastic about the work of Reinhardt and Piscator. It is after visiting Berlin in 1930 and, presumably, seeing their work, that he first mentions the idea of creating "un théâtre d'action et de masses" (*OC*, 3: 217). It is not clear if he knew about the *Thing* project.

34. Ritual would be another critical avenue to pursue here in thinking about the "real" invoked by these theaters. This is the route Erika Fischer-Lichte takes in her examination of mass theaters in *Theatre, Sacrifice, Ritual*, which draws on Richard Schechner's description of different forms of performance in theater, ritual, play, and more in *Performance Theory*. Since my comparison here is like with like in terms of form—theater with theater—I assume them to have comparable levels of "reality." Fischer-Lichte, however, provides a valuable perspective in thinking about varying levels of efficacy and permanence of community among different mass theaters, drawing distinctions between a "limited aesthetic community" and theaters with "lasting" social and political agendas.

CHAPTER 5

1. Serge Moscovici recalls Solon's declaration that a single Athenian is a wily fox but a group of Athenians is a flock of sheep, and the Roman proverb:

"Senatores omnes boni viri, senatus romanus mala bestia" (Senators are all good men, the Roman senate is an evil beast) (*The Age of the Crowd: A Historical Treatise on Mass Psychology,* trans. J. C. Whitehouse [Cambridge: Cambridge University Press, 1985.], 14). This book is a comprehensive study and overview of crowd theory.

2. Gustave Le Bon, *The Crowd: A Study of the Popular Mind* (Mineola, N.Y.: Dover, 2002), ix.

3. Theodor Adorno, "Freudian Theory and the Pattern of Fascist Propaganda," in *The Culture Industry,* ed. J. M. Bernstein (London: Routledge Classics, 2001), 132–57; Mosse, *Nationalization of the Masses;* Moscovici, *Age of the Crowd.*

4. Serge Moscovici, "The Discovery of the Masses," in *Changing Conceptions of Crowd Mind and Behavior,* ed. Carl F. Graumann and Serge Moscovici (New York: Springer-Verlag, 1986), 5–25, at 15.

5. Elias Canetti, *Crowds and Power,* trans. Carol Stewart (New York: Farrar, Straus and Giroux, 1984), 77, 79.

6. Le Bon writes: "The fact that [individuals] have been transformed into a crowd puts them in possession of a sort of collective mind which makes them feel, think, and act in a manner quite different from that in which each individual of them would feel, think, and act were he in a state of isolation" (*Crowd,* 4).

7. José Ortega y Gasset, *The Revolt of the Masses* (New York: W. W. Norton and Co., 1930), 52 and *passim.*

8. Translated in Nicholas Hewitt, *The Life of Céline* (Oxford: Blackwell Publishers Ltd., 1999), 196.

9. For a classic articulation of the feeling of individual anonymity particular to the time, see Karl Jaspers, *Man in the Modern Age,* trans. Eden Paul and Cedar Paul (London: Routledge and Kegan Paul Ltd., 1959) (published in German in 1933).

10. Sigmund Freud, *Group Psychology and the Analysis of the Ego,* trans and ed. James Strachey (New York: W. W. Norton and Co., 1959), 20.

11. Sigmund Freud, *The Standard Edition of the Complete Psychological Works of Sigmund Freud,* trans. James Strachey (London: Hogarth and the Institute of Psycho-Analysis, 1966), 1: 82.

12. "I propose to treat the spectators like the snakecharmer's subjects and conduct them *by means of their organisms* to an apprehension of the subtlest notions" (*TD,* 81).

13. Moscovici stresses that individuals cease to be motivated by self-interest in a crowd: "When individuals are lost in the mass, they forget their own interests and accept common desires, or those desires which their leaders tell them are common to all" (*Age of the Crowd,* 31).

14. Translated in Greene, *Antonin Artaud,* 109.

15. William McDougall, *The Group Mind* (New York: G. P. Putnam's Sons, 1920), 35.

16. "The obvious conclusion to be drawn from this [the organic and persistent nature of crowd formation] is that man's nature is not, as a rule, fully realized in the individual" (Moscovici, "Discovery of the Masses," 18).

17. Koch argued persuasively that the form of Artaud's works is simply

the transmission of an impulse and therefore never complete: "These works do not, properly speaking, have a form: like the discourse to which they are phenomenologically related, they are potentially interminable" ("On Artaud," 36).

18. Alison Winter, *Mesmerized: Powers of Mind in Victorian Britain* (Chicago: University of Chicago Press, 1998), 48. This fascinating book studies animal magnetism, its uses, and its politics in Victorian England.

19. Alan Seymour, "Artaud's Cruelty," *London Magazine* 3, no. 12 (1964): 59–64, at 61.

CHAPTER 6

1. Helen Krich Chinoy, "The Emergence of the Director," in *Directors on Directing: A Source Book of the Modern Theater*, ed. Toby Cole and Helen Krich Chinoy (Indianapolis: Bobbs-Merrill, 1963), 1–77. This valuable book contains, in addition to Chinoy's introductory essay, translations of major texts by over thirty influential theater directors.

2. "Dans le tragédie grecque, dans les mystères, dans la Commedia dell'Arte, sous Elizabeth, sous Louis XIV, . . . on pouvait se passer de cette direction, occulte. La mythologie, la foi chrétienne, la joie populaire ou des goûts qui forment l'esthétique intangible d'une société fermée—voilà quels étaient les vrais metteurs en scène" (J. Kessel, quoted in André Veinstein, *La mise en scène théâtrale et sa condition esthétique* [Paris: Flammarion, 1955], 119).

3. Frederick Brown, *Theater and Revolution: The Culture of the French Stage* (New York: Vintage Books, 1989), 288.

4. Fischer-Lichte argues that the experiments by directors such as Reinhardt before the war attempted to build community with no political agenda, and that theaters after the war used those same strategies, but added an agenda to them. I think it is important to recognize that Reinhardt and others did not support the political uses made of their work, but it is also imperative to recognize the ways that work naturally turned toward successful implementation by the fascists. I am also not sure that it is possible to orchestrate crowds of people and not see that as a political act, but that is a larger question.

5. Essentially. There was also one performance at the Jarry Theater on 5 Jan. 1929, and some manifestos were written the following year.

6. The process of concentrating artistic as well as technical control over a production in one person had begun in the late eighteenth century with figures such as Goethe in Weimar and Garrick in Drury Lane, and new production methods such as extensive rehearsal periods, integrating scenic elements, and selective casting made this kind of consolidation increasingly possible.

7. Lee Simonson, quoted in Cole and Chinoy, *Directors on Directing*, 25.

8. Translated in Cole and Chinoy, *Directors on Directing*, 93, 91.

9. "The Art of the Theatre," first dialogue, was published in pamphlet form in 1905.

10. Translated in Cole and Chinoy, *Directors on Directing*, 46.

11. John Osborne, *The Meiningen Court Theatre, 1866–1890* (New York:

Cambridge University Press, 1988), 172. Saxe-Meiningen ran his company with the assistance of his wife, Ellen Franz, and his stage manager, Ludwig Chronegk.

12. See Patrick Carnegy, "Wagner and the Theatre of the Early Nineteenth Century," in *Wagner and the Art of the Theatre*, 3–45, for a discussion of Wagner's attempts to bring production elements under the composer's control in his operas.

13. Edward Gordon Craig, *On the Art of the Theatre* (London: Heinemann, 1957), 99. The other "masters," according to Craig, include the theater proprietor; the business manager; the stage-director; business men; leading actor and actress; the other actors; scenic, costume, and lighting designers; the technical worker; and general staff.

14. Translated in Cole and Chinoy, *Directors on Directing*, 41.

15. The displacement of the play did not occur in the United States (with artists such as the Living Theatre, the Performance Group, and others) until the 1950s and '60s. *The Theater and Its Double* had been translated into English in 1958 and was being read by these artists.

16. Translated in Cole and Chinoy, *Directors on Directing*, 31.

17. Translated in Cole and Chinoy, *Directors on Directing*, 94.

18. Translated in Cole and Chinoy, *Directors on Directing*, 90.

19. Translated in Cole and Chinoy, *Directors on Directing*, 55.

20. Martin Esslin, "Max Reinhardt: High Priest of Theatricality," *The Drama Review* 21, no. 2 (1977): 3–24, at 7.

21. Translated in Cole and Chinoy, *Directors on Directing*, 68.

22. Translated in Cole and Chinoy, *Directors on Directing*, 33.

23. Translated in Cole and Chinoy, *Directors on Directing*, 41.

24. Brown notes how frequently the language of the early French directors echoes that of the Terror, in the creation of a secular religion that demanded absolute immersion in the shared spirit of *le peuple*. Festivals that celebrated such secular-divine concepts as "The Supreme Being" and "Unity and Indivisibility" were inspired by the words of leaders such as Robespierre and Saint-Just, whose belief in the absolute need for unity of *le peuple* manifested itself as despotism. See *Theater and Revolution*, 298 and *passim*.

25. Quoted in Irène Eynat-Confino, *Beyond the Mask: Gordon Craig, Movement, and the Actor* (Carbondale: Southern Illinois University Press, 1987), 166.

26. Translated in Cole and Chinoy, *Directors on Directing*, 46. Copeau's sense of divine purpose was not just aesthetic: he converted to Catholicism in 1925, under the guidance of the fervently Catholic Paul Claudel.

27. See Virmaux, *Antonin Artaud et le théâtre*, 239–42, for a complete list of Artaud's theatrical engagements.

28. They performed in off-seasons when they could rent the space from other theaters. What we know of the performances comes to us from reviews, the creators' writings and correspondence, a few photographs, reflections by some of its many spectators and participants, production plans, publicity announcements, and reconstructed scripts of performances. Much of the material about this theater is accessible in the notes to *OC*, vol. 2; much in the BNF, Département des Arts du spectacle, Théâtre Alfred Jarry box, RT 3800. An overview of the Jarry Theater can be found in Virmaux and Virmaux, *Artaud:*

Un bilan critique. I have written at more length on each production of the Alfred Jarry Theater in "The Theatre before Its Double: Artaud Directs in the Alfred Jarry Theatre," *Theatre Survey* 46, no. 2 (2005): 247–73. In-depth analyses of Artaud's directing techniques can be found in Virmaux, *Antonin Artaud et le théâtre.*

29. Vitrac also contributed to their manifestos and tracts, although his primary focus was on playwriting. Aron was more managerial in function and dropped out of the project around 1927.

30. Antonin Artaud, *Collected Works,* trans. Victor Corti (London: Calder and Boyars, 1971), 2: 31 (hereafter *CW*).

31. *OC* 2: 20.

32. Production plans for Strindberg's *Ghost Sonata* and Vitrac's *Le Coup de Trafalgar* can be found in *OC,* 2: 101–22 and in *CW* 2:97–115.

33. "Le metteur en scène est le mandataire spirituel de l'auteur" (Paul-Louis Mignon, *Charles Dullin* [Lyon: La Manufacture, 1990], 90). The fruits of this approach are evident in the valuable series: Collection "Mises en scène," published by Éditions du Seuil in the 1940s, to which Dullin, Baty, and Stanislavski, among others, contributed studies and descriptions of stagings of classical plays. The chef d'oeuvre of this series is Barrault's 225-page study of *Phèdre,* which creatively and academically covers the history of the drama; analyzes it line by line; describes in detail lighting, costume, and gestural choices suggested by the text; explains Alexandrines; and, in all, is a remarkable document of a director engaging fully with a text and attempting to bring the theatrical possibilities the text opens up to life.

34. "Le metteur en scène doit mettre au jour l'esprit original"; "extérioriser tout ce qu'il y a dans le texte et derrière le texte" (Mignon, *Charles Dullin,* 92).

35. "Suprématie de la mise en scène" (Mèredieu, *C'était Antonin Artaud,* 419). See also Mignon, *Charles Dullin,* 92.

36. Edward Braun, *Meyerhold: A Revolution in Theatre* (Iowa City: University of Iowa Press, 1995), 221.

37. "La mise en scène doit s'inspirer de cette sorte de double courant entre une réalité imaginaire, et ce qui a touché un moment donné à la vie" (*OC,* 2: 101).

38. An exact correspondence. His scenarios can be found in *OC,* vol. 2. The same is true of his production plans: we only have texts of plans that were never executed; the plans for the ones he did stage are no longer extant.

39. "Une brève hallucination sans texte ou presque" (Crémieux, in *OC,* 2: 51 [*La gazette du Franc,* 1927]). See a reconstruction of this piece (based on interviews) in *OC,* 2: 280–81.

40. "Il utilisait la lumière d'une manière étonnante, qui transfigurait aussi bien les objets que les acteurs" (Robert Aron, cited in Virmaux and Virmaux, *Artaud: Un bilan critique,* 29). The music included, among other styles, a funeral march and a tango and relied heavily on bass and percussion.

41. "Une impression d'étrangeté . . . forte et persistante" (Crémieux, in *OC,* 2: 51 [*La gazette du Franc,* 1927]).

42. The opening night was met with the review: "Il faut louer immédi-

atement la mise en scène de ce spectacle: les trouvailles de M. Antonin Artaud sont presque toujours excellentes" (Marcel Sauvage, *Comoedia*, 3 June 1927, Arts du Spectacle). For the performance of Vitrac's *The Mysteries of Love*, Crémieux wrote: "Les mises en scène de M. Artaud sont ce qui m'est apparu de plus valable" (*OC*, 2: 53 [*La gazette du Franc*, 1927]).

43. "Voilà vingt ans que Craig, Tairoff, [et] . . . Copeau ont créé le miracle moderne qu'est la régie, la redécouverte du théâtre, sa seule forme actuellement possible, et cependant aucun d'eux n'a délibérément osé *rompre* avec le texte" ("Lettre ouverte à Antonin Artaud," 1930, printed in Michel Carassou, "Fondane-Artaud, même combat!" *Europe: Revue littéraire mensuelle* [Nov.–Dec. 1984]: 84–93, at 88).

44. "[Si] vos décors, vos éclairages, vos costumes, votre jeu scénique, soient l'étoffe même du texte, soient le texte même" (Fondane, "Lettre," 89).

45. The exaggerated size or the spare nature of set pieces could evoke this "violently real" feeling. See the review of *Ghost Sonata* by Benjamin Crémieux, *La gazette du Franc*, 11 Aug. 1928 (cited in Virmaux and Virmaux, *Artaud: Un bilan critique*, 32).

46. Virmaux, *Antonin Artaud et le théâtre*, 62–63 and *passim*. Camille Dumoulié also discusses Artaud's work in terms of *décalage* in *Antonin Artaud* (Paris: Seuil, Les Contemporains, 1996), 34–35.

47. One reviewer wrote of the "caractère d'irréel et de rêve de la pièce" (Paul Achard, "Les Surréalistes manifestent, mais Le Songe n'est pas ce qu'ils en firent," *Paris-Midi*, 5 June 1928; cited in Virmaux and Virmaux, *Artaud: Un bilan critique*, 31).

48. Benjamin Crémieux, translated in *CW*, 2: 215. "L'univers que parvient ainsi à évoquer M. Artaud est un univers où tout prend un sens, un mystère, une âme" (cited in Virmaux and Virmaux, *Artaud: Un bilan critique*, 32).

49. "Le désordre, l'anxiété, la menace" (described by Artaud in "Le Théâtre Alfred Jarry et l'hostilité publique," *OC*, 2: 55).

50. Nin also asked "if his madness was not really like a Way of the Cross, in which each step, each torment, was described to make one feel guilt; and whether Artaud was desperate because he could not find anyone to share his madness" (*Diary*, 234).

51. Artaud wanted to work in the Grand Guignol and sought to procure an invitation to perform from de Lorde (to no avail). See Mèredieu for a discussion of this connection (*C'était Antonin Artaud*, 200–203).

52. August Strindberg, *Ghost Sonata*, in *Five Plays*, trans. Harry G. Carlson (New York: Signet Classic, 1984), 303; Artaud, "Production Plan for Strindberg's *The Ghost Sonata*," *CW*, 2: 97–105, at 104. Artaud's production plan for *The Ghost Sonata* was written in 1930. It bears a close resemblance to the production of *A Dream Play* that Artaud directed for the Jarry Theater in 1928.

53. Virmaux, *Antonin Artaud et le théâtre*, 61–63 and *passim*.

54. Artaud, "Production Plan for Strindberg's *The Ghost Sonata*," *CW*, 2: 100.

55. "Chez Artaud, en fait, les déformations et agrandissements rele-

vaient . . . d'une recherche de déséquilibre et de dissonances, qui visait à priver le spectateur de ses refuges habituels" (Virmaux, *Antonin Artaud et le théâtre*, 76).

56. Virmaux, *Antonin Artaud et le théâtre*, 60.

57. *Victor* ran three nights: 24 and 29 Dec. 1928 and 5 Jan. 1929 at the Comédie des Champs-Elysées.

58. Artaud, "Letter to Ida Mortemart, alias Domenica, Second Version, 1929," *CW*, 2: 65.

59. This two-sided character draws from the *commedia* tradition of having a *bifronte* marionette, or sometimes a masked character, with two different faces available for quick changes or for a character's lazzo of disguise. *Commedia* characters were in vogue at the time, used widely by other Parisian theater directors and discussed in almost every issue of Edward Gordon Craig's periodical *The Mask* (1908–29).

60. The extravagant violence is made possible by the dummies themselves—Harlequin later picks up his limbs and reattaches them. Virmaux points out that mannequins both serve a practical purpose and function as articulations of the characters' hidden doubles (*Antonin Artaud et le théâtre*, 60–61).

61. "Une lenteur désespérante, une lenteur à vomir" (*OC*, 1*: 71). A similar direction is given in the scenario *The Philosopher's Stone*, in which a line is delivered with increasingly lengthened pauses after succeeding words. See *CW* II, 75.

62. "Frontière infranchissable qui sépare Artaud de *tous* les grands animateurs de son temps" (Virmaux, *Antonin Artaud et le théâtre*, 144).

63. Descriptions of these disruptions, such as calling Paul Claudel "an infamous traitor," describing a Strindberg piece as "vomit" against Swedish society, and more, can be found in the notes to related sections in *OC*, vol. 2.

64. See an interview with the actress Alexandra Pecker (interviewed anonymously, but she is easily identifiable by the information she gives in the interview), "Une amie anonyme d'Antonin Artaud," in Alain Virmaux and Odette Virmaux, *Antonin Artaud: Qui êtes-vous?* (Lyon: La Manufacture, 1986), 127–43; interviews with Artaud's actors in the chapter on Strindberg in Randolph Goodman, *From Script to Stage: Eight Modern Plays* (San Francisco: Rinehart Press, 1971); and Mèredieu, *C'était Antonin Artaud*, 390–92.

65. "Son contact était stimulant" (Alexandra Pecker, in Virmaux and Virmaux, *Antonin Artaud: Qui êtes-vous?*, 116).

CHAPTER 7

1. Some critics have considered Artaud's deep involvement with his subjects representative of a fundamental urge to identify with another self. John C. Stout's *Antonin Artaud's Alternate Genealogies: Self-Portraits and Family Romances* (Waterloo, Ont.: Wilfrid Laurier University Press, 1996) argues that Artaud's "rewritings of the lives of literary and historical figures" form "part of the general search for self-presence that animates much of his work" (vii).

Anaïs Nin has a concise diary entry on the topic: "Artaud sat in the Coupole pouring out poetry, talking of magic, 'I am Heliogabolus, the mad Roman emperor,' because he becomes everything he writes about" (*Diary*, 229).

2. Artaud used Léon de Wailly's 1840 translation as the foundation for his own version.

3. "Je me crois et je suis une force de la nature. Pour moi, il n'y a ni vie, ni mort, ni dieu, ni inceste, ni repentir, ni crime. J'obéis à ma loi" (*Les Cenci, OC*, 4: 153).

4. Artaud, Blin, and others, "Antonin Artaud's *Les Cenci*," 97 (hereafter *TDR* 16). Artaud's interviews and essays promoting *The Cenci* are translated in this "dossier" that appeared in vol. 16 of *The Drama Review*, along with correspondence, photographs, blocking notes, and reviews of the project.

5. All found in *TDR* 16.

6. There was no official credit given to a lighting designer, but Artaud appears to have been solely responsible for the lights. He frequently refers to his ideas for the lights in publicity interviews, saying: "I attach great importance to the lights, and my lighting will be worthy of merit, I hope, because of its excellence" (*TDR* 16, 100). Balthus designed the sets and costumes, which generally received praise for their striking beauty and eerily desolate atmosphere.

7. André Frank, who oversaw the financial side of the show, recalled that the debts and poor sales pushed their finances "à la catastrophe" (cited in Virmaux, *Antonin Artaud et le théâtre*, 159).

8. Lady Iya Abdy, who played Beatrice, helped finance the production. She had a Russian accent so thick that it was difficult to understand her. Cécile Denoël, who played Lucretia, Count Cenci's wife, was married to Robert Denoël, who also helped finance the production.

9. The failure of *The Cenci* is well documented in *TDR* 16, which includes translations of its scathing reviews. Also see Virmaux, *Antonin Artaud et le théâtre*, 157–61. As the rehearsals advanced, Artaud stated that it would not yet be the realization of the Theater of Cruelty, but only "a preparation for it" (translated in *TDR* 16, 103).

10. Virmaux's phrase ("ambition totalitaire") is in reference to Artaud's idea, put forth in many letters to Jean Paulhan, that he must be granted complete control—commercial and artistic—of a theater company housed at the *NRF* (*Antonin Artaud et le théâtre*, 157).

11. Stendhal's text was written as a chronicle of the historical events in 1837 and later published in his *Chroniques italiennes* in 1839. Shelley's dramatic version was written in 1819 and translated into French in 1887 by Félix Rabbe (Nouvelle Librairie parisienne, ed. Albert Savine). Artaud condensed the last two acts, cut most of the monologues, and added stage directions, calling his work "an original play" (*TDR* 16, 94), but the work is, on the whole, a paraphrased version of the Shelley.

12. "Je ne saurais résister aux forces qui brûlent de se ruer en moi" (*OC*, 4: 153).

13. "J'ai fini par lui ressembler" (*OC*, 4: 210).

14. A recent attempt to revive Artaud's play at the Ohio Theater met with a scathing review of the text in the *New York Times* by Neil Genzlinger (13 Feb.

2008) that affirms the continuity of this negative critical response: "There's a reason that references to [Artaud's] 'The Cenci' generally come with the words 'rarely seen' attached."

15. "Pour que son expression devienne plus véritable, plus saisissante." Artaud reportedly was furious at her refusal: "Et la colère d'Artaud est terrible" (cited in Virmaux, *Antonin Artaud et le théâtre*, 331–32). From André Frank, *La revue théâtrale*, no. 13 (Summer 1950): 32.

16. Cécile Denoël, who played the role of the wife, Lucretia, reportedly had to cover up bruises on her neck inflicted in a rehearsal when Artaud tried to strangle her with too much "reality." Barrault dropped out of the production (he was playing the role of Bernardo and assisted in rehearsals) partway through, and the resulting correspondence between him and Artaud points to irreconcilable temperaments evident during the process. Artaud also reportedly told Abdy to get screwed by a mammoth ("aller vous faire enculer par un mammouth") when he couldn't get something he wanted from her in a rehearsal (see Mèredieu, *C'était Antonin Artaud*, 513–16).

17. This paved the way for what we would now call "auteur" directing. Indeed, Gabrielle Cody and Rebecca Schneider place Artaud at the beginning of their section entitled "Auteur Theater," which includes the directors Robert Wilson, Richard Foreman, and Reza Abdoh, among others, in their directing sourcebook *Re: direction: A Theoretical and Practical Guide* (New York: Routledge, 2002).

18. From an interview with Charles Marowitz, transcribed and translated in *Artaud at Rodez* (London: Marion Boyars, 1977), 76. A reproduction of Act I, scene 3, of Blin's rehearsal notebook can be found in *TDR* 16, 112–25. A color reproduction of two pages (text and blocking for one moment in Act IV, scene 1) can be found in *Antonin Artaud* (Catalogue de l'exposition présentée à la bibliothèque nationale de France sur le site François-Mitterrand du 7 novembre au 4 février 2007), ed. Guillaume Fau (Paris: Bibliothèque nationale de France/Gallimard, 2006), 121, showing Blin's attention to detail with colored crayons and drawings. The entire notebook is housed in the Bibliothèque Nationale de France (BNF), Manuscrits, fonds Artaud, NAF 27443, as "Cahier de la mise en scène des *Cenci*."

19. *TDR* 16, 135, modified with text from the complete original review published in *Le journal*, 12 May 1935.

20. Artaud wanted to use life-size dummies in the production, and they are included in Blin's blocking notes, but it's not easy to say with certainty that they made it into the actual performance. There are no mentions of them in any review, and they don't appear in a photo of Act I, scene 3, a scene in which the rehearsal notebook calls for them.

21. Artaud worked closely with the sound designer Roger Désormière, who supplied the necessary technical skills. The sound track (Désormière recorded the sounds, which were then played over loudspeakers) is housed in BNF, Manuscrits, fonds Artaud, under "Musique de scène pour *Les Cenci*."

22. Translated in *TDR* 16, 97. The first publicly available Martenot was produced in 1928.

23. Denis Hollier, in an essay on Artaud's "sound system," notes: "Artaud's ultimate . . . sound effect . . . occurs when the spectator feels sur-

rounded to the point of surrendering. *Le Théâtre et son double* is filled with references to such an enveloping and powerful curvature of the sound space" ("The Death of Paper, Part Two: Artaud's Sound System," *October* 80 [Spring 1997]: 27–37, at 34).

24. Or the bells of Chartres; Artaud names both in separate interviews.

25. Roger Blin, Artaud's assistant on *The Cenci*, recalled: "It was the first time stereophonic sound was used in the theatre, with the sound of bells on tape and speakers placed in different points of the auditorium. That had never been done before" (translated in *TDR* 16, 110).

26. Translated in *TDR* 16, 97.

27. Translated in *TDR* 16, 102.

28. "Le but premier d'Appia et de Craig, c'est le théâtre lui-même, c'est rendre le théâtre à lui-même"; "Toutes les réflexions d'A[rtaud] sont orientées par cette préoccupation: susciter chez les spectateurs une véritable passion salvatrice au moyen du théâtre" (André Veinstein, in Virmaux, *Antonin Artaud et le théâtre*, 302).

29. Graver's essay is useful in its historical situation of Artaud's work vis-à-vis that of his contemporaries, including the Cartel.

30. *SW*, 299, translation modified. "Et l'intérêt que susciteront à priori les spectacles que je réaliserai sera lié à la confiance qu'on me fera, au crédit qu'on m'accordera en tant que créateur, inventeur d'une réalité théâtrale absolue et qui se suffit à elle-même" (*OC*, 5: 88).

31. Artaud wrote that Barrault had put too many of his own ideas into the actors' choices.

32. "L'Homme va retrouver sa stature. Et qu'il la retrouvera *contre* les Hommes" (*OC*, 7: 126).

33. "*A Adolf HITLER/en souvenir du* Romanischès café *à Berlin un après-midi de mai 1932/et parce que je prie DIEU/de vous donner la grâce de vous ressouvenir de toutes les merveilles dont IL vous a ce jour-là GRATIFIÉ (RESSUS-CITÉ)/LE COEUR*" (*OC*, 7: 424).

34. Artaud praises the "animated sorcery" of Oriental theater for demonstrating its connection "with all the objective degrees of universal magnetism" (*TD*, 73); the new theater language operates "by its use of man's nervous magnetism" to realize actively "a kind of total creation" (93); the theater must operate by a "fiery magnetism" (84).

35. Cited and translated in Brown, *Theater and Revolution*, 370.

36. This description is from an account of mesmerism in Victorian England cited in Winter, *Mesmerized*, 54.

37. Influential in the minds of Marat and others during the Terror, mesmerism took on a different character after the Revolution finally ended, bound up with the sinister rather than the frivolous element of human susceptibility: "After the Terror mesmerism wed Gothic fiction and melodrama. Embodied by the Great Outsider, by the wizard, by the Director . . . mesmeric power became the instrument of a nature hidden from view and fraught with occult intentions" (Brown, *Theater and Revolution*, 373).

38. "I do not believe," Artaud wrote to Barrault one month after *The Cenci* closed and months before he renounced the theater, "that I am only a vulgar theoretician" (*SW*, 343).

39. See Romain Rolland, *Le théâtre du peuple*, ed. Chantal Meyer-Plantureux (Brussels: Éditions Complexe, 2003).

40. Cited and translated in Brown, *Theater and Revolution*, 292.

41. LeBon compares this to the theater, where the audience demands excessive virtues and heroics from its characters. The art of appealing to crowds parallels that of pleasing audiences; in order for a manager to judge a play's future success, "they should be able to transform themselves into a crowd" (*Crowd*, 23).

42. Cited and translated in Brown, *Theater and Revolution*, 334.

43. Cited and translated in Brown, *Theater and Revolution*, 335.

44. Artaud wrote a letter to Hitler in 1939 from the asylum at Ville-Évrard that evoked, again, a memory of meeting in Berlin in 1932, saying. "Les Parisiens ont besoin de gaz" (reproduction in Fau, *Antonin Artaud*, 44).

45. Hannah Arendt, "On the Nature of Totalitarianism," in *Essays in Understanding* (New York: Schocken Books: 1994), 328–60, at 346.

46. "Je suis un fanatique, je ne suis pas un fou" (quoted in Claude Roy, "Antonin Artaud: Un certain État de Fureur," *Le nouvel observateur*, no. 527, 16–22 Dec., 1974, pp. 68–69; translated in Shattuck, "Artaud Possessed," 186.

47. His last work, a radio piece, was entitled *Pour en finir avec le jugement de dieu*.

48. Friedell noted this also, in 1927, in terms of the genius artist and the criminal leader, asking if "the 'monsters' of world-history—Caligula and Tiberius, Danton and Robespierre, Caesar Borgia and Torquemada—what were they but artists cast adrift in reality?" (*Cultural History*, 69).

CONCLUSION

1. Examples of each: The Living Theatre and its inheritors exemplify the belief that loss of order will open the door to an agreeable socialism. Performance art's frequent invocation of Artaud shows how breaking personal boundaries has been seen as self-expression. Eric Sellin provides an exemplary existential interpretation of Artaud's "cruelty": "By cruelty Artaud meant a metaphysical experience shared by the actor and the viewer, and not morbidity or sadism as such. . . . Artaud felt that destruction is a transforming force and that cruelty . . . is a means of transforming the audience" (*Dramatic Concepts*, 128–29).

2. Terry Eagleton, *Holy Terror* (New York: Oxford University Press, 2005), 45.

3. Elinor Fuchs, for one example in theater theory, makes a compelling argument that the techniques of postmodernism have been resourcefully adopted by traditionally marginalized groups. See Elinor Fuchs, "Postmodernism and the Scene of Theater," in *The Death of Character* (Bloomington: Indiana University Press, 1996), 144–57.

4. Foucault writes of the possibility that in the future "man would be erased, like a face drawn in sand at the edge of the sea" (*The Order of Things: An Archaeology of the Human Sciences* [New York: Vintage Books, 1973], 387).

5. The intellectual historian Richard Wolin makes an extended (and

controversial) case for the philosophical connections between postmodernism and fascism in *The Seduction of Unreason: The Intellectual Romance with Fascism from Nietzsche to Postmodernism* (Princeton: Princeton University Press, 2004).

6. Friedrich goes on: "The depersonalisation and dehumanisation that constitute totalitarianism are the ugly forms that the deconstruction of the self and antihumanism of postmodern theory have taken in political praxis" ("Deconstructed Self," 294).

7. Euripides, *The Bacchae,* trans. C. K. Williams (New York: Farrar Straus Giroux, 1990), 33.

8. Félix Guattari, "Everybody Wants to be a Fascist," in *Chaosophy,* ed. Sylvère Lotringer (New York: Semiotext[e], 1995), 225–50, at 237.

9. Richard Schechner, "The Politics of Ecstasy," in *Public Domain: Essays on the Theater* (Indianapolis: The Bobbs-Merrill Company, 1969), 209–28, at 217.

10. Peter Brook, *The Empty Space* (New York: Touchstone, Simon and Schuster, 1996), 54.

11. See Sontag, "Fascinating Fascism," 91.

12. Robert Brustein, reported in Tytell, *Living Theatre,* 241. Oddly, Brustein did not make this critique of Artaud himself. He writes that Artaud "turns [the] negative attitudes [of the Surrealists and Dadaists] into positive acts, transforming the nihilism, sterility, and buffoonery of his predecessors into profoundly revolutionary theory" (*The Theatre of Revolt* [Boston: Little, Brown, and Company, 1964], 366).

13. David Roberts provides an excellent analysis of this dynamic in a discussion of Canetti's *Crowds and Power* and Adorno and Horkheimer's *The Dialectic of Enlightenment* in "The Natural History of Modernity," in *Elias Canetti's Counter-Image of Society* (Rochester: Camden House, 2004), 27–58, at 50.

14. Gautam Dasgupta's otherwise cogent overview of why Artaud's theatrical practice appealed in the 1960s assumes such a constructive community: "The core of Artaud's philosophy," Dasgupta writes, "is predicated on a communal ethos." But Dasgupta's examples—such as his mention of the "portraits of friends and the 'spells' that he [Artaud] cast on various people"—lose their force when we consider that these spells on friends were frequently curses, and that the "community" addressed in these letters includes Hitler ("Remembering Artaud," *Performing Arts Journal* 19, no. 2 [1997]: 1–5, at 4).

15. Recently, Michael Hardt and Antonio Negri have argued for a "multitude," that is, a collection of peoples working in collaboration, as opposed to a "people" comprised of individuals generalizing their voices within a hierarchical system. See *Multitude: War and Democracy in the Age of Empire* (New York: Penguin Press, 2004). In a similar vein, but with a psychoanalytical focus, Guattari posits a group of people who attain their goals not by subsuming their desires into one "totalizing unity" but by attaining a "univocal multiplicity of desires"; in other words, the group would represent "the univocity of the masses' desire, and not their regrouping according to standardized objectives" ("Everybody Wants," 231).

16. See esp. Serge Moscovici, who admits that the study of mass psy-

chology is "a painful one. At every turn, one discovers a rather unflattering picture, to put it mildly, of public life, leaders and masses" (*Age of the Crowd*, 9).

17. The original, from "Ci-gît," is worth knowing, as there are many neologisms: "Et maintenant / vous tous, les êtres, / j'ai à vous dire que vous m'avez toujours fait caguer. / Et aller vous faire / engruper / la moumoute / de la parpougnête, / morpions / de l'éternité" (*OC*, 12: 85). "Morpion" could also be translated as "pubic louse."

18. "C'est la groume qui a fait les choses. / Et la groume à nez, qu'est-ce que c'est?/L'excavation du ventre naître / râpé rouge et désespéré, / hémorroïde vaginale qui hurle dans son claque de crasse contre dieu qui la fait puer" (*OC*, 14*: 44).

19. "Dieu est-il un être? / S'il en est un c'est de la merde . . . / Or il n'est pas, / mais comme le vide qui avance avec toutes ses formes / dont la représentation la plus parfaite / est la marche d'un groupe incalculable de morpions" ("Pour en finir avec le jugement de Dieu," *OC*, 13: 86).

20. "Il y aurait sept à huit cents millions d'êtres à anéantir . . . qu'est-ce que c'est sur trois ou quatre milliards qui vivent sur la terre. La plupart des êtres passent leur vie à ne rien faire" (Jacques Prevel, *En Compagnie d'Antonin Artaud* [Paris: Flammarion, 1974], 191); translated in Esslin, *Antonin Artaud*, 110–11.

SELECTED BIBLIOGRAPHY

PRIMARY SOURCES

MAJOR EDITIONS IN FRENCH

Artaud, Antonin. *Antonin Artaud.* Catalogue de l'exposition présentée à la Bibliothèque nationale de France sur le site François-Mitterrand, 7 November–4 February 2007. Ed. Guillaume Fau. Paris: Bibliothèque nationale de France/Gallimard, 2006.

Artaud, Antonin. *Artaud: Oeuvres.* Ed. Évelyne Grossman. Paris: Quarto Gallimard, 2004.

Artaud, Antonin. *Oeuvres complètes d'Antonin Artaud, nouvelle édition revue et augmentée,* vols. 1–26. Paris: Gallimard, 1976.

Artaud, Antonin. *Pour en finir avec le jugement de dieu.* Original recording. Ed. and intro. Marc Dachy. Compact disc. Sub Rosa/aural documents, 1995.

LIBRARY HOLDINGS

Fonds Artaud. Bibliothèque Nationale de France, Manuscrits.

Théâtre Alfred Jarry. Bibliothèque Nationale de France, Département des Arts du spectacle, RT 3800.

MAJOR EDITIONS IN ENGLISH

Artaud, Antonin. *Antonin Artaud: Works on Paper.* Ed. Margit Rowell. New York: Museum of Modern Art, distributed by H. N. Abrams, 1996.

Artaud, Antonin. *Artaud on Theatre.* Ed. Brian Singleton and Claude Schumacher. London: Methuen, 1989.

Artaud, Antonin. *The Cenci.* Trans. Simon Watson Taylor. New York: Grove Press, 1969.

Artaud, Antonin. *Collected Works of Antonin Artaud,* vols. 1–4. Trans. Victor Corti. London: Calder and Boyars, 1968–73.

Artaud, Antonin. *Selected Writings.* Trans. Helen Weaver. Ed. and intro. Susan Sontag. Berkeley: University of California Press, 1988.

Artaud, Antonin. *The Theater and Its Double.* Trans. Mary Caroline Richards. New York: Grove Weidenfeld, 1958.

SECONDARY LITERATURE ON ARTAUD

BOOKS

Adamov, Arthur, Jean-Louis Barrault, and others. *Antonin Artaud et le théâtre de notre temps.* Paris: Gallimard, 1969.

Barber, Stephen. *The Screaming Body.* London: Creation Books, 1999.

Baudrillard, Jean. *Oublier Artaud.* Paris: Sens and Tonka, 2005.

Bermel, Albert. *Artaud's Theatre of Cruelty.* New York: Taplinger Publishing Co., 1977.

Bonardel, Françoise. *Antonin Artaud: Ou la fidélité à l'infini.* Paris: Balland, 1987.

Borie, Monique. *Antonin Artaud, le théâtre et le retour aux sources: Une approche anthropologique.* Paris: Gallimard, 1989.

Brau, Jean-Louis. *Antonin Artaud.* Paris: La Table Ronde, 1971.

Camus, Michel. *Antonin Artaud: Une autre langue du corps.* Saucats, France: Opales/Comptoir d'édition, 1996.

Charbonnier, Georges. *Antonin Artaud.* Paris: Pierre Seghers, 1959.

Costich, Julia F. *Antonin Artaud.* Boston: Twayne Publishers, 1978.

Derrida, Jacques, and Paule Thévenin. *The Secret Art of Antonin Artaud.* Trans. and preface Mary Ann Caws. Cambridge: MIT Press, 1998.

Dumoulié, Camille. *Antonin Artaud.* Paris: Seuil, Les Contemporains, 1996.

Dumoulié, Camille. *Les Théâtres de la cruauté: Hommage à Antonin Artaud.* Paris: Éditions desjonquères, 2000.

Durozoi, Gérard. *Artaud, l'aliénation et la folie.* Paris: Larousse, 1972.

Esslin, Martin. *Antonin Artaud.* London: John Calder, 1976.

Fock, Holger. *Antonin Artaud und der surrealistische Bluff: Studien zur Geschichte des Théâtre Alfred Jarry.* Berlin: Tiamat, 1988.

Galibert, Thierry, ed. *Antonin Artaud: Écrivain du sud.* Aix-en-Provence: Édisud, 2002.

Galibert, Thierry, ed. *La bestialité.* Cabris: Sulliver, 2008.

Goodall, Jane. *Artaud and the Gnostic Drama.* Oxford: Clarendon Press, 1994.

Gouhier, Henri. *Antonin Artaud et l'essence du théâtre.* Paris: Vrin, 1974.

Greene, Naomi. *Antonin Artaud: Poet without Words.* New York: Simon and Schuster, 1970.

Hahn, Otto. *Portrait d'Antonin Artaud.* Paris: Le Soleil Noir, 1968.

Hayman, Ronald. *Artaud and After.* Oxford: Oxford University Press, 1977.

Knapp, Bettina. *Antonin Artaud: Man of Vision.* New York: Swallow Press, 1969.

Larrouy, Mireille. *Artaud et le théâtre: 1920–1935 quinze ans de bonheur.* Toulouse: CRDP Midi-Pyrénées, 1997.

Lévêque, Jean-Jacques. *Antonin Artaud.* Paris: Henri Veyrier, 1985.

Lotringer, Sylvère. *Fous d'Artaud.* Paris: Sens and Tonka, 2003.

Marowitz, Charles. *Artaud at Rodez.* London: Marion Boyars, 1977.

de Mèredieu, Florence. *C'était Antonin Artaud.* Paris: Fayard, 2006.

de Mèredieu, Florence. *La Chine d'Antonin Artaud/Le Japon d'Antonin Artaud.* Paris: Blusson, 2006.

Morfee, Adrian. *Antonin Artaud's Writing Bodies.* Oxford: Oxford University Press, 2005.

Penot-Lacassagne, Olivier. *Antonin Artaud: "Moi, Antonin Artaud, homme de la terre."* Croissy-Beaubourg, France: Éditions Aden, 2007.

Penot-Lacassagne, Olivier, ed. *Artaud en revues.* Lausanne: l'Âge d'homme, 2005.

Penot-Lacassagne, Olivier. *Artaud et les avant-gardes théâtrales.* Paris: Lettres modernes Minard, 2005.

Penot-Lacassagne, Olivier. *Vies et morts d'Antonin Artaud.* Saint-Cyr-Sur-Loire, France: Christian Pirot, 2007.

Plunka, Gene A., ed. *Antonin Artaud and the Modern Theater.* Cranbury: Associated University Presses, 1994.

Prevel, Jacques. *En compagnie d'Antonin Artaud.* Paris: Flammarion, 1974.

Scheer, Edward. *Antonin Artaud: A Critical Reader.* London: Routledge, 2004.

Sellin, Eric. *The Dramatic Concepts of Antonin Artaud.* Chicago: University of Chicago Press, 1975.

Sollers, Philippe, ed. *Artaud.* Paris: Union Générale d'Éditions, 1973.

Stout, John C. *Antonin Artaud's Alternate Genealogies: Self-Portraits and Family Romances.* Waterloo, Ont.: Wilfrid Laurier University Press, 1996.

Thévenin, Paule. *Antonin Artaud, ce désespéré qui vous parle.* Paris: Seuil, 1993.

Virmaux, Alain. *Antonin Artaud et le théâtre.* Paris: Seghers, 1970.

Virmaux, Alain, and Odette Virmaux. *Antonin Artaud: Qui êtes-vous?* Lyon: La Manufacture, 1986.

Virmaux, Alain, and Odette Virmaux. *Artaud: Un bilan critique.* Paris: Belfond, 1979.

Virmaux, Alain, and Odette Virmaux. *Artaud vivant.* Paris: Nouvelles éditions Oswald, 1980.

ARTICLES AND BOOK CHAPTERS

"Alfred Jarry Theater: Portfolio of Photographs." *Theater* 9, no. 3 (1978): 20–24.

Arnold, Paul, Antonin Artaud, and others. *Tulane Drama Review* 8, no. 2 (1963): 15–84.

Artaud, Antonin, Roger Blin, and others. "Antonin Artaud's *Les Cenci.*" *The Drama Review* 16, no. 2 (1972): 91–145.

Baker, Geoffrey. "Nietzsche, Artaud, and Tragic Politics." *Comparative Literature* (Winter 2003): 1–23.

Béhar, Henri. "Lettres d'Antonin Artaud à Roger Vitrac." *La nouvelle revue française* 12, nos. 136–38 (1964): 765–76.

Bersani, Leo. "Artaud, Birth, and Defecation." *Partisan Review,* no. 43 (1976): 439–52.

Blanchot, Maurice. "Artaud." *La nouvelle revue française* 4, no. 47 (1956): 873–81. Also in Blanchot, Maurice. *Le livre à venir.* Paris: Gallimard, 1959.

Brasillach, Robert. "La Chronique des théâtres: *Les Cenci.*" *L'action française,* 17 May 1935.

Carassou, Michel. "Fondane-Artaud, même combat!" *Europe: Revue littéraire mensuelle* 62, nos. 667–68 (1984): 84–93.

Chin, Daryl. "The Antonin Artaud Film Project." *Performing Arts Journal* 19, no. 2 (1997): 23–28.

Cohn, Ruby. "Surrealism and Today's French Theatre." *Yale French Studies*, no. 31 (1964): 159–166.

Crombez, Thomas. "Artaud, the Parodist? The Appropriations of the Théâtre Alfred Jarry, 1927–1930." *Forum modernes theater* 20, no. 1 (2005): 33–51.

Dasgupta, Gautam. "Remembering Artaud." *PAJ* 19, no. 2 (1997): 1–5.

Deak, Frantisek. "Antonin Artaud and Charles Dullin: Artaud's Apprenticeship in Theatre." *Educational Theatre Journal* 29, no. 3 (1977): 345–53.

Deleuze, Gilles. "Le schizophrène et le mot." *Critique*, nos. 255–56 (1968): 731–46.

Demaitre, Ann. "The Theater of Cruelty and Alchemy: Artaud and *Le Grand Oeuvre*." *Journal of the History of Ideas* 33, no. 2. (1972): 237–50.

Derrida, Jacques. "Artaud, oui . . ." *Europe: Revue littéraire mensuelle* 80, nos. 873–74 (2002): 23–38.

Derrida, Jacques. "La parole soufflée." In *Writing and Difference*, trans. Alan Bass. Chicago: University of Chicago Press, 1978. 169–95

Derrida, Jacques. "The Theater of Cruelty and the Closure of Representation." In *Writing and Difference*, trans. Alan Bass. Chicago: University of Chicago Press, 1978. 232–50.

Dubech, Lucien. "La chronique des théâtres." *L'action française*, 24 May 1935.

Esslin, Martin. "The Theater of Cruelty." *New York Times Magazine*, 6 March 1966, 22–23, 71–74.

Finter, Helga. "Antonin Artaud and the Impossible Theatre: The Legacy of the Theatre of Cruelty." *The Drama Review* 41, no. 4 (1997): 15–40.

Foley, Kathy. "Trading Art(s): Artaud, Spies, and Current Indonesian/American Artistic Exchange and Collaboration." *Modern Drama* 35, no. 1 (1992): 10–19.

Fotiade, Ramona. "Fondane-Artaud: Une pensée au-delà des catégories." *Europe: Revue littéraire mensuelle* 76, no. 827 (1998): 143–50.

Fotiade, Ramona. "The New French Theater: Artaud, Beckett, Genet, Ionesco." *Sewanee Review* 67, no. 4 (1959): 643–57.

Friedrich, Rainer. "The Deconstructed Self in Artaud and Brecht: Negation of Subject and Antitotalitarianism." *Forum for Modern Language Studies* 26, no. 3 (1990): 282–97.

Garner, Stanton B., Jr. "Artaud, Germ Theory, and the Theatre of Contagion." *Theatre Journal* 58, no. 1 (2006): 1–14.

Graver, David. "Antonin Artaud and the Authority of Text, Spectacle, and Performance." In *Contours of the Theatrical Avant-Garde: Performance and Textuality*, ed. James M. Harding. Ann Arbor: University of Michigan Press, 2000. 43–57.

Greene, Naomi. "'All the Great Myths Are Dark': Artaud and Fascism." In *Antonin Artaud and the Modern Theater*, ed. Gene A. Plunka. Cranbury: Associated University Presses, 1994. 102–16.

Grotowski, Jerzy. "Il n'était pas entièrement lui-même." *Les temps modernes* 22, no. 251 (1967): 1885–93. Translated as "He Wasn't Entirely Himself." In *Towards a Poor Theatre*. London: Methuen Drama, 1994. 85–93.

Guicharnaud, Jacques. "The Gaping Mask." In *Modern French Theatre: From Giraudoux to Genet*. New Haven: Yale University Press, 1967. 283–91.

Halm, Ben. "Antonin Artaud: Forms of 'Total Art' and Their Peculiar Means for Disalienating the Occidental Self- and-World." In *Theatre and Ideology*. London: Associated University Presses, 1995. 132–58.

Harries, Martin. "Forgetting Lot's Wife: Artaud, Spectatorship, and Catastrophe." *Yale Journal of Criticism* 2, no. 1 (1998): 221–38.

Ho, Christopher. "Antonin Artaud: From Center to Periphery, Periphery to Center." *Performing Arts Journal* 19, no. 2 (1997): 6–22.

Hollier, Denis. "The Death of Paper, Part Two: Artaud's Sound System." *October* 80 (Spring 1997): 27–37.

Innes, Christopher. "Antonin Artaud and the Theatre of Cruelty." In *Avant-Garde Theatre 1892–1992*. New York: Routledge, 1993. 59–94.

Jannarone, Kimberly. "Exercises in Exorcism: The Paradoxes of Form in Artaud's Early Works." *French Forum* 29, no. 2 (2004): 35–53.

Jannarone, Kimberly. "The Theatre before Its Double: Artaud Directs in the Alfred Jarry Theatre." *Theatre Survey* 46, no. 2 (2005): 247–73.

Jouve, Pierre-Jean. "*Les Cenci* d'Antonin Artaud." *La nouvelle revue française* 23, no. 261 (1935): 910–15.

Knapp, Bettina. "Anaïs/Artaud-Alchemy." *Mosaic* 11, no. 2 (1978): 65–74.

Koch, Stephen. "On Artaud." *Tri-Quarterly*, no. 6 (1966): 29–37.

Lyotard, Jean-François. "The Tooth, the Palm." Trans. Anne Knap and Michel Benamou. *SubStance* 5, no. 15 (1976): 105–10.

Peters, Julie Stone. "Artaud in the Sierra Madre: Theatrical Bodies, Primitive Signs, Ritual Landscapes." In *Land/Scape/Theater*, ed. Elinor Fuchs and Una Chaudhuri. Ann Arbor: University of Michigan Press, 2002. 228–51.

Savarese, Nicola. "1931: Antonin Artaud Sees Balinese Theatre at the Paris Colonial Exposition." *The Drama Review* 45, no. 3 (2001): 51–77.

Scarpetta, Guy. "Artaud écrit ou la canne de Saint Patrick." *Tel Quel*, no. 81 (Fall 1979): 66–85.

Seymour, Alan. "Artaud's Cruelty." *London Magazine* 3 (March 1964): 59–64.

Shattuck, Roger. "Artaud Possessed." In *The Innocent Eye*. New York: Farrar Straus Giroux, 1984. 169–86.

Sollers, Philippe. "Saint Artaud." *Nouvel observateur*, no. 2080, 16–22 September (2004): 57–58.

Spreen, Constance. "Resisting the Plague: The French Reactionary Right and Artaud's Theater of Cruelty." *MLQ: Modern Language Quarterly* 64, no. 1 (2003): 71–96.

Thévenin, Paule. "Antonin Artaud dans la vie." *Tel Quel*, no. 20 (Winter 1965): 25–40.

Thévenin, Paule. "Letter on Artaud." *Tulane Drama Review* 9, no. 3 (1965): 99–117.

Villeneuve, André. "La chronique des spectacles: Le théâtre de la cruauté." *L'action française*, 14 October 1932.

Virmaux, Alain. "Artaud and Film." *Tulane Drama Review* 11, no. 1 (1966): 154–65.

Virmaux, Alain, and Odette Virmaux. "Dieu merci, Artaud n'est plus à la mode!" *Europe: Revue littéraire mensuelle* 74, nos. 813–14 (1997): 207–11.
Ward, Nigel. "Twelve of the Fifty-One Shocks of Antonin Artaud." *New Theatre Quarterly* 15 (February 1999): 123–30.

SPECIAL JOURNAL ISSUES DEVOTED TO ARTAUD

Antonin Artaud: Textes, documents, témoignages. Paris: K Editeur (1948). Series: K revue de la poésie; no. 1–2.
Cahiers de la Pléiade, no. 7 (Spring 1949).
84, no. 5–6 (1948).
Europe: Revue littéraire mensuelle 62, nos. 667–68 (1984).
Europe: Revue littéraire mensuelle 80, nos. 873–74 (2002).
Obliques, nos. 10–11 (1976).
Obsidianes, no. 5 (March 1979).
Planète plus, no. 7 (February 1971).
La tour de feu, nos. 63–64 (December 1959). Reprint, no. 112 (December 1971).

GENERAL

Adorno, Theodor. "Freudian Theory and the Pattern of Fascist Propaganda." In *The Culture Industry*, ed. J. M. Bernstein. London: Routledge Classics, 2001. 132–57.
Antliff, Mark. *Avant-Garde Fascism: The Mobilization of Myth, Art, and Culture in France, 1909–1939.* Durham: Duke University Press, 2007.
Antoine, André. *Le théâtre libre.* Paris: [unknown], 1890.
Arendt, Hannah. *Essays in Understanding: 1930–1954.* New York: Schocken Books, 1994.
Aronson, Arnold. *The History and Theory of Environmental Scenography.* Ann Arbor: UMI Research Press, 1981.
Aschheim, Steven E. *The Nietzsche Legacy in Germany, 1890–1990.* Berkeley: University of California Press, 1992.
Béhar, Henri. *Roger Vitrac: Un réprouvé du surréalisme.* Paris: A. G. Nizet, 1966.
Benjamin, Walter. "The Work of Art in the Age of Mechanical Reproduction." In *Illuminations*, ed. Hannah Arendt, trans. Harry Zohn. New York: Schocken Books, 1968. 217–51.
Bennett, Susan. *Theatre Audiences: A Theory of Production and Reception.* London: Routledge, 1997.
Berghaus, Günter. ed. *Fascism and Theatre: Comparative Studies on the Aesthetics and Politics of Performance in Europe, 1925–1945.* Oxford: Berghahn Books, 1996.
Berghaus, Günter, ed. *Futurism and Politics: Between Anarchist Rebellion and Fascist Reaction, 1909–1944.* Oxford: Berghahn Books, 1996.
Berlin, Isaiah. "Joseph de Maistre and the Origins of Fascism." In *The Crooked Timber of Humanity*, ed. Henry Hardy. New York: Alfred A. Knopf, 1991. 91–174.

Berlin, Isaiah. *The Magus of the North: J. G. Hamann and the Origins of Modern Irrationalism*. Ed. Henry Hardy. London: John Murray, 1993.

Blackadder, Neil. *Performing Opposition: Modern Theater and the Scandalized Audience*. Westport, Conn.: Praeger, 2003.

Blavatsky, Helene Petrovna. *The Secret Doctrine: Synthesis of Science, Religion, and Philosophy, Part I*. 1888. Whitefish, Mont.: Kessinger Publishing, 2003.

Bradby, David, and John McCormick. *People's Theatre*. London: Croom Helm Ltd., 1978.

Breton, André. *Entretiens, 1913–1952*. Paris: Gallimard, 1952.

Brook, Peter. *The Empty Space*. New York: Touchstone, Simon and Schuster, 1996.

Brown, Frederick. *Theater and Revolution: The Culture of the French Stage*. New York: Vintage Books, 1989.

Brown, Kenneth H. *The Brig, with an Essay on the Living Theatre by Julian Beck and Director's Notes by Judith Malina*. New York: Hill and Wang, 1965.

Brustein, Robert. *The Theatre of Revolt*. Boston: Little, Brown, and Company, 1964.

Butsch, Richard. *The Making of American Audiences: From Stage to Television, 1750–1990*. Cambridge: Cambridge University Press, 2000.

Canetti, Elias. *Crowds and Power*. Trans. Carol Stewart. New York: Farrar, Straus and Giroux, 1984.

Carnegy, Patrick. *Wagner and the Art of the Theatre*. New Haven: Yale University Press, 2006.

Céline, Louis-Ferdinand. *Bagatelles pour un massacre*. Paris: Denoël, 1937.

Chinoy, Helen Krich, and Toby Cole, eds. *Directors on Directing: A Source Book of the Modern Theater*. Intro. Helen Krich Chinoy. Indianapolis: Bobbs-Merrill, 1963.

Craig, Edward Gordon. *On the Art of the Theatre*. London: Heinemann, 1957.

Deleuze, Gilles, and Félix Guattari. *Anti-Oedipus: Capitalism and Schizophrenia*. Trans. Helen R. Lane, et. al. Minneapolis: University of Minnesota Press, 1983.

Eagleton, Terry. *Holy Terror*. New York: Oxford University Press, 2005.

Eksteins, Modris. *Rites of Spring: The Great War and the Birth of the Modern Age*. Boston: Houghton Mifflin Company, 2000.

Fischer-Lichte, Erika. *Theatre, Sacrifice, Ritual: Exploring Forms of Political Theatre*. London: Routledge, 2005.

Foucault, Michel. *Madness and Civilization*. Trans. Richard Howard. New York: Vintage Books, 1988.

Freud, Sigmund. *Civilization and Its Discontents*. Trans. Joan Riviere. London: Hogarth Press, 1982.

Freud, Sigmund. *Group Psychology and the Analysis of the Ego*. Trans. and ed. James Strachey. New York: W. W. Norton and Co., 1959.

Friedell, Egon. *A Cultural History of the Modern Age*. Trans. Charles Francis Atkinson. New York: Alfred A. Knopf, 1964.

Friedländer, Saul. *Reflections of Nazism: An Essay on Kitsch and Death*. Bloomington: Indiana University Press, 1993.

Fussell, Paul. *The Great War and Modern Memory*. New York: Oxford University Press, 1975.

Gentile, Emilio. *The Struggle for Modernity: Nationalism, Futurism, and Fascism*. Westport, Conn.: Praeger, 2003.

Goodman, Randolph. *From Script to Stage: Eight Modern Plays*. San Francisco: Rinehart Press, 1971.

Goodrick-Clarke, Nicholas. *The Occult Roots of Nazism: Secret Aryan Cults and Their Influence on Nazi Ideology*. New York: New York University Press, 2004.

Gropius, Walter, ed. and intro. *The Theater of the Bauhaus*. Trans. Arthur S. Wensinger. Middletown, Conn.: Wesleyan University Press, 1961.

Guattari, Félix. "Everybody Wants to Be a Fascist." In *Chaosophy*, ed. Sylvère Lotringer. New York: Semiotext[e], 1995. 225–50.

Hays, Michael. *The Public and Performance: Essays in the History of French and German Theater, 1871–1900*. Ann Arbor: UMI Research Press, 1981.

Heed, Sven Åke. *Le coco du dada: Victor, ou les enfants au pouvoir de Roger Vitrac: Texte et représentation*. Lund, Sweden: CWK Gleerup, 1983.

Hewitt, Nicholas. *Les Maladies du Siècle: The Image of Malaise in French Fiction and Thought in the Inter-war Years*. Hull: Hull University Press, 1988.

Jaspers, Karl. *Man in the Modern Age*. Trans. Eden Paul and Cedar Paul. London: Routledge and Kegan Paul Ltd., 1959.

Jünger, Ernst. *Storm of Steel*. Trans. Michael Hofmann. London: Penguin Books, 2004.

Kaplan, Alice Yaeger. *Reproductions of Banality: Fascism, Literature, and French Intellectual Life*. Minneapolis: University of Minnesota Press, 1986.

Kershaw, Baz. "Oh for Unruly Audiences! or, Patterns of Participation in Twentieth-Century Theatre." *Modern Drama* 44, no. 2 (2001): 133–56.

Kirby, Michael, and Victoria Nes Kirby. *Futurist Performance*, with manifestos and playscripts translated from the Italian by Victoria Nes Kirby. New York: PAJ Publications, 1986.

Kristeva, Julia. "Le sujet en procès." In *Artaud*. Paris: Union Générale d'Éditions, coll. 10/18, 1973. 43–108.

Le Bon, Gustave. *The Crowd: A Study of the Popular Mind*. Mineola, N.Y.: Dover, 2002.

Lehmann, Hans-Thies. *Postdramatic Theatre*. Trans. Karen Jürs-Munby. New York: Routledge, 2006.

London, John, ed. *Theatre under the Nazis*. Manchester: Manchester University Press, 2000.

McClelland, J. S. *The Crowd and the Mob: From Plato to Canetti*. London: Unwin Hyman, 1989.

McDougall, William. *The Group Mind*. New York: G. P. Putnam's Sons, 1920.

Mignon, Paul-Louis. *Charles Dullin*. Lyon: La Manufacture, 1990.

Moscovici, Serge. *The Age of the Crowd: A Historical Treatise on Mass Psychology*. Trans. J. C. Whitehouse. Cambridge: Cambridge University Press, 1985.

Mosse, George L. *The Culture of Western Europe: The Nineteenth and Twentieth Centuries*. Boulder: Westview Press, 1988.

Mosse, George L. *Masses and Man: Nationalist and Fascist Perceptions of Reality*. New York: Howard Fertig, 1980.

Mosse, George L. *The Nationalization of the Masses: Political Symbolism and Mass Movements in Germany from the Napoleonic Wars through the Third Reich.* New York: Howard Fertig, 1975.

Nietzsche, Friedrich. *The Birth of Tragedy* and *The Case of Wagner.* Trans. Walter Kaufmann. New York: Vintage, 1967.

Nin, Anaïs. *The Diary of Anaïs Nin, Volume One, 1931–1934.* Ed. and intro. Gunther Stuhlmann. New York: Harcourt Brace and Company, 1994.

Nye, Robert. "Savage Crowds, Modernism, and Modern Politics." In *Prehistories of the Future: The Primitivist Project and the Culture of Modernism,* ed. Elazar Berkan and Ronald Bush. Stanford: Stanford University Press, 1995. 42–55.

Ortega y Gasset, José. *The Revolt of the Masses.* New York: W. W. Norton and Co., 1930.

Osborne, John. *The Meiningen Court Theatre, 1866–1890.* New York: Cambridge University Press, 1988.

Paxton, Robert O. *The Anatomy of Fascism.* New York: Vintage, 2005.

Roberts, David. "The Natural History of Modernity." In *Elias Canetti's Counter-Image of Society.* Rochester: Camden House, 2004. 27–58.

Rolland, Romain. *The People's Theater.* Trans. Barrett H. Clark. New York: H. Holt and Company, 1918.

Rolland, Romain. *Le théâtre du peuple.* Ed. Chantal Meyer-Plantureux. Brussels: Éditions Complexe, 2003.

Schechner, Richard. "The Politics of Ecstasy." In *Public Domain: Essays on the Theater.* Indianapolis: Bobbs-Merrill Company, 1969. 209–28.

Schnapp, Jeffrey T. *Staging Fascism: 18BL and the Theater of Masses for Masses.* Stanford: Stanford University Press, 1996.

Sontag, Susan. "Fascinating Fascism." In *Under the Sign of Saturn.* New York: Farrar Straus Giroux, 1980. 73–105.

Sternhell, Zeev. *The Birth of Fascist Ideology: From Cultural Rebellion to Political Revolution.* Princeton: Princeton University Press, 1994.

Sternhell, Zeev. *Neither Right nor Left: Fascist Ideology in France.* Trans. David Maisel. Berkeley: University of California Press, 1986.

Strobl, Gerwin. *The Swastika and the Stage: German Theatre and Society, 1933–1945.* Cambridge: Cambridge University Press, 2007.

Tarde, Gabriel. *L'opinion et la foule.* 1901. Paris: Les Presses universitaires de France, 1989.

Trevor-Roper, Hugh. *The Last Days of Hitler.* New York: Collier Books, 1970.

Tytell, John. *The Living Theatre: Art, Exile, and Outrage.* New York: Grove Press, 1995.

Wagner, Richard. *The Art-Work of the Future and Other Works.* Trans. William Ashton Ellis. Lincoln: University of Nebraska Press, 1993.

Willett, John. *The Theatre of the Weimar Republic.* London: Holmes and Meier, 1988.

Winter, Alison. *Mesmerized: Powers of Mind in Victorian Britain.* Chicago: University of Chicago Press, 1998.

INDEX

Artaud, Antonin, works by
(*continued*)
complètes d'Antonin Artaud, 3, 20;
Philosopher's Stone, The (*La pierre
philosophale*), 155–56; poetry, 3–6,
16–17, 21, 125–29, 197–98; *Revolution surréaliste, La*, 15; *Selected Writings*, 7–8; "Theater and the Plague,
The" (see *Theater and Its Double,
The*); "Théâtre de séraphin, Le,"
167; *To Have Done with the Judgment of God* (*Pour en finir avec le
judgment de dieu*), 13, 16–17; "Umbilicus of Limbo, The," 152
Aschheim, Stephen, 27
Atelier, 5, 94, 157, 165–66. *See also*
Dullin, Charles
audience: agitation techniques, 82–84,
92, 99, 120; audience/director relationship, 24, 137, 142, 144, 150,
152–53; audience/performer relationship, 79–80, 84–85, 89, 92–96,
111–12, 121–22, 216nn15–16; avant-
garde audience, 23, 75, 79–85,
92–95, 97, 216nn15–16; behavior, 77,
215n6; comfort, 76, 78, 80–81; control, 75, 79–80, 84, 86, 88–90, 116–17,
158, 168, 171–72, 230n41; immersion techniques, 80, 84–85, 89–90,
92, 95, 99; as *organisme*, 87–88, 91,
95, 114, 116; and the spectacle,
78–79, 113–14, 116, 123, 124, 169,
171–72, 215–16n7; and "total theater," 89–91, 111–14, 144. *See also*
crowd theory; theater; *Theater and
Its Double, The*; Theater of Cruelty
avant-garde: and the audience, 23, 75,
79–85, 92–95, 97, 216nn15–16; as
cultural movement, 32–33, 37, 45;
and primitivism, 33, 58, 114; theater, 40, 58, 85, 93–95, 116, 194–95.
See also Naturalism; Symbolism

Bacchae, The. See Euripides
Balinese theater, 57, 58, 59, 60, 69,
170–71, 172, 203n22, 211n17
Barrault, Jean-Louis, 94, 135, 142,
151, 158, 165, 174

Baty, Gaston, 94, 138, 139, 140, 142,
149, 157, 164
Bauhaus artists, 90, 111
Bayreuth Festspielhaus, 80, 89, 95
Beck, Julian (the Living Theatre), 11,
13–15, 197
Benjamin, Walter, 70, 207n17
Berezin, Mabel, 104–5
Bergson, Henri, 61
Berlin, Isaiah, 51, 55, 66
Bibliothèque Nationale, Artaud ret-
rospective, 18–19
Birth of Tragedy, The. See Nietzsche,
Friedrich
Blackadder, Neil, 77, 78
Blanchot, Maurice, 10, 16
Blavatsky, (Madame) Helene Petrov-
na, 63–64
Blin, Roger, 166, 171, 228n20, 229n25.
See also *Cenci, The*
body, the: antipathy toward, 1, 15,
31, 197–98; effects of plague on,
38–40, 42, 43; in Theater of Cru-
elty, 121, 124, 169–70, 185–86
bourgeoisie: audience, 23, 76–79, 96,
111–12, 119, 120; "crisis of bour-
geois theater," 76–79, 84, 99–100;
theater, 76–78, 81, 89, 106–7, 111,
215n6
Brasillach, Robert, 69
Braun, Edward, 145
Brecht, Bertolt: Brechtian theater vs.
Theater of Cruelty, 87–88; Epic
Theater, 83–84, 134, 178–79
Breton, Jacqueline, 184, 195
Bridet, Guillaume, 19, 20
Brig, The, 14
Brook, Peter (*The Empty Space*), 2, 11,
135, 137, 194, 223n24
Brown, Frederick, 134, 140, 180, 181
Brown, Norman O., 193
Brustein, Robert, 195

Cabaret Voltaire, 45, 83
Cage, John, 11
Camus, Albert, 12
Canetti, Elias, 11, 117, 118, 122, 123,
128, 185, 186–87, 196

44–45; theatrical philosophy of, 85, 87

Symbolism, 80–82, 89, 91–92, 116, 216nn15–16. *See also* avant-garde

synaesthesia, 81, 89, 91–92, 113, 147

Tarahumara Indians, 5, 15, 59, 203n22

Tel Quel (journal), 2, 16

theater: and the audience, 75–84; audience/director relationship, 24, 137, 142, 150; building design, 78–79, 89–90; as expression of vital forces, 61, 63; production as mise-en-scène, 56, 78, 145, 146, 149, 153, 169, 170; production control, 23–25, 45, 76–79, 131, 136–40, 144, 176; proscenium, 23, 80, 81, 89, 90; psychological drama, 55, 102; seating, 80, 89. *See also* audience; director; Theater of Cruelty; theatrical elements

Theater and Its Double, The: on the audience, 85, 87–88, 89, 94–95, 121–22; autobiographical material in, 9–10; on the avant-garde, 32–33, 94–95; "On the Balinese Theater," 57–60, 69, 170–72; cataclysmic events, 32–34, 39–40, 48, 61, 115, 162; commentary about, 8–10, 51–52; *Conquest of Mexico, The,* 58–60, 109, 123–24, 163; on control of the performance, 159, 171–72, 176, 179, 186; on counter-Enlightenment thinking, 23, 44–45, 52–58, 68, 120; on cruelty, 37, 41, 44, 62, 71, 123, 198–99; on the director as "creator" of the event, 133, 151, 170; on evil, 37, 44, 49, 53, 61, 123, 197; on freedom, 24–26, 48, 69, 85–86, 120, 123, 147, 192, 194; on individual psychology, 55–56; influence of, 11–15; and irrationalism, 57–58, 65, 190; on "Myth" and eternal truths, 59–60, 106–10, 163, 176–77, 184; "No More Masterpieces," 109–10; on occult practices, 58, 63–64; pho-

tographs in, 7; publication of, 7, 8; reactionary viewpoint in, 58, 65–66, 71, 186; "readings" of artworks, 56–57; on science, 52–54, 210n8; on "shock" as theatrical technique, 87; on suffering, 33, 36–38, 43–44; "Theater and the Plague, The," 23, 32–39, 41, 44–49, 122–23, 126; on theater and vitalism, 61–63, 211–12n21; on theater as an event, 42–43, 48, 63, 128–29, 157; on theater as spectacle, 49, 78–79, 113–14, 116, 124, 169–70, 215–16n7; on "total theater," 89–91, 94, 111–14, 122, 126–29, 143, 157, 172–73, 217n29; on "true culture," 33–34; on violence, 47, 61, 186. *See also* audience; plague; Theater of Cruelty

Theater of Cruelty: anti-intellectual approach, 50, 55–56, 66, 87–88, 95, 96, 99, 113–14; apocalyptic themes, 23, 35, 44–46, 106, 115; audience agitation techniques, 82–84, 92, 95, 99, 120; audience as crowd, 23–24, 49, 99, 106, 116, 123–25, 129, 192, 196; audience as *organisme,* 87–88, 91–92, 95, 114, 116, 121, 179; audience immersion techniques, 80, 84–85, 89–90, 92, 95, 99; audience/performer dynamic, 75, 85, 94–95; avant-garde context, 84–90, 94–95; the body, 121, 124; vs. Brechtian theater, 87–88, 178–79; control of the audience, 79, 82, 84, 88–89, 91–92, 116; Cruelty manifestos, 68, 161, 164, 166, 168; director in sole control, 48–49, 88–90, 94, 110, 126–29, 133, 143, 169–72, 178, 186; fascistic aesthetic, 44, 68, 99, 106–7, 110–14, 186; influence of, 11–12, 13–14; intensity of the experience, 61, 62–63, 82–83, 86–90, 92–93, 95, 111, 115, 119–20, 123, 129, 169, 182; "invisible" forces, 113, 121, 176–78; "Myth" and heroes, 99, 106–11, 113, 115,

Printed and bound by CPI Group (UK) Ltd, Croydon, CR0 4YY

09/06/2025

14685669-0002